When You Walked
Back Into My Life

When You Walked Back Into My Life

Hilary Boyd

W F HOWES LTD

This large print edition published in 2014 by
W F Howes Ltd
Unit 4, Rearsby Business Park, Gaddesby Lane,
Rearsby, Leicester LE7 4YH

1 3 5 7 9 10 8 6 4 2

First published in the United Kingdom in 2013
by Quercus Editions Ltd

A CIP catalogue record for this book is available
from the British Library

ISBN 978 1 47126 686 7

Typeset by Palimpsest Book Production Limited,
Falkirk, Stirlingshire

Printed and bound in Great Britain
by TJ International Ltd, Padstow, Cornwall

MIX
Paper from
responsible sources
FSC
www.fsc.org   FSC® C013056

For Don, with forty years of love.

PROLOGUE

September 2009

She had slept without meaning to, then woken with a start. As soon as her eyes were open, she automatically tried his mobile number. Again it went to answer. The clock read nearly five-thirty in the morning, and she failed to stop herself imagining the worst: a bike accident, a fall on one of his climbs.

It had been a hurried goodbye, before she went to work the previous day; they'd made love when she should have been getting dressed, and she'd been late.

Her shift at the hospital finished at seven and he'd said he'd be home, that he'd pick up some fresh fish for supper, that he'd fix the lamp on her bike. But he hadn't been home, wasn't home now.

She was a nurse in a Brighton hospital A&E, she knew what could happen to people: the blank eyes dulled by the paramedics' morphine, the twisted limbs, the flesh ripped and jagged, bulging dark with blood.

Please, please don't let that be Fin.

She thought of all the places he might go – a climber by profession, there weren't many places he could climb locally. He sometimes went along the coast to the chalk cliffs at Hope Gap. Or the climbing wall if he was teaching. But he'd only taken his pedal bike. The sleek, powerful Triumph was still here, parked in the alley that led to the tiny back garden of their house and shrouded in its metallic-silver cover.

Had he mentioned anything different about his day? She tried to recall his exact words as she hunched inside a rug on the sofa, cold and worried, staring obsessively at the display on her phone, willing it to light up. But she couldn't remember, the sex had distracted her.

She'd already rung her own hospital to check if he'd been brought in. Should she call the police now? But they wouldn't do anything, she knew. It was too soon. Too soon for most people, who would assume just a drunken night out. But Fin never got drunk, barely touched alcohol when he was in training, which was most of the time. A bit of dope here and there, but nothing serious. He'd never stayed out late without her, let alone all night. And he always called or texted her constantly, all day.

In the end she fell asleep again, still clutching her mobile, waking an hour later with the dawn light and immediately checking for a missed call. She knew she'd never concentrate at work so she rang in sick and asked for a second time if someone

2

called Fin McCrea had been brought in overnight.

By teatime she was down at the police station. The constable on the desk took careful details.

'Has he ever done this before?' he asked.

'Never. Not once. We've been together eight years and he's always told me where he was.'

'And you didn't have a row or anything?'

'Nothing.' She wasn't going to tell him about the lovemaking, although it seemed to prove something about their closeness.

'Have you rung his friends? Family?'

She said that she had: his dad in Scotland, a few climbing mates. He went on asking questions, which she answered mechanically. No, he wasn't on any medication; yes, his bike was missing; no, she didn't know if he'd taken his passport.

'Well, Miss, we'll make a few enquiries, check the other hospitals. I don't think you should worry too much. It's early days. There'll be a perfectly simple explanation, practically always is.'

'Like what?' she demanded.

The young policeman sucked his teeth. 'Well, you know the thing . . . a bit too much to drink and finds himself on a mate's couch in the back of beyond with no signal; maybe a sudden illness in the family, mobile on the blink . . .'

Give the man credit, she thought, he's doing his best.

'Seen it all,' he added, giving her an encouraging smile.

'So what shall I do?' she asked, on the verge of tears.

'Go home. Have a good look round, see if he's taken stuff – his passport, clothes, that sort of thing. Might've been called away suddenly. We'll keep in touch, let you know as soon as we get any news.' As she turned to go, he called after her, 'Don't forget to tell us if he turns up.'

She did as the policeman suggested. At home she went straight to the drawer in the desk where they kept their passports. Fin's was gone. Then she checked his clothes, searched for the backpack he used for travelling. It was gone too, plus his climbing boots, his favourite Patagonia jacket, his waterproof trousers. She found his computer on the floor beside the bed. Logging in, she checked his emails, brought up his recent history. The emails were from days ago, just brief communications with mates, the usual bike sites, climbing blogs. Nothing that told her his plans – if he had any.

For a while she sat, numb, refusing to face the obvious: he wasn't missing, he wasn't lying at the bottom of a ravine. He'd just gone climbing, left her without a word.

She began inventing excuses for him, just as the policeman had. Perhaps he'd got word of a fantastic climb, leaving immediately – she knew September was the start of the climbing season, post-monsoon, in Tibet – in some inaccessible place on the globe where there was no mobile

4

signal. Maybe at the airport his phone had been lost or stolen and he had no time to call. Or a note gone missing . . . Had he left a note that had been blown off the table when she opened the door? She looked at once, scrabbling under the kitchen table, then under the bed. It's barely twenty-four hours, she kept telling herself.

But when she woke the next morning and still her mobile was silent, she recognised her excuses for what they were. What she could not yet face were the implications of his absence.

She went downstairs to make a cup of tea, then punched in the number of the police station.

'Umm, I'd like to cancel the missing persons report I made yesterday.' She gave the reference number, feeling humiliated, a total fool.

'Oh, hello Miss Bancroft. So you've found him then?' She recognised the young PC's voice.

'Not exactly, but I think I know where he is.'

The policeman said nothing for a moment.

'OK . . . so you're sure you don't want us to go on looking?'

'Quite sure. Thank you.'

'Right you are then, I'll take it off the system. Let us know if you need any more help.'

She carefully laid her phone down on the kitchen table. With shaky steps, she climbed the stairs back up to bed and crept under the duvet. No tears now. Nor rage. Just nothing, nothing, absolutely nothing.

CHAPTER 1

10 September 2012

'I'm just nipping out to the shops for about forty-five minutes. You've got your glasses on, the phone is right here. Will you be OK?' Flora fiddled with the things on the small side table, placing the phone in the most accessible position, then laid the newspaper across the old lady's lap, open at a page about Pippa Middleton's antics. She knew that when she came back the page would not have changed, but Dorothea Heath-Travis, aged ninety-three, liked to maintain the illusion that she read the paper in the morning.

'I expect I shall.' Dorothea spoke slowly and carefully – her speech had not completely recovered after her last mini-stroke.

'Ring me if you need me. Or Keith. Speed-dial one for me, two for Keith.' Flora said this every morning as she went off to do the shopping, never sure whether Dorothea would remember, if the need arose. In the two years she'd been working there, however, it never had.

The old lady looked up at Flora from her

armchair by the window, an amused expression on her face; she hated fuss. But she didn't reply, just bent her head to the paper, her white hair, thin now, neatly rolled in a small French pleat. The room was quiet, and filled with morning light that showed up the worn chair covers, the faded wallpaper and carpet – all good quality in their day, but not new now for at least fifteen years. Rene Carmichael, Dorothea's friend, who had power of attorney for the old lady's affairs, was always tut-tutting about the tatty state of the flat, but Dorothea seemed not to notice or, if she did, not to care.

Flora went through to the hall, taking her cardigan from the coat stand by the front door, and pulling it on over her shapeless, pale-blue uniform dress. She checked herself quickly in the ornate oval mirror on the wall and frowned. Her brown-gold eyes seemed huge in her face, which she knew was too pale, too thin. But it had been one of the wettest summers on record, barely a ray of sun until late July, and she couldn't afford to go away . . . had no one she particularly wanted to go away with . . . Yanking the band from her pony-tail, she allowed her dark hair to fall about her shoulders before scraping it back and off her face again. She preferred not to go out dressed like this unless she had a proper coat to hide the uniform, but she swallowed her pride; it was pointless to change just for a quick trip to the supermarket, and who would see her?

'Morning, Florence.' Keith Godly, porter for the block, poked his head sideways from behind his computer.

'Hi, Keith. Good weekend?' Flora asked the question without thinking. She knew what the answer would be; Keith never had a good weekend.

The porter, predictably, let out a groan and dropped his voice, flexing his muscle-bound shoulders in his dark suit. 'Nah. Just same old, same old. Bloody whingeing tenants with leaking toilets or lost keys. That new woman in number twenty-four phoned me three times on Saturday night because a dog was howling his bloody head off somewhere! It was annoying the hell out of me too, but it wasn't even in our block. Did she think I was fucking Superman?'

Flora nodded sympathetically. 'The problem is you're a sitting duck, living right under their noses.'

'Not the only problem in my life though, eh?'

Flora gave him a wave and moved off towards the main entrance. She liked Keith, he was endlessly kind to Dorothea, helping her out with small tasks in the flat whenever Flora asked, such as fixing the bathroom light or recalibrating the Freeview box, but she didn't feel inclined to listen again to the tale of his miserable life since he'd been forced out of the Army – his one and only passion. His back, the cause of his discharge, was fine now, he insisted. But for him, life was over.

'Will you be here for the next half an hour?'

'For you, Florence, I'll be here a million lifetimes.'

His attempt at flirting was accompanied by a theatrical sigh that made her laugh, and even brought a smile to Keith's heavy, lugubrious features.

As soon as she was outside she took a long, slow breath, happy to be in the open air on this late-summer's day, the air sharp with a hint of approaching autumn but still pleasantly warm. Twelve hours in the flat, always on duty even when Dorothea was having her afternoon nap, was wearing, and she relished these brief moments to herself. She turned right down Gloucester Road, towards the Underground station, crossed the busy Cromwell Road and entered the arcade on the corner. The supermarket was at the far end, and she dawdled . . . checking out the face cream in Boots, which she decided she couldn't afford, peering into the expensive jewelry boutique.

The store wasn't busy yet. She took a handbasket and began in the fruit and vegetable section. A Bramley apple or some plums to stew, leeks – Dorothea's favourite – carrots, a couple of potatoes for mash. Maybe she'd get some chicken today . . . a change from the endless poached fish. She was picking out tomatoes for her own lunch, when an arm reached rudely across her and plucked a bag of organic carrots from the box to the left of the tomatoes. No 'excuse me', no apology. Flora, irritated, turned to glare at the owner of the arm,

10

and froze. For a moment she held her breath, then her heart began to beat twenty to the dozen.

'Fin?' She was surprised that any sound came out.

The man, obviously equally taken aback, just stared at her for a moment.

'Flora.'

She knew her pale cheeks were flushed, she could feel the warmth. She brushed a hand self-consciously across her hair, collecting the dark strands that had come loose from the band and smoothing them flat.

'God, Flora. Is it really you?' Fin McCrea kept staring at her.

He looks just the same, she thought, just as beautiful. Tall and athletic, he stood well over six feet, his hair, sun-bleached, sticking out from his head in a wild tangle she was painfully familiar with. He wore jeans, and a faded red T-shirt sporting a Save the Children logo, the ubiquitous black daypack slung across his broad shoulders.

'What . . . what are you doing here?' he was asking.

'Shopping?' She smiled and so did he, his light grey eyes creasing with amusement. 'How about you?' she added. 'Not your usual neck of the woods, West London.'

Flora talked, but she hardly knew what she was saying. It had been all but three years – she knew almost to the hour how long – since she had seen him last.

11

Fin put his basket down by his feet and shook his head. 'Long story. I'm staying with a mate at the bottom of Queen's Gate. I had a pretty bad fall in January.'

'What happened?' She asked more to give herself time than because she wanted the grisly details.

'I was in Chamonix, guiding this old Italian, and the ledge I was standing on collapsed . . . sodding rock just fell off the side of the mountain. He was OK, miraculously, but I smashed into the rock face and just broke up. They flew me back to the UK and it was all mending fine, except the pin in my leg's playing up now. I had to go back into hospital.'

As he talked, she just watched him, watched every movement of his face, noted his square hand clutching the strap of his bag and the golden hairs on his permanently tanned arms.

'But everything else is OK?'

He shrugged. 'S'pose . . . I had a bust pelvis, compound fracture of my thigh.' He tapped his right leg. 'Two cracked lumbar vertebrae, God knows what else – the docs got bored of telling me. Can't stand London, as you know, but it's easier to be near the hospital for all the follow-up stuff. They've put more metal plates in me than a Sherman tank.' He looked questioningly at her, as if he were waiting for her story now.

'Sounds as if you're lucky to be alive.'

'Lucky to be alive *and* walking, so the doctor says,' he agreed, his face breaking into an uncertain grin.

There was a paralysed silence. Flora didn't know what to say, where to look; adrenaline was coursing through her body making her shaky and cold. She clung to the black plastic handle of the basket as if it were her lifeline.

'I'd better get going. I'm on duty,' she said eventually, but remained rooted to the spot.

'You're not at the Charing Cross are you? That's where I've been . . . on and off all year. How weird would that be? Us in the same place and not knowing it.'

'No, no, I'm doing private nursing at the moment – just down the road. I needed a break.'

Finlay McCrea and her, standing in the middle of a London supermarket, making polite conversation as if they were old mates catching up? She suddenly needed to get away from him.

'Flora.' As she turned to go, he reached out and touched her arm, sending a shock through her body as if he'd been electrically charged. 'It's . . . incredible to see you. Seems like a lifetime. Don't go without telling me how I can get hold of you.'

She felt a spurt of anger. 'What for?'

He looked surprised at her tone. 'Well, er, I thought we could meet up. Have a drink or something while I'm around?'

A drink? It sounded so normal. As if going for a drink could ever contain the maelstrom of feelings she had for this man. 'Sorry . . . it's . . . it's not such a good time. I've got a lot on.'

She noted his crestfallen expression. 'But it's

been good to see you too,' she added, hearing the formal, almost prim tone of her voice as she hurried away and instantly regretting it.

The rest of the shopping was conducted in a blur. She moved up and down the aisles, plucking the necessary items mechanically from the shelves, not daring to look up from her task in case she saw him again. She felt lightheaded, but she kept focused until she was safely out of the store, then almost ran back to Dorothea's flat as if the devil were on her tail.

Keith hadn't moved from his desk. He looked up as she shot round the corner.

'No need to panic. I haven't heard a peep out of her.'

'Oh . . . thanks, thanks for keeping an eye.'

'You OK?' He peered at her through the gloom of the hall.

'Fine, yes.' She smiled brightly and hurriedly closed the door of the flat behind her, only able to relax when she had a physical barrier between herself and Fin McCrea.

That evening Flora stood in her sister's immaculate, state-of-the-art kitchen, telling her about the supermarket encounter. It was nearly nine – Flora only finished work at eight, and Prue was just back from a gallery opening in the West End.

Prue took a wine glass from the cupboard and set it on the polished black granite worktop with a sharp click. She poured out red wine from an already opened bottle of Australian Shiraz and handed it to Flora, her face set and angry.

'Bloody man.'

Prue, three years Flora's senior, was about as unlike her sister as it was possible to be and yet still be related. She looked good for her forty-four years, her clothes classic and expensive, giving only a passing nod to trend. Her hair, short, layered and tastefully blonde, framed a round face, seldom seen without extensive make-up; her nails were long, manicured, and varnished a rich, shiny crimson. The only similarity to her sister was her gold-flecked brown eyes. Financially ambitious from an early age, Prue was now an interior designer of considerable fame and popularity amongst the international set with homes in London; she never stopped working. Her husband, Philip, a lawyer, was usually the one at home making supper for their teenage daughter, Bel.

'He wanted to have a drink with me,' Flora said. She had somehow managed to get through the rest of the day with some semblance of normality. Rene had come round for tea with Dorothea, the doctor had visited, Mary, the night nurse, had bent her ear about what they would all do if Dorothea died. So she hadn't yet had time to make sense of what had happened.

'And you said no, right?' Prue asked, not really concentrating as she checked her BlackBerry and replied at once to whatever message she'd just received – Prue's phone was never more than

15

grabbing distance from her hand. Laying it temporarily on the counter, she opened the fridge and pulled out a box of butternut squash and sage ravioli, a bag of watercress, a lemon and a block of Parmesan cheese. 'Have you eaten?'

Flora shook her head. 'Where are Philip and Bel?'

'Bel's staying with Holly . . . getting up to some unspeakable fifteen-year-old mischief, no doubt. And Philip is having dinner with an old college mate.' Prue stopped what she was doing to peer closely at her sister. 'You didn't give him your number, did you?'

'No, no, of course I didn't.' And then she burst into tears.

'Darling . . . come here.' Prue wrapped Flora in her arms and held her close. 'Poor you, it must have been a terrible shock.'

Flora rested in her sister's embrace for only a moment before pulling away and wiping the tears away with the back of her cardigan sleeve. Prue made a disapproving face and passed her a piece of kitchen roll.

'It *was* a shock.'

'What was he doing in Waitrose in the Cromwell Road for Christ's sake? He spends his entire life up a mountain.'

'He had a bad fall, he said. He was in Charing Cross Hospital getting his leg fixed.' Flora took a gulp of wine and pulled herself up onto one of the high beechwood stools that lined a side of the square island in the centre of the kitchen. Her sister's house always amazed her. She realised, of course, that it was Prue's calling card for her design business, but still, there was no mess anywhere, none of the normal clutter, nothing out of the cupboards and drawers at all. Just clean, blank lines and gleaming surfaces, punctuated by an occasional art work, an elegant vase of flowers, some tasteful arrangement of fruit. Not even salt and pepper mills or a bottle of olive oil sullied the black polished perfection of the kitchen.

'Serves him right, stupid sod.' Prue smacked a pan of water down on the stove, repeatedly jabbing at the controls of the black ceramic hob until the halogen plate was glowing.

She leaned across the central island. 'You don't *want* to see him again, do you? After what he did? You'd be insane.'

'No . . .' In the face of her sister's indignation, Flora wasn't going to argue – too much like hard work right now – but it didn't seem as black and white to her. Part of her wanted more than anything else in the world to sit with Fin McCrea and talk and laugh – and perhaps experience the intense sexual energy that had always existed between them. But part of her wanted to run a million miles in the opposite direction, so terrified was she at the thought that she might depend on him in any way again.

Prue looked at her suspiciously. 'You don't sound at all certain.' She topped up Flora's glass and went to check on the water. It had boiled, and she tipped in the ravioli, prodding with a wooden spoon to separate the pouches.

'I suppose I'm not.'

'Uh?' Prue spun round, letting out a gasp of horror. 'Flora!'

Flora held up her hand. 'OK, OK, I know what you're saying and I agree, of course I do. But . . .'

'But nothing. You can't go there, darling. You really can't. Eight years together and he walked out on you, never called you, never even wrote. Just disappeared up one of his sodding, bloody mountains.'

Flora met her sister's angry stare. 'I know all that.'

'No, you can't. Not if you're even contemplating spending a single second in that bastard's company.' Prue paused, as if she were gathering together her arsenal before an attack. 'He broke your heart. He wrecked your career. He made it unlikely you'd have the children you always wanted, and he sent you into a depression that you're only now recovering from. What part of this sounds like a good idea to you?'

Flora had to admit Prue was right, but that didn't mean that meeting Fin hadn't triggered all the feelings that, for nearly three years, she'd been trying to quash. Mostly unsuccessfully. The therapist to whom she'd been assigned when she'd been depressed had said she needed 'closure', to be able to draw a line under the relationship. But how

18

could she do that without learning why he'd walked out on her so suddenly? Perhaps, she thought, it was important to see him again: to realise for herself what a selfish bastard he was, rather than just being told so by everyone else. She ignored the voice in her head, which said, 'That's my excuse and I'm sticking to it.'

'Hello? Speak to me . . .' Prue was waving the spoon in front of her sister's face.

Flora smiled. 'Sorry. Just thinking. You don't need to worry. It's not like he's after me any more. If he was he'd have got in touch years ago. He knows where you live.'

Prue looked away for a moment. She seemed to be about to say something, then apparently changed her mind.

'Anyway, I didn't give him my number.'

'Bloody good thing too,' Prue pursed her lips, glaring off across the room. 'It's not *his* agenda I'm worried about . . .' she added.

After supper, Flora made her way downstairs to the flat in the basement of her sister's large Cornwall Crescent house near Ladbroke Grove. However irritated Flora got with what she considered her sister's blunt, pragmatic approach to life, it had been Prue who had scooped Flora up after Fin's defection and brought her to live with her and Philip. Later, when she fell badly behind with the mortgage payments on the house in Brighton, Prue had suggested she sell up and stay with them, rent the basement flat on a 'mate's rates' basis. Flora had reluctantly agreed, helpless in the face of her incapacity. Her only certainty back then, which had been a steady beacon in her darkness, was the absolute certainty that Fin would come back – today, tomorrow, next week . . . But as the months passed and he didn't, her depression deepened.

Up until that September day three years ago, Flora had considered her life a good one. She loved her job in the A&E department, relished the frantic, unpredictable, life-or-death nature of the work – so much more exciting than the more mundane pace of ward life. And she had Fin.

True, his work – and obsession – was climbing mountains, and there weren't too many of those in Brighton, so he was away a lot. And when he was home, he was restless from day one, champing to get out of the city again. As soon as she was off duty for a few days, he would whisk her away, both of them astride his sleek Triumph America. They had seen the dawn rise from the top of Mount Snowdon, they had camped out in Swiss mountain huts with the goats, hiked up Kilimanjaro, driven across the desert to Timbuktu, literally. If her duty rota meant they were stuck at home, he would smoke a bit of dope, tinker with the bike and make mostly botched attempts at renovating their tiny terraced house, seven minutes' walk from the sea. And threaded through all the adventures was that powerful sexual charge, which Flora sometimes felt controlled her as much as any drug. She and Fin might be having supper, getting up in the morning, walking along the seafront, and one look would catapult them both into an almost unseemly desire to possess each other. When he came back from one of his expeditions, perhaps having been away for a month or two, they would spend whole weekends in bed. Fin wasn't just a boyfriend: for eight years he had been a way of life for Flora.

Thankful to be home, away from Prue's nagging, Flora ran a bath and sank into the too-hot water with relief. She had drunk a lot of red wine but barely touched the butternut ravioli; she felt muddled and a bit queasy. All she could see as she lay still, the water almost up to her neck, was those light grey eyes she knew better than her own, their expression always containing vanity and a certain vagueness, a detachment from the reality around him, but also a balancing humour and charm, which was how he connected with the world.

She wondered if he had changed. But what does it matter if he has or he hasn't? she asked herself. I blew him out, he won't bother to try and find me. And acknowledging that, she felt an almost painful sense of loss.

CHAPTER 2

'Would you like to go to the park today?'
Flora asked Dorothea the following
morning. 'It's so beautiful out there.'
She had just finished giving the old lady a bed
bath and was dressing her, pulling on the navy
elastic-waisted slacks that Rene bought from
Marks and Spencer in bulk, along with cardigans
and blouses in beige, and horrible pastel shades
of blue, pink and green, which she found at knock-
down prices at various outlets of Edinburgh
Woollen Mill. 'Every time I see a branch, I go in.
There's always something on offer,' Rene told
Flora proudly.

'I . . . might like to,' the old lady replied uncer-
tainly, struggling weakly with the arm of today's
pink cardigan. She looked up at Flora. 'But . . .
Maybe Dominic said he would come round.'

'Oh, OK.' Flora suppressed her annoyance.
Dominic was Dorothea's great-nephew and, in
Flora's opinion, a smarmy creep. 'Did he say
when?'

Dorothea gave a small shrug. 'Perhaps not till this afternoon.'

'You don't have to go to the park if you don't want to,' Flora said, as she helped her off the bed, propping her inside the semicircle of her aluminium frame for the agonisingly slow walk to the armchair in the sitting room.

'I think I would like it,' Dorothea smiled up at Flora, her pale old eyes large behind her glasses.

Keith jumped up from his desk as soon as he saw Flora pushing Dorothea's wheelchair out of the flat.

'Go-o-od morning, Miss H-T. And how are we today?'

'*I* am quite well, Mr Godly. I can't speak for Flora, I'm afraid.'

Keith laughed. 'Touché!' He grinned at the old lady, whose face lit up in response. 'I deserved that.'

Never underestimate Dorothea, Flora thought with satisfaction. The small stroke she had suffered about a month ago had taken it out of her, as had the several other transient ischaemic attacks she'd experienced. Each time she lost a bit of ground physically, but mentally, although her speech was so slow, she seemed as sharp as ever.

The flower-walk in Kensington Gardens was worth the long haul with the wheelchair. Peaceful, and lined with blooms for most of the year, filled with small wildlife, it was a haven in the hectic urban surroundings. Nowadays it was Dorothea's only real experience of the outside world, and she revelled in it.

'Look . . .' Dorothea held out her hand to a squirrel standing inches from the wheelchair, observing the old lady. 'Do we have some bread?'

Flora passed her a handful of crumbs from a plastic bag slung on one of the chair handles. A small child saw the squirrel too and came over, sitting quietly on her haunches to watch. Dorothea passed the little girl some bread, which the squirrel grabbed eagerly, making the child laugh. The sound sent the squirrel darting off into the bushes.

Normally, Flora would have taken pleasure in the scene, but today she was distracted. Since she'd woken up, Fin had never been out of her thoughts. She had begun looking around as soon as she left Miss Heath-Travis's flat, hoping and dreading in equal measure that she might bump into him. She had no idea how long he would be living with his friend, he hadn't said. But she knew Fin never stayed in one place very long.

'Flora, lovely to see you.' Dominic Trevellick, Dorothea's great-nephew – her sister's daughter's son and only living relative – held his hand out.

'Hello, Dominic.' She reluctantly shook the limp, moist hand that was offered and forced a smile. Dominic was short and plump. An antique dealer by trade, he was about her age but dressed like a fogey in a navy blazer, butter-yellow cords, a matching silk waistcoat with paisley bow tie, and tan loafers. His blond hair, neatly parted, was darkened by hair product and barbered too short, his large tortoiseshell spectacles giving him an owlish air which seemed to overwhelm his watery blue eyes.

'How is she?' Dominic lowered his voice, a look of studied concern on his face.

'She's very well.'

'Good-good.' He waited, looking awkward. 'May I go in?'

Flora nodded. 'She's expecting you.'

She went into the kitchen to make the tea and unwrap the Jamaican ginger cake Dorothea always asked her to get for her great-nephew. She heard him making conversation with his aunt, his plummy tones loud in the quiet flat. He had barely visited in the first eighteen months that Flora was working for the old lady, but since then he had been round more frequently and more regularly. Flora knew from an unguarded moment with Rene that he stood to inherit from Dorothea, so perhaps he was just keeping tabs on his legacy. Although Dominic had done nothing specific to warrant it, Flora didn't entirely trust him. His aunt, however, seemed always delighted by his company.

She carried the tea tray in and set it on the sideboard. Dominic, ever on guard about showing his 'breeding', insisted on the habit of putting the milk in last. This seemed daft to Flora because you then had to stir the tea; whereas, if you put the milk in first, the tea mixed itself. But she played along and handed Dominic his cup of tea, then offered him the milk jug.

'Marvellous. Thank you so much.' He beamed up at Flora from his seat on the ancient chintz sofa. 'I've said it before, but I'll say it again: you're a very lucky lady, Aunt Dot, to have this special girl looking after you.' He splashed milk into his cup and handed the jug back to Flora. 'But I'm sure you know that.'

Dorothea nodded slowly. 'She *is* wonderful,' she said, speaking slowly but with deep sincerity, and Flora found herself blushing.

'I'll be in the other room if you need me,' she told the old lady, escaping gratefully to the kitchen.

When she went back into the sitting room, Dominic was standing over by the French doors that led to the balcony and then, via some iron steps, to the communal gardens behind the flats. He still carried his cup and saucer in one hand, but with the other he was lovingly stroking the surface of a small walnut box-table wedged next to the window.

'This is a pretty little piece, Aunt Dot. I never noticed it before.'

Dorothea twisted round as much as she could and cast an eye on the table. 'It's Georgian, I think. A sewing box. Open it up, the inside is quite interesting.'

Dominic turned the small metal key and lifted the lid. Flora had never seen inside. It was neatly laid out into fretwork sections, some still containing spools of coloured thread, a cloth tape measure, tiny gold-coloured scissors and a thimble. The lid was lined with delicate floral marquetry.

'Splendid.' Dominic bent to inspect the detail. 'And it's in such good condition. Must be worth a couple of hundred at auction.'

'My mother's. I don't care for it much,' Dorothea told him, her tone unusually disdainful. Flora had seldom heard her mention her mother. Her father, yes. She talked about him a lot, and always with great fondness. His portrait hung above the fireplace. He was a handsome Edwardian, with Dorothea's hawk nose and an impressive waxed moustache. It was almost a swagger portrait in style – with his puffed chest, his head thrown slightly back and his hand resting on the marble mantelpiece as if he were at least a captain of industry – when in fact he'd been something in insurance.

Dominic came and sat down. 'Well, if you ever need some extra cash, I'm sure I'd be able to sell it for you.'

His great-aunt raised her eyebrows and looked at Flora questioningly, but she didn't know how to reply, so went on collecting up the teacups, the teapot, the plates littered with crumbs from the ginger cake. She obviously couldn't get involved in anything to do with her patient's finances, but if she had her way she wouldn't let Dominic anywhere near the walnut sewing box.

As she left the room she heard Dorothea say in

her slow, laboured way: 'Maybe you should. I never use it. I don't really need things any more.'

'Flora?'

She jumped. The tap was running as she rinsed out the brown teapot, and she hadn't heard Dominic come up behind her in the small kitchen.

'Sorry, I startled you.'

Flora turned, hands wet, still clutching the pot. 'Everything alright?' she asked.

'Fine, fine. I just wanted to tell you that I'm taking the sewing table with me.'

'Now?'

'Might as well. Aunt Dot wants it sold. She says she wants to clear stuff out before she dies. Make things simple. I've got an auction coming up in a few weeks, so I'll need to get it down to the sale room to be catalogued.'

'Oh . . . OK. Will you tell Rene or shall I?'

Dominic looked puzzled. 'Does she need to know?'

'It's just I don't want her accusing the nurses of making off with stuff in the flat,' Flora explained.

'Ah. No, no, of course not. Hadn't thought of that. I'll give her a bell when I get home.'

'Thanks.'

Dominic hovered. He had this odd habit of saying something then waiting, even when she had answered him, peering at her through his owl glasses as if he was expecting her to speak again. And often, just because of the silence, she obliged.

'Can you carry it yourself?'

'It's not heavy. I'll just bring the car round. Won't be a tick.'

As soon as he'd left the flat, she went through to Dorothea.

'Dominic's taking the table now. Is that the plan?' Flora asked, wanting to make sure the old lady realised what was happening.

Dorothea looked blankly at her for a moment.

'Your mother's sewing table in the corner? You asked Dominic to sell it.'

The old lady nodded. 'I never liked it. Reminds me of those dreadful samplers I was made to sew as a child. Cross-stitch reduced me to tears. I never got the hang of it.'

'So you're happy for him to sell it?' Flora paused, not knowing quite how to phrase what she wanted to say. 'I . . . don't think you need the money, if you were worrying about that.'

Dorothea shook her head. 'I don't suppose I do . . . But it's better to get rid of things now, perhaps, than leaving it to be sorted out when I'm dead. And he's so kind, going to all that trouble for me.'

The front-door bell rang that evening as Flora was sitting on the sofa with a bowl of mushroom soup on her lap, watching catch-up *Holby City* on the television. She glanced through the barred window leading out to the area steps up to the pavement, and saw her niece pulling a comical face at her as she huddled close to the door to avoid the rain. Flora let her in.

'Hi, darling. Lost your keys again?'

Bel nodded, grinning ruefully as she gave her aunt a hug. 'Yup, second time this month. Mum'll kill me.'

'They're probably upstairs somewhere.'

Bel shook her head. 'That'd be too lucky.'

'Worth looking before you tell Mum.'

Her niece plonked herself down on the sofa and peered at the soup. 'Is there any more of that? I'm starving.'

The room was open plan, the small kitchen running the length of the window with the sitting room space behind, then a bedroom and bathroom underneath the stairs that led up to the main house. Flora had been allowed by her sister to decorate it as she pleased, and the result was a random collection of furniture, cushions and rugs from the Brighton house that gave a cosy, slightly bohemian, air to the tiny place.

Flora heated up the remains of the soup and cut some brown bread.

'Toast?'

Bel nodded enthusiastically and curled up contentedly in the only armchair. She was small for her age, wiry and sporty like her father, with a puckish face and lively brown eyes. She had recently had her waist-length brown hair restyled in a gamin cut which feathered prettily around her face – an act that made her mother weep for days. But Bel's clothes were Prue's real Armageddon. To her intense distress and irritation, her daughter had no interest whatsoever in what she wore – usually a pair of jeans and an old T-shirt or sweater often plundered from a friend's drawer. She never wore make-up and looked more like twelve than fifteen. With the equivalent money her friends were spending on clothes and lip gloss, Bel was buying books about the theatre, tickets to the theatre or attending theatre workshops at the weekends and in the school holidays. She wanted to be a stage designer, not an actress or a director – small comfort to her parents, Flora knew, who had pegged law as the route to their daughter's glittering future.

For a while they sat and ate in silence.

'Mum said Fin's back,' Bel said, shooting a cautious look at her aunt.

Flora wished Prue hadn't said anything. The more everyone talks about the man, the more real his presence becomes, she thought.

'Yes. Well, he's not back. I just bumped into him in the supermarket.'

'Aren't you going to see him? Mum seems to think you are. She's going mental.'

Flora laughed. 'She obviously doesn't trust me to stay away.'

Bel was frowning. 'But do you think you still love him?' Fin and Bel had got on well. He wasn't interested in relating to her as a child, but he would take her off swimming or to the park as soon as lunch was over – ever keen to escape confinement and social interchange – on the rare

31

occasions he and Flora came up to London to visit the family.

She flinched at Bel's question. 'No . . . how could I?' she said eventually.

Her niece watched her and waited, a worried look on her face.

'I suppose maybe I still love the man who loved me back then,' she added.

'Wow.' Bel frowned. 'That's complicated. But . . . maybe he still does love you. You don't know.'

The television, put on pause, suddenly sprang to life and startled them both. Flora reached for the remote and turned it off.

'I know people stop loving each other, but I don't really understand how,' Bel said. 'I mean, if you have this intense feeling that takes you over like you can't breathe . . . where does it go?'

Flora smiled and shrugged. 'Where indeed.'

'And can it come back at any time, if it's been there once?' Bel persisted. 'What if I fell in love with someone now, and it didn't work out for whatever reason? And then I met him again, say in twenty years' time – when I'm old and married to someone else – why wouldn't I, potentially, have the same feelings for him that I had before? It could be really dodge.'

Flora laughed. 'You could. But mostly it doesn't work like that. I suppose your feelings for the new person supersede the old love. Or the things that went wrong in the first place – the anger and

32

resentment and stuff – change your feelings. Kill them in most cases.'

'Like with you and Fin.'

'No . . . not like with me and Fin. We were happy, and then he left. There were no bad feelings to kill the love.'

'So if . . .' Bel paused.

'It's late and I'm really tired,' Flora interrupted, before Bel could say any more. 'I think I should get to bed.'

'Yeah, sure. Sorry.' Bel leapt to her feet. 'Time to face the music about those dumb keys, I guess.'

Flora smiled and gave her a hug. 'Good luck with that.'

'If you hear Mum attacking me with a meat cleaver, you will come, won't you?'

'Only if you scream loudly enough. Your mum's floor insulation is second to none.'

CHAPTER 3

14 September

Flora could have turned north up Gloucester Road and gone to the Marks and Spencer on Kensington High Street for the groceries. She had done so before, and Dorothea loved the lemon mousse from there. But she turned right towards the arcade.

It was five days since she had seen Fin, and every day she struggled valiantly to dampen the volcanic emotions his presence had triggered. But, even in her most sensible moments, she couldn't help feeling the tantalising breeze of hope. What if . . . what if . . . she asked herself in the silence of the early hours. And today she made a conscious decision to take one more look.

She spent longer than usual filling her basket. She checked every aisle, lingered in the vegetable section, and was pleased that there was only one cashier on the tills so that the small queue held her up for a few moments more. But there was no sign of Fin and disappointment stung her, made her want to cry. As she walked dispiritedly back to Dorothea's flat, she was aware of the dark shadow hovering at the edge of her brain like a gang of black figures ready to pounce. It frightened her.

When depression hit her a few weeks after Fin had left, she thought she had a physical illness, like flu or M.E. She had been poleaxed, literally unable to get out of bed. It had been three days before Sal, a friend from the hospital, had come round and persuaded Flora to let her in. She had taken one look at her and called the doctor. Flora remembered none of this, but apparently she had been taken into hospital for tests – her GP thinking too that she was the victim of a mysterious virus.

By this time Prue was in charge and had immediately arranged for her to come and stay at Cornwall Crescent. It wasn't until weeks later that depression was finally diagnosed, then more time before the SSRI antidepressants kicked in and Prue felt she was safe to be left alone during the day. But even in her bleakest moments of despair and nihilism, Flora had never considered suicide. Just the task of getting herself dressed or preparing a simple meal had seemed insurmountable; any decision – big or small – impossible.

Flora was hardly back from the shops when the bell rang.

'Simon Kent,' said the voice over the intercom, and she let the doctor in.

'Hi, Flora.'

'Hi.'

'I've just popped in to tell you I've booked an x-ray for her stomach. The appointment should come through in the next week, I said it was urgent. I think we need to check out the pain she keeps complaining about.'

'So you don't think it's just wind?'

'It might be, but it seems too localised. And you say she's not constipated.' He paused, dropping his black case on the floor by the wall. He was dressed in a dark-grey suit and tie today, although often he wore chinos and a casual jacket. 'Nothing else to report?'

Flora shook her head. 'She seems better than usual, less tired. We've been up to the park a lot, which always perks her up.'

She and the doctor had taken a while to become friends, both wary of the professional nature of their situation. But when their patient had been very ill with a bladder infection a few weeks back, he had developed the habit of dropping in to check on her – his surgery was just around the corner – on his way to or from another visit. Flora liked Simon Kent. He made her laugh, and they had gradually developed a sort of soundbite friendship based on the few minutes together as he came and went. But they never met outside the workplace, and she knew virtually nothing about his private life.

'Not being funny,' he said, looking at her questioningly, his head on one side and a slight frown on his brow. 'But you look a tad gloomy today.'

'That obvious is it?' She gave him a rueful smile.

'Not that it's any of my business.'

His gaze didn't waver and Flora found herself blushing. Dr Kent sometimes had a very direct way of looking at her with his dark, intense eyes that she found disconcerting. He was handsome – not with Fin's assured confidence – but quietly good looking: thick dark hair, strong cheekbones, very long dark lashes around his brown eyes, a slim, fit physique. He was one of those men who, although always friendly, was often in a hurry, but would then suddenly stop and just be there. And in those moments, she had a sense that she could confide in him, tell him anything, although she never had thus far. But today she felt fragile and lacked her usual self-control.

'If you really want to know,' she said, 'I bumped into an old boyfriend – well more than a boyfriend really – in the supermarket a few days ago, and I can't get him out of my head.'

He gave a small frown. 'Well, you know what they say. Getting back with an ex is like eating a Mars Bar again and expecting it to have morphed into a Twix.'

She smiled. 'Do they say that?'

'All the time.'

'And do you think "they" are right?'

'My experience is limited to one. But if she's anything to go by, I'd say spot on.'

'OK . . .' She waited for him to explain, but he didn't. Instead, he said, 'Perhaps you need diversion.'

'Like what?'

'Well, I was thinking a bit of ballroom dancing?'

Flora laughed. 'Yeah, sure. That'd do it.'

'Friday night any good?'

'You're serious?'

The doctor looked awkward now, his face suddenly clouded. 'Not a date or anything. I didn't mean that. There's a gang of us go most weekends to a place in Earl's Court. It's fun, gives you a chance to let your hair down. You might enjoy it.'

It was Flora's turn to be embarrassed. 'Thanks, but I can't dance.' She remembered the last time she'd had to, at a friend's wedding. 'I just shuffle about pretending I'm too cool to try any harder.'

'Know the feeling. But you don't have to be able to dance. A couple are full-on Fred Astaire wanna-bees, but the rest of us are just muddling through, having a laugh.'

Flora didn't reply for a minute. Part of her wanted to go, wanted, as Simon said, to divert her thoughts, even for a few hours, away from Fin McCrea. But they were work colleagues . . . it might be awkward.

'I'm afraid I can't do Friday,' she said.

'OK,' he replied with a quick smile. 'Another time, perhaps.'

She nodded. 'That'd be good.'

★   ★   ★

Flora couldn't wait to get Dorothea into bed for her nap that afternoon. She herself felt much more tired than the old lady seemed to be. As soon as she was settled, she went through to the kitchen and made her own lunch: toast and cheese and a tomato. She took her plate and a cup of peppermint tea through to the sitting room and sat down on the sofa with a sigh of relief. I should have said yes to Dr Kent, she told herself as she munched her toast. She hardly ever got out these days; usually she was too knackered after a twelve-hour shift to even consider it. And given that it took time to change and get ready, then to travel somewhere, and she only got off work at eight, the evening was almost over. But I could have made the effort, she thought. He was only trying to be nice.

Her mobile rang and she dug it out of her uniform pocket, swallowing her mouthful before speaking.

'Rene, Hi.'

'I need to have a word with you about something, Flora.' The high-pitched voice on the other end of the phone sounded anxious as usual. 'Is Dorothea asleep? Can I drop round now for half an hour? I don't want her worried.'

'Of course. See you in a minute,' Flora replied. What else could she say to her employer? But she was thoroughly irritated at having her break interrupted. She wondered what Rene wanted to talk about. She made it sound terribly important, but then everything was a drama with Rene.

Dorothea's friend made her customary whirl-wind entrance. She was around sixty, Flora thought, small and very thin, with wild sandy-grey hair wisping around her long face like an over-balancing halo. She dressed invariably in a denim skirt or jeans, with a pastel T-shirt (perhaps also picked up as a bargain in Edinburgh Woollen Mill) topped with a sleeveless, navy padded body-warmer and sensible lace-ups. She had been friends with Dorothea for over thirty years. They had met at an art class, both pupils of a man they called 'the Maestro' – Flora had no idea what his actual name was – who apparently took them for sketching trips to France. When Dorothea had begun getting a little frail, Rene had offered to take over some of the paperwork and bill paying, and it had eventually led to her having Dorothea's power of attorney.

'How is she?' Rene whispered, before dashing through to the sitting room and closing the door behind them with exaggerated care.

'Good, I think. She's seems quite bright today,' Flora told her.

Rene sat down on the sofa and gestured to Flora to do the same.

'I wanted to talk to you without Dorothea overhearing.'

Flora nodded.

'Has she said anything about Mary to you?'

Mary Martin was the nurse who worked almost every night, refusing to take time off because she

40

said she slept most of the time and didn't need to. Bel had developed a dramatic theory that she didn't actually have a home, and that during the day she wandered from café to café, or sat on park benches until it was time to go on duty again.

'No one,' Bel insisted, 'would want to stay in that dingy old flat every single night otherwise.'

'They might if they needed the money, like me. Anyway,' Flora had added, 'she's always banging on about her cat, Millie, so she must have a home somewhere.'

'No, why?' Flora asked Rene now.

'Well, I came over for tea on Saturday, as I usually do. Pia went across the road for some cakes while I had a nice chat with Dorothea, and I took the opportunity to ask her how she was and if she was happy.' Rene paused, giving Flora a glance laden with significance. 'She said yes at first, then she looked towards the door, as if she was worried to say anything else. I told her we were alone but she still seemed nervous. When I pressed her, though, she eventually said, "The nurse . . . is sometimes a bit cross with me."'

Rene pursed her lips and looked wide-eyed at Flora.

'Are you saying she meant Pia?' Flora asked. 'Because I can't imagine she'd ever be unkind to Dorothea. She wouldn't hurt a fly,' she added, in support of the gentle middle-aged Filipina woman who did weekends.

'She wouldn't tell me,' Rene went on, smoothing

her hands over her denim skirt. 'But as you say, it can't be Pia, surely, and certainly not you. She absolutely adores you. I was wondering about Mary.'

'Oh, come on, Rene! Mary's been working here as long as I have. If she was abusing Dorothea, surely she'd have said something before now. And they seem really fond of each other.'

'Well . . .'

'We had that Australian girl for a week when I was ill in the summer and Pia was on holiday.'

Rene frowned. 'Would she remember that far back?'

'Maybe she's confused, or she hasn't had a chance to say anything before.'

Dorothea's friend nodded slowly. 'Maybe . . . but what do you think of Mary . . . as a nurse?'

'It's hard to say. We don't actually work together, just hand over at the beginning and end of shifts. But she seems like a good person to me.'

'So from what you see, Dorothea gets on with Mary alright?'

'Yes, absolutely fine. Mary has some bizarre ideas, like fish making Dorothea pee more in the night, but I've never seen her be anything but kind to her.'

Rene laughed. 'I agree with you, I've always thought her a kindly soul. But perhaps it's different in the middle of the night. It's easy to be grumpy when you're woken up. I mean, Mary's no spring chicken.'

'I don't know how we can find out, unless Dorothea says something more specific.' Although Flora hated the idea that the old lady was being treated unkindly and was too scared to say anything, she thought Rene was making a bit of a drama out of Dorothea's remark. She couldn't imagine any of the nurses being mean in that way.

'Well, that's what I was going to ask you,' Rene said. 'Will you try and talk to her? Be very discreet, but ask her what she thinks of Mary and Pia.'

Flora didn't think this was a particularly discreet line of questioning, but she agreed to try. The bell from Dorothea's bedroom tinkled and Flora got up.

'I won't stay,' Rene whispered, 'I've got to be home to let the cleaner in. Give her my love.' They both went through to the hall. 'And Flora, don't upset her, will you?'

As if, Flora thought, seeing her visitor to the door with some relief. She admired Rene's dedication to the old lady, but her habitual state of anxiety was disconcerting.

As she closed the door, Flora realised she hadn't mentioned the walnut sewing table. She wondered if Dominic had rung Rene.

The weekend stretched ahead of Flora, blissfully empty except for a drinks party upstairs on Saturday night to celebrate Philip's fifty-second birthday.

'I've got someone I want you to meet,' Prue had

told her enthusiastically, on the phone the night before. Those dreaded words. Flora knew her sister meant well and was only trying to distract her from thoughts of Fin, but the string of men lined up over the past two years had caused Flora cringing embarrassment. Philip had fielded a few from the law world, including Derek, whose breath smelt hideous even from across the table, and James, who was recently divorced and clearly hated the entire female sex as a result. From Prue's corner came Freddy, the slimy (and unnervingly rich, according to Prue) music producer from Azerbaijan; Julian, who had followed her to the loo and tried to have sex with her an hour after making her acquaintance, and Robbie, the highly amusing but unashamedly gay design associate. It wasn't encouraging.

'Pleeeese,' Flora had begged, 'do I have to come? I know it's Philip's birthday, but I can see him during the day. I'm just not in the mood for a party right now.'

But Prue was having none of it. 'Nonsense! Getting dressed up and making an effort will do you good. Nothing's to be gained by sitting all alone on a Saturday night, moping about that bloody man.' (Prue, Flora noticed, never mentioned Fin's name these days without attaching the epithet 'bloody'.)

'I've got nothing to wear,' Flora stated, unwisely thinking this might prove the swing vote.

'Well, that's no excuse. I've got cupboards full

of clothes as you well know. Come up in the morning and we'll find you something.' Prue sounded thrilled at the prospect, but Flora knew she risked ending up in a two-thousand-pound designer dress that would make her look like Nancy Dell'Olio, or worse.

'OK, OK, I'll come to the party. I've got the black dress, I can wear that.'

There was a silence at the other end of the phone.

'You look great in the black, of course, but you do wear it a lot. Borrow something of mine for a change,' said Prue.

So Flora sat in bed now, a cup of tea in her hand, summoning up the energy to get dressed and go upstairs to brave her sister's walk-in ward-robe. She could still wear the black, she told herself, and probably would, but she felt obliged to go through the motions for the sake of family harmony.

On her way up, she paused in the black and white marble-tiled hall to check if there was any post. The postman never bothered to deliver to the basement, so her mail was put on the hall table beneath the large Italian-designed mirror broken up into nine squares of glass, some concave, some convex, which distorted the image and always fascinated Flora. For a moment she stared at herself, enjoying the bizarrely broken-up configuration.

There was one letter from the bank, nothing

more. Part of her hoped, each day she checked, that there might be a note from Fin. If he was at all keen to see her, he knew he could contact her through Prue: a Please Forward tag would be worth a try . . . if he was keen. Flora stood turning the bank letter over in her hand, feeling the familiar desire to cry. She was on the point of running back down to the safety of her little flat when a voice stopped her.

'There you are!' Prue was standing at the top of the stairs, dressed in a strawberry-pink Juicy tracksuit, her bare toes gleaming with damson nail polish. 'I was just about to come and get you.'

Flora reluctantly followed her sister to her first-floor bedroom suite where, laid out in rows on the huge double bed, were about ten dresses, still attached to their padded silk hangers. The room was otherwise immaculate: soft white walls, pearl and white appliqué bed cover, a stunning contemporary wardrobe in bleached wood inlaid with charcoal geometric marquetry. The only hint of colour was a washed-out grey-pink, picked out in squares on the rug by the bed, and again in the tiny button beading around the cushions on the white slub-linen sofa.

'Where's Philip?' Flora asked, brandishing his wrapped present – a book from the Booker short list he'd said he wanted.

'Running in the park. He'll be back soon.' Prue spoke dismissively about her husband, clearly impatient to be getting on with the fashion show.

She held out her arm with a flourish to indicate the spread. 'Ta-da!' She chuckled. 'This is going to be fun.'

And it was fun, in that it was like dressing up as they'd done as children. Many of the frocks technically looked good on Flora – she was slim with a small bust, slightly above medium height and held herself well.

'Perfect!' Prue shrieked, not for the first time, as Flora twirled in front of the mirror in a Donna Karan halter-neck jersey dress which clung to her like a bandage. 'That's the one! That is *the* one.'

'It looks great, I admit . . . if I was somebody else.' Flora was stubborn.

Prue groaned and threw herself onto the sofa, burying her head in her hands. 'Christ, darling. You look like a fucking supermodel and you're still not satisfied. I give up.'

'I'm not being difficult, honest,' Flora pleaded, wriggling out of the soft scarlet jersey. 'It's just it's your wardrobe, your style. I'd feel a fake in this gorgeous dress, but on you it looks spectacular. It looks like *you*.' She really appreciated Prue's efforts to dress her more stylishly, but, as with Bel, her sister's task would always be an uphill one. Flora liked good clothes, she just wasn't particularly interested in wearing them herself.

Her sister was somewhat mollified and gave a nonchalant shrug, moving to gather the dresses up and begin replacing them in the wardrobe which ran along one end of the bedroom.

'Well, you know where they are if you change your mind. Let's get a cup of coffee and wait for the birthday boy. Go and dig that lazy niece of yours out of bed, will you?'

Flora went out after lunch and walked over the hill to Holland Park. It was drizzling and cold, but she was frightened of staying alone in the basement for too long and sliding into the pit that she was sure awaited her if she persisted in moping about Fin. But how can I stop myself, she wondered, as she trudged up Ladbroke Grove. It was a known fact that the more you tried not to think of something, the more you found yourself doing so. And that glimpse of him had been so unsatisfactory: both tantalising in that it had immediately triggered the memories, the familiarity, and pointless because it led nowhere.

Waitrose on Cromwell Road had now acquired this bizarre significance. It seemed an island in her thoughts, an anchor to the one person in the world she longed to see. She was tempted to go there now, to hang around on the off chance he was getting food for the weekend. But her pride wouldn't permit it.

Instead, she sat on a newspaper on a damp bench, the hood of her mac low over her face, and gave in to memories.

The first time she ever saw him, it had been as if a light had gone on in her brain. She seemed to recognise him instantly, although she was sure she'd never met him before in her life. She'd been off duty when he'd been admitted to her ward, men's orthopaedic, with a broken arm and collar bone – knocked off his bike on the South Downs by a four-by-four on a tight corner. He was asleep, lying propped against the pillows, naked from the waist up. His muscular torso was golden from the sun, his right arm encased in a fresh, snow-white long-arm cast, bent at the elbow and resting on a pillow. She had picked up his chart from where it hung on the end of the bed, wanting to check his obs, but all she could do was stare.

Cath, a high-spirited junior nurse, came up behind her.

'Fancy a bit, do you?' she'd whispered cheekily, digging Flora in the ribs and adding, 'Get in line,' as she hurried off to deal with another patient.

Flora hadn't replied, bewildered by her response to the man in the bed. She'd glanced at the sheet attached to the clipboard. His name, it seemed, was Finlay McCrea. When she looked up again she was aware of a pair of light grey eyes, clouded with sleep, boring into her.

'Bugger . . .' she heard him say as he eyed his cast, and she couldn't help smiling.

'Could put it like that,' she said, hanging his chart back on the bed.

Then he smiled, his eyes coming alive, full of wry humour. 'I thought you might be heavenly for a moment there. Morphine fucks with your head. Love it.'

49

'Heavenly? In this get-up?' Flora indicated her shapeless royal-blue cotton tunic and trousers with distaste.

'Well . . . who's to say angels only come in white?'

She blushed in the face of his casual charm and made an effort to pull herself together.

'You'll be discharged later today, once you've seen the doctor. They only kept you in overnight in case you had a head injury.' She attempted a businesslike tone. 'Do you need any more pain relief? You're due for some.'

Fin had shaken his blond head. 'Nope, seems OK at the moment.' He paused for only a fraction of a second before peering at the name tag on her uniform and saying, 'Will you give me your number before I go, Nurse Bancroft?'

His bold request, after barely five minutes' acquaintance, took her breath away. But she'd given it to him nonetheless.

'James, you know Flora don't you?' Prue didn't wait to find out the answer before moving off to greet another guest.

James looked blankly at her and then gave a vague smile.

'We met at one of Prue's dinners,' Flora reminded him – she had no trouble remembering his vituperative rant about his ex, and the obvious boredom with which he'd greeted her attempts at conversation. She wasn't in the mood tonight.

50

'Yeah . . . I'm sure you're right,' he drawled as he looked over her shoulder at the people coming into the room.

Flora stood awkwardly for a moment, a glass of champagne warming in one hand, then suddenly found herself overwhelmed with annoyance. She did what she never normally would have done: she walked away without another word. Out of the corner of her eye, she saw his look of surprise with some satisfaction.

She went and joined Bel and two of her friends, who hovered, giggling, in the hall just outside the drawing room.

'Havin' a good time, honey?' Bel spoke with a bad American accent, her expression full of mischief. All three girls were flushed from champagne, Bel's two friends touchingly self-conscious in their tiny skirts, tottering heels and red, glossy lips. Bel had managed a glittery T-shirt over her black jeans and pumps.

'Bit on the grim side so far,' Flora replied, making them all giggle some more. 'I think I'll sneak off in a moment. Prue won't notice.'

'What won't I notice?' Prue was suddenly at her side, tugging at the sleeve of the black dress. 'I thought you'd be skulking out here. Come on. I've got someone you're going to totally adore.'

She was towed back into the party behind her sister, glamorous in the red Donna Karan Flora had earlier discarded. I'm glad she listened to me, Flora thought, as she glanced round at Bel and her friends and mouthed 'Rescue me', like a prisoner on the way to the scaffold.

'Flora, I'd like you to meet Jake. Jake, this is Flora, my little sister.'

Flora duly shook hands with the man she was going to adore. And Jake *was* cute, no question – almost pretty with his neat features and wide blue eyes, his light-brown hair in soft curls. He looked like another designer in the way he was dressed: all in black except for his super-white shirt, which had black edging on the inside of the collar and cuffs, and mother-of-pearl stud buttons down the front. He gave Flora an amused smile.

'Hi. I never knew Prue had a sister.'

'You work with her?'

'Sort of. I design kitchens. I did the one here.'

'Oh, *that* Jake.'

'Cursing me from here to kingdom come, was she?'

Flora nodded and laughed. 'The black marble being a month late was a bit of a challenge, I seem to remember.'

He grinned. 'Not my finest hour. But the end result is fantastic, don't you think?'

'It certainly looks lovely . . .' Flora hesitated.

'But?'

'I suppose it's a bit severe for my taste.'

'Yeah, me too. My own kitchen's mostly wood.'

'Prue loves it, though,' she added quickly, in case he was offended.

But Jake just shrugged. 'All that matters in the

end . . . that the client is happy.' He took a gulp of champagne. 'So what do you do?'

For a while they stood together, chatting. Flora found him attractive. He was easy to talk to, teasing and a bit flirtatious – although she was sure he had no real interest in her – and she wished she could just fall in love with him then and there. She could live with him in his wooden kitchen with all his black clothes and forget that Fin even existed. But Fin's departure seemed to have built a wall around her, sealing her off from the cells in her body that responded to another man's sexual advances.

Conversation was stopped by Prue clapping her hands for silence. She held onto the sleeve of her husband's bespoke suit as she began to speak, as if she were worried he'd escape.

'Philip didn't want me to say anything. He didn't want me to give him a party. He didn't want to have another birthday, or be a year older. But, as usual, I *persuaded* him it was for the best . . .' There was raucous laughter and some barracking from the guests at the commonly accepted pretence that Prue wore the trousers in the family. And Philip, as always, beamed genially at the crowd, accepting the spotlight with his usual unflappable calm. Flora adored her brother-in-law. He was a kind, non-judgemental man, patient with his bossy wife, a good father to Bel, and had been Flora's friend through thick and thin. But she knew that the amiably charming façade he showed to the

53

world hid a cutting intellect that had fooled many an opponent, both in and out of court. Now he shot the cuffs of his white shirt, smoothed his blue-patterned tie, and began his witty reply.

When the speeches were over, Flora and Jake had been separated. She looked around for him and saw him laughing in the corner of the room with a skinny redhead. So she crept away before her sister could stop her, a bit irritated with herself for not making more effort to be charming to Jake.

CHAPTER 4

17 September

As Flora made her way down Gloucester Road just before eight the following Monday, she decided that Fin was no longer in town. It was a week since she'd bumped into him and there had been no sign of him since, no word left at Prue's house, nothing. He'll be off on another climb, she told herself, professing a certain relief that she could start to put him behind her again, to begin living the life she intended to live, but was somehow perpetually putting on hold. Prue had been on the phone to her early Sunday morning, her voice squeaky with excitement.

'Darling, breaking news! Jake *adores* you. *And* he fancies you like mad. His very words: "She's gorgeous." He was very distressed you disappeared without saying goodbye.'

'Really?' Flora had asked, not believing her sister's hyperbole one bit. He'd seemed so young and too self-consciously trendy to be interested in someone like her.

'Yes, really. You *are* gorgeous, I keep telling you. So? Did you like him?'

'I did. I . . . I thought he was very attractive,' she was trying to tell the truth without getting her sister's hopes up. It didn't work.

'Bingo! That's the first time you've said that about *anyone* since that bloody man whose name we won't mention in case I have a stroke. Anyway, I hope you don't mind, I gave him your number.'

Prue sounded as if she'd already married them off and Flora hadn't wanted to burst her bubble. He probably won't call, she thought, but if what she said was true and Jake did like her, perhaps she *should* see him. Just do it, find out if she could.

Dorothea was sitting up in bed, eating a bowl of cornflakes on the bed table in front of her.

'Morning, Dorothea.' Flora gave her arm a quick stroke, but the old lady seemed almost alarmed to see her. She blinked nervily behind her glasses and jabbed uselessly at the cornflakes with her spoon.

'Are you alright? Did you have a bad night?' Flora enquired softly.

The old lady stared at her. 'I think . . . I did.'

'Was something bothering you?'

Mary Martin popped her head round the door. 'See you a minute before I go?'

Assuring Dorothea she would be back, Flora went through to the kitchen where Mary was washing up her tea mug.

'Up and down like Tower Bridge she was,

56

sometimes barely an hour in between,' Mary told her. 'Said she wanted to wee, but mostly she didn't.' She was a tall, heavily built Irish woman, with short, dyed brown hair pinned back from her face with incongruously girlie clips, usually in pink or blue. She was always dressed in a maroon fleece and black tracksuit bottoms, never bothering with a uniform dress. 'I thought perhaps it was the fish again, but Pia said she'd given her scrambled eggs last night.'

'And was she distressed?'

'Like she is now. I'm not sure she slept at all.'

Mary put her mug back in the cupboard. They all had their own particular mugs. Mary's was a thick, blue pottery one, large and round. Flora's was made of thin white china with 'Mad Aunt' written on the side in pink; Bel had given it to her for Christmas.

'Do you think she's in pain? Maybe her stomach again?'

'I asked and she said no, but it's hard to tell. I hope she's not building up to another TIA. She doesn't have a temperature but she definitely isn't herself. I think the season change can affect old people. They see the light fade and think of winter and–'

'I'll ask Dr Kent to drop in, perhaps.' Flora interrupted Mary before she could expand on another of her wacky theories. And no doubt the onset-of-winter speculation would have segued neatly into the need to keep the patient alive till the following summer. It was always hard to get new jobs in the winter, Mary said, because none of the nurses were taking holidays, and the patients died more often. It didn't make sense, but that didn't stop her repeating it on an almost daily basis.

Mary chuckled to herself. 'You realise I'm in love with the man, don't you?'

'Dr Kent?'

'Mmm. What a dreamboat. So kind and handsome.' Mary had had to call him out recently when Dorothea was taken ill in the night.

Flora laughed. 'Do you think?'

'Well, don't you?'

'Never thought about him like that. But I like him, he's brilliant with Dorothea.'

Mary shook her head in mock despair. 'You've got no taste, you. Anyway, I'd best be getting back to little Millikins.' She yawned. 'Christ, I'm knackered. Not used to having to work for my living.' She gathered her black backpack from the hall floor and went to say goodbye to her patient.

Dorothea seemed to settle down during the morning. Flora suggested she stay in bed until lunchtime, and the old lady slept. She seemed a little dazed, however, when Flora got her up and into the sitting room.

'Is Peter coming?' Dorothea asked, as Flora collected the tray with the remains of her fish, broccoli and mashed potato. She hadn't eaten much, but Flora didn't want to force her.

'Peter?' The old lady had never mentioned a Peter before.

Dorothea gave a small laugh. 'Er, you know . . .' She waved her right hand in the air. 'Is it Peter I mean . . . the man . . .' She lapsed into silence.

'Dominic? Your nephew?' Flora suggested, but Dorothea shook her head.

'No. Not him.' The arm was up again as Flora watched her struggle with her memory.

'Keith Godly . . .? Dr Kent?' She couldn't think of any other men that visited the old lady.

Dorothea shook her head again and gave a small giggle. 'Silly old me,' she said. 'I think . . . I was remembering someone else.'

The doorbell rang.

'That might be Dr Kent,' Flora said, and went to let him in.

'She's not herself,' Flora told him.

'I'll take a look.' He seemed in a rush, as was often the case, and went on through to the sitting room.

'Flora tells me you didn't sleep well last night?' He spoke so gently to her, and the old lady gave him a radiant smile.

'It . . . wasn't anything . . . much,' she said, almost apologetically.

The doctor bent to take her pulse. For a second there was silence in the room, only the laboured ticking of the long-case clock by the fire-place. He turned to Flora.

'What's her temperature?'

59

'Normal.'

Flora helped Dorothea take off her cardigan; Dr Kent fixed the blood-pressure cuff around her right upper arm and pressed the button.

'Hmm.' He watched the display on the Boots sphygmomanometer. 'OK, that's it. How are you feeling now, Dorothea? Do you have a headache or anything? Is your stomach bothering you?'

The old lady took a long, slow breath. 'I . . . don't think so.' She stared ahead, as if she was unaware the doctor and Flora were there at all.

He got up and motioned Flora to join him outside.

'Her blood pressure's a bit raised, but nothing alarming. I can't find any sign of anything serious.'

'Sorry to drag you out.'

'No, no, not at all. I was on my way to another patient anyway. Maybe she's just got something on her mind?'

'We've asked her, but she won't say. She's not of the generation to complain.'

Dr Kent smiled. 'No, bless her. She's a sweetheart.' He glanced at Flora as he put on his coat. 'Did you sort out the boyfriend problem?'

'I did . . . sort of.'

'You missed a good night of ballroom.'

She smiled. 'I was stupid. I should have come.'

She closed the door behind him, suddenly wondering what his private life was like. She realised she didn't even know if he was married or had children. If he's asking me to go dancing with him, he's probably not married, she decided.

Her mobile rang as she was walking to the bus stop that night.

'Flora?'

'Yes.'

'It's Jake. Jake Hobley, from the other night.'

'Jake, hi.' She was taken by surprise at hearing his voice, and couldn't think of what else to say.

A bus roared past and she missed his next words. He repeated them: 'Just wondered if you felt like a drink sometime?'

Flora took a deep breath, pressing the phone hard to her ear against the traffic noise. 'Yes, I'd like that.'

They arranged to meet that Thursday at a bar in Notting Hill. She felt anxious as soon as she'd ended the call. Was this a date? The thought was terrifying. She immediately wanted to ring and cancel. I don't have to go, she told herself, I can make some excuse on the day. But that didn't seem to soothe her. At some stage, if she wasn't to spend the rest of her life alone, she knew she would have to cross the line.

When Flora got home, Prue was standing on the doorstep of the main house, silhouetted by the light from the hall behind her. Despite it being so late, her sister was still in her work clothes – a charcoal tailored suit and cream shirt – talking to a blonde girl who was clutching an armful of giant folders containing what looked like fabric samples. The girl said goodbye when she saw Flora, and clattered down the steps into the night.

'Darling, come in for a sec.' Prue held the door open. 'God, I'm whacked. Amy promised me those samples at nine this morning. People are so casual. Does she really think the client'll give a toss that UPS went to the wrong house?'

Flora looked sympathetic and waited for the inevitable.

'Well, has he called?' Prue asked, as soon as the door was shut.

'Just now. We're meeting for a drink on Thursday.'

Prue squealed with delight, clasping her hands in front of her in anticipation. 'Quick glass? You can fill me in.'

'OK.' She could do with some wine to steady her nerves. 'But there's nothing to tell.'

They perched on the stools in the kitchen.

'What do you know about him?' Flora asked, after giving Prue a verbatim account of her very brief phone call from Jake.

'Not much really, except that he's single.' Prue laughed. 'All you need to know really.'

'Why isn't he married?'

Prue shrugged. 'Why aren't you married?' She must have seen Flora's face fall, because she hurried on. 'He's only thirty-seven. Lots of men aren't married by then. Plus he never stops working.'

'So you don't know about any girlfriends?'

'Doh! He wouldn't be asking you out if he had a girlfriend, now would he?' Prue did one of the eye rolls she kept specially for anything to do with Flora's frustratingly single status.

'I certainly hope not.'

Prue frowned. 'You will go, won't you? I know you, Flora Bancroft. You'll invent some feeble excuse and cry off at the last minute.'

How perceptive, thought Flora. 'OK . . . just one drink. But I reserve the right to not like him enough and not go out with him ever again, no matter what you say.'

'Christ, darling! You'd think I was forcing you on a date with Quasimodo . . . or worse, Simon Cowell. Jake's a poppet. How bad can it be, having a drink with a cute guy in a cool bar of a Thursday night?'

'Put like that,' Flora grinned.

'No helping some people,' her sister chuckled, looking pleased with herself.

By Thursday, Flora was a bag of nerves. The old lady had recovered her spirits over the course of the week, and they had settled back into their normal routine – but neither Flora nor Mary had managed to get to the bottom of what had been bothering Dorothea.

Flora was meeting Jake at nine. She could have gone straight from work, but that would have meant changing and getting ready in Dorothea's flat.

Instead, she raced home and had a shower, threw almost her entire wardrobe on the bed before deciding on black jeans, a lacy cream top and black pumps. It would do, she told herself.

He was already there when she arrived, sitting at a table in the corner of the room. The bar was manic: loud and drunk and young and very Thursday night. Flora wasn't used to the noise or the crowded space, but she was grateful for it nonetheless. It masked her nervous tension.

Jake, on the other hand, seemed perfectly at ease. He rose to greet her, his boyish face breaking out into a big smile.

'Hi, there. Great you could make it. What'll it be?' He pulled a face as a guy stumbled drunkenly into the table as he went past, clutching an empty cocktail glass. 'Bit crazy in here. Would you rather go somewhere quieter?'

Flora shook her head. 'No, it's fun.' She didn't want to seem her age, even if she felt it in this melee of twenty-somethings. She asked for a beer.

'Nothing stronger? How about a cocktail? They do fantastic margaritas here.'

She hesitated. She hadn't eaten, but the thought of a heavy shot of alcohol right now was very appealing. 'Oh, OK. Make it a margarita then.'

Jake smiled approvingly. In for a penny, Flora thought.

'You look great,' Jake said later, eyeing her over his drink, a flirtatious smile hovering around his mouth.

'Thanks,' she muttered, not believing a word and concentrating hard on the purple tortilla chip in her hand, a bowl of which had been delivered with the order.

'Where has Prue been hiding you?' he asked. 'You weren't in the basement when I was doing the kitchen, were you?'

'No, I was living in Brighton at the time.'

'Why did you move back? Not sure I'd swap life by the sea for a basement in Ladbroke Grove.'

He was very direct with his questioning, but she didn't mind. It was better than just making small talk about who they knew and what they did.

'I had a breakdown,' she said, the alcohol making quick work of her normal reticence. 'And Prue took me in.'

Jake raised his eyebrows. 'OK . . . and now I ask you why and you say it's none of my business.'

She laughed. 'It's not a secret. The man in my life walked out on me and I didn't handle it very well.' She saw him nodding.

'But I'm fine now,' she added. 'It was three years ago.'

'I've not really done the relationship thing,' he said, draining the last of his Margarita and checking her glass. 'You sort of have to give it time and attention I reckon, and setting up my business has taken all of that so far.'

Flora hesitated. She didn't want him to think she was concerned about whether he wanted a relationship now or not, because she wasn't. Her reply was neutral: 'I know how many hours Prue puts in. I can imagine it's not easy.'

'Another?' he asked.

'Thanks.' She drained her glass too.

The second cocktail seemed to go down even faster than the first. No tortilla chips with this one. She knew, vaguely, that she should eat, but things were going well. He was flirting, she was flirting back. It wasn't so hard; she hadn't forgotten.

God knows what time it was when Jake got up and dragged her to her feet. 'Come on. Let's go back to mine. I only live two streets away.'

'So do I . . . well, four or five streets anyway.'

'Mine's closer then. Closer's better.' He guided her through the room, which had thinned out considerably since they'd arrived.

Jake's flat was on the first floor of one of the large terraced houses off Westbourne Park Road. The ceilings were high, the sash windows in the open-plan living room/kitchen making a bay which looked over the street. The space was uncluttered, sparse, as if Jake spent very little time there. The kitchen cupboards were a warm oak – as promised – the furniture low and modern, the old floorboards stripped. Flora was feeling even more heady than she had in the bar. The night air had seemed to double the effect of the cocktails to dangerous levels. But when Jake produced a bottle of champagne from the fridge she didn't argue.

They both sat on the black leather sofa.

'What made you choose kitchens . . . to design I mean?' she asked, for something to say. The change of venue, the fact they were now alone, seemed to have created an awkward constraint between them.

'I'm a cabinetmaker by trade, and when I was putting in kitchen cupboards I noticed how lost most people are when it comes to organising their kitchens so they function properly.' He shrugged. 'They basically haven't a clue. So I thought, hmm, bit of an opportunity here.'

'But how did you know how a kitchen functions?' Flora was trying hard to keep track of what he was saying. The champagne was cold and refreshing, and she found herself doing what she seldom did: living in the moment.

Jake laughed. 'Well, I didn't, but it wasn't rocket science. And then I got busy, too busy to do it all myself, so I started Hobley and Star with my mate Gus.'

They talked on for a while, the conversation getting more and more disjointed as the bottle level dropped. She had no idea what they were talking about, the world had become a pleasant, hazy, floating place.

'When we met at the party, I thought you were too trendy for me,' she said, leaning back against the low back of the sofa as she met his eye. 'I find those clothes slightly intimidating.'

Jake grinned as he glanced down at his dark shirt

and skinny black jeans, waggling the long points of his lace-up shoes. 'That's the idea.'

'To be intimidating?'

'Yeah. It puts a sort of handy buffer between you and the client.' He paused. 'Look, I'm an ordinary guy. I made cabinets. I never took my jeans off . . . but they came from the Blue Harbour sale back then. Now I have to relate to rich people who hang out with – or are – celebrities and the super-cool. They care about dumb things like status and appearance. So I do too. I play the game.'

Flora smiled. 'But you like the clothes too.'

'Yeah, I suppose I've come to like them . . . quite a lot, I'm afraid,' he admitted with a shy grin.

'Nothing wrong with that,' she said. And as she spoke he reached for her, laying his hand against her cheek in a gentle caress.

'Is it OK if I kiss you?' he asked.

The light from the uncurtained window woke her. Jake's clock read five past seven. For a moment she stared at it, blinking. Then she stared at Jake, who lay beside her, his face childlike in sleep, his light curls crushed into the pillow. She remembered the sex almost with surprise. Surprise that it had happened at all, and surprise that she had enjoyed it, drunk as she was. Jake had made it fun, lighthearted, just two people getting together for mutual pleasure. But for Flora it was much more than that. Not because she thought herself in love with him, but because he was the first person she'd had sex with, the first person she'd kissed, or even touched in that way since Fin.

She pushed the duvet back and began to slide carefully out of bed, not wanting to disturb Jake. She would be late for work if she didn't hurry. Her uniform was in Dorothea's flat, but she couldn't go to work looking this wrecked. She went through to the bathroom and tried to make the shower work. But the state-of-the-art controls were beyond her in her dazed state, and she gave up, just sluicing her face with some water and borrowing Jake's comb to tidy her hair.

'You weren't going to leg it without saying goodbye again, were you?' Jake stood leaning on the bathroom doorway in his boxers, rubbing his eyes.

'I was, actually.'

'Very bad manners,' he said. 'Won't you even have some coffee before you go?'

Flora shook her head. 'I have to be on duty at eight, and I've got to run home and change first.'

Jake shrugged. 'Couldn't you pull a sicky and come back to bed?'

Flora shook her head. That was the trouble with private nursing, the sense of obligation you developed for your patient. If she didn't show, the people who would suffer most would be the night nurse, who had to hang around until a replacement was found – and Dorothea.

For a moment they stood and looked at each other in silence.

'Thanks . . . thanks for last night,' Flora said. 'I had fun.'

'Yeah, me too.' He moved aside to let her go.

As soon as Mary saw her, she raised her eyebrows, giving an amused smile.

'Rough night, eh?'

'Is it that obvious?'

'Perhaps not to most. But I'm from a family of professional drunks, me. Curse of the Irish. I'd recognise that jazzy look about the eyes at forty paces.'

Flora sat down heavily on the wooden chair in the kitchen.

'Coffee?' Mary moved to the kettle. 'Water's just boiled.'

Flora nodded gratefully.

'Don't forget it's the stomach x-ray today. Rene rang last night to say she'll be here to pick you up at nine-thirty.'

Flora's eyes flew wide open. 'Oh, no! Not today . . . please, please don't let it be today. I'd totally forgotten.'

Mary laughed as she handed Flora her steaming mug of instant coffee. 'Must say, I don't envy you the outing.'

Flora looked at her watch in a panic. 'I'd better get her dressed or we won't be ready in time. Did she have a good night?'

'Yes, pretty normal. I thought I heard her cry out at one point, but when I went in she was fast asleep. She seems quite bright this morning.'

'Does she know about the x-ray?'

Mary nodded. 'Not sure she took it in, but I told her.' She went into the hall to get her backpack. 'Sure you'll be OK? You look pretty rough. I could stay and help with getting her ready if you like.'

'Thanks, Mary. That's a really kind offer, but I'll be fine once the coffee kicks in. You get off.'

The morning was hell for Flora as she struggled with her pounding head and incipient nausea, still reeling from the previous night. Sex with a man on a first date, when she wasn't sure she even fancied him that much? She had shocked herself.

She went through the routine of the bed-bath mechanically, rubbing the warm flannel around the old lady's body, quickly drying her before she got cold. But she remembered the moment when Jake had laid his hand against her cheek. She knew she had hesitated for a fraction of a second before leaning into his caress. Then she'd made the decision to go with it, with him. And yes, she had felt a drunken desire, which grew as she gradually let herself go, as she gave in to his enthusiastic lovemaking. But she knew she was not in love with him.

Might love grow? she asked herself, doubtful. But the spectre of Fin, never far from the surface, chose that moment to rise up and offer a rude comparison. The head-over-heels obsession they had had for each other made her feelings for Jake Hobley pale into insignificance. But does it always have to be like that? she wondered, as she bent to tie the laces on her patient's beige shoes, suddenly disheartened by the likelihood of ever finding such strength of feeling for another man.

Rene drove up to the entrance of Charing Cross Hospital in her battered Volvo and stopped in the drop-off parking bay.

'Could you not get too close to the pavement?' Flora asked, knowing from past experience that it was easier to lift Dorothea into her chair from the road. 'Just here would be great.'

'I'll park somewhere and find you. First floor, isn't it?' An obsessive stickler for rules and regulations, Rene's gaze darted fretfully about, on the lookout for officials.

Flora did her best to hurry, but it wasn't easy getting Dorothea out of the front seat and into the wheelchair.

'Put your hand up here.' She swung the old lady's legs, encased in the navy polyester slacks, out onto the road, placing her hand on the top of the door as she hauled her up. 'Hang on tight.' She eased Dorothea round until she could sit back into the chair. The old lady had been completely silent on the journey to the hospital, just staring out of the window at the passing traffic. Now she looked up at Flora, her face a mask of bewilderment and anxiety.

'It's OK, we've done it.' Flora gave her a reassuring smile as she tucked the rug securely around her patient's knees.

The x-ray department was packed. Flora asked how long it might be until they were seen, but the unsmiling receptionist, clearly used to this question, merely shrugged. 'We're running late,' she intoned, pointing to the blackboard on the wall on which was scrawled in chalk, *Current waiting time, approx one hour.*

Flora pushed the chair to the end of a row of seats and put on the brake.

'Might be a long wait,' she told Dorothea.

'I . . . don't mind. I find waiting rooms entertaining.'

'You do?'

Dorothea's eyes flickered with a smile. 'I don't get out much these days.'

Flora grinned back. 'True. Well, Rene will be here soon. Do you want anything to drink? I've brought some water.' But the old lady waved her hand to indicate she didn't.

Flora drank some water herself. She wasn't feeling any better, she was just functioning on autopilot, looking forward to the moment when she could lie horizontal again, and sleep. Blurred thoughts of Jake strung through her brain, making her feel alternately uneasy and liberated; her body felt almost bruised. But perhaps, whatever happened next between them, Jake's touch might have begun to expunge the memory of Fin's.

The x-ray, when it finally happened, was over in minutes; undressing Dorothea and dressing her again seemed to take hours and was exhausting. Rene fussed around her friend, making everything more stressful for Flora, and probably for Dorothea too, but it was finally done, and Flora wheeled the chair out towards the exit with relief. Rene moved ahead to open the door to the lifts.

'Flora . . . Flora, wait.' The voice came from behind her and a tall figure leaped to her side.

CHAPTER 5

Flora stopped, clinging onto the chair handles as she realised who it was. She saw Rene waiting, holding the door open, but she couldn't move.

Fin was grinning from ear to ear. 'God, is this a stroke of luck or what! I've been dying to see you again after the supermarket, but I didn't know where you were.'

'You're here for an x-ray?' She asked, realising how stupid her question was. Why else would someone like Fin be hanging around a hospital x-ray department?

He nodded. 'I'm still getting pain when I walk, and they thought it might be some gruesome condition where the hip begins to crumble because the blood's been cut off . . . altogether too much information.'

'Avascular necrosis?'

Fin looked impressed. 'That's the one.'

'And is it?'

'They haven't told me yet.'

Rene was watching her impatiently.

'Listen, I've got to go,' Flora said, beginning to move the wheelchair forward.

Fin glanced over at Rene and gave her a charming smile before turning his attention back to Flora. 'Hey, don't rush off again without telling me how I can get hold of you. Please.'

'If you can manage the doors,' Rene was calling, 'I'll go ahead and get the car round to the front.'

'Thanks, I'm just coming.' Flora was flustered, her heart jumping in her chest. 'I'm at Prue's,' she muttered to Fin as she walked.

He frowned. 'You're living with your sister?'

'In the basement flat,' she said.

'OK . . .' He followed her, propping the door open as she moved towards the lift. 'Could you give me your number though? I'm not sure I still have hers.'

She waited by the lift, hardly daring to meet his eye. She knew she looked a wreck, and all she could think of was Jake's hands all over her naked body. The lift was taking a bloody age. Fin hovered, his eyes searing into her. Can he tell what I've been doing? she wondered. Not that he had any right to judge.

'Flora?' His tone softened to hardly more than a whisper, and she felt his hand on her shoulder. 'Please. Can we meet up? Just once?'

She looked up at him finally. Their eyes met, and a frisson of pure longing passed through her tired body as she took in his familiar face, his expression both boyish and pleading. She tore her gaze away.

'OK . . .' She rattled her mobile number off. His face looked panicked as he tried to remember it while rooting around in his Eastpak for a pen, quoting the number back to himself. She relented, and repeated it more slowly. He found a pen and wrote hastily on the back of his hand. She remembered him often writing stuff on his hand or the inside of his wrist, and also her frequent, light-hearted advice to him that this wasn't the best way to file information.

The lift doors opened and she wheeled Dorothea into the crowded interior, everyone pressing themselves against the sides to make room for the chair. There was no space for Fin, and she didn't turn round as the doors closed.

Flora had thought she would sleep like the dead that night. When she got home, almost dizzy with exhaustion, she just ate some toast, drank a large glass of water and was in bed before nine o'clock. But minutes later her mobile pinged with a message. Fin, she thought, as she reached across for it, and suddenly she was wide awake.

Last night great. Should do it again soon? Best, Jake, read the text.

She fell back on the pillows, disappointed, and then cursed herself for giving in and letting Fin have her number. She felt suddenly on the back foot, as had so often been the case in the past – waiting for him, in thrall to him, however willingly. And although she wanted him to ring, part of her also dreaded hearing what he had to say: perhaps that he had moved on, or that he just wanted to exonerate himself, no more than that. Fantasies that he still loved her were nothing short of imbecilic, she knew. And here was Jake, willing to take her on.

Yes, I enjoyed it too. Bad head now! See you soon, she texted back to Jake on the spur of the moment.

Fuck Fin, she thought. I need to have some fun with someone who appreciates me, not spend the rest of my life angsting about a selfish moron who's too stupid to see what he had when he had it. She smiled to herself. I'm beginning to sound like my sister, she thought, as she finally drifted into sleep.

Flora mooched around for the rest of the weekend, checking her mobile a ridiculous number of times, and gradually getting more and more angry with Fin. Why did he ask for my number if he wasn't going to use it? she asked herself repeatedly. What does he want from me? But however much she talked herself down, the feeling that she might see him again drove her heart to race, put her off her food, made her languish on the sofa, dreaming, like a lovesick teenager.

She was glad when it was Monday again.

'Morning Keith,' she said, stopping by the porter's desk.

Keith's face lit up. 'Florence! Haven't seen much of you recently. How's it all going?'

'Not so bad,' Flora replied. 'You?'

For once Keith Godly didn't pull a face. 'Yeah. Not so bad my end either. Been out a bit . . .' He looked embarrassed and hurried on. 'Nothing serious yet.'

'Know the feeling.' Flora decided the porter did look different this morning, his heavy face topped with the dark buzz-cut somehow brighter, a light in his normally troubled eyes.

'Do you now? So you've got something brewing too?'

'You could put it like that,' she laughed.

Keith nodded approvingly. 'Nothing like a bit of action to lift the spirits, eh?'

Mary looked relieved to see her and immediately pulled her into the kitchen before she even had time to take off her coat.

'Happened again. Sunday night, just like last week. She was as twitchy as hell all night. Calling out all the time, saying she was uncomfortable, or wanted a wee, anything and nothing. Seems she just wanted me there.'

'But she didn't seem ill?'

'I took her blood pressure, which was quite high, but it often is. And she doesn't have a temperature. I'm saying, it's just like last time.'

Both of them stood thinking for a while.

'You don't think it has anything to do with Pia do you? I mean, that's two weeks running that she's been like this on a Sunday night. And Pia stayed over Saturday night both weeks, didn't she?'

Mary nodded, reaching for the kettle and filling it. 'Pia said she needed the extra work, and I must say it was grand having the night off.'

'So Pia was here all weekend each time.'

Mary looked at her, frowning. 'Are you thinking there's something going on?'

Flora told her about what Rene had said.

'But can you imagine Pia being mean to anyone?' Mary countered.

'No, but that doesn't mean she isn't, does it?'

'Should you talk to Dorothea again?'

'I suppose. But I don't want to put something into her mind about Pia if it's not true.'

'Christ,' Mary muttered. 'Pia seemed very bright and breezy about the day when I came on. How can we find out then?'

'I'll try again, and I'll tell Rene. Not sure what else we can do.'

Mary's brow darkened. 'If anyone's bullying that sweet old lady, she'll have me to answer to.'

'Well, hold on. Let's establish some facts first. It's probably nothing to do with any of us.'

Flora waited till she had settled Dorothea. It was a gloomy day, and she put the lamp on next to the old lady's chair, then sat down opposite her on the sofa.

'Dorothea, I . . . er . . . I wanted to ask you about Pia.' This wasn't the first time she had asked, but the old lady was always vague in her replies.

'Pia?' She looked blankly at Flora.

'You know, the nurse who looks after you at the weekend.'

Dorothea looked away, then down at her hands.

'Dorothea?'

'What is it that you want to know?' she eventually replied.

'Well, I was wondering if you like having her here.'

There was a very long pause.

'I think she's . . . helpful.'

Flora was puzzled by the word. 'So you do nice things together do you? She said in the report that she took you to church on Sunday . . . in Eldon Road?'

Another pause.

'She . . . No, she didn't.'

Flora was surprised, but maybe Dorothea had forgotten. It was possible. Surely Pia wouldn't lie about something like that?

'So you didn't see Reverend Jackson?' She knew how much Dorothea loved the charismatic vicar of her church.

'I . . . don't think so,' the old lady replied.

'You know that Rene can stop Pia coming if you don't like having her here.'

Dorothea looked at her, her expression suddenly alert.

'We can easily get another nurse to look after you at the weekends,' Flora added.

'Can you?' Her pale eyes looked doubtful.

'Yes. It would be no problem. You wouldn't have to see her again.' It would be a problem, in fact, finding a really good nurse to take over weekends. But Flora knew Rene would go to the ends of the earth to protect her friend, if that's what was needed.

Dorothea seemed sunk in thought, to the extent that Flora began to wonder if she had forgotten what they were talking about.

'I don't think that would be a very good idea.' The old lady spoke slowly but firmly.

'So Pia is kind to you. You like having her here.'

Her patient stared at her for a long time. 'I . . . think it's best to leave things as they are,' she said.

Flora didn't know what to think. Surely, if Pia was the problem Dorothea would have said something to one of them by now. She and Rene had given her every opportunity.

On her way out to the shops, she questioned Keith.

'I'm not up here much on the weekends,' he told her. 'I know who you mean . . . small Asian lady, plumpish. We've said hello once or twice.'

'So you wouldn't know if she took Miss Heath-Travis to church on Sundays, for instance?'

Keith shrugged. 'Not sure how she'd get the chair down those steps, she's only a wee thing. She hasn't asked me, but maybe one of the residents helped her out?'

Flora sighed.

'Problem?'

'Not sure.' She wasn't going to point the finger, but Keith had understood anyway.

'I can check on them next weekend if you like. Wouldn't be a problem to make up some excuse to drop in. I've got a key.'

Flora thought about this. 'That might be helpful. Can I let you know when I've talked to Rene?'

Dorothea slept for almost two hours that afternoon. Flora took the opportunity to ring Rene and tell her what had happened, but she wasn't sure what to do either.

'Keep an eye,' she told Flora in her breathless high-pitched voice. 'Let me know what you think by Thursday, so we have time to get something else organised if necessary. I'm going to ring Pia and see if she can throw any light on it all. We mustn't fall into the trap of blaming her unless we're absolutely sure. I must say, I find it hard to believe . . . Dorothea might just be going a bit dotty.'

As Flora finished the call, she found a text from Jake: *Do you fancy music and pizza Tuesday eve? Got friend playing jazz in Soho caff. Might be a laugh. Jake x*

Without hesitation she replied, *Yes, love to. What time?*

Starts eight. Later ok. You say.

Flora told him she'd be there by eight-thirty. She'd ask Mary to come half an hour earlier, and she'd make it up the following morning. They'd done it before.

Great, Flora thought. That sounds like fun. There had been nothing from Fin, and each passing hour of silence chipped away at her burgeoning dreams, making her angrier, more determined than ever to put him behind her and begin enjoying her life.

When Dorothea woke up she seemed disorientated and still anxious.

'You . . . are here today?'

Flora nodded. 'All week.'

'Every day?' Dorothea asked, working her fingers together as they lay on the bedcover.

'Yes, every day.'

'You said something . . . about another nurse coming?'

'Not for my days.' Flora wanted to make it very clear. 'I am coming all week, every week. That's not changing. I was only asking you if you wanted another nurse for Saturday and Sunday when I'm not here.'

Dorothea nodded and seemed to relax. 'I'm so sorry . . . I wasn't quite sure . . .'

Flora was getting Dorothea's supper, beating the eggs in a plastic bowl, when the doorbell rang. It was Dr Kent.

'Hi, Flora. Bad time?'

Flora shook her head. 'No, come in. I was just getting her supper.' The sound of canned laughter blared from the television in the sitting room. '*Dad's Army*. Her favourite,' she explained with a long-suffering grin.

'Could be worse, could be *Nightmare on Elm Street*. I was just passing and I hadn't seen you . . . well, Dorothea, for a few days. How is she?'

'Do you want a cup of tea? I'd like to tell you something.'

'Such a difficult thing to call,' Simon Kent said, when she'd finished explaining. He was leaning against the counter in the kitchen, cradling his cup, as Flora got on with setting Dorothea's tray. 'From what you say, she does seem to be getting more confused since the last TIA, and perhaps the Sunday night thing is just coincidence. Someone ought to talk to Pia in any case. Find out what she has to say about what Dorothea's like in the daytime.'

'Rene's doing that, but according to the report, she's fine. It says they do things together, like go to church and to the park, but when you ask Dorothea, she says they didn't.'

'Ill-treatment of the elderly is rampant,' he said, 'and it's notoriously difficult to prove, unless they speak out.' He watched her as she melted butter in the small pan and dropped the eggs in for scrambling.

'I'm glad you don't put milk in. Ruins it,' he commented.

She smiled. 'Mum used to put loads in, and it dribbled out of the egg all over the plate.'

'Don't complain. You're lucky your mother made scrambled eggs at all. I don't think mine even knew where the kitchen was.'

Flora was surprised. 'You had servants?'

'Nooo, me and my brother just looked after ourselves most of the time. She had . . . hard to put this delicately . . . a drink problem.'

'And your father?'

'He couldn't handle it. He left, came back, left again. He did his best for a while, but then he met someone else and moved away. You know how it is.'

Flora took some sliced brown bread from the plastic packet and spread butter on it, then cut it up into quarters and laid them round the edge of the plate before spooning the egg into the middle.

'Your brother's older?' she asked.

'Younger. He's a research scientist at Cambridge – DNA stuff.' She could hear the pride in his voice.

'God, must have been such a responsibility for you.'

The doctor gave a short, harsh laugh. 'Could say that.' He put his empty mug in the sink and ran some water into it. 'It was my daughter's fourth birthday at the weekend, and I suppose it made me think about the whole fathering thing. Nothing, literally nothing on this planet, would make me lose touch with Jasmine.'

Flora put the plate on the floral-patterned plastic tray and added a glass of water. She waited for a moment, not sure what to say.

'Sorry, don't know why I'm laying my dismal past at your door,' he went on as he moved aside to let her through, the expression in his eyes suddenly miles away.

'Don't apologise. It's good to find out something about you. I feel we've known each other for years without knowing anything at all.'

'I haven't found out anything about you though, except your mum put too much milk in the scrambled eggs – and you can't dance.'

Flora grinned. 'No, well, you might want to keep it that way.'

He shook his head.

'Anyway, about Dorothea. Do you want me to talk to her?'

Flora considered this. 'Thanks, but leave it for now. Both Mary and I have been on at her and she's just clammed up. I don't want to upset her.'

'Of course not. Well, let me know if there's anything I can do.' He picked up his black bag. 'I'd better let you get on.'

They said goodbye, leaving Flora with memories of her mother absent-mindedly doling out their supper in the family kitchen in Kent. The house was a 1930s suburban four-bedroom, the furniture and decor mostly reproduction and without much style, but the garden, sloping up to a small copse, was a work of art. Prue always said she and Flora were surplus to requirements for their parents. Linda Bancroft went through the motions of mothering in a conscientious way, but always seemed happier alone in her garden.

This passion had begun when their father had

gone to work in Saudi on a lucrative engineering contract. He'd wanted them all to join him, apparently, but her mother had refused – she didn't like the restrictive society there, particularly for a woman – and her parents eventually drifted apart. Flora was eight when her father began working abroad. He would come back at first, with exotic presents such as camel-skin pouffes, silver bracelets and elaborately embroidered scarves. Flora and Prue would be wound up with intense excitement for days before his arrival, their enthusiasm slowly dwindling as the visit progressed: Frank Bancroft, career-driven and introverted, wasn't much interested in children, not even his own.

The time between his visits grew longer, and eventually they stopped altogether. Her parents never divorced, never settled with other partners, just lived apart – Frank eventually in Dubai – until they both died, her mum from bowel cancer when Flora was seventeen, her father not until much later. But she hadn't seen him in the ten years before his death. Prue, on the rare occasions when they talked about their father, made clear that she despised Frank for his lack of parental concern. Flora wasn't sure what she felt. Perhaps nothing much.

CHAPTER 6

25 September

As Flora hurried home on Tuesday night, she knew she should have changed at Dorothea's flat, but she hated doing that. It meant deciding what to wear in the morning, which might feel completely wrong when she put it on in the evening, then lugging it all to work with her, often forgetting a vital bit of kit – shoes, for instance, or mascara. And Jake, with his smooth outfits, made her more self-conscious about her appearance. Not that she had a great selection in the wardrobe. Shopping for clothes had always been low on her priority list, and the dip in her wage packet since leaving hospital didn't help.

She jumped into the shower as soon as she got home and rushed to get dressed. She knew she was going to be late, but was leaving it till the last moment to tell Jake, sort of hoping some miracle would occur to slow time. Tonight it was black jeans again, a thin pearl-grey jumper with buttons on the sleeves, and the black pumps.

She put her hair up in a loose knot and applied some mascara and lip gloss. Not very thrilling, she thought, as she peered dispiritedly in the bathroom mirror – the only one in her flat and quite inadequate for the purpose. She looked tired. It'll have to do, she told herself, gathering her keys, her purse, her Oyster card, her lip gloss into her black bag.

Slinging her leather jacket on and wrapping a patterned pink scarf around her neck to alleviate the gloomy black, she hurried out of the flat. And almost screamed in fright.

Coming down the area steps was Fin McCrea.

'Fuck, you scared me!'

Fin stopped in his tracks and grinned broadly. 'Nice way to greet an old friend.'

'What are you doing here? Why didn't you ring?' Her voice sounded tinny and thin, her breath caught in her throat.

'Oh, the usual . . . me being a total idiot. I went to wash my hands at the hospital and I was being careful of your number, but it was one of those lever taps that gushes out and sprays all over the place and the last three numbers ran so I couldn't read them. I tried every combination but all I did was irritate all the poor sods with the wrong combos.'

He was at the bottom of the steps now, his broad shoulders and height looming in the darkness and the damp, cramped space.

'You're going out?'

'Well, yes. Obviously,' she retorted. His presence was so unsettling.

'Can't you cancel, Flo? I really, really want to talk to you.'

'No! Of course I can't. Why would I?'

Fin pulled a face.

'It's a bit bloody late to drop in on someone unannounced, anyway.'

He looked upwards towards the rest of the house. 'I thought it best to come under cover of night.' His voice dropped to a dramatic whisper. 'I . . . wasn't so sure I wanted to be spotted by your sister . . . yet. I'm sure she hates me.'

Flora gave a short laugh. 'No, I can see why you wouldn't.'

There was silence.

'Listen, I'm late already, I've really got to go.' She moved towards the steps.

'Will you be long? I could come back.'

Flora just looked at him. 'Fin, I am going on a date. I have no idea if I'll be back at all tonight.'

It was as if she had slapped him.

'I see.'

Exasperated, she said, 'Did you think I was just sitting at home these last three years, waiting on the off-chance for you to drop by?' She had been, in fact, but that was beside the point.

He shook his head. 'No, no, sorry, of course not. Look, I know I fucked up with the number thing, Flo, but I swear I went to Waitrose every morning that week I bumped into you, in the hope you might show up again. I'm desperate to see you. Can I come round tomorrow? Or can we meet somewhere else? I don't mind what we do as long as we can talk.'

She was halfway up the steps, thinking of Jake sitting waiting for her in Soho. 'OK. Let's meet at Gloucester Road station at eight-thirty tomorrow. We can have a drink somewhere round there.' She was no more keen than he was to have Prue on their case.

Fin perked up at the prospect. Following her up the steps, he repeated, 'Eight-thirty tomorrow at Gloucester Road station.'

'Don't write it on your hand this time,' she said, before running off towards Ladbroke Grove.

The rest of the evening was a blur. She couldn't concentrate. Jake was sitting at a table with some friends – two women and another man – so at least the pressure wasn't on for her to engage on a one-to-one basis. And the music was loud, the basement space small; no one was able to talk much. Jake's friend was the singer in the band. Tiny, and beautiful in a boyish way, she had a pure, distinctive voice that gave the soft jazz songs an appealing edge. The packed audience loved her.

'She's good, eh?' Jake grinned at Flora during a break in the music.

She nodded. 'Love her voice.'

'Glad you could make it,' he said, but after a

hello kiss, he had made no move to hold her hand or be physically close to her, for which she was grateful. Watching him as he talked and laughed with his friends, she realised that she hardly knew him – not least when she compared his face to the intensely familiar lines and contours of Fin's.

One thought vibrated in her head: seeing Fin.

There was a move afoot to go on to a club. The singer had joined them at the table, clearly on a high from her performance and wanting to party.

'You'll come, won't you?' Jake took Flora's hand for the first time as they got up to go. 'It's just over in Greek Street.'

'I'd love to, but I think I'd better get off. I have to be on at eight and I'm a bloody lightweight. Going to work almost killed me after our night last week.'

He laughed. 'Yeah, know what you mean, but we were in thrall to Margarita last week. Come for a bit? Go on, it'll be fun.' He pulled her up the stairs behind him. The others were already waiting on the pavement and began moving off down the street when they saw Jake.

Flora just wanted to be home. She wanted to think about what Fin had said: 'I went to Waitrose every morning . . .'

She held Jake back. 'Sorry, Jake. Listen, you go. I'm afraid I'm being a party pooper, but thanks for a great evening. Your friend was brilliant.'

Jake grinned good-naturedly. 'OK, if you're sure I can't persuade you.'

They kissed each other goodnight, chaste and on each cheek, as if the intimacy of the other night had never existed.

'You're going to Tottenham Court Road?'

Flora nodded.

'Let's talk later in the week,' he said, 'maybe do something at the weekend?'

She knew from the way he looked at her what he had in mind, and she felt her face freeze in a noncommittal smile.

''Night, Jake,' she said.

The day dragged by, Flora making every effort to contain her expectations. We are just meeting for a drink, she kept telling herself. He wants to apologise, nothing more. But her heart told her different.

'Are you meeting your young man?' Dorothea asked her when she went to say goodnight. Flora had changed as soon as Mary arrived. She deliberately didn't dress up, just wore her jeans and a jumper, kept her hair down and put on a bit of make-up. She didn't want to be seen to be trying.

'Umm . . . he's not really my young man.' Flora found she was blushing, not missed by Dorothea.

'Perhaps you'd like him to be?' Her eyes sparkled with interest.

'It's complicated, I'm afraid.'

'It can be. I had . . . a few boyfriends in my time.' She paused, her head turned on her pillow towards the wall. 'But only one that mattered.' She didn't go on.

'It didn't work out?' Flora had never liked to ask the old lady why she hadn't married.

'He died.' The old lady's voice was soft.

'Oh, I'm so sorry. Was it in the war?'

Dorothea turned back to look at Flora, her expression still veiled by the past. 'No . . . no, not the war. It . . . was an accident, they said.'

Puzzled, Flora didn't like to ask what this meant. But Dorothea wanted to speak.

'He was an artist. A very talented man. But he had . . . he had times when he couldn't cope. And one time . . . one time he . . . well, he fell.' Her eyes filled with tears. Flora had never seen such emotion from the old lady before. 'He fell from the bridge . . . so they said.'

'How awful.' Flora was shocked.

'We were engaged to be married.'

'I'm so sorry.'

The old lady gave her a sad smile. 'It was a long time ago now. But he was such a man. So beautiful. The brightest of stars. You've never seen the like.'

'You must have loved him very much,' Flora said.

Dorothea didn't answer. For a moment there was silence, only the sound of her hands rubbing backwards and forwards on the quilt.

'Sometimes you have to look beyond the complications,' she said, almost to herself.

Flora squeezed her hand. 'Mary's here. Good

night, Dorothea, see you in the morning. I hope you sleep well.'

'I hope I do too,' said the old lady, smiling.

'Another date?' Mary looked Flora up and down. 'Two nights running. Must be serious.'

'This isn't the same one as last night.'

'Oooh. Two fellas at once. Go, girl.'

'No . . . no. Well, not in the way you think.'

Mary laughed. 'I'm not saying a word!'

'Tonight's just a friend.' Flora heard the insistence in her voice.

'Right. Well, you enjoy yourself, whatever he is.'

'Thanks. See you tomorrow. Nothing happened, it's all in the report.'

It was blustery outside. The welcome blast of fresh air hit Flora as she left the block. She walked quickly, although it would only take her minutes to reach the station. She felt hollow and cold, anticipation holding her body tense. Please let him be there . . . she felt unable to wait another minute.

And he was. Standing at the entrance, wearing a navy pea jacket that had seen better days, jeans, and heavy black boots she remembered from when they were together.

'Flora.' He moved towards her, then stopped.

'Hi, Fin.'

They both hovered, unsure.

'Where shall we go?'

She shook her head. 'Don't know. I work in Gloucester Road, but I don't hang out round here much.'

'Well, there's one of those bar chains just along a bit on the left. It's probably OK.'

'Fine. Let's do it.' She didn't care where they went.

They walked along the pavement, side by side. Flora was so aware of his body next to her, it was as if they were actually touching. The wine bar was not full, but there was something depressing about the space. It was over-lit and smelled of toilets and chip fat. They glanced at each other and Fin pulled a face.

'Not liking this.'

'Me neither.'

They turned on their heels and found a pub on the other side of the street which felt cosier, choosing a seat against the back wall.

'Glass of red?'

'Thanks.'

He hadn't forgotten. For a second it was as if none of the events of the past three years had happened; she and Fin were just going out for a casual drink as they always had. She shook herself, suddenly frightened by the distance she had travelled from reality. You are *not* together now, she told herself firmly, trying to marshal her thoughts about what she wanted to say to him.

Once he was back, seated, the two glasses of red wine on the wooden table between them, there was another awkward silence.

Fin fixed his eyes on Flora.

'Can I go first?' he asked.

She nodded, holding her breath as Fin seemed to be preparing himself for a speech.

'Listen, I'm so, so sorry, Flora. It was a terrible thing I did, disappearing like that. I want you to know that I've regretted it almost since the day I left.'

'Why, Fin? Why did you do it? There wasn't even a note.'

He sucked his lower lip, almost gnawing on it. 'I just freaked about us agreeing to have a baby – the whole trapped, commitment thing.'

Flora shook her head. 'Not good enough. I can understand you freaking out, but couldn't you just have said that to me? Told me you weren't ready?'

'But you were in your late thirties, I knew it was then or never.'

'Yeah, well it turned out to be never, didn't it?' Flora made no attempt to keep the bitterness out of her voice. 'You left me without a single word, Fin. Nothing, nada. Just walked out. That's a terrible thing to do to anyone, especially someone you said you loved. I had no idea where you were, what was going on. I thought something terrible had happened to you. I rang the hospital, filed a missing persons report . . . it never entered my head that you'd left me. It was Mick who finally rang me, nearly two weeks later, and mentioned he'd seen you in Tibet.'

Fin's face was rigid with tension as he listened to her diatribe. 'I know, I know all that, I asked him to call you. And believe me, I don't feel good about any of it. But I came back, Flo, less than a year later, and you were already engaged to someone else. What was I supposed to think?'

She stared at him, stopped in her tracks.

'Sorry . . . you *came back*?'

'Yeah . . . you . . . didn't you know?'

'Wait. What do you mean, you "came back"?'

'Well, obviously I went to our place, the Brighton house. And the woman who opened the door told me you'd sold up about two months before. I'd tried your phone and email, but they were all cut off, so in the end I rang your sister.'

'You talked to *Prue*?'

'Eventually, yes. I rang for days, and she wouldn't return my calls. But then eventually I tried from a friend's phone and caught her. She was livid with me, understandably. She said you wanted nothing more to do with me, that I'd made you ill, but that you were fine now and you'd met someone else and were really happy. She said you'd just got engaged, and that if I came anywhere near you she'd call the police.'

'When was this?' Flora asked, in a small voice.

'I know exactly when it was, because I'd just got back from a climb in Peru. It was August of the following year.'

'She told you I was *engaged*?' She spoke almost to herself, a growing spike of anger forming in her gut.

Fin was staring at her. 'You mean . . . you weren't?'

'Of course I wasn't. I hardly went outside the door for the year after you left, even to work.'

'That bad?'

'I got depressed, I mean seriously. A sort of body-shock thing.'

'Because of me . . . that's terrible.'

There was silence.

'I wish I'd known.'

'You would have if you'd called.'

'I *did* call. I'm telling you.'

'After a year? I wouldn't call that concern for my welfare exactly.'

'No, well . . . I was mostly in Tibet, then South America . . . there was a lot happening . . .'

He ground to a halt, clearly seeing the dangerous look in Flora's eye.

'OK, I get it. I fucked up. I know that, and I can never apologise enough to you. I was a complete arse, a selfish moron, running away. But Prue shouldn't have said that, about you getting engaged.'

'She shouldn't, I agree.' It was hard to know what she felt about hearing that her sister had so radically taken over the managing of her life. 'But she saw how ill I was, and blamed you. She was just trying to protect me.'

'Still.' Fin drained the last of his wine and looked across at her glass. She'd hardly touched it. 'I'm getting another.'

While he was at the bar, she tried to compose herself. She felt as if a hurricane had blown through her, laying waste to the reconstructed emotions she'd so carefully and laboriously put in place since her breakdown. What was Fin really saying, she wondered, beyond his desire to apologise and be forgiven?

'Drink up, Flo. You look awful.'

'Thanks.'

She looked at him. His sun-bleached hair, usually wild and sticking out in all directions, had been combed into a parting, smoothed uncharacteristically flat. But as the evening went on, the hair was beginning to claim back its natural shape, the sides creeping inexorably outwards. It looked comical, but Flora was suddenly touched that he should have made the effort for her.

'What's so funny?'

'Your hair.'

Fin self-consciously ran his hands over his head, then laughed.

'My friend, Paul, the one I'm staying with, said I should try and look smart if I was seeing you. He thought the hair was the main problem.' As he spoke, he ruffled his hair until it took on its usual rumpled, chaotic contours. 'Better?'

She nodded and they both began to laugh.

'Flo . . .' Fin reached across to take her hand, and for a second she allowed it to sit there, the familiar touch tearing at her heart.

'Don't,' she said, pulling away.

Fin's look was questioning.

'I don't even know why you're here,' she said,

almost angrily. 'Is it just to hear me say I forgive you?'

'Well, yes. I do want you to forgive me.' He looked down at his glass, twiddling the stem between his fingers, his tall figure, always out of place in urban surroundings, slumped awkwardly on the low bar stool. 'But not for the sake of it. Not just to make me feel better. That'd be pointless . . . and futile.' Now, he looked up at Flora, fixing his grey eyes on her face, and said, 'I want you to forgive me, Flo, because I still love you. I never stopped.'

There was a loud shout of laughter, male, from somewhere behind her. Other voices joined in. Flora turned her head towards the sound, as a reflex. But she didn't see what she was looking at, wasn't aware of any more external noise. All she heard were Fin's words, echoing, clanging, clamouring for attention in her head.

'Flo?' Fin was peering at her, his expression tense, waiting. 'The date . . . the man you were meeting the other night. Is it serious?'

She found her voice enough to reply. 'No.'

He didn't say anything, managing not to look relieved as he kept his face carefully neutral.

'So . . . do you still have feelings for me?'

Flora could see he was struggling. This sort of conversation was as unfamiliar to Fin as if she were speaking Chinese. During their eight years together they had never delved into the whys or wherefores of their relationship, just got on with it.

She felt the tears behind her eyes and fought

102

against them. But the tension of the past couple of weeks, since that day in Waitrose, had taken its toll.

'Flo . . . please, don't . . . I can't bear it when you cry.' This time when he took her hand she didn't resist. 'I can't tell you what it means to me, to be sitting here with you again. You have no idea how much I've missed you . . .' His words were delivered softly, a note of reserve in his voice as he watched her.

'Yes, but you loved me before, didn't you?' She tore her hand away from his and looked for a tissue in her coat pocket. 'If that's what you mean by love, you can bloody well keep it.' She paused to blow her nose. 'How could you have done that, Fin? How?' She knew she was raising her voice, but she didn't care.

Fin sat there, his expression stoical, as if he'd been expecting this, and worse.

'You say you came back to find me as if I should award you a fucking medal. You even blame Prue. But it was NEARLY A YEAR after you left before you made any attempt to get in touch. Is that really love? Tell me: *is* it?'

He hung his head. 'No, no of course it's not.' His eyes met hers again. 'But I've changed, Flo, really I have. This fall last winter, I nearly died on that mountain. Then spending so much time pinned to a hospital bed with my leg in traction . . . I had time to think. And all I could think about was you.'

103

Flora gave a short, sarcastic laugh. 'Oh, I see. It's only when you're almost dead that you remember you love me. When your full-time mistress, those bloody mountains, has finally let you down.'

'Fair comment. But that's not the way it was. I've never, ever stopped loving you. I knew it then, and I know it now. I was just a pathetic idiot running away from responsibility, and once I'd gone it was harder to come back. By that time I was living a different life, trying not to think of what I was missing. Because I knew, even as I ran, what I'd done to you. I may behave like an idiot, Flo, but I'm not stupid.'

'I think I need to go home,' she said. She felt suddenly exhausted.

Fin looked panicky. 'Flora, please. I knew this meeting would be hard for both of us. But we needed to talk, to get it all out into the open at last. You will see me again, won't you?'

She hesitated. Can I do this? she asked herself. Can I risk loving him again? But as she asked herself the question, she knew the answer: she had never stopped loving Fin McCrea; even in the darkest throes of rage and despair, she had always hoped.

'Give me your number.'

His face broke into a smile. 'Great, that's great.'

She wrote it down and they both rose to go.

'Just one more thing,' he laid his hand on her sleeve. 'I meant everything I said tonight. I can't take back what I've done, but please believe me, I would never, ever behave like that again. I told you, I've really changed.'

Flora couldn't face waiting for a bus. She walked for a while, the breeze cooling her hot cheeks, happy to be away from him and have time to think about what he had said. Because on paper it was so clichéd: the never-stopped-loving-you line, the I-don't-know-how-to-say-how-sorry-I-am line, the one that bleated 'I've changed, I've changed.' She knew he was sincere, but *had* he really changed? Did anyone ever properly change? It was the sixty-four-thousand-dollar question.

She saw a taxi and hailed it. Fuck the expense, she thought, as she sank back gratefully into the seat.

She didn't sleep well. She would doze off and then start awake, the conversation with Fin churning in her mind. And then there was Prue. The more she thought of it, the angrier she became. OK, she knew her sister had done what she thought was best, *and* she'd been the one at the sharp end of Flora's illness. But not to tell her that Fin had been in touch . . . that was wrong. Wouldn't it have been better for her emotional health to have dealt with Fin back then, to talk to him, have it out, as they had tonight? Get it all behind her? Or get back together, perhaps, when there was still time to have a family. Instead, his ghost presence had festered in her psyche for two more years, never fading, everything still unresolved. It had been a major obstacle in her getting her life back.

Flora wished she had someone she could talk to. She had lost touch with most of her friends in Brighton when she'd been ill – mental illness had a devastating effect on friendships – and anyway, she and Fin had led such an exclusive life together, there had never seemed the need for anyone else. Now she suddenly felt very alone. But she knew the reaction she would get, the advice she would receive, if she told anyone about Fin. Don't touch him with a bloody bargepole, would be the resounding response.

CHAPTER 7

27 September

T hursday was quiet. Dorothea seemed in good spirits. Dominic was coming to tea, the ginger cake was in. Flora, tired from the broken night, plodded through the day, asking herself the same question over and over again: Is it safe to love him? Her heart told her it didn't matter if it was safe or not. She loved him, end of. Her brain told her that she absolutely *could not* risk being ill like that again – the thought of sliding into that grey, exhausted hopelessness was hideous. Depression could recur, she knew that, but deliberately to put herself in the path of the person whose behaviour had triggered it seemed perverse, insane even.

As soon as Dorothea was in her bed for her afternoon nap, Flora sank onto the sofa without even bothering to make herself some lunch. Fin loves me. The words sounded so unbelievable that they brought tears to her eyes. And the tears progressed to crying – quiet, stifled sobs she couldn't control. They felt like sobs of relief, as if the long years of holding that crushing loss were finally over.

Then she heard the doorbell. She got up to answer it, cursing to herself as she hastily wiped her eyes and blew her nose on a tissue from her pocket. It was Dr Kent.

'Hi, Flora. Umm . . .' He paused, obviously noting her distress. 'Sorry to drop by unannounced. I haven't got long, but I was passing and I thought I'd let you know the results of the stomach x-ray,' he said, delving in his bag to retrieve the report. 'Baffling really. It says there's no evidence of any abnormality.'

She held her finger to her lips and pointed to Dorothea's bedroom.

'Oops, sorry.' He dropped his voice.

His eyes rested on her teary face, but he rushed on, making no comment.

'She hasn't been complaining about it for a few days,' Flora whispered.

The doctor shrugged. 'Maybe it was wind then. But palpating her stomach, it certainly seemed tender on the right side – both times I checked it.'

'At least we know there's nothing serious.'

'True, and I don't think there's any point in doing an ultrasound unless it gets worse again.'

There was silence between them.

'So . . . everything OK?'

She smiled. 'Sort of yes and no.'

'Want to talk to Dr Simon about it?'

'I shouldn't but, in brief, old love who – as I

told you before, I bumped into in the supermarket – leaves me broken-hearted, comes back three years later and declares his undying love. But can I believe him?'

'Hmmm. Tricky one. Back to the Mars Bar.'

'But can't people change?'

'Not in essence, no, I don't think so. Although – to use the better-known leopard/spots analogy – it's possible to be mistaken about someone's real spots in the first place.'

'Explain.'

'I mean you can misjudge people, either for good or bad. We do it all the time.'

'So this guy behaves badly, but at heart is a saint. Hmm . . . like it.'

'I'm afraid in my experience the other option's more likely. The putative saint-at-heart is usually a reprehensible cad.' A shadow passed across his features. 'Do you love him?'

She hesitated, suddenly not wanting to tell him the answer.

Dr Kent held up his hands. 'Sorry, this is getting a bit personal.'

'No, I started it. I did love him. And, yes, I suppose I do love him still. If you can love someone in any realistic way, when you haven't seen them for three years.'

'So you're thinking of getting back with him?'

'Not yet.'

He gathered up his bag. 'Love's a bit of a lottery, Flora. You *could* win, but most of us don't.'

Despite the lightness of Simon Kent's tone, Flora heard an uncharacteristic cynicism. She wondered what had happened to him.

She went back to the sofa much calmer. Fin made one mistake, she told herself. He's really sorry. Everyone makes mistakes.

'Is he here yet?' Dorothea was fretting; Dominic was late.

'No, but I'm sure he will be very soon.'

'He said three.'

'He'll have got held up in traffic probably.'

Dorothea's glance held a touch of scepticism. 'You think so?'

'Shall I make you a cup of tea now?'

She shook her head. 'I'll wait.'

It was nearly four when Dominic finally turned up.

'How's Aunt Dot?' He employed his usual stage whisper when Flora opened the door.

'She's fine. A bit worried when you weren't here at three.'

Dominic raised his hands in horror. 'Heavens, did she think I was coming at three? I said four.' He must have seen Flora's sceptical glance. 'Honest to God, Flora, I really did say four.' The expression in his owl eyes looked hurt.

'Anyway, go through, I'll put the kettle on.'

'Did you manage to sell . . . my mother's sewing table?' Dorothea was asking her great-nephew as Flora brought the tea tray in.

Flora saw Dominic hesitate. 'Not yet, but the

auction isn't for another week. I'll let you know as soon as it's over.'

'I . . . I seem to remember my mother saying it was quite valuable,' the old lady went on. She hadn't mentioned this before, in fact she'd seemed quite dismissive of the table when Dominic first drew attention to it. Flora never got used to the strange tricks old age played on the brain. It made it so hard ever to know her patient's thought processes, or work out what she remembered and understood minute by minute, day to day.

'It's a nice piece, Aunt Dot. But don't get your hopes up. The auction house has put a fair price on it, around the two hundred, two hundred and fifty mark. It's just not popular at the moment, that sort of Victoriana.'

'I think Mother said . . . it was earlier than that,' Dorothea said slowly, the glance she gave her nephew suddenly beady. 'Georgian perhaps?'

Flora caught a tiny flicker in Dominic's eye before he replied.

'Georgian, of course. Silly me. Been one of those days.' He sighed theatrically and wiped his hands on his voluminous white cotton handkerchief.

After tea, Dominic had insisted he carry the tea tray to the kitchen for Flora.

'Did you tell Rene . . . about the table?' she asked.

'I did, yes.'

'Great. Thanks.'

Dominic hovered. 'So . . . is Aunt Dot getting on alright?'

'How do you mean?' Flora began clearing the tray.

'Weeell . . . in herself she seems fine, a bit slower perhaps. But medically, is she in good health?'

'As good as someone of her age with her health problems is likely to be,' Flora replied. 'She sees the doctor every week, and apart from the small strokes she keeps having, she's doing well. There's nothing much we can do about that, except give her the right drugs.'

Dominic nodded. Up and down, up and down went his neatly combed head. 'Good-good, glad to hear the old girl's bearing up. Remarkable lady, my aunt.'

'She is indeed.'

'Splendid,' he muttered vaguely, pursing his lips as he stood there, watching her run hot water into the washing-up bowl. 'Well, better be off. I'm stopping you from your valuable work.'

Flora felt she needed a good bath once the oleaginous Dominic had gone. She wondered if the apparent concern for his aunt was in fact code for 'Is she going to die soon?' And she was pleased she had played it straight.

That night Flora settled herself down with a cup of camomile tea and, hands shaking a little, phoned the number Fin had given her. He answered on the second ring, and she felt her heart suddenly large in her chest, beating at double speed.

'Flora . . . So glad you've called,' he said.

'How are you?'

'I'm OK. Much better for hearing your voice.'

'Not sure what to say,' she admitted, and heard him laugh softly.

'I know. Weird, after all this time.'

'Sort of like we don't know each other.'

'Except we do . . . very well.'

'We did,' she corrected.

'Have you changed, Flo?'

She thought about this, and realised the huge gulf that existed between the naïve, trusting person she'd been before he left her, and the wary recluse she had become since.

'A lot,' she replied.

'Was it my fault?' Fin's question was tentative, as if he were terrified of opening the door to an avalanche of distress.

'Don't let's get into the blame thing again. I've told you how I felt when you left, and we all have to take responsibility for our own lives.' She was sick of hating him for what he'd done. Sick of being the victim.

'You're being very generous,' she heard him say quietly.

'Well . . .'

'Shall I come over?'

'Now?' The thought of being with him, close, alone, intimate again, was overwhelming.

'Umm . . . perhaps it's a bit late?' Fin, a man totally unfamiliar with caution, was suddenly striking a careful note.

She laughed. 'I think you've changed too.'

'I told you I had,' he said, sounding childishly pleased.

'Maybe we could meet up at the weekend?' she suggested.

'Great, any time. I'm doing absolutely nothing except waiting for your call.'

That night she lay in bed, hugging Fin's words close, repeating each detail of their conversation over and over as she fell asleep.

Flora woke on Saturday possessed with an energy and enthusiasm she hadn't felt in years. Even the thought of confronting her sister seemed paltry in the light of having Fin back in her life. Her phone beeped a text and she grabbed it eagerly.

Any chance of a re-match tonight?! Promise to go easy on the cocktails. Jake x

Jake. She stared at the screen. She had forgotten about Jake. Should she ring and tell him? Or text? She didn't know what to say, so she said nothing. It was early, she would reply later – when she'd spoken to Prue.

Her sister was in the kitchen, grinding coffee.

'Hi, sis,' Prue didn't immediately turn round from her task, and Flora perched on one of the stools beside the marble-topped island.

'So . . .' Prue set a cup of coffee in front of

Flora and went to get the milk from the vast, gleaming, black Smeg fridge before sitting down opposite. 'What's up?'

Flora had prepared her speech, but inevitably the lines deserted her and words came tumbling out in a blast of pent-up nervousness.

'I . . . Fin and I, we met up the other night for a drink. And he apologised, said he was sorry, *really* sorry, for how he'd treated me. I . . . it was just great to talk to him at last and get it all out into the open. He explained what had happened, admitted he'd been selfish and stupid. He was so, so sorry, Prue . . . you'd have believed him if you'd heard it.' She paused, watching her sister's face fall, seeing the fixed expression which could only mean trouble. 'Don't start.' Flora held her hand up. 'There's more, let me finish and then you can have your say.'

Prue's face remained stony, but she did as she was told.

'And he said he'd spoken to you. About a year after he'd left? He said he'd called the house when he couldn't find me in Brighton, and you'd said I'd moved on . . . that I was happy. He said you'd told him I was engaged.'

Prue wasn't looking at her, and the room had gone very still.

Flora watched her sister push her fingers through her short blonde hair, the brick-red nails stark against the paleness of her skin.

'Did you?'

Prue finally met her gaze. 'OK, yes, I did. I said you were engaged. I would have said you were dead if it'd meant that bloody man stayed away from you.'

Flora took a deep breath and tried to control her anger. 'I understand why you did that at the time, but shouldn't you have told me, instead of letting me believe he didn't care?'

Prue threw her arms in the air.

'You were fucking ill! You were almost destroyed by depression. You always deny it, but there were weeks when I thought you might kill yourself. There was no way on this earth I'd've given you foolish hope. Not about a man who'd treated you like that.'

'OK, but what about afterwards? Couldn't you have told me later, when I was better?'

Prue's face was suddenly flushed from her frustrated attempts to explain. 'And how do you think you'd have reacted? What would you have done, Flora? You'd have done exactly what you're doing now. You'd have forgiven him everything and gone straight back to him. Wouldn't you?' she shouted. '*Wouldn't* you? Admit it!'

'Well, maybe I would, but it's *my* life. You had no right to make that decision for me.'

There was the sound of footsteps on the stairs, and they both turned to see Bel standing in the doorway in her pyjamas. She looked anxiously from one to the other.

'What are you shouting about?'

Prue got up and stamped across the kitchen to get the cafetière.

'Mum?'

'Hey, Bel,' Flora got up and gave her niece a hug. 'Sorry, your mum and I are having a bit of a discussion.'

Prue snorted. 'Hardly a discussion. Your aunt has just informed me that she's planning to get back with that bastard, Fin McCrea.'

Bel stared at Flora, her eyes wide. 'Are you?'

'I didn't say that. I said I'd had a drink with him, that's all.'

'Oh, yes, and he was soooo sorry, and soooo lovely, and changed from being a bloody prick, and such a good, good person all of a sudden.'

'I didn't say that, either.'

'So you're not getting back with him?'

'I don't know what I'm going to do. I've only seen him once, I told you.'

Prue sighed, slumping defeated on the other side of the island, the handle of the coffee pot still clasped in her hand.

'Wow,' said Bel.

Prue began again, this time her voice was controlled and deliberately calm. 'Flora . . . listen, please. Yes, maybe I *was* out of order, telling him to fuck off like that. I was taken by surprise when he called and I said the first thing that came into my head. But I was only trying to do what's best for you, and Fin is not best, darling. Really he's not. He wasn't then and he isn't now. Leopards don't change their spots.'

'I'm very familiar with the spots argument.'

'Well then. You'll know I'm talking sense. If you—'

'But if they still love each other . . .' Bel interrupted her mother.

Prue glanced over at Bel with exasperation. 'Darling, I know you mean well, but please, stay out of this. You don't understand.'

Bel shrugged, and padded over to check out the contents of the fridge.

Flora sipped her coffee. It was cold and tasted bitter, but Prue preferred a strong Italian blend, even for breakfast.

'If you get back with him, you know what'll happen, don't you? Things'll be marvellous for a few months, you'll be "In Love", it'll be all sweetness and light and you'll wonder why you were ever apart. And then he'll get bored and do the same fucking thing again. You can't trust him not to. Can you risk that, Flora? Can you really risk being ill again?'

For a few moments they stared each other out in silence. Flora could see the frustration on her sister's face. And the concern.

'This isn't about me being right or wrong,' Prue said. 'If I did the wrong thing, then I'm sorry. This is about your health. And that man will never, ever be good for anyone's health – certainly not yours. Believe me.'

'Toast, anyone?' Bel was waving a couple of slices of brown bread, poised over the toaster, her young face tense. Flora and Prue shook their heads.

'I hear you,' Flora said, wearily, 'but I think you're wrong. I know what he did. *He* knows what he did. Can't people make mistakes? We were happy for years before this happened, remember. And he explained what happened. He panicked about having a baby, and the responsibility and—'

'Please, I don't need to hear his pathetic justifications,' Prue broke in, waving her hand at Flora as if to wipe away her words. She seemed about to say something else, but just shook her head.

'So you'll never forgive him? One mistake and you'll never forgive him.'

Prue pursed her lips, her face stubborn. 'I'd hardly call it a "mistake". I hate the man.'

That's a strong word, Flora thought. 'I promise I'll be careful with him, Prue. I won't rush into anything.'

Her sister nodded slowly.

'Well, I've had my say. And you're right, it's your life.'

Flora got up. 'I . . . I want to live. I want to have a life again. And if that's with Fin . . .'

Prue's face softened. 'I want you to have a life too, darling. You know that.' She got up and came round the island, pulling Flora into a strong embrace. 'But what about Jake, for instance? Couldn't you have a life with him? He's a good man. You could trust him.'

'I agree, he is a good man. But I'm not in love with Jake, Prue.' She spoke with quiet emphasis.

Her sister just shook her head, the fight gone out of her. 'You haven't given him a chance.'

'Dad died. Last year.'

She was sitting with Fin in a café in Notting Hill. It was one of a chain – French farmhouse chic with exposed brick walls, chunky wooden tables, good bread and apricot jam. They had chosen a table by the window, and at this time of the evening, before six, it wasn't full.

'I'm sorry,' Flora said. She knew Fin had been as close to his father as he was, perhaps, to any other human being. Angus McCrea was a climber too, a weather-beaten Highlander of few words who, even in his late eighties, walked the Scottish hills near his home in Inverness alone, almost daily. 'Had he been ill?'

Fin shook his head. 'Pneumonia. He got a cold and didn't take it seriously. By the time they got him to hospital he was past help apparently. I was in Chamonix and didn't know till two days later.'

'Horrible for you . . . not to be there . . . not to have known. But he was so independent, he never complained about anything. You probably couldn't have done much.'

'I keep telling myself that.'

'Well, it's true.'

'Maybe . . . but I hadn't seen him in six months.

I kept meaning to go up, but I had this guiding gig, which was good money, considering the crap they normally offer, and I thought I'd stay on while it lasted.' He looked off across the café, obviously struggling with emotion.

Flora said nothing. Story of his life, she thought, sadly. Always meaning to do the right thing, but never quite managing it.

He must have sensed what she was thinking because he said, 'I've changed Flora. All these things in the last few years – you, Dad, the accident – have really woken me up to what an arse I've been in the past. I've taken things for granted too much.' He gazed at her, his eyebrows raised questioningly. 'Can you ever forgive me . . . do you think?'

For a moment she resisted the pleading, almost childlike expression in his keen grey eyes. But as she returned his look she found herself weakening, his eyes a magnet drawing her in, triggering a moment of pure desire, long suppressed, which coursed through her body making it hard to breathe. Fin must have seen it. He quickly reached over to take her hand.

'Oh, Flo. I'm so, so sorry. I hurt you, I know. What can I do to make amends?'

'Get me a large glass of red,' she said, the tart reply a cover while she got herself under control. But her hand remained, tentatively, beneath his.

He laughed with relief. 'Coming up,' he said, waving at the pretty, black-clad Frenchman who had shown them to the table and ordering a bottle of house red.

They talked about normal things: friends, work, family, the summer of sport, the wine gradually taking the edge off Flora's nerves. And her struggle to hold herself separate from the man sitting opposite, who was promising her the world if she would just forgive him, was weakening by the moment.

'How long will you stay with your friend?' she asked, as she picked at some olives and salami laid elegantly on a wooden board between them.

'Not a whole lot longer, looks like. It was fine till Paul hooked up with this girl. But Jenna doesn't like me being around, she's made that clear, and I understand. I wouldn't want me around if I was her.'

Flora waited for him to go on. She didn't want him to think she was asking for her own sake.

'The bugger is, my leg's not right yet. I don't have the grisly disease they thought I had – the necro-whatsits thing – which I suppose is good. But that doesn't solve the problem. It's bloody painful still and no one knows why. So I suppose I have to wait around until that's sorted. I'd be daft to change doctors at this stage, have to start explaining the whole sorry state of my bones to someone else . . .'

'So what'll you do?'

Fin shrugged. 'In the long term I reckon I'll go and live in Dad's house in Inverness. He left it all to me, and it's a great place. It'd suit me.'

Inverness. Flora jumped ahead in her mind. Angus McCrea's house, which she'd only visited once, was in a comfortable Victorian terrace right beside the River Ness. Could she live there? She loved Scotland, but Inverness was so far from everything and everyone she knew.

'I need to know if I can climb again first, of course,' Fin was saying. 'And if not – which heaven forbid – then perhaps I can open a climbing shop up there, or mountain bikes, run walking tours . . . stuff like that.' He grinned at her. 'Not sure how good a businessman I'd be, but I'll have to earn my living somehow if the worst happens. I know I've got the small income from my flat in Fort William . . . Richie's still there. But it's not enough to live on.'

He's making light of it, she thought, but she wasn't fooled. 'So you're going back for more tests?'

Fin nodded gloomily. 'Bloody endless.'

'You only had the accident this year. It takes much longer than you think for your body to get back to normal.'

'So they say. And I have to believe them, Flo, because it terrifies me, the thought of never being able to climb again.'

'Of course it does. But you used to tell me all the time about people who'd been much more badly injured than you, who went up mountains regardless. People with one leg. Or no legs even.'

Fin laughed. 'True.'

'So? If they can do it . . .'

'OK, OK, take your point.' He sighed. 'I just miss it so much. That freedom thing, the physical and mental strength, the exhilaration I get on a mountain . . . you know what I mean. I feel I've gone soft.' He held his hand to his right bicep and flexed his arm experimentally.

'I'm just saying you have to give it time.'

Fin's head sank lower, his broad shoulders slumped over the table.

'Sorry to whinge, Flo,' he said after a moment, raising his head again. 'That's not what I intended for tonight.'

She smiled at him. 'What did you intend?'

'Oh, you know . . .' He grinned back. 'Just hanging out, having fun like we used to. Getting to know each other again.'

There was another silence. Flora wanted that too. But more than anything she wanted certainty, maybe a sign from the universe – a bolt of lightning would do – something that would make it clear to her whether or not she should commit to Fin again. And she wanted that sign before they made love. Because she knew that afterwards she would be lost.

Fin was gazing at her again, his eyes soulful and penetrating.

'I wish you wouldn't do that,' she said, without much force.

'Do what?' he asked, all innocence.

She didn't respond immediately, just looked away.

'Fin,' she said quietly, 'please. Can we not rush this?'

He immediately looked contrite and sat up straight, his hands folded demurely on the table in front of him, his face determinedly composed, but failing to hide his obvious delight that she still found him so attractive.

'Flora Bancroft, I will do whatever you ask.'

Flora couldn't help laughing. 'That'd be a first.'

Fin saw her home, despite her protests. It was a warm early-autumn night, and they didn't say much, just walked side by side along the broad avenue which led over the hill to her street. She was acutely aware of his presence and tempted at times to move closer to him, to take his large hand, permanently callused from climbing ropes, in hers. But she didn't. Have some pride girl, she told herself. Don't just go running at the first click of his fingers. Give yourself time to think this out. But her heart still beat out the rhythm of her excitement.

When they reached the crescent, her sister's house loomed large, all lit up, three doors along on the right. Fin stopped.

'Better not risk it,' he whispered, nodding his head towards her home.

Flora was reluctant to let him go, but she said, 'Yes, better not.' She didn't want the evening ruined by some hostile interchange with Prue.

They stood face to face on the corner for a moment.

'Thanks, tonight was . . .'

Fin didn't let her finish. He laid his hands gently either side of her face, lifting it to his, and kissed her. The kiss was so brief that Flora had no chance to respond before Fin had dropped his hands and moved back.

'Sorry, sorry . . . didn't mean to do that, just couldn't help myself,' he said, making no effort to suppress a mischievous smile.

When Flora didn't say anything, he added, obviously fearful he had offended her. 'Just to say goodnight.'

'Goodnight, Fin.' Flora turned away before she had a chance to change her mind and ask him in.

'Ring me tomorrow,' she heard Fin's voice behind her, and she waved a hand in acknowledgement before hurrying down the area steps to her flat.

Her mobile rang as she was unlocking the door. She smiled, sure it was Fin, and answered it.

'Flora?' She heard Jake's voice with surprise, then remembered she hadn't replied to his last text. 'Just checking in. Wondered what you were up to next week.'

She hesitated. 'Umm . . .'

'Thought we might take in a film or something?'

'That would have been fun . . . but the thing is,' she spoke carefully, not wanting to offend him. 'You know the man I told you about? The one I had a relationship with before? Well, he's turned up suddenly.'

'O-kaaay . . . This is the one who let you down? Made you ill.'

'Yes . . .' she sighed. 'I know, it's daft.'

Jake gave a short laugh. 'Not judging, Flora. Shame though. We had fun. Let me know if it doesn't work out.'

'I will.'

She put her phone down on the table. She liked Jake a lot, but Fin blotted out any possible alternative. They had been together for nearly six hours this evening, and it had passed in a flash. As always. Think this out, she told herself, as she sat on the sofa, wide awake. But each time she began to make a mental list of the pros and cons of trusting Fin McCrea again, her mind wandered back to his eyes, his big square hands, his sheer – albeit wounded at present – physicality. And thoughts of their past lovemaking played over in her brain, setting her on fire again, making it difficult for her to concentrate on anything but memories of his naked body pressed hard against her own.

CHAPTER 8

1 October

'**M**orning Dorothea.' Flora put her head round her patient's door, making the old lady jump.

She was sitting up in bed, the cornflakes in front of her on the bed table, a spoon clasped in her hand. But she was making no attempt at eating.

'Sorry, I startled you.'

The old lady stared at her. 'Are you . . . here now?'

Flora nodded. 'All week. Do you want some help with your breakfast?'

Dorothea looked down at the bowl and back up to Flora. 'I . . . don't think so.'

'OK, well I'll just have a word with Mary. I'll be back in a minute.'

'She wet herself last night.' Mary held out a cup of coffee to Flora. 'She's never done that before.'

'God. She must have been really upset.'

'I'd have thought so too. But she didn't seem to realise what had happened.'

'Maybe she was too deeply asleep?'

'Yeah, that's what I thought. She was quiet when I came on, and did seem really tired. Didn't want to talk about the day. Pia said they'd been busy, going to church again, and Rene'd dropped by for tea. So she was asleep early. Then I didn't hear a squeak from her until about one o'clock. That's when I found she'd wet herself.'

The two nurses pondered the news.

'She seems a bit dazed this morning. Did she sleep after that?'

'She didn't call until six, so I suppose so.'

'And Pia? How did she seem?'

Mary shrugged, cradling her pot-bellied blue mug in her large hands. 'Same as usual, butter wouldn't melt.'

Flora frowned. 'You suspect her, don't you?'

'Do I? I don't know, I change my mind every few minutes. It's a terrible thing to think about someone. But it's just so strange that Dorothea's always upset – different, you know – when Pia's been on. I mean, when I got here Saturday, Dorothea was definitely twitchy. She held my hand when I went in to say goodnight, which she's never done before. As if she didn't want me to leave. And she woke four times in the night.'

'Maybe that's why she slept so heavily last night?'

'Probably. But she's never like this in the week, when you're here.'

'Perhaps she is, it's just we don't notice . . . now we're looking for stuff to condemn Pia.'

'I'm not, though. I don't want Pia to be abusing the old lady. But something's up, Flora.'

Flora undid the buttons of Dorothea's pyjama top and peeled it off her frail body. The bowl of hot water sat on the bed table, and she began to wash her patient's breasts, her arms, her stomach. The bedroom was very hot, but Flora laid a towel over the old lady to keep her warm until she was ready to be dressed.

'We had nurses for my father when he got too much for me and Mother. One of them was responsible for killing him, my mother always said.'

'Killing him?'

'The silly girl left the bar fire too close to the bedroom curtains. It was only a tiny fire, but Mother said the shock killed him.'

'How awful. Did he die immediately after?'

Dorothea chuckled. 'No, about eleven months later. But Mother liked to apportion blame!'

Flora grinned at the old lady. 'Roll over.' She helped Dorothea turn towards the wall so she could wash her back. As the old lady did so, Flora saw her wince.

'Are you alright?' she asked.

'I . . . I'm fine,' came the muffled reply.

But Flora saw immediately the cause of Dorothea's pain. Across her lower ribs on the left side was a large bruise. It looked recent, a reddish purple spread beneath the old, thin skin, not yet yellowing. And it hadn't been there on Friday.

'God, Dorothea, how did you get that?'

'What?'

'The bruise on your back. It's huge.'

Dorothea tried to turn her head, then gave up. 'I . . . didn't know I had one.'

'You didn't know? But it must be so painful.'

The old lady didn't reply, and Flora gently washed and dried her back around the bruise, dusted her with talcum powder, then rolled her back against the pillows.

'Maybe you knocked yourself, getting in and out of the wheelchair?' Flora thought about this as she spoke, but couldn't actually see how it was possible, doing any of the things that the old lady did in a day.

'I expect I did,' Dorothea said, not looking at Flora.

'You didn't have a fall, did you?'

Her patient shook her head slowly. 'I . . . don't think so.'

As soon as Flora had dressed Dorothea and settled her in her armchair in the sitting room, she called Rene.

'What sort of a bruise?' Rene asked, the pitch of her voice immediately rising.

'Well, a bruise. Large, about the size of the palm of my hand, just below her ribs.'

'And Mary didn't mention it?'

'She wouldn't have seen it. And another thing. She wet herself last night. First time.'

There was silence at the other end of the phone.

'Always a Sunday night.'

'But surely . . . surely Pia isn't hitting her? I just can't believe it,' Flora said.

'I'll call her now and ask her about the bruise. If it's recent, it must have been on her watch. Dorothea couldn't injure herself without the nurse knowing, could she? At night, perhaps? Trying to get out of bed? Old people do bruise very easily, especially when they're on anticoagulants.'

'Well, I suppose she could. But Mary didn't hear anything.'

'Will you call Dr Kent, please. Better be safe. Not because he'll do anything, but if there *is* something going on, we'll need a witness.'

Flora brought Dorothea a cup of tea. She sat with her, searching her face for signs of distress, but the old lady seemed calm, a faraway look on her face.

'Did you have a good weekend? Pia says you went to church again. You must have enjoyed seeing the reverend.'

'I . . . didn't.'

Flora laughed. 'Didn't enjoy it? Why not? You love Reverend Jackson. Or wasn't it him this time?'

'I . . . haven't been to my church in a long time.'

'Haven't you? Not yesterday? The report said Pia took you.'

Dorothea raised her eyebrows. 'Well, she didn't.' Her voice was firm. No vagueness. No argument.

'OK . . . so you're saying you didn't go to church?'

She looked at Flora patiently, as if she were hard of hearing. 'No . . . I told you.'

Dr Kent said he would drop round late morning. As Flora waited for him, her thoughts returned to Fin. She'd called him on Sunday and they'd talked for hours. He'd wanted to meet up again that afternoon, but she knew he would end up in her flat, and she knew if he did – as night follows day – they would make love. She wasn't ready for that. Ready physically, yes – her body cried out to be with him again – not ready mentally. But would she ever be? Perhaps she just had to take the plunge. What good would a bit more time do? she asked herself.

The doctor raised the powder-blue cardigan, and the blouse beneath. He didn't touch Dorothea, just bent close, then pulled her clothes back into place.

'It must be sore,' he said to the old lady.

She raised her hand and waved it dismissively. 'Not really,' she replied.

'Do you remember how you did it?' he asked.

Dorothea giggled nervously. 'I . . . don't . . . think so. I bump around a bit these days.'

'It's a nasty bruise.'

'Is it?' she asked, without much interest.

'Her skin's so thin and she's on the Clopidogrel. It could have been caused by even the slightest bump.'

Flora nodded. 'I know. I just wonder.'

'About one of the nurses hurting her?'

They stood in the kitchen, their voices low. The doctor was in casual clothes today, jeans and a light blue shirt. He always smells so clean, Flora thought, as she handed him a cup of coffee.

'I don't think you can take the bruise as a sign of it, necessarily. Or wetting the bed, either. She's old, Flora.'

'Yeah, I know. I just want to make sure. Sorry to drag you out again.'

'Always a pleasure to see you both,' he said, smiling at her, and setting his half-drunk coffee on the draining board. 'You look a lot happier.'

Flora couldn't help the blush. 'I am.'

'Worked out, did it? With the Mars Bar?'

She laughed. 'I wish I could answer that. I suppose I'm looking for certainty. I want to know for sure that I'm doing the right thing, but I know that's dumb.'

'Weeell . . . not dumb. A bit unrealistic perhaps.'

'Are you married?'

'Was.'

'Oh . . . sorry.'

'Don't be, we've been divorced a year now.' He shrugged. 'Not sure you should take my advice though, because at the time I thought Carina was completely the right thing . . . and she turned out completely not to be.'

'So if she suddenly came back and said she loved you, would you believe her?'

134

'That's about as likely as me becoming the next Olympic pole-vaulting champion.'

'That bad.' She wished she hadn't asked now. He was almost squirming with discomfort at discussing his private life.

'But to get back to your dilemma. Obviously, it's really hard to trust someone again who's let you down badly. But not impossible, if the will's there.'

'I think we both want to make this work.'

'Well, follow your instincts, Flora. You won't forgive yourself if you walk away without trying.'

As she opened the door for him, she asked, 'So you don't think I should worry . . . about Dorothea?'

'I didn't say that. I just said bruising's a common side effect of the drugs she's on, and incontinence, similarly, one of old age.'

'Thanks. Now I know exactly what to do.'

He grinned. 'Always glad to be of service.'

Fin texted her as she made her way home on the bus: *How was your day?*

OK. Usual, she texted back.

Shall I come round?

She hesitated before replying, *Bit tired. Later in the week maybe?* She waited.

OK, ring me if you like. x

She realised one of the things she missed most about not living with someone was that there was no one to talk to about the day. Even though he

135

was away a lot, when she and Fin had been together, she would come back from the hospital and relate stuff that had happened, good, bad or merely trivial, and listen to his news in return. Since then, she often felt that events at work lay heavy on her, bottled up, blown up, made worse than they really were – the Pia issue, for instance. She had got used to being alone, but she knew she didn't want to be by herself any more.

She was looking in the fridge to find something for supper when there was a knock on the door at the top of the stairs, and her niece's voice called out.

'Mind if I come down, Flora?'

'Of course not.'

Bel galloped down the wooden stairs and threw herself onto the sofa. She looked worried.

'Sorry, sorry . . . I know you've just got in, but I had to talk to you.'

Flora sat down opposite her. 'It's fine . . . Go ahead.'

Bel pulled a face. 'It's Mum.'

Flora had known it would be. Bel, over the years, had often confided in her about altercations with her mother. Now her niece hesitated, searching Flora's face anxiously before speaking.

'Well, not just about Mum. This Fin business,' she began, 'she's so wound up about it. Keeps banging on about how horrible he is and how he's going to ruin your life again and how it's not fair on her. She's in a vile bait all the time.'

Flora didn't know what to say.

'And I'm worried . . . not just about Mum, but about you. I get that she's protective about you, but she seems so certain he's a bad person. What if she's right?' Her brown eyes were round with concern.

'Listen, Bel, I have no idea what will happen between me and Fin. But I still love him, as I told you before. And I want to give it a go.'

Her niece sighed, drawing up her legs to clutch them to her body. 'And you're sure, totally positive, he's not bad like Mum says?'

'You've met him. Did he seem bad to you?'

Bel shook her head slowly.

'It's early days. We've met a couple of times for a drink, that's all. I promise I'll take it really, really slowly, darling, not rush into anything. Promise.'

'Do you think he really loves you this time?' her niece asked.

'This time . . . I don't think I know.'

'Mum says you can't tell with people like him. They say one thing and mean another.'

Flora sighed. 'On paper, Fin *is* a bad bet. But sometimes you have to take risks in life, Bel, because we can never be certain about any outcome.'

'But you won't rush?'

'I won't. Promise.'

Bel seemed to relax a bit. 'OK. I guess I'll just have to wait it out. Hope Mum calms down a bit.'

'She will.'

Bel raised an eyebrow. 'OK for you to say. You don't quite live with her. She's getting more and more like Chucky every second. I reckon she keeps electrodes in her bag in case she bumps into Fin.'

Flora giggled. She'd watched *Child's Play* with Bel on sufferance, her head under the cushion.

When Bel said goodbye, she leant against her aunt, unwilling to let go. 'I just want it all to be OK with everyone,' she whispered. But as she drew back, both of them heard a noise, something tapping against the window. Bel's eyes widened in alarm.

Flora moved cautiously towards the barred window and peered out into the darkness. Fin's face peered back, wreathed in an expectant smile. Flora silently cursed him.

'It's OK, it's just Fin.'

Bel looked hard at her.

'I didn't ask him round. I promise I didn't.'

Her niece just turned and ran for the stairs.

'Bel?' Flora called, but she didn't reply and the door to the main house slammed loudly behind her.

Flora said nothing as she let Fin in. He stood in the middle of the room, looking around, a faint air of satisfaction on his face as if he'd breached the barricades.

'You sounded a bit down in your text,' he said, looking intently at her. 'Thought you might need some company.'

She glared at him. 'I said I was tired. I've just

had Bel down here, worrying about you and me being together. And I said I was taking it really slowly . . . then you pitch up in the dead of night.'

Fin looked contrite. 'Oops. Bad timing, eh? Sorry about that.' He sank down onto the sofa, and patted the brown seat cushion. 'Recognise this,' he said.

Flora didn't reply. She remembered him so well, lounging on that same sofa in the Brighton house, looking up at her just as he was now. And suddenly she was tired of fighting her feelings.

'Drink?' she asked.

He nodded.

'Tea? Wine? There's some red left . . . not sure how old it is.'

'Tea's good.'

They didn't talk as she boiled the water.

'Sit beside me,' he requested, as she set the mugs on the coffee table.

They sipped their tea, still in silence. But the silence was not quiet to her, it was charged with the pulsing, beating clamour of her desire. She didn't dare look at him.

Fin put his mug down. He turned to her and took her own mug from her hands, placing it on the table.

Gently tracing his finger across her forehead, moving her hair aside, he bent to kiss her. First just beside her ear, then moving across her skin, with small, delicate kisses, to her mouth. For a second he paused, then laid his lips against hers, this time firmly, fiercely, forcing her mouth open. She could hear her breath, shaky and shallow, feel her body trembling uncontrollably as his hand moved down her neck, his finger exploring briefly the dip of her collar bone before resting familiarly around her breast.

'Oh, Flora,' he whispered against her mouth.

The first time they made love it was almost brutal, neither of them able to get enough of the other, each desperate to consume every inch of flesh, taste every drop of pleasure, seize the long-withheld desire – and purge the years of loss. Afterwards, exhausted, they lay apart, only their hands touching, in the light from the bedside table. She rolled over until she was resting her head against his shoulder. Fin pulled the duvet over them, and cradled her body against his own. Neither spoke, and within minutes he was kissing her again.

When she woke in the morning, to the maddening chirrup of her alarm, Fin was already awake, lying on his back looking up at the ceiling. He turned as he heard her stir.

'Hi,' he said.

She smiled. 'Hi.'

'Did you sleep?' he asked, drawing her towards him again.

'Like a log. You?'

'Yeah, not bad.' He shifted beside her. 'My leg aches at night.'

She'd forgotten his injury. 'Do you take stuff for it?'

'When I remember. I had other things on my mind last night.'

She laughed. 'Bloody cheek, I call it. Knocking on a girl's window in the middle of the night and expecting sex.'

'If I'd waited for said girl to ask me to bed, I'd have been too old for sex, or anything beyond incontinence.' He began stroking the skin of her shoulder, but she pulled back.

'I have to go. I'm late already.' But she didn't get up at once. 'Did you . . . have you . . . been out with people . . . since us?'

Fin laughed. '"People"? Not really. Well,' he paused, 'the odd girl in a tent I suppose . . . nothing memorable. Just once or twice.' He glanced down at her, but she didn't look up. She was feeling a sudden pang of jealousy, imagining the intimacy and isolation of a base camp somewhere, the adrenalin rush, the shared sense of living on the edge. Not real life, but something she'd never been part of. 'Nothing that came close to you, Flo.'

'I've got to get up,' she kissed his cheek, wrenching herself away from his warm body.

He didn't object, just lay there until she'd returned from her shower, and watched as she pulled on a clean pair of pants, did up her bra, zipped her jeans, poked her head through the neck of a blue T-shirt and laced her trainers over some black socks.

'Come on, get up,' she urged. 'I need to lock up after you.'

Reluctantly, Fin dragged himself out of bed. Not like him, Flora thought. In the past, he would be up before six most mornings and on his bike for an hour or so, coming back with some fresh bread or croissants for breakfast.

'What are you doing today?'

Fin yawned and stretched, his long arms touching the low ceiling of the basement. 'Oh, the usual: bugger all.'

'Won't be for much longer, will it?'

He just shrugged.

'Hi, Keith.' Flora went over to the porter's desk when she arrived at work. Fin had come on the bus with her, walked her to the door of the flats.

'Meet me in Waitrose at ten-thirty?' he'd asked.

'There might be enough food here. I don't go out every day. And anyway, I don't know when it'll be.'

'OK . . . well, see you tonight? I can pick you up.'

'I need to sleep tonight,' she'd told him. 'And anyway, we were going to take it slowly, remember?'

'Can't bear not to be with you,' he said, his face a picture of dejection. It's all or nothing with Fin, she reminded herself, realising too that his own day would be empty of the only thing he wanted to do: climb. She didn't want to leave him either. It had seemed so natural, waking together, dressing, walking to get the bus. And last night had been extraordinary. She had worried that the sexual chemistry might no longer exist, worn away by all that had happened. She needn't have worried, but she knew now that everything was different. She could no longer pretend to herself that she had any control over her feelings for him.

'I'll call you later,' she'd told him, almost wanting to pinch herself. Fin McCrea was back in her life. The knowledge created an aura of happiness around her whole body, as if she were floating separate from the world.

Keith dragged his gaze from the computer screen.

'Morning Florence. You're looking very gorgeous this morning. Things good?'

'They are, yes.' She felt a hotness in her cheeks, unable to divorce herself from the almost tangible feel of Fin's body against her own, and hurried on. 'Listen, I just wanted to ask you something, Keith. The CCTV here in the hall. It's always on, isn't it?'

Keith raised his eyebrows. 'Yeah, sure. Why?'

'Even at weekends?'

'Twenty-four-seven. It's part of the insurance for the building. We get the odd glitch, but mostly it's on.'

'And you can access it presumably?'

'You want me to? Just say the word.'

Flora hesitated. 'You remember I asked if Miss Heath-Travis's weekend nurse had asked you for help with the chair on Sundays?'

He nodded.

'Well, it's just a bit odd. The nurse says she takes Dorothea to church, but Dorothea says she doesn't. And I was wondering if you could check for me. See if they went out this last Sunday.'

Keith frowned. 'Because you think she's lying, or because you think the old lady's losing her marbles?'

'Well, either, I suppose. It'd just be good to know one way or the other.'

'Odd thing to lie about, taking Miss H-T to church. No one's making her, are they?'

'No, of course not. And I agree, it is odd. This is why we need to know. Perhaps Dorothea's mental state is worse than we think.'

'Not much you can do about it if it is,' Keith said gloomily.

'No. But would you be able to check for us, please?'

'Sure. No problem. I'll give you a shout when I've found it.'

Dorothea had a quiet day. She seemed lost in her own world much of the time, hardly noticing what went on around her.

'I'll put the tea on,' Flora said, when she'd got her up from her rest and settled her in the armchair with a thin rug over her knees.

'No cake,' Dorothea said, her voice suddenly cross.

Flora was taken aback. 'OK. I haven't got one today anyway.'

Dorothea stared at her, her brow furrowed. 'I don't want cake.'

Puzzled, Flora repeated, 'There isn't any cake, Dorothea.'

'You haven't made me one?'

'No.

Her patient looked away, her hands frantically working the edge of the rug. Flora went over to her.

'There isn't any cake today.'

The old lady's eyes blinked up at her.

'I'm . . . glad there isn't.'

Flora was baffled. 'I thought you liked cake.'

She still gazed at Flora, bewilderment replacing the previous agitation. 'I expect I do, if you say so.'

Flora waited, but Dorothea seemed to calm down. What was all that about, she wondered, as she nipped outside to see what Keith had found.

He beckoned her round the side of the desk, so she could view the screen. He pointed to the time and date code in the top left-hand corner.

'See . . . ten thirteen last Sunday.'

Flora peered at the grainy black and white image. There was the top of Pia's head, Dorothea in the wheelchair, waiting by the steps leading to the front door. Dorothea was wrapped up in the tartan rug. For a while nothing seemed to happen. Then a man and a woman came into the hall from the lift, and it was clear, as Keith fast-forwarded the image, that the man was helping Pia bump the chair down the steps.

'Put your mind at rest has it?'

'Yeah . . . yeah, I suppose it has. Thanks.'

Mary, when Flora told her about the CCTV that night, looked disconcerted.

'Well, I suppose I'm glad Pia wasn't lying.'

'You don't sound it,' Flora said.

Mary laughed. 'Perhaps I'm not really. I must have worked it up in my mind that's she's a bad lot, and now I'd better un-work it.' She paused. 'But just because she was telling the truth about church, doesn't mean she isn't being mean to Dorothea behind our backs, does it?'

'No. But we could be exaggerating the problem.'

'You don't see her when she's had a day with that woman. I do. She's not herself.'

Flora sighed. 'Well, maybe one day she'll tell us the truth, if there's one to be had with her brain deteriorating at this rate.'

She went in to say goodbye to the old lady.

'I'll be back in the morning.'

Dorothea smiled, her head resting peacefully against the pillows.

'Seeing your beau again tonight?'

'He asked me, but I'm tired.'

'My mother said I should never make excuses about being tired or ill when a young man asked me out. If I wasn't well, I just jolly well had to grin and bear it.'

'Your mother sounds a bit fierce.'

Dorothea stared off into the distance. 'She was . . . firm. But then everyone had different

146

standards in those days.' She looked Flora up and down, taking in the jeans and black boots, her face registering curiosity rather than disapproval. 'She wouldn't have let me out of the house dressed like that.'

Flora laughed. 'No, well, she was probably quite right. Standards have definitely slipped.'

'In my day, a young man would take you to supper and then dancing.' She gave Flora an amused smile. 'But I don't suppose . . . you will be dancing in those shoes.'

'Did you go to clubs?' Flora asked, trying to imagine Dorothea being swept round the dance floor of a West End club.

'Oh, yes. We drank champagne and danced, smoked too much. Such fun. The men would be in black tie, the girls in evening frocks . . .'

'Bet you looked gorgeous,' Flora replied, but the old lady's concentration had gone and her eyelids had begun to droop.

'Sleep well,' Flora whispered.

CHAPTER 9

4 October

Fin came round again on Wednesday and they sat for hours, just smiling at each other, talking about nothing. Flora felt almost dizzy with pleasure as she looked into his beautiful grey eyes, unable to believe he was there in front of her again, in the flesh, no longer the tormenting image of loss.

But Thursday night she had been summoned to supper with the family. She dreaded it. What might Bel have said to her parents . . .? She had a long shower and slowly made her way upstairs.

When she reached the ground floor, the others were already gathered for a kitchen supper around the black marble island. They had obviously been talking about her, because they stopped when she came in, their faces stiff with guilt.

'Flora!' Philip got off his stool and came to embrace her. He had changed out of his work clothes and was padding around the kitchen in bare feet, his blue striped shirt hanging out of his jeans. Prue followed suit, her hug slightly less enthusiastic. Bel looked up, but didn't move.

'Hi, Bel,' Flora said, and went to give her a kiss. 'Hi,' the fifteen-year-old muttered, and continued to tear up her bread and dip it in the saucer of olive oil in front of her.

Prue indicated the place laid for Flora and they all sat down. Prue pushed a glass towards her, and Philip poured some red wine into it. There was a small silence before her brother-in-law spoke.

'How are you? How's work?' he asked brightly.

She saw Prue shoot him an irritable glance.

'Look,' Flora said. 'Let's talk about him.'

Prue pursed her lips. 'What, in a *We Need to Talk about Kevin* sort of way?'

'Fin's hardly a serial killer.'

Flora saw Bel give a small smile.

'I know I've upset Bel,' she addressed Prue, 'because Fin came round on Monday night, unannounced, and she thought I'd asked him to come, at the same time as I was promising her we were taking things slowly.'

'Well, you have a very loyal niece, because she didn't tell *me* that.' Prue now turned the glare on her daughter.

'Bel has a right to be annoyed with me.' Flora wasn't finished yet. 'I intended to take it slowly, but I haven't. Fin spent the night on Monday and yesterday.'

Philip was keeping his head down, pushing his finger into a drop of wine on the marble.

'And?'

'And I intend to get back with him. Make a go of it.'

'Live with him.' Her sister's voice was leaden.

'Yes, live with him.'

'Right.'

No one spoke for a moment.

'I don't want that bloody man in our house.'

'Prue!' Philip's head shot up. 'Come on, that's not very reasonable. Or respectful.'

Prue put her head on one side and gave him a questioning look. 'And I should be respectful to Fin McCrea, why?'

'Not to Fin, specifically. To Flora.'

She snorted.

'You won't stop her seeing him.' Philip said. 'She'll just move away and we won't speak to each other for years and years. Is that what you want?'

'Don't be ridiculous. She isn't moving anywhere with Fin. He hasn't a pot to piss in.'

Flora took a large gulp of wine.

'He has, in fact,' she said. 'His father died and left him his house in Inverness. He's planning to live there anyway, and I'll go with him.'

Flora was surprised by her own bravado. There had been no talk about going to Scotland together. They hadn't discussed the future at all, only endlessly made love. But the information took the wind out of her sister's sails.

'Inverness?' Bel asked. 'Isn't that Scotland?'

'The north, yes,' Philip told her.

Flora was shocked to see Bel's eyes fill with tears. 'Please, Flora, don't go. Don't go to Scotland. We'll never see you again, like Dad says.'

'Darling . . . sorry, sorry, I didn't mean to upset you.' She got up and went round the island to put her arms round her niece's shoulders. 'I'm not going anywhere at the moment, I swear. I have a job, and I won't leave Dorothea. But Fin can't live in a city; he's a mountain climber.'

The atmosphere in the kitchen was thick with unspoken anger and hurt, which hung in the air like a physical weight. Prue got up and went to open the oven door, taking out an earthenware baking dish of roasting chicken quarters, sliced onions and potatoes, dotted with sage and black olives. She laid it on a wooden block beside the stove, prodding one of the chicken quarters with a knife and peering at the juice running out. It must have been ready, because she switched the oven off.

'Are you saying you don't want Fin to even come to the flat?' Flora asked.

Prue turned, but didn't meet her eye.

'You rent the flat. I suppose you've the right to have anyone you want down there,' she answered evenly.

'Can we stop this?' Philip's voice broke the silence that followed. They both looked at him.

'The last thing I want is for this to cause trouble in the family,' Flora said.

151

Prue took longer to speak, and Flora could see her biting back another angry response.

'Nor me, obviously. So let's hope I'm wrong about him.'

Flora held her tongue. Fin would have to earn their respect himself, she knew that. Nothing she could say would change Prue's opinion.

Flora called Fin when she got home. It was late, but she knew he would be up, probably watching a movie about derring-do on some lone, ice-bound rock face: men falling to their deaths, suffocated by an avalanche, cutting the rope to save a friend.

'I've told her,' she said when he answered.

'That you're seeing me?' He gave a wry laugh. 'Bet she was thrilled.'

'Over the moon. But it's my life.'

'So can I risk meeting her? Or will she run at me with a claw hammer?'

Flora remembered Bel likening her mother to Chucky.

'I think electrodes are the weapon of choice.'

'Electrodes?'

'Never mind.'

She heard him chuckle. 'I've just spent months putting my body back together, only to be burnt to a crisp by your psychotic sister. Great.'

'No need to meet her yet.'

'Not planning to . . . so shall I come over?' he added softly.

'It's a bit late . . . but yeah, come round, I'd love it.'

It had been cold and blustery for days, the wind tearing at the autumn leaves, laying them in drifts across the London pavements. Nevertheless, Flora decided to risk taking Dorothea for a half-hour walk around the block.

Once outside, she turned left, then left again into the quiet residential streets lined with pretty, semi-detached Georgian villas. She walked slowly, thinking of Fin. He'd spent most of the weekend with her. For much of it, they had just sat and talked, on and on, catching up on details of the missed years. For the rest they had made love. She felt dizzy, almost euphoric with happiness. She was with Fin, they were together again; he loved her.

The only shadow on Flora's horizon was the fact that Bel stayed away. She hadn't expected it to be different, but it pained her to think she might lose the precious closeness she'd built up with her niece since coming to live in the basement flat.

'At fifteen it's all black or white,' Fin said, when she told him of her concern.

'But I hate it that she might not trust me now.'

'Of course she trusts you. Who wouldn't? She's just got caught in the middle of you and her mother.'

'But that's not fair.'

He'd stroked the hair back from her face as they

both lay against the sofa cushions. 'It's not, but it's as much Prue's fault as it's yours.'

Flora had pulled herself upright. 'I don't want this to be about blame. We've all played a part in what's gone on, and we can't go back, but surely Prue won't turn Bel against me, just because I want to be with you?'

'Hey . . . you're making this up. Bel's not dropped in this weekend because she knows I'm here. That's all. When I'm not, ask her down. She'll come. Don't be so sensitive.'

Flora had relaxed. 'OK, yes, that's a good idea. I'll do it one night next week.' Her thoughts were interrupted by a hearty greeting.

'Miss Heath-Travis, how splendid to see you.' It was Reverend Jackson, the vicar of Dorothea's church. He was large and very bald, around sixty, and his face wore a permanent (and apparently genuine) beam of Christian pleasure above his dog-collar. 'I've been meaning to drop in on you for weeks now, but you know how it is . . . busy, busy.' He laughed at nothing in particular.

Dorothea, clearly a bit startled by this onslaught, giggled in sympathy, her eyes blinking furiously as he grabbed her hand and held it between his two big paws.

Now the reverend turned his attention to Flora. 'And nice to see you too, er . . . I always want to call you Florence, but that might just be association of ideas.'

Flora smiled. 'Flora, actually.'

'Flora, Flora, of course. Well . . . better get on. Hope to see you both at church soon.' He patted Dorothea's hand. 'Although I know it must be difficult for you to get out much these days.'

'She comes most Sundays.' It sounded as if he were implying she hadn't.

Reverend Jackson cocked his head to one side and looked at her as if she was pulling his leg.

'To Christ Church?'

'Umm, the one at the end of Victoria Road? Yes, the other nurse brings her.'

He shook his head. 'I don't think I've seen her at Sunday service since the spring,' he said. 'You haven't been to see us, have you, my dear?' he asked Dorothea directly.

The old lady shook her head. 'Not recently . . . I . . . don't think so.' She paused. 'I would like to come.'

He looked at Flora and raised his eyebrows.

'So she wasn't at church last Sunday?'

He shook his head, obviously not sure what the problem was.

'Anyway, must get on. Let me know if she'd like a visit.'

'Thanks . . . yes, I will.'

She watched as he strode purposefully off down the street, leaving her puzzled – and worried – by what she'd heard. What was Pia up to?

'I . . . he's very charming,' Dorothea was saying.

★　★　★

Flora heard Rene sigh on the other end of the phone. 'But why would Pia lie?'

'I can't imagine. As Keith Godly said, there's no pressure to take her to church. But she obviously takes her *somewhere*, so why not to church? And if not, why lie?'

'Maybe she wants Brownie points for being a caring person.'

'That's what she's employed to be. There's no bonus incentive.'

'Could the reverend have missed her? It's a popular church by all accounts.'

'I don't see how. He stands by the door when you go out. And anyway, she's in a wheelchair.'

'I'll have to talk to her.' Rene paused. 'Would you be able to be there? I'd like her to hear what the vicar said from the horse's mouth – if you'll excuse the expression. I don't want to leave her with any wriggle room.'

Flora would rather Rene dealt with it alone. She knew it was cowardly of her, but, as a fellow nurse, she didn't feel it was up to her to be part of the inquisition.

'Alright, if you think that's best,' she told Rene reluctantly. 'I suppose no real harm's been done. I mean Pia's told a stupid lie, which isn't great, but Dorothea hasn't been harmed really, has she? Perhaps Pia just wanted to be seen to be doing her best, worried about her job or something.'

★　★　★

156

Pia arrived at one. Flora had made sure the old lady was safely tucked up for her nap before either Rene or the other nurse arrived.

She looked worried. 'I think Miss Rene is angry with me?'

'Better wait till she gets here,' Flora said. 'Do you want a cup of tea?'

Pia shook her head. She was dressed in jeans and a red wool jacket, a small, neat middle-aged Asian woman who didn't look as if she had a mean bone in her body.

Rene bustled in, her expression set and determined. They sat in the sitting room, the door firmly shut.

'Now,' Rene clasped her hands together. 'Pia . . .'

The nurse looked anxiously between Rene and Flora.

'It's about church.'

Flora watched Pia's face, but all she saw was bewilderment.

'Church?'

'Yes. You say in the report that you take Dorothea to church every Sunday. She says you don't . . .'

'She forget . . .' Pia interrupted, casting a pleading glance at Flora.

'You say that, but Flora here bumped into Reverend Jackson this morning. He said he hadn't seen Dorothea since the spring.'

'Reverend Jackson?' Pia looked puzzled again. 'Who is he?'

Rene sighed impatiently. 'The vicar of Dorothea's church? The man who takes the service?'

'Oh . . . the priest. Yes, he there, he very friendly to my lady.'

A thought suddenly came to Flora. 'Pia, you go to the church at the end of Victoria Road, don't you? Christ Church?'

Pia shook her head vehemently. 'No, I not go to that one. The path to the door, it no good. The wheelchair get stuck. I take her to St Stephen . . . near the bank.' She paused. 'I am in trouble? You no like me take her there? Is no Catholic, the church.'

Rene let out a long breath. 'No, no that's fine. It's not her church, but if she enjoys it . . .'

Pia was still looking worried; she clearly didn't understand what the problem was.

'I am very careful with Miss Travis. I not take her if she no want to go.'

'No, I'm sure,' Rene said. 'Well, that's it. That's all I wanted to ask you.'

Pia looked at her hard, light suddenly dawning. 'You think I lie? You think I say I take Miss Travis to church and I no do it?'

'You can see how it looked, Pia,' Flora said. 'Dorothea said she hadn't been, and the vicar the same, but you were saying the exact opposite.'

Pia's eyes filled with tears, which she hastily wiped away. 'I am a very honest person. I no lie, never.'

'No, no, I'm sure you don't.' Rene was

158

flustered. 'But I have to check these things. We're dealing with a very vulnerable patient, as I'm sure you understand.'

Pia didn't look as if she understood at all. 'You ask anyone. I tell truth always.' Her voice was thick with indignation.

'I'm sorry, Pia. I know it's never nice being accused of something you haven't done. But my job is to protect Dorothea.'

Pia sniffed. 'I never do anything to hurt Miss Travis. I love my lady.'

Flora thought 'love' was a step too far, but perhaps Pia's language problem made more of the word than she meant.

Rene got up. 'Well, anyway. Apologies. I'm really sorry I doubted you.'

The Filipina nurse got up too, still looking injured.

Understandable, thought Flora. I'd be mortified to be accused of lying. Whatever her mother's shortcomings in the scrambled egg department, Linda had been an obsessively honest person.

'Even a small lie makes you a dishonest person,' she told them over and over again throughout their childhood.

After the door had shut behind Pia, Rene and Flora looked at each other.

'Stupid. I should have thought of that . . . Pia taking her to a different church,' Flora berated herself.

'So should I. But don't forget, Dorothea was still insisting she hadn't gone at all.'

'Maybe she did say she hadn't gone to *her own* church . . .' Flora thought back.

Rene let out a long sigh. 'Who knows? I feel terrible now, accusing the poor woman of lying when all she was doing was finding a church that was easy to get into.' She paused and gave a wry smile. 'Although I think St Stephen's is pretty high. Not sure Dorothea would approve.'

'High?'

'High Anglican . . . whiff of the Pope's knickers, incense, mass, that sort of thing. Probably why Pia chose it.'

'Better not tell the reverend!'

'Quite. And I think we should all drop this suspecting Pia business. We've been a bit carried away there and got the wrong end of the stick.'

CHAPTER 10

12 October

'Bel, Bel!' Flora saw her niece on the corner, just about to cross the road, as she was coming back from work on Friday night.

Bel turned, and seeing Flora hurrying towards her, waved and smiled.

'Hi, hi darling,' Flora gave her a hug. 'Off out on the razz?'

Bel laughed. 'Me? Hardly. I'm going round to Holly's for a pizza.'

Flora bit her lip. 'Umm . . . I was hoping you'd come down for supper one night soon? Haven't seen you properly in a while . . . without the arguing thing.'

'Yeah, well, it's been a bit challenging at home. But I reckon Mum's going to have to accept the inevitable.'

They stood in silence for a moment, the usual easy banter between them suddenly constrained.

'Look, Bel. I hate what's happening with us all over the Fin thing. It's my fault. I'm foisting someone on the family who you all distrust, and for perfectly good reasons. But I don't do it lightly.'

Bel said nothing, just looked down, fiddling with the strap on her leather bag.

'All I'm asking is that you give him a chance, let him earn your respect . . . at least let him try.'

Her niece looked at her hard, a small frown on her forehead. 'Do you really, really love him, Flora? Like, can't live without him sort of love?'

Flora smiled. 'Yes. I do.'

'And he feels the same?'

'He says so.'

Bel sighed. 'OK. Well, I guess that's good enough for me.' She paused, pulled a face. 'But he'd better not fuck you around.'

'I'm with you on that.'

Bel suddenly threw her arms around Flora and hugged her tight.

'Love you,' she said and immediately looked embarrassed. 'Better get going. Holly'll have eaten all my American Hot.'

'Love you too,' Flora said. 'Supper next week?'

Bel nodded, and waved as she ran across the road.

'So what do you think?'

Fin and Flora were walking in Holland Park. It was a soft, misty autumn Sunday, the air still chilly so early in the morning, but all around them, lining the wide avenues of the park, was the breathtaking landscape of foliage turning to rich golds, reds and bronze.

'About what?' she asked, as they scuffed slowly through the fallen leaves, their arms linked. Fin's leg had ached all night and he hoped gentle exercise might help.

'About us.'

Flora glanced sideways at him, saw his questioning smile.

'In what respect?'

'Well . . . us. You and me.'

Flora couldn't answer. Thoughts tumbled around her brain: too soon; living together; Prue; Inverness; trust; babies. Because she wasn't yet forty-two there was still an outside chance that she could have a child, if she was very lucky – if they were lucky. Although she hardly dared bring the subject up: the last time she did was ten days before Fin disappeared. At the time, she was pretty sure – when she finally worked out that he'd made the choice to go – that their decision to start a family must have been the catalyst.

As she'd approached her thirty-eighth birthday, she had sat him down one evening.

'I think it's time we started trying for a baby,' she'd said.

'Now?' He'd seemed shocked.

'Well, yes. We need to get on with it, just in case there are problems conceiving at my age.'

'OK, but . . .' His expression was suddenly wary. 'I mean, with me travelling so much . . . is it a good idea? You'd be alone a lot, with the baby.'

'You do want children, don't you? You said you did.'

'I do . . . of course I do . . . but I'm just thinking of you.'

Flora thought this unlikely, as he wouldn't even look at her.

'If you don't want kids, you should say so now,' she said, trying to keep her tone light, but she didn't know what she would do if he said no. He got up and began pacing about the room that served as a kitchen-sitting room in their Brighton house, and opened out onto a tiny paved patio.

'Fin?'

Still pacing about, he had paused by the sink, leaned back against it, and faced Flora.

'Yeah . . . of course I want children, you know I do, Flo.'

His reply was completely unconvincing, despite the fact that on a number of occasions they had discussed having a family. But it had always been at some nebulous point in the future, never pinned down in the here and now. She got up too, went and stood in front of him and took his hands in hers.

Looking directly at him, Flora had said, 'You have to be honest, Fin. If you aren't, you'll get landed with a baby you don't want.'

At that, he'd seemed to wake up, his gaze

suddenly focused on her, and a slow smile crept around his light eyes.

'Of course I want a baby . . . your baby, Flo . . . our baby. Of course I do. Just a bit scary for a man like me.'

And that time she'd believed him.

Now, here they were, three years on, and Fin was saying, 'I know, I know. We've got to Take It Slowly,' laying heavy emphasis on the words. He threw his arms up in the air. 'But what does "taking it slowly" mean exactly? I don't really get it. We love each other. We've lived together for years, so that's no biggie.'

'We need to work out whether this is what we really want.'

'Yes, but how can we do that if we don't get on with it and see? What other way is there?'

Flora saw his point. 'But there are things, practical things, that we need to work out.'

He shook his head. 'All that stuff's not important. What matters is that we're committed to each other.' He stopped and pulled Flora round to face him, the expression in his grey eyes spirited and passionate.

'You are, aren't you . . . committed to me?'

As she gazed back, she knew that what Fin had said about Bel went for him too: everything was black or white. He was here now – committed, passionate, in love, the complete package – or he was gone, cut off, alone, doing his own thing. He didn't do balance, only extremes. This was what

165

she feared most about him, and what she found most appealing.

Her hesitation triggered doubt in his eyes.

'Flo?'

She took a deep breath. 'Yes, Fin, I am. I am committed to you.'

He drew her into a close embrace, breathing fiercely into her hair the words: 'I love you love you love you, Flora Bancroft.'

'How's it going with Paul?' Flora asked, when they were settled in a café after their walk.

He pulled a face. 'Not great.'

'But he's not chucking you out?'

He looked peeved. 'He hasn't said as much, but the writing's on the wall. Problem is, I can survive, just, on the rent from the Fort William flat, but I certainly can't afford my own place, not at London prices. And I need to be here, just for another couple of months until the leg's sorted.' He tapped the table nervously with the fingers of his right hand, glanced up at her. 'So I was thinking, since you mention it . . . if you're OK with the idea, maybe I could move in with you . . . just temporarily, while we see how things go?'

She didn't have time to reply before he added, 'Paul's come to the end of his tether, keeping me and Jenna apart.'

'You fight?'

Fin looked sheepish. 'Not fight, exactly. More

snipe. I know it's childish, but she takes every opportunity to wind me up.'

'Like how?'

'Oh, you know. Waving my dirty mug at me and raising her prim little eyebrows. Sulking if I'm in at the weekend. Saying things like, "Oh, how strange, I could have sworn I bought some milk yesterday." All sarky because I finished the bottle before she got out of bed.'

Flora laughed. 'Flat-sharing at its best.'

'Can't be doing with it.' He drained his cup of black coffee. 'Another?'

'Please.'

While he went over to the counter to order more coffee, she tried to concentrate. He'd just asked if he could move in. She understood he didn't have many options, but their relationship still felt so new, so delicate. Moving in together might be like stepping on a young shoot with a hobnail boot.

Fin put the mugs down on the table. 'Coffee these days . . . drop by drop it must be more expensive than champagne.'

She laughed. 'Probably, if you think the froth takes up most of the cup.'

Neither of them spoke for a while. He was waiting, she could tell, for her to comment on his suggestion, but she was suddenly overcome with panic.

'You don't want to live with me?' Fin asked quietly, when she didn't say anything.

'Fin . . . I don't know. It's so soon. We only met up again a few weeks ago. And it's a very small flat. Would we drive each other crazy? And with Prue upstairs?'

He looked hurt. 'You don't have to make excuses, Flo. Just say if you don't want to live with me.'

'I didn't say that. I do want to be with you, of course I do. But in my sister's flat?'

'Why not?'

'Well, for a start, she lets me have it for less than half the market rent, so I feel sort of beholden. I don't want her to think I'm taking the piss, moving you in.'

Fin frowned. 'We could offer to pay more.'

'Could we? I'm stretched as it is.'

'Yeah, me too.'

There was a dispirited silence, then Fin brightened up.

'Let's just run away, Flo. We could go to Inverness, live in my dad's house. It's nice, you've seen it. And free, all paid for, just needs a bit of paint. I'll get the Scottish docs to fix me up – I'm sure they'd be as capable as this lot – and I can teach kids climbing or something until my leg heals. You can find a job at Raigmore. Why not?' He was in his stride now. 'Bel could stay in the holidays. It's perfect. What's keeping us here?'

'Just the small matter of Dorothea.'

He looked surprised. 'It's just a job, Flo. Anyone can look after an old lady. Sure, she'd miss you for five minutes, but you say she's going dotty anyway. Would she notice?'

'Thanks a lot.'

Fin looked puzzled at her expression. 'What have I said?'

'Oh, just that my job can be done by any moron, that I'm redundant.'

'Hey . . . I didn't mean that. I just meant that things happen, people change jobs. Dorothea will understand.' He hesitated. 'Won't she?'

'She might. But I'm not leaving her.'

'OK, fair enough. But, realistically, she'll probably die soon. And anyway, don't you want to get back to some real nursing? You were so brilliant at it. You loved A&E. You used to say the wards were deadly dull. Surely looking after an old lady is worse than dull?'

Flora suddenly felt close to tears. It seemed as if Fin was riding roughshod over her life, dismissing it as if it were totally irrelevant.

He saw at once that she was upset, although she wasn't sure he knew why. He held her hands tight across the table.

'Flo, Flo don't, please. I'm a clumsy arse sometimes. I was only thinking you were a bit wasted in that job, that you deserve better. But I totally understand that you really care about Dorothea. Of course you don't want to walk out on her.'

'I don't feel wasted,' she said.

'No, I'm sure you don't. I'm so sorry. I'm in a weird space at the moment. All this waiting around

169

in town is doing my head in.' He squeezed her hands. 'Forgive me. I just want to be with you so badly, and suddenly the thought of living together, just us, in our own place was so tempting.'

She smiled. 'But I can't go yet. You understand? The family, Dorothea. It wouldn't feel right to just up and leave them.'

Fin nodded. 'But shall we try it out, Flo, living together in your place? If we know it's not for ever, and if we can get Prue and the family on side, couldn't it work?'

He got up and came round, pulling a chair from the table next door and sitting close by her side, his arm round her shoulder. She resisted for only a second before relaxing into his shoulder. His body felt strong, his embrace so familiar, so protective. She inhaled the rough, masculine smell of him. How she'd missed being held like this, being loved. Suppressing all her misgivings, she replied, 'Maybe. Yes. Why not?'

She heard Fin let out a small sigh.

'You won't regret it.' He dropped a kiss on the top of her head.

'And how'll we deal with my sister then?'

'We don't have to. She's got no hold over you. You pay rent.'

'I'll have to tell her.'

'Of course. But what's she going to do about it? Chuck you out? Never speak to you again? I don't think so.' He laughed, his tone suddenly light and playful. 'This is exciting, Flo.'

But Flora didn't share his excitement. She could already feel the icy waves of disapproval coming off her sister, and she dreaded the conversation.

Dominic arrived, brandishing a cheque for two hundred and fifty pounds, his round face alight with self-importance. He seemed to think selling the table was a superhuman achievement.

'Not a good market for these things at the moment, Aunt Dot, as I said. But I really ferreted around until I found this specialist furniture sale . . . a mate of mine helped me out. And I said it was for you, and he waived the VAT. Marvellous, eh?' He laid the cheque in his great-aunt's lap.

Dorothea picked it up and peered at the sum. 'Thank you,' she said, smiling up at him. 'It's very kind of you to go to all that bother.'

Dominic puffed out his chest. 'An absolute pleasure,' he crooned, bending to kiss Dorothea on the cheek.

Flora completed the tea ritual, without the ginger cake as she hadn't had time to get one, offering instead some chocolate digestives normally reserved for the nurses.

When she came in to collect the plates, Dominic was hovering over a wooden corner chair with a faded tapestry seat, which sat by the fireplace.

'What about this, Aunty?' he was saying as he squatted down on his plump haunches and ran his hand along the curved arms, turning the chair to examine the back. 'Looks in pretty good

171

condition, although the tapestry's a bit faded. They're immensely popular at the moment, as decorators' pieces.'

Dorothea was watching him. 'Decorators' pieces?'

He stood up, dusting off his trousers where he'd knelt on the carpet. 'Interior decorators,' he explained.

'Oh.'

'People who do up rich people's houses. They buy a lot at auctions.'

The old lady nodded. 'So you think you could sell it?'

'Definitely. It's George II, if I'm not mistaken, mahogany. Look at the delicate carving on the two splats. Beautiful thing. And corner chairs are much rarer.'

'It is pretty,' Dorothea agreed, 'but you can take it. I don't need it.'

Dominic cocked his head, fixing her with a serious look. 'Are you absolutely positive, Aunt Dot? I don't want you turning round one day and wondering where all your furniture's gone.'

She shook her head. 'I said, I don't need things any more. I . . . don't think I shall be around for much longer.'

Dorothea spoke without any drama or pathos. It was just a fact, but Dominic jumped on her words.

'Oh, Aunty, don't say that! You've got years left in you. I wouldn't be selling off your stuff if I thought you were about to . . . well, you know.'

She gave him a wry smile. 'I *am* ninety-three, Dominic.'

'Don't. Please. I can't bear to think of you not being around any more. What would I do without our teas?' He rushed over and gave her another hearty kiss on the cheek, then retreated to the sofa looking deliberately sad.

Flora thought she might puke.

'I'm sure you'll manage,' Dorothea said.

'I most certainly won't! Anyway, you mustn't dwell on things like that, Aunt Dot. It isn't good for you.'

'It's quite hard . . . not to,' she said slowly. 'But it doesn't bother me any more,' she added, giving one of her characteristic waves.

Dominic didn't stay much longer. He put the chair in the hall while he brought round the car.

'I feel this sort of thing cheers her up,' he said earnestly to Flora. 'It's not about the money, of course, more something she can look forward to.'

Flora didn't dent his fantasy. 'What do you think you'll sell it for?'

He gave an airy shrug. 'Oh, perhaps as much as four, perhaps five, hundred pounds? Depends on who's in on the day of course.'

'Wow, that's a lot.'

'Worth it, don't you think, if she doesn't want the thing around any more.'

'Don't forget to tell Rene,' Flora said, as he disappeared round the front door.

★   ★   ★

173

On her way home that evening, she caught Keith on the steps having a smoke.

'It'll kill you,' she said.

He looked hard at his cigarette. 'No kidding! Sneaky little bastard. Can't trust anyone these days.' He dropped it on the step with a grin and ground it out with the toe of his shoe, then bent to pick it up, mindful of keeping the area clean.

'All quiet on the Western Front?' he asked. 'No more church-outing dramas?'

Flora wondered if Keith was taking the piss. It must seem a bit melodramatic to him, she thought, spying on a nurse taking an old lady to church.

'No. At least that particular one's sorted.'

'My offer still stands, Florence. If you want me to nip up and check on how she's doing at the weekend, I'm up for it. Just say the word.'

The first thing Flora did on Saturday morning was clean the small flat thoroughly. Like most nurses, she was good at making the place look surface-tidy, but housework wasn't her forte. She had told Fin he couldn't stay the previous night, which she knew was ridiculous, especially as no one would know. But now they had decided to be together, she wanted to get her sister's sanction for him to be there before he moved in, almost like a bride before her wedding – so she'd invited the family down to dinner that evening.

'I'll cook,' Fin had said, and she hadn't argued. She was the sort of cook who had three staple recipes, all of which produced good enough results and could be prepared in advance, just heated up at the last minute – anything more complicated made her sweat. But Fin saw cooking as a performance art. He was instinctive and flamboyant, throwing together often bizarre combinations with abandon – sometimes successfully, sometimes less so. But he didn't care. For him the process was the thing. How it tasted was secondary to his enjoyment.

'So what are we having?' she asked, as he came through the door with three large carrier bags.

'Tibetan curry,' he grinned, dumping the bags on the draining board. 'Bet your family have never had that before.'

'Bet they haven't.'

'It's got seaweed in it. I had to go into town for it, to that Japanese store in Brewer Street. That's why I took so long.'

Flora looked at her watch. It was already nearly five and she remembered what an age it normally took Fin to prepare a meal. She was on edge at the prospect of the evening ahead.

'Hadn't you better hurry up?' she asked.

Fin grinned and took her by the shoulders, planting a lingering kiss on her mouth. 'Hmm, nice,' he pulled her closer, but she shook him off.

'They'll be here at seven-thirty.'

'Relax, we've got plenty of time. Won't take long once I get going. This is one-pot cooking, none of that fancy French stuff. Help me chop and it'll be done in a flash.'

As they stood side by side, she grating root ginger, Fin slicing a pile of onions, Flora looked up at him.

'Aren't you nervous?'

Fleetwood Mac was playing in the background, Fin singing along, '*Go your own way* . . .' 'Yeah, sort of. You know me, not one for a fight. But hey, what's the worst that can happen?'

Flora didn't answer.

'She says I can't live here,' he went on, wiping an onion-induced tear from his cheek. 'She says you can't live here . . . She hates us both . . .'

'None of that's exactly brilliant.'

Fin put his knife down and wiped his hands on the tea towel hanging from his jeans pocket. Turning to Flora he tipped her chin up and stared into her eyes. His expression was resolute.

'Whatever happens, we've got each other,' he said, and dropped a kiss on the end of her nose.

She reached up, put her hand around his neck, feeling the warm skin and running her fingers up through his hair. What did it matter what her sister thought? She felt reckless and happy. No one could give her guarantees about what would happen, but suddenly she didn't care.

Flora watched as Prue greeted Fin. Philip had already shaken his hand, given him his usual quiet smile, treating him as he might someone he had nothing against but didn't know very well. Bel had been shy, hardly looking at Fin, just saying 'Hi' and moving quickly away, as if she were worried he might hug her – as he would have done in the past.

Both Prue and Fin seemed to draw themselves up, tight and separate, creating a solid distance between each other. Yet their outward manner was worthy of an Oscar, each delivering smooth, polite fluency as if they were reading from a script.

'How are you?' This from Prue, but she didn't offer her hand.

'I'm well, thanks, apart from my stupid leg. You?'

'Busy, as usual. But good busy.'

'Not affected by the recession?'

Prue shrugged. 'I'm lucky. Most of my clients are so rich they're recession-proof.'

Polite laughter from Fin. 'Lucky them.'

'I wouldn't think climbing was much affected,' Prue went on. 'Although I suppose sponsors are a bit challenged at the moment.'

Flora winced and held her breath, the unsaid made more potent by this glossy cover-up.

'Drink?' She moved to open the fridge. 'We've got Prosecco.' She knew this was one of her sister's favourites. Philip had already handed her a bottle of red for later – he didn't trust her, quite reasonably, to buy high-quality wine.

'So, Flora says you had a bad fall?' Philip had led the conversation from early on, since Prue's initial effort seemed to have taken its toll. She was largely silent as they sat down to supper at the cramped, drop-leaf IKEA table, which Fin had insisted on dragging into the middle of the room and covering with an ancient blue cloth he'd found in the airing cupboard.

Fin related the details of his fall, and Flora could see Bel's interest piqued. She was listening intently as he told of how he felt the rock suddenly give way beneath his feet, how the rope jerked violently, jolting him as he was swung hard against the rock face. How it took them nearly three hours to rescue him, by which time it was freezing cold and getting dark.

'So you were hanging there all that time?' Bel asked, her eyes round with horror. 'With a broken leg?'

'Well, I didn't know it was broken at that stage. I was going in and out of consciousness, so most of it's a blur. But I do remember the cold being intense, really painful. And the Italian I was guiding, the one who called the PGHM – that's Chamonix mountain rescue – shouting at me in Italian all the time from above to stay awake and not give up.'

Philip laughed. 'Lucky you understood him.'

'Yeah. I'll never forget it . . . *non mollare, non mollare mai*. Even if I hadn't spoken Italian I would have got the gist.' Fin suddenly had a glimmer of tears in his eyes. 'I reckon I owe him my life.' There was silence around the table for

178

a moment. 'Because when you get really cold,' he addressed Bel, 'your body just shuts down, and you lose consciousness, like going to sleep. And once that happens, unless you're rescued pretty fast, well . . .'

'You die, you mean?'

Fin nodded slowly.

'Awesome.'

'But *you* clearly lived to tell the tale.' Prue's tone was sardonic.

Fin raised an eyebrow. 'Sorry to disappoint you,' he replied.

They had finished the Tibetan curry. It was a success – rich and spicy and delicious – even with Bel, who wasn't the most adventurous of eaters. Flora rose to collect the plates, unable to sit still in the face of the sudden tension.

'I wouldn't wish that end on anyone, but I'm not going to pretend I'm thrilled you're back in Flora's life.' The anger had gone from Prue's tone, to be replaced by a weary resignation, as if she'd been battling to keep Fin at bay for a lifetime.

Flora carefully rinsed the plates off under the cold tap, stacking them to wash later.

'Mum,' she heard Bel plead.

She took the ice cream out of the freezer and carried the tub and five bowls to the table. The others watched as she took off the lid and peeled back the paper seal, tapping the creamy vanilla surface with a tablespoon. It clinked like sheet ice.

'Sorry,' she muttered into the silence, 'I should have taken it out earlier.'

'No hurry,' Philip said.

'I got some chocolate fudge sauce too,' Fin grinned at Bel. 'Your favourite.' As he got up to retrieve it from the cupboard, Flora realised the last time Fin had seen Bel she was still a child of twelve. Nonetheless, her niece nodded her approval, clearly awkward under her mother's chilly eye.

They sat round the table, eyes glued to the tub, as if their collective stare might somehow soften the ice cream. Flora shot a quick glance at her sister, but her face was closed and set. It was Fin who broke the silence.

'We're not asking for your approval, or expecting it, Prue. Your position's entirely fair. I messed up. I'm just sorry I put you all through it.'

Prue looked at him suspiciously. 'Approval for what?'

Fin smiled encouragingly at Flora and reached over to take her hand. It was a relief to have someone deal with her sister, not to be the brunt and focus of Prue's annoyance for once.

'We wanted you to know that we've decided to live together again. And it makes sense for us to be here, in your flat, until the hospital have finished with my leg.'

Flora saw Prue give Philip an 'I told you so' look, but Philip kept his face completely neutral.

When Fin and Flora had discussed this conversation, she had wanted him to ask Prue if it was

OK for him to move in. But Fin had objected. 'I won't beg from your sister,' he'd stated.

'I've told Flora, it's not up to me who she lives with.'

'We just thought you should know,' Flora said, matching her sister's *froideur*.

They ate the ice cream in silence, no one with much appetite. Flora wished they would just go, and she was sure it was only politeness that kept them there.

'I took Bel to see *Madame Butterfly* the other night.' Philip's words seemed to balance on the tension, but were unable to dent it. 'She wasn't too impressed.'

'I was, Dad . . . the soprano was brilliant, and it was cool to hear that famous aria live. But it's such a dumb story, a girl of my age who falls in love with a guy she's only seen for ten minutes, pines for him for three years then he comes back and she kills herself. All seemed a bit turgid and sentimental to me.'

Philip and Bel talked on about the opera, but no one else joined in.

'We should probably go,' Prue said eventually.

Flora and Fin both threw themselves onto the sofa as soon as they heard the door at the top of the stairs close.

'That went well.' He let out an exasperated sigh, and pulled her close against him.

'She can be such a bitch,' Flora said, closing her eyes.

Fin let out a low chuckle. 'Christ, that look she gave me. No wonder the ice cream wouldn't melt.'

'I'm fed up with pandering to her. I don't give a fuck if she never comes round to us being together.'

'We mustn't let it affect our happiness.'

'Happiness.' Flora turned the word over on her tongue. Not a word she'd felt applied to her till now. She seemed on the edge of something wonderful, but also frightening in its intensity: a daredevil leap into the unknown.

'Kiss me,' she said, turning her face up to meet his lips.

They made love for a long time that night. At first Flora had to force herself not to think about her sister's coldness, but gradually the touch of his fingers tracing the contours of her body, his lips urgent on her own, his body hard and strong as it entwined with hers, drove her into a place where there was no room for anything but absolute abandonment to the senses, to the physicality of desire. And her thoughts were finally stilled.

CHAPTER 11

22 October

'Dorothea?' Flora had just said goodbye to Mary Martin the following Monday morning, and had gone in to collect the old lady's breakfast tray. At first she thought she was asleep, but her right hand was clutching at the duvet. 'Dorothea?' she repeated, going closer. But Dorothea didn't answer, just stared at Flora, her expression bewildered and disoriented.

Flora noticed at once the droop on the left side of her face, and the dribble of saliva travelling from the corner of her drawn-down mouth.

'Can you move your arm?' she asked, laying her hand gently on Dorothea's left hand. The old lady shook her head weakly, but then managed to lift it slightly.

Drawing back the covers, Flora said, 'And your left leg? Can you lift that?'

Dorothea struggled, succeeding only in twitching her foot weakly. 'I . . . can't feel it . . . much.' Her speech was slurred.

Flora covered her up, making her comfortable

and mopping her chin with the napkin. 'I think you've had a bit of a turn,' she said. 'I'm just going to call the doctor. I'll be back in just a minute.'

After Simon Kent had examined Dorothea carefully, he said, 'Looks like another TIA. Nothing much we can do, she's on all the drugs already. Just give her lots of rest . . . usual stuff, and see how things go.' He paused. 'Of course this might be a precursor to a much bigger stroke.'

'I hope if it is that it's really huge.'

The doctor nodded. 'Everyone's worst nightmare, hanging on in some semi-paralysed state.'

'Her father did just that, for almost two years apparently. She's often said it's what she fears most.'

'Well, let's hope for the best. I'll drop by later on, on the way back from my morning visits. Should be around one?'

'We'll be here,' she said with a smile.

'I feel . . . not very well,' Dorothea said later, as Flora gave her face and hands a quick wash to freshen her up.

'You look a bit better than you did earlier,' Flora said encouragingly.

'I don't know . . . what happened.'

'I think it was just another of those funny turns you have. I'm sure you'll be fine by tomorrow. But I think you should stay in bed at the moment, have a bit of a rest.' She didn't want to mention the word 'stroke', in case it frightened her.

The old lady stared at her as if she were having trouble understanding what Flora said.

'I . . . would like to sleep.'

She dozed on and off during the morning, and when the doctor came back she was once more asleep.

'Can you stay for a minute, see if she wakes? I could make you a sandwich.'

'Umm . . .' he checked his watch. 'Yeah, that'd be great, thanks.'

Flora made him a ham and tomato sandwich, and they went through to the sitting room.

The doctor eyed her as he ate. 'You're really close to her, aren't you?'

Flora nodded. 'I've always done hospital work before, mostly A&E. You don't have time to get attached. But I've been with Dorothea all day, every day for two years now. We really get on.'

'Why did you give up A&E? Was it burn-out?'

'No. I . . . got ill. This job was a stepping-stone back.'

He hesitated, perhaps about to ask about her illness. Instead he said, 'Will you do the hospital thing again?'

'I'll have to. I need to earn more. I'm living off my sister's charity at the moment, but that's got to stop. Not least because she hates my boyfriend.'

Dr Kent looked surprised. 'Why?'

'She doesn't like how he behaved in the past. Which I suppose is fair. But it's all a bit tense between us right now.'

Prue had hardly spoken to her since the night of the curry, over a week ago now. Flora had gone up on the following morning, but her sister had just brushed off any mention of Fin. 'Nothing more to say,' she kept repeating. She'd been barely polite, obviously just waiting for Flora to go. Flora hadn't bothered again, but the problem was a shadow over her life. Prue had never done this before, held her at arm's length. It reminded her how much her sister meant to her; the only real family she had.

'Was he unfaithful?' The doctor's question was tentative.

'No, no. Never. Fin's not like that.' She sighed. 'He . . . oh, you don't want to hear.'

He waited, maybe thinking she would tell him anyway.

'I should get back for afternoon surgery. Thanks for the sandwich. I'll check on Dorothea before I go, see if she's awake.'

But she wasn't.

'Call me tomorrow and tell me how she is. I'll drop by if I can.'

Flora thanked him and walked with him to the door.

'Families . . . can't live with them, can't live without them,' the doctor muttered.

She laughed. 'It's normal I suppose.'

He turned to her. 'It is . . . but you need your family.'

She saw the sadness in his eyes before he turned away.

★   ★   ★

Rene sat beside Dorothea, holding her hand.

'You poor old thing.'

Dorothea smiled. 'I think . . . I feel a little better.'

'Good. Glad to hear it.'

Flora stood by the door. 'Would you like some tea?'

Rene nodded, her wild hair bouncing around her face. 'Lovely idea. Yes, please.'

'Dorothea?'

The old lady stared solemnly at her. 'I . . . don't think so,' she said slowly.

When Flora brought the mug of tea for Rene, Dorothea had turned her head to gaze at her friend.

'I thought . . . perhaps . . . I might be going.'

'Going where?' Rene asked.

Dorothea lifted her right arm heavenwards, her finger outstretched and gave a wry smile.

Rene looked horrified. 'Darling, please. You're very far from dead and you shouldn't joke about it.'

Flora sighed inwardly. Why did they all keep up this ridiculous pretence that Dorothea, unlike every other mortal on the planet, would live for ever?

'That's what Dominic said. But, as I told him, I'm not afraid.'

Rene squeezed her hand tight. 'I'm glad you're not, but I suppose I just don't want to lose you.'

'Nor I you,' Dorothea replied. 'That seems to be the most difficult thing about death . . . leaving the people you care about.' She paused, her gaze far away. 'You've all been so kind . . . even dear

Dominic, going to the bother of selling the things I don't want . . . tidying up for me.'

Rene looked puzzled. 'What things, dear? What has Dominic sold?' She glanced across at Flora, a small frown on her face.

Flora nodded, indicating that Rene should come outside.

'What's she talking about?'

'Dominic promised he'd told you,' Flora began. 'He sold the walnut sewing table, and now he's taken that wooden armchair. Dorothea seemed quite happy about it.'

'Hmm. But he's given her the money presumably? What did he get for them both?'

'I don't think he's sold the chair yet – I think he said it might be worth about five hundred – but he got two hundred and fifty for the table.'

Rene gasped. 'The one in the corner? The Georgian one? Two hundred and fifty? It's worth ten times that!'

'Oh God, I'm so sorry, I should have told you myself. But he swore he'd talked to you.' Flora cursed him under her breath. 'Maybe he left a message you didn't pick up?'

'I doubt it.' Rene sighed. 'But even if he did, there's still the fact that the table is worth way more than a measly two hundred and fifty pounds.'

'Surely he wouldn't deliberately rip Dorothea off?' Even though Flora had never trusted the man, it seemed truly shocking that he would fleece the old lady so blatantly, and to that extent. Perhaps

Rene didn't know as much about antiques as she thought, she told herself. Or maybe Dominic was incompetent, for all his pompous blustering. 'I suppose it's his stuff, technically . . . if he's her heir, as you said.'

'That's hardly the point! He might assume, but he doesn't know for certain.' Rene shook her head, her expression pained. 'I'm surprised at you, Flora.'

'I didn't say *I* thought it was right. I certainly don't. I just said perhaps *he* had reason to think it was.'

'Yes, well . . . but I must talk to him anyway.' She sighed dramatically, her face a mask of anxiety. 'Nothing's easy when you take on the care of an old person,' she muttered, gathering her coat from the hook in the hall. 'As soon as someone's vulnerable, it seems to be open season.'

The following morning, Mary and Flora stood leaning against the work surface in the kitchen, drinking their tea.

'Tell me, then. Which man did you go for in the end? A or B?'

Flora laughed. '"A" I suppose . . . the old boyfriend.'

'So what was it made him "old" in the first place?'

'Oh, you know . . . just the usual. We were together eight years before we . . . split up. Anyway, he's just moved in. Last week.'

Mary's eyes widened. 'Whoa, fast worker, you!'

'Not really . . . sort of taking up where we left off.'

189

'And this fella's the one is he?'

'I hope so,' Flora heard the hesitation in her voice. Even now that Fin had moved in, it seemed unreal, almost like a game.

'Where's the rest of your stuff?' Flora had asked him, as she surveyed the small pile on the sitting-room floor – including one backpack, one medium holdall and a cardboard box containing his boots and some climbing gear – that represented Fin's possessions.

'That's it,' Fin had grinned. 'You know me, always travel light.'

They had stood, then, just looking at each other. She thought his eyes seemed to be gauging her mood, checking perhaps if he was really welcome. She had moved towards him, put her arms around him. 'I'm so glad you're here.' She had almost said I love you, but the words, which she had yet to speak out loud, seemed too weighted, too significant.

That was over a week ago now, and he had settled in as if he'd never been away. When she went off to work every morning, he walked her to the bus stop. When she came home at night, he had cooked supper. She looked forward to seeing him when she left work, anticipating the evening ahead like an excited child. But it was also true that his presence seemed very big in the small space, almost caged, as if he were waiting to burst out. She hoped it wouldn't be too long before they could make other arrangements.

'Well, I'm dead jealous. But you never know, perhaps we'll make a double wedding of it. You with yer man A, me and the dishy Dr Kent.'

Flora laughed. 'Yeah, why not? Look forward to it.'

'What did you do today?' she asked when she got home a couple of evenings later.

'Oh, you know. Nothing much.' He looked tired.

This was always what Fin said when she asked, but this time she didn't let it go.

'What, though?'

He looked up from the map he'd been studying.

'Why the third degree? Are you worried I'm becoming a layabout?' His smile seemed forced.

'No, of course not.'

He bent his head to the map again.

'Fin? What's the matter?'

For a moment he seemed to ignore her, then he raised his head. 'If you really want to know, I don't do a damn thing. Absolutely fucking nothing. I watch crap TV, I go to the shops, I doze on the sofa. I sometimes walk, but mostly my fucking leg hurts like hell if I go too far. I wait. For you.' His tone was verging on the desperate, the expression in his eyes pained.

She sat down beside him. 'I'm sorry. I wasn't trying to needle you.'

'OK . . .'

'Your leg's getting better, isn't it?'

191

He sighed. 'I don't know any more. Some days I think it is, then I have days when it hurts more than it did before. And they keep changing their minds about what the problem is and what they should do about it.'

She put her arm round him. He didn't shake her off, but he didn't respond, and for a moment they just sat there in silence. She realised her heart was beating fast.

'Say something, Fin.'

Still he was silent. She felt his body tense beneath her touch. Then he turned to her.

'I'm sorry. I shouldn't take it out on you, Flo. But I hate hate *hate* being cooped up like this. I'm going mad.'

'What did they say at the hospital?'

'Nothing. As usual. Now they just want me to be patient while they monitor the pins. They say it's inflammation which'll settle down eventually.'

'Should you see someone else? Get a second opinion?'

'No point. Listen, Flo . . . I'm thinking of going up to Scotland for a few days . . . check on Dad's house. Will you come with me?'

Flora was just about to say that she couldn't, when she stopped herself. She hadn't had a holiday for months.

'OK,' she said slowly. 'OK, why not? I'll talk to Mary.'

Fin's face lifted. 'Brilliant! That's wonderful. We could drive up.'

'Except we don't have a car.'

'Good point.'

'We could take the train, hire something up there.'

'Dad had an old Vauxhall that I left with Jimmy, the neighbour. We could use that.'

'It'll be freezing,' she said, a broad smile on her face.

'Brass monkeys,' he agreed, laughing as he gathered her to him. 'It'll be brilliant . . . just to get out of London, get away from here.' He bent to kiss her. 'Scotland, just the two of us. Bliss. When can we go?'

That Saturday, as Flora was coming up the steps onto the pavement, Philip and Bel were standing beside their car, a black Audi. Bel, who looked unusually subdued, came up to Flora at once and gave her a hug.

'Hi Flora,' Philip said. 'You haven't forgotten it's Prue's birthday next weekend?' he asked.

'No . . . no, I haven't forgotten.'

The three of them looked at each other in silence, none of them wanting to be the one to mention the problem.

'She didn't want a big drama this year,' Philip went on. 'So we're just doing Nobu. Eight on Saturday.'

'Great.'

Bel was silent, scuffing her boots on the pavement.

'Should be fun.' Philip's voice was leaden, more

as if he were selling tickets to a public hanging than dinner at one of the most up-market restaurants in London. He must have heard himself, because he laughed and added, 'No, really. It should be. Food's fabulous.'

'Is Fin asked?' Flora finally put the question, speaking softly, worried that Prue might overhear in the building behind; Fin was out at physio.

Bel pulled a face. 'Dad?'

'Well . . .' Philip puffed his cheeks out, exhaling his breath in a sharp burst of air. 'Let's look at it from both angles.' He pushed them down the street a way, until they were out of earshot. 'If he comes and they behave as they did the other night, it will be hell for everyone. However, if we don't ask him, are we setting a precedent?'

'Perhaps we could ask him next time? Just not for Mum's birthday?' Bel looked apologetically at Flora. 'Sort of start the precedent later.'

Flora didn't know how to respond. She was with the other two, in that she had no desire to struggle through an evening of phoney civility, covert jibes, tension – and expensive tension at that; Nobu's prices were extortionate in her opinion. But Fin, as her partner, had a right to be asked.

'God make me good but not yet, you mean.' Philip was smiling at his daughter. 'I don't know. I think, on balance, we probably should ask him. If we don't, things will never have a chance to get any better between them.'

'Or between me and Prue.'

Her brother-in-law nodded. 'Yes, there's that too.'

'Mum's not angry with you, Flora. Just Fin, for coming back.'

Philip raised an eyebrow. 'Not quite true, darling. I think Mum *is* angry with Flora for taking him back, as much as she is about him being here.'

Flora threw her arms in the air. 'But what can I do? Short of breaking off with the man I love, I can't see how to pacify her.'

They both looked at her sympathetically, but neither came up with any suggestions.

'And don't say she'll come round. I'm sick of hearing that.' Her voice rose in frustration.

'I'm sure you are. But the truth is she probably will.'

'Whatever.' Flora knew she sounded like a sulky teenager. 'So . . . your professional advice is to ask him and hope for a light sentence?'

'Yup,' Philip replied with an encouraging grin. 'That'll be two thousand pounds please.'

'Cheque's in the post.'

'I'm not bloody coming to your sister's birthday just to be her whipping boy. Forget it. Not going to happen.'

Flora had met up with Fin at the supermarket after his physio appointment. He looked flushed and exhausted, gulping from a bottle of water as they walked along the aisles.

'So you want to be left out of all family gatherings, despite the fact that we live together now?'

Fin twisted his mouth, wiping his hand back over his unruly hair, still damp with sweat.

'No, but what's in it for me? She'll just give me the ice-queen treatment; Philip will make jolly conversation about suicidal sopranos while treating me like one of his defective clients; Bel will look tortured. What's the point? They all loathe me.'

Flora stopped pushing the trolley and turned to face him. 'The point is that they're my family . . . for better or worse. And at some stage you and Prue are going to have to make it up.'

'Tell *her* that. I have no problem with any of them. It's her who's digging her heels in.'

They stood looking at each other for a moment.

'Anyway,' Fin went on, 'I don't have any clothes to wear. You can't go to some poncey gaff in a ten-year-old T-shirt and frayed jeans.'

Flora laughed. 'Oh, I don't know. Nobu's kind of rich international blingy types: Russian oligarchs, Saudi princes . . . they often wear jeans.'

'Yeah, designer ones, with a naff crease down the front and a pink sweater tied over their shoulders.'

'Can't wait to see you dressed like that!'

They both began to laugh.

'But seriously, you could go to the charity shop on Notting Hill Gate and pick up a good shirt for a fiver.'

Fin pulled a face. 'Loathe charity shops. They smell of old people.'

'Don't be cruel. Anyway, there aren't any old people in Notting Hill, except the rich, scented variety.'

She began pushing the trolley again and they walked in silence.

'Please . . . please come. I don't want a situation where Prue thinks it's OK to leave you out of everything.' She picked a couple of tins of plum tomatoes off the shelf. 'I don't want to go on my own.'

Fin harrumphed. 'OK. I'll come. But I'm warning you that I'm not going to make nice if she starts to pick on me. I don't care if it's her birthday, I'll just get up and leave.'

'And the shirt? I'll come with you if you like. We can go after this.'

'If I must,' he gave her a grin as he pulled her against him and ran his hand down over her bottom, bending to kiss her on the lips.

'Stop it,' she hissed, trying to wriggle out of his grasp, looking to see if anyone had noticed.

'Relax, Flo. Nobody's looking.'

He held on tight, kissing her again, a deliberately long and lingering one.

CHAPTER 12

31 October

'So. I spoke to Dominic. And he says the sewing table had water damage along the back. That's what made it sell for so little.'

'Water damage?'

'Did you notice it? All along the back panel, he said. It was quite badly warped.'

'Sorry, I didn't look at it closely. He never mentioned that at the time. But it was crammed by the window, so I suppose, if someone left the window open, it could have got wet. He took it so suddenly . . .'

She heard Rene give one of her long-suffering sighs on the other end of the phone.

'I wish you'd stopped him. I could have checked it myself.'

'I can't really challenge him,' Flora replied, stung by the criticism.

'No, no. Of course not. I didn't mean to get at you, Flora. I just don't like him making off with her things like that.'

'Maybe there *was* water damage?'

'Maybe. Anyway, there's not a lot I can do about it.'

'Unless there's proof,' Flora said.

'Unless, as you say, there's proof.' There was another heavy sigh. 'Tell me about Dorothea. How is she today?'

The shirt that they'd found in the charity shop was a Ralph Lauren. It appeared to be almost new: a fine, soft cotton, very pale blue with a button-down collar.

'You look great,' she said, as Fin emerged from the bedroom looking self-conscious.

'Well, I feel a dick,' he said, pulling at the sleeve to do the cuff button up.

'Why? It's just a shirt.' Flora had also tried to persuade him into a pair of black trousers in the charity shop, but they were way too short for his long legs. He had on his newer pair of jeans now, the bottoms of which were not yet frayed.

He finished doing the button up and suddenly noticed Flora. 'Wow! You look stunning.'

She smiled shyly. It was only the black dress again, but Fin hadn't seen it before.

'Are we sharing a taxi with them?'

'No, they've gone on earlier. Philip's taking Prue to the new cocktail bar at Brasserie Zédel. I think we're all hoping if she downs a couple of martinis it'll grease the wheels.'

When they arrived at the restaurant, the other three were already there. Philip got up when he saw them and pulled out the chair next to him for Flora.

'Happy Birthday,' Fin said to Prue as Flora bent to kiss her sister.

'Thanks.' Prue eyed them both up and down. 'You look smart.' The surprised note in her voice wasn't entirely flattering.

The swarm of chic, grey-uniformed staff hovered around them, pouring water, swishing napkins onto knees, handing menus.

'How was the journey?' Philip asked, a look of concern on his face as if they'd trekked from Outer Mongolia to be there.

'Fine, we got the bus.'

Silence.

'Great.'

Bel's head was buried in the menu.

'What'll you both have to drink?' Philip again.

'What have you got?' Flora asked her sister, checking out the pink, fizzy concoction in her tall glass. 'Looks good.'

Prue waved her glass at her. 'It's delicious . . . have a taste.'

'Love the necklace,' Fin smiled charmingly at her sister, who patted her new necklace lovingly.

Prue had obviously had enough alcohol to make her forget she should be cross with him, and she smiled back. 'Can't go wrong with Tiffany. I love every single thing in that shop.'

'Pity I didn't know that earlier,' Philip said. 'I'd

have settled on a key-ring and saved myself a whole heap of money.'

Prue pouted at him. 'Meanie. No one sees a key-ring.'

'I'll have your Ralph Lauren one then, Mum.' Bel giggled as she sucked her Coke through a straw.

'In your dreams.' Prue looked at Fin. 'But I see Mr McCrea has upped his game and gone for a touch of Ralph himself this evening.'

Fin looked down at his shirt. 'Like it? Cost a fortune.'

'Yes. Suits you. You look quite handsome.'

Is she flirting with him? Flora caught the look that passed between Prue and Fin with disbelief.

'The climbing industry must be doing well,' her sister added.

'That, or the charity shop business,' Fin replied, and they all laughed.

'So far, so good,' Bel said, as she and Flora made their way to the Ladies' later.

'I know. Not quite what I expected.'

'Mum's drunk.'

'That doesn't always make her so benign.'

'True. And it may not last.'

Bel was right, it didn't. When they got back to the table, the three were sitting in total silence. And it wasn't a companionable silence; each face was rigid and constrained.

'Pudding anyone?' Philip asked, waving the dessert menu at his daughter. 'Bel?'

'Er . . . I'm OK Dad.'

'What? Not even an ice cream?' her father cajoled her, but she shook her head.

'Couldn't.'

Prue wasn't even looking at the menu, just fiddling with her BlackBerry – a rudeness at table that Flora knew she abhorred, and was always nagging Bel and Philip about.

Fin suddenly got up. 'I think we should get going Flo.'

But before she had a chance to respond, a waiter appeared, phalanxed by three more, bearing a plate with an exquisite meringue cake, decorated with delicate sprays of fruit, candles lit in a circle around the centre. As he placed the cake in front of Prue, all four waiters began to sing 'Happy Birthday'.

Flora wished the floor would swallow them all up, but she'd underestimated her sister. Prue's expression was instantly transformed to one of surprised delight. She held her hands clasped before her like a child, her eyes sparkled, she beamed at the waiter and his pals, at the family round the table, as if this was the most thrilling moment of her life. The rest of them joined in weakly, sheepishly – even Fin, who had no option but to sit down again. Flora kicked him under the table to get his attention, but he just shot her a blank look.

Prue blew the candles out and handed the cake back to the waiter to cut up.

'Thank you so much. How wonderful. It looks completely delicious,' she crooned. But as soon as the table staff had moved away, her face shut down again.

'Lucky we didn't order pudding,' Philip said.

'Well, presumably you knew they were bringing a cake.'

Philip looked at his wife, raising his eyebrows just a fraction. 'I didn't, actually. Darcy booked.'

'Who's Darcy?' Bel asked.

'The woman whose house your mother's doing up. She's friends with the owner of Nobu and got us the table at the last minute. Normally you have to book months in advance,' Philip told her.

The cake was served. They ate in silence. Prue didn't even touch hers. Flora struggled with a few mouthfuls, but the atmosphere turned the feather-light meringue to dust in her mouth.

Prue suddenly pushed her chair back, gathered her bag from the floor. 'I'll meet you downstairs,' she said, and swept out of the room.

Once they were out on the pavement, Fin offered an abrupt thank you to Philip, nodded good night to Bel, and, grabbing Flora's arm, dragged her off down the street towards Piccadilly.

'Bitch,' Fin muttered, still clutching her arm. 'She waited till you and Bel weren't there, then just laid into me.'

'What did she say?'

'Usual snippy bollocks . . . "Why can't you just leave my sister alone . . . you're just using her because it's convenient . . . as soon as your bloody leg is OK, you'll be off, breaking her heart again . . . she's totally

203

in thrall to you, you realise that, don't you, so it has to be me who speaks out . . . she never will." That's what she said.'

Flora, appalled, digested this for a moment. 'That's . . . horrible,' she said, subdued.

'Flo, we should just get away. Bugger your sodding job, I can't stay another night under that woman's roof. She sees me as some ligger, taking advantage of you, and you're my poor abused victim. I just can't stand the sight of her.'

'Calm down, please, Fin. We can't just leave—'

He interrupted her. 'Why not? Why can't we? The old lady will be fine. If you were ill she'd have to find another nurse. Say you're ill, just leave. We could get an early morning train and be out of here for ever. Sod your fucking sister.'

Flora pulled him to a standstill. They were outside the RAF Club on Piccadilly, in amongst the tourists milling round the Hard Rock Café on the corner. She pushed him to the side, against the railings.

'Fin, I am not leaving my job. And I am not just walking out on my family.'

He stared at her coldly. 'OK. Well, I guess that tells me. Your sister's never going to accept me, so if they're more important to you than I am, then I don't reckon we've got much of a future together.'

Flora felt her heart lurch uncomfortably in her chest. 'Stop it. Don't say that. You know how I feel about you.'

'Do I? Do I really? I say I love you a hundred times a day, but you haven't said it once. Not once.

You've said you're "committed" to me, but that's not the same at all. Do you love me, Flo? *Do* you?'

A couple walked past, the man eyeing them curiously. She stared him down and he turned away.

She swallowed hard. 'Yes . . . yes, I do. You know I do.'

'But? I hear a but.'

'But nothing. Except I feel . . . just that it's all happening so fast.'

'So you agree with Prue, that I forced you to let me move in? Christ!'

'No . . . no, that's not what I said. I just mean I'm not ready to leave my entire life yet. It's too soon.'

Fin shook his head. 'Well, I'll tell you this for free. I'm not staying in this fucking city a second longer. There's nothing for me here.'

Flora felt close to tears. His cruel tone bit into her like a physical wound, made her want to run away, just leave him there on the pavement and forget she'd ever seen him again.

'Can we not do this . . . please.'

They both stood stiffly, two wooden statues, the solid exterior belying the turmoil throbbing beneath the surface. Then his arms were round her, holding her in a powerful embrace. His mouth was buried in her neck, kissing her skin, whispering in her ear until she was dizzy with it. 'Oh, Flo, forgive me. Forgive me, darling. I love you so much. I didn't mean a word of what I just said. I was angry, upset at Prue attacking me like that. Of course I'll wait,

I'll never leave you. We don't have to live in Inverness if you don't want to. We can live anywhere, as long as it's in the fresh air, where I can breathe. Flo, Flo, say you forgive me.'

She rested wearily in his embrace, the fight gone out of her. 'Take me home,' she said.

Sunday morning passed without either of them saying much, both of them still shell-shocked from the previous evening. But Flora knew she had to square it with the others before she could have any peace of mind.

'I'm going up,' she said, late morning.

Fin raised his eyes from the paper. 'I'll come with you.'

'No . . . I'd rather do this alone.'

But Fin got up. 'We're in this together. I'm coming whether you like it or not. Otherwise Prue will always play one of us off against the other.'

So they both trailed reluctantly up the stairs to the main house.

Prue was alone in the kitchen, reading the *Sunday Times* on the polished worktop, a cup of coffee and her BlackBerry at her side.

'Hi.'

'Hi.' Flora sat down on the opposite side of the island. Fin hovered behind her.

'Where are Bel and Philip?'

'They've gone swimming.'

'Can we talk?'

'Fine.'

Flora detected a slight hesitancy, an uncharacteristic nervousness in her sister's face. There was no sign of the anger of the previous night. She wondered if Philip had given her a dressing down.

Then Flora realised she had no idea what she was going to say. All sorts of accusations and blame that had been churning about her brain all night sprang to her tongue, but she firmly rejected them. In the end she just blurted out, 'I love you. I can't bear this . . . arguing with you.'

She watched as her tough sister's eyes filled with tears. 'And I love you too.'

Flora felt Fin go very still behind her, as if he was holding his breath. Then his hand slowly came to rest on her shoulder.

'Please, can we talk this through, try to resolve our differences?'

Prue shook her head wearily. 'There aren't really any differences, except that I'm terrified you'll be hurt again. And worrying about it is making me crotchety.'

Flora got up and went to her sister. She put her arms around her, and for a while they just stayed like that. Flora could feel the tension gradually leave Prue's shoulders.

Fin spoke: 'I promise, from the bottom of my heart, that I will never do what I did to Flo three years ago. Never. You have my solemn promise.'

Prue looked up at Fin, letting out a long breath.

'You can trust me,' he added, leaning earnestly across the marble towards her.

Prue shrugged, gave him a small smile. 'I certainly hope so.'

'The last thing I want is to take her away from you all, that was never the intention.'

'Alright . . .' Prue reached for Flora's hand, clasped it tight. 'OK. Well . . . I'm sorry for being a cow, but my sister means everything to me. I was only trying to protect her.'

'I understand. Really I do.'

'Phew! All this soul-baring is a bit exhausting, eh?' Prue got up. 'Shall we celebrate?' She opened the fridge door and drew out a bottle of the inevitable Prosecco, waving it at Flora and Fin.

'Love some,' Fin said.

Flora would have liked to just crawl downstairs and go to sleep for a week, but she smiled and nodded, hugged her sister again and went in search of three glasses.

'I could do Friday . . . then Monday, Tuesday, Wednesday if you like.'

Mary was checking the pages of her pocket diary.

'Are you sure?' Flora counted the days. Six. Alone with Fin. Out of London. She took an excited breath. 'It would mean three days and four nights without going home. What will you do with Millie?'

Mary winked. 'I'll bring her here. I've done it before, remember, and Dorothea adores her.'

Flora frowned. 'When was that?'

'When you took that week off at Easter? Rene

was fine with it. She knows how much the old lady loved her cats in the past.'

'Oh, thank you, Mary. Thank you so much. I really appreciate this.'

The night nurse smiled. 'All in the cause of true love. Give me a chance to have a bit of a tryst with the good doctor too.'

'Dorothea, I'm going away tomorrow for a few days,' she told the old lady that Thursday morning as she got her dressed.

'Going away?' Dorothea stared at her. 'Where are you going to?'

Flora pulled her patient's trousers up into place and pushed her back gently so she was sitting on the edge of the bed. She bent down and reached for her shoes.

'I'm going to Scotland with my boyfriend.'

Dorothea's eyes lit up with interest. 'So you have a young man now. Was there a problem . . . something not quite right . . . you were telling me?'

'I didn't know, because we'd been apart, how he felt about me.'

'If he has any sense . . . he will love you a great deal.'

Flora was touched, Dorothea spoke with such sincerity.

'He says he does.'

'But?' The old lady raised her eyebrows.

'Nothing really.'

Dorothea didn't reply at once. Then she smiled,

almost a girlish smile. 'Love is . . . so marvellous, isn't it? You feel so . . . alive.'

For a moment Flora had a glimpse of what she must have been like as a younger woman. Her enthusiasm lit up her face, temporarily masking the drooping lines of old age.

'It *is* marvellous,' Flora agreed. But her voice must still have held a noticeable reticence.

The old lady's eyes were upon her. 'Although things didn't work out . . . as I had hoped . . . I never doubted him.'

Flora remembered the story of the man 'falling' to his death from the bridge. The ultimate betrayal in her eyes, yet Dorothea had never doubted him. And she realised in that minute that it wasn't Fin she doubted – she really did believe he loved her and meant to do the best by her this time – it was herself she was unsure of.

She finished tying Dorothea's shoe laces. 'Mary will be here when I'm away.'

'Mary . . .' Dorothea seemed confused suddenly. 'Mary?'

'The night nurse? The Irish lady who looks after you every night?'

Dorothea nodded. 'Oh yes.' Flora began easing her to her feet, positioning her frame so she could grasp it easily. 'I hope you won't be away for too long,' the old lady said.

CHAPTER 13

9 November

The terraced house stood just across the road from the River Ness. They had taken a taxi from the station in the pouring rain, and as Flora opened the door of the cab, the wind tore at it, snapping it back. She struggled out, dragging her backpack after her, stiff from being bent up in the short bunk on the sleeper. Fin had insisted on sharing with her and neither of them had got any sleep. She looked over at his late father's house. From the outside, it was an attractive red-brick terrace, with a white gable window.

No one had lived in it since Angus McCrea had died the year before. Only Jimmy, the man next door, who was using Angus's ancient Vauxhall, dropped in to check once in a while and remove the piles of junk mail from the mat to the hall table. As they opened the front door they were met by an overpowering smell of mustiness and damp. Flora shuddered.

'Better get the heating going,' Fin said, and went

off to the kitchen to light the gas boiler while Flora peered cautiously into the sitting room. As she remembered it from the few occasions she'd visited with Fin, it had been a cosy room, tidy and warm, filled with the reassuring presence of Angus McCrea. She could recall the tea tray and the battered Scottish shortbread tin full of digestive biscuits; the knitted, striped tea cosy over the brown teapot; the pile of local papers, the scattering of yellowing Ordanance Survey maps – collecting them had been his hobby. Now, stripped of Angus's personality, the room seemed sad – and a little creepy. She wandered in and sat gingerly on the brown sofa, trying to imagine living here with Fin. In her mind she stripped the faded wallpaper and painted the walls a light, clean colour – white, pale blue? – took up the swirly-patterned beige carpet, replaced the furniture with her own . . . But it wasn't happening. He said we don't have to live here, she thought, and prayed he had meant it.

That night, after a supper of fish and chips, cramped together in one of the single beds in the spare room, under the faded blue floral sheets – probably bought in the Seventies and smelling stale and dusty – neither of them could sleep.

'What are you thinking?' Fin asked. The river, swollen with the rain, sounded loud outside the window.

The house had warmed up slightly – physically at least – during the day. But the atmosphere was still cold and dead, as if the four walls were resisting them, reluctant to let go of the previous occupant and allow them to be at home there. Flora snuggled closer to Fin.

'I'm thinking I don't like being here,' she said. All day she'd pretended it was fine, that it only needed a small amount of polishing up and clearing away to make it habitable. She didn't want to hurt Fin's feelings about his father's house, conscious that he was still sensitive about not having been there for Angus when he was dying. But now, tired and dispirited, the dream of their days alone together marred by this drear and ghostly house, she could no longer hold her tongue. She heard Fin chuckle, the sound reverberating in his chest as she lay against him.

'Pretty grim, eh?'

She laughed too, relieved. 'It's horrible.'

'What shall we do then?'

'We could stretch to a B and B perhaps? Can't be very expensive in Inverness at this time of year.'

'It seems so stupid, when we can stay here for free. But I get what you're saying.'

'Maybe it'll get better . . . in the morning. When it's had time to warm up properly.'

'I doubt it. Could we camp?'

'Ha, ha.'

'No . . . OK . . . maybe not. We'll think of something when we wake up.'

He began stroking her shoulder, bringing his hand up under her arm to cup her breast, trailing his finger to and fro across her nipple, and within minutes they were making love, everything outside the immediate vicinity of their tangled bodies suddenly irrelevant.

The bed springs, rusty with age and disuse, shrieked alarmingly. There was no room to move and the sheets came loose almost immediately, rucking up under their bodies, but Flora was hardly aware of it until Fin suddenly pulled away, flopped back on the pillow.

'Condoms,' he muttered. 'I forgot the bloody condoms.'

Breathless from their lovemaking, her whole body crying out to have him inside her again, Flora groaned.

'We don't need to worry. There's almost no chance I'll get pregnant from one night, at my age.' She wasn't even sure when her last period had been, they'd been erratic since her depression, when they'd stopped altogether for a few months.

'You sure?'

'At this moment? Yes, I'm sure.' She laughed, pulling him towards her again, covering his skin with a line of kisses which slowly reached down the length of his body until he was hard again.

But at his moment of climax he withdrew, coming against her stomach, and part of her was disappointed.

She woke early the next morning, before it was light. She padded through to the bathroom for a pee, hurrying back to the warmth of bed.

'Hey,' Fin said sleepily, gathering her close. 'Did you sleep?'

'I did . . . surprisingly. It's still early.'

'That was beautiful last night,' he said.

'It was . . .' She hesitated, loath to ruin a moment. 'You were . . . really careful.'

'I thought it'd be risky.'

'Yeah, I get that. But . . . but has your feeling about children changed?'

'Children in general, or children in particular? Can't stand the little blighters in general.'

She dug him in the ribs. 'You know what I'm talking about.'

He didn't reply immediately.

'It's sort of not really the right time, is it? What with me still off sick, not a bean between us and neither of us with a place to live.'

'I have got a place to live. We have. The flat is my home as long as I want it to be. Prue's always said that.'

'Yes, but a small basement in the middle of London? You can't bring a kid up there.'

'That's not really what I asked.' She shifted to lie on her back, her head perched uncomfortably on Fin's outstretched arm. She realised her heart had suddenly upped its beat.

'Umm, well . . . we always said we'd have children one day, didn't we?'

'Still not answering my question.'

She heard his long sigh.

'God, Flo. I don't know. Aren't we too old for

kids? They're bloody hard work, if other people's brats are anything to go by. And, as I've always said, I'm away all the time. You'd virtually have to bring it up on your own.'

Flora sat up, pulling the thin duvet over her shoulders. She turned to face him.

'So you're saying you don't want them? Be honest, Fin. I'd rather you were honest.'

He looked flustered, shaking his head. 'Please, don't give me that look. I'm just saying it won't be easy, that's all. If you want a baby, then we should have one.'

'If *I* want a baby?' She crawled over his body and began to get dressed.

He grabbed her arm. 'Come on, come back to bed. That's not what I said. I just said that we have to think this out carefully. Wait till we get somewhere to live that's ours. Wait till I know if I'm going to be away so much. I might not be able to climb again, not professionally. In which case I'll be around more. But we don't know yet.'

Flora sat down on the bed in her knickers.

'Obviously, right now would be stupid, I totally agree. But Fin . . . perhaps you haven't noticed a small but significant fact: I'm in my forties. I don't have time to wait for everything to be perfect and in place. If I don't get pregnant in the next year or so, it's over. Even now it might be too late, and it's already dangerous . . . for the baby and possibly for me.'

'Dangerous?'

'Potentially, yes. Down's Syndrome, premature birth . . .'

He looked horrified. 'Well, why risk it then?'

She sighed. 'Women do have babies well into their forties, always have. And these days, if they're healthy and get good antenatal care it mostly works out. Anyway, the risks are irrelevant if you don't want children.'

Fin reached for her, pulling her down onto the bed and grabbing the duvet. He wrapped it round her tenderly.

'You're freezing.'

Flora felt suddenly tearful. 'Please, Fin. Can we just clear this up once and for all? You don't want children. Right?'

'No . . . no, not right. Not right at all. I love you to bits, Flora Bancroft, and a little version of you running around the house would be the most beautiful thing on the planet . . .'

'It might look like you.'

'Even better! But seriously, if it was just me and my life that I had to take into consideration, children wouldn't be a priority. But that's not how it works. I don't want it to be just me and my life, I want a life with you. And if that means a baby, then I will love every inch of it for as long as I live.'

Flora lay very still, shivering slightly, despite the duvet. The passion with which he spoke touched her heart. And in the moment he said those words, she was sure he believed them utterly. But what would he do, faced with the relentless demands of a small baby?

'Cousin Tommy!' the caption read, as if there were something intrinsically funny about being Tommy. But the man in the picture looked far from amused or amusing, his shoulder-length Seventies hair framing a heavy, almost sullen face as he stared at the camera.

'Not sure who he was . . . perhaps a cousin of Mum's.' They were sitting on the brown sofa later that morning, looking through a pile of albums Fin had found in the bottom drawer of his father's desk.

Fin seldom spoke about his mother. She had been a teacher in a teacher-training college in the Lake District, where Fin was brought up. But when he was thirteen, he'd told Flora, she had gone into hospital for a routine operation to remove a small, benign tumour in her neck. The operation went well, apparently, but two days later she collapsed and died from a pulmonary embolism.

Flora peered at a photo of her, standing with her hand on Fin's shoulder beside a tarn, a picnic rug spread out under their feet. He must have been about eight at the time. She was tall, slim, her blonde hair in a ponytail, with an open, laughing face. She looked very young.

'Where were you when she died? You've never said.' Flora asked.

'At school. I was dragged out of a maths lesson.'

'It must have been so dreadful.'

'To be honest, I can't remember much about that day. I remember the funeral . . . and everyone asking me if I was alright, and me saying I was because I didn't know what else to say.'

'How did your father cope?'

Fin sat back against the sofa. 'Oh, you know Dad. Didn't say much. Just went on as if nothing had happened. So I did too.'

'Not good for either of you.'

She felt Fin's hand rubbing her back. 'No, well, probably not. But it's a long time ago.'

They went out for a walk in the afternoon, along the river-bank. 'Wish I could just take off. Spend the day in the hills,' Fin sighed, looking off towards the mountains. 'Christ, I miss it.'

'You're sure your leg's not up to it? Even a gentle hike?'

'Don't want to risk it. And anyway, it aches even on a stroll like this.'

'I can't tell because you don't limp, and you never say unless I ask.'

'I'm supposed to be a brave and fearless mountaineer, remember? Able to withstand loneliness, avalanches and frostbite. Whingeing's not an option.' He swung her hand as they walked.

'I reckon by next year you'll be back on the slopes.'

Fin pulled her to a stop. 'And how will you be

with that, Flo? If I have to be gone for weeks at a time like I was before?'

'I won't mind. I never did. As long as I'm not stuck somewhere I don't know anyone.'

'Like here, you mean.'

'Not necessarily. I just don't know it very well yet.'

They walked on, the winter sun warm on their faces, but an uneasy tension marred her pleasure.

'You want to stay in London, don't you? Close to your sister?'

'No . . .'

'So where do you want to live?'

'I don't know . . . we were happy in Brighton, weren't we?'

Fin gave an irritated sigh. 'Yeah. But if I'm not doing the grand stuff – the Himalayas etc – I'll have to do more teaching – local climbs, guiding, that sort of thing. And I'll need to live in an area with mountains and hills. Brighton's climbing wall is hardly a career option.'

'One minute you say you're going to be away all the time, the next that you'll be working round the corner. Make up your mind.'

There was a tense silence.

'I suppose I had this dream . . . when we were back in London, that you would fall in love with Inverness, with Dad's house. It would make it so simple, us being here.'

Flora didn't reply at once. When she and Fin had met again, she had thought it would be simple:

either they would be in love, or they wouldn't. And if they were, then love would be enough. She hadn't considered the details, how a life together would actually be lived.

'You said it yourself, we can't resolve anything until you know what's happening with your leg. No point in discussing it till then, is there?'

'You were the one that brought up the kids thing,' he said, 'and you're the one who hates Dad's house.'

'That's not fair! I don't hate it. You agreed with me that it's grim as it is at the moment.'

'I don't know how to make you happy, Flo,' Fin said with a martyrish air. 'I'll do anything you want, but I can't live in London.'

'OK, OK, I hear you. You don't have to keep repeating it over and over like a stuck record. You seem to think I'm some spoilt princess for not wanting to just up sticks and move to this freezing, dreary town.'

Fin threw his hands up in the air. 'Look around you! *Look* at it. It's beautiful. The sun is shining, the river looks incredible, the mountains are breathtaking. Hardly freezing or dreary.'

Flora had to laugh. 'OK . . . but it was yesterday.'

'And it probably will be tomorrow,' Fin grinned.

'Truce?'

'Truce.'

Dominic was back with another cheque for his great-aunt.

'Nearly five hundred this time . . . well, four-fifty once you've taken off the commission.' He brandished the cheque in front of Dorothea before handing it to her.

'What is this for?' she asked.

'For the corner chair, Aunt Dot. Remember? I took it last time I was here because you said you didn't want it any more. Good result, eh?'

She peered at the writing and nodded. 'Thank you so much.'

'Bet you never thought I'd get that amount.'

The old lady looked at him with a wry smile. 'I thought . . . perhaps you'd get a lot more.'

There was a shocked silence. Flora stopped pouring the tea and looked over at Dominic. He was staring at his great-aunt, a look that Flora couldn't at first decipher on his plump face. Calculating, she thought, that's what it is. He looks like a child with his hand in the sweet jar, who has to come up with a good explanation, fast.

'Heavens, Aunt Dot! Five hundred pounds is a lot for that chair.'

'Well, I think you said it was George II . . . didn't you? My father collected George II furniture, and he always bought the highest quality.'

Flora was staggered once again by the way one minute the old lady couldn't remember Mary's name, and the next she could exactly recall not only the chair that had been gone for weeks now, but its provenance to boot.

'It was a lovely item, but there was a small break

on one of the arms that had been clumsily mended,' Dominic told her, his face a mask of earnestness.

'Really? I don't remember that. But . . . I imagine it's still valuable.'

Dominic tut-tutted. 'Aunt Dot, nearly five hundred pounds for a chair *is* valuable! Especially in today's market, when no one is buying the top-end stuff until this tiresome recession is over.'

'Tea?' Flora handed him a cup and saucer, hovered with the milk jug.

'Thank you, thanks so much, how kind you are, Flora,' he gushed, resorting to an excess of manners to hide his embarrassment. 'I thought you'd be pleased,' he said to his aunt, feigning hurt.

'I am glad you got rid of it,' Dorothea said. 'I didn't want it any more.'

Dominic beamed. 'Easy to get in a muddle about this sort of thing. Especially when you don't spend a lot of time in the salerooms like I do.'

'Am I in a muddle?' she asked, her pale eyes suddenly sharp.

When he left, he didn't come into the kitchen as he normally did, just called goodbye from the hall. Flora went to see him out and noticed that he had a small painting tucked under his arm – the farm landscape from the wall above the desk in the sitting room. Flora had no idea who it was by.

'Umm . . . Aunt Dot asked me to sell this next.

Seems to be on a roll, trying to get rid of all her worldly goods.'

'Right . . . Dorothea mentioned to Rene that you were selling some of her things and Rene didn't seem to know about it. You told me you'd talked to her.'

'I know, she called me. I definitely left her a message. She must have wiped it by mistake or something.'

'Will you make sure you actually talk to her this time, please? As I said before, it'd be really awkward if there was a problem and us nurses were accused of nicking things.'

'Of course I will, but you know, Flora, Rene can be a bit tricky.' He lowered his voice conspiratorially. 'I mean, she's doing a splendid job, and I'm endlessly grateful to her for it, of course, but I sometimes think she's a bit possessive of Aunt Dot.' He eyed her, carefully gauging her reaction.

'She's just trying to protect her,' Flora replied.

'Yes, yes, naturally. And I said I admire her tremendously for doing it. I just think she's sometimes unnecessarily suspicious of us all. As if I would even dream of cheating anyone, let alone my dear old aunt. It really is unthinkable.' He stood silently for a moment, looking injured in just the way Pia had.

'So what's the picture worth, do you think?'

He shrugged, bringing it up to the light. 'Not a lot. It's a John Bowman . . . he's a not very important Victorian artist, although he has a small following still. Landscapes aren't really the thing at the moment, but she wanted it gone, so I'm obliging her. Should be able to make a few hundred, bring the grand total so far up to a thousand. Not to be sniffed at.'

'No, indeed,' Flora agreed, wondering how many thousand he was pocketing for himself. Or if he was, in fact, just doing his best for his aunt.

Fin was asleep on the sofa when Flora got home from work that night. Since returning from Scotland two weeks ago, he had been increasingly morose. The remaining days of their holiday had been magic. The weather held and the house began to feel more lived in. Both of them tacitly put a moratorium on any mention of the future, and they laughed and loved and walked in the sunshine as if they were carefree, the days speeding past too quickly.

'Hey . . .' He raised his head from the cushion at her touch, then flopped back. 'Christ, what time is it?'

'Quarter to nine. Are you OK?'

He pulled himself upright, rubbing his face with both his hands. 'I must have dozed off. Sorry . . . I haven't even started supper.'

'Doesn't matter. What did the hospital say?'

'They said what I thought they'd say, that it's finally on the mend.'

'That's brilliant . . . isn't it?'

225

'Yeah . . . yeah, it is. Of course it is.'

She sat down next to him. 'But?'

'Well, so it's better. So what?'

She was taken aback by the despair in his voice.

'Flo, I haven't got a life any more. I'm as weak as a kitten. I don't have a job or any money. I don't have a future. And so my leg is better, which is good. But the doc said it would be months before I would be properly fit to climb again, and then I'd have to be careful of my back. And I'm bored to tears, hanging around here being nothing more than a dumb housewife.'

Flora, seeing he was in distress, tried not to be offended by his words. 'Well, maybe you should take off, go back to Inverness for a while and get fit.'

'Will you come with me? Nothing except that dying woman is stopping you.'

She stared at him, her stomach fluttering with anxiety. He had kept the pressure up, constantly referring to the life they would have once they settled in Scotland. And each time Flora had to hold the front line, keep repeating that it was too soon, that she had a job.

'OK . . .' he was saying. 'So what happens if she lives for another two, three, even four years? It's quite possible, with you looking after her as well as you do. Will you still be there in four years' time?'

'She won't. But yes, I suppose I might.'

'Might?' Fin looked triumphant. 'So it's not

written in stone, then. You *might* leave if it goes on too long, but you *won't* leave now.' He threw his arms in the air. 'Don't get it.'

Flora got up. Is Dorothea an excuse? she wondered. If she died tomorrow, would she be happy to go wherever Fin took her? She took a long breath, trying to be sympathetic because she understood how frustrated he must be.

'I didn't mean it like that. I said "might" because we're talking about a situation where neither of us knows the outcome. So yes, I might still be there if she doesn't die. But she's getting weaker physically all the time. I noticed it when I got back.'

Fin began pacing about the small space. He stopped in front of Flora, his hands on his hips.

'You don't trust me. That's it, isn't it? That's why you won't come away with me.' He stared at her. 'Isn't it?'

'You know the reason.'

'How much longer are you going to make me pay for my sins, Flo? I can only say I'm sorry so many times. I made a mistake, but can't you forgive and forget, let us get on with our life? We were so happy in Scotland together.'

He reached out to put his arms around her shoulders, but she twisted away.

'This isn't about you, Fin, or forgiveness. It's about *my* life. I've said it a million times: I'm not walking out on Dorothea. And it's all well and good us running off to Scotland, but neither of us has a job up there. How's that going to work?'

She moved past him, her whole body trembling with indignation.

'Thanks for reminding me.' Fin's voice behind her was sullen and tired. He followed her into the bedroom where she had flopped down on the edge of the bed.

'Sorry, Flo, sorry. Please, come back . . .'

'You keep hassling me about my job,' she said. 'It's not fair.'

He sat beside her. 'I know, I know. Flo, look at me, please. I'm sorry. I was horrible just now. I think it was the back thing that freaked me out. The doctor went on about my spine being weak and not to put too much strain on it. And when I asked how long it might take to be OK again, he just said "Maybe never, you sustained very serious injuries, you know." Like I hadn't noticed.' He sighed. 'And then he said, giving me this really stern look, "You don't want to end up in a wheel-chair" . . . Christ.'

He prised her right hand away from the left as she clenched the two together in her lap and kissed it gently, turning it over and burying his mouth in the palm of her hand.

'I love you . . . so much. You love me, don't you? Say it, please . . . say you love me, Flo.'

She looked up at him, saw the pain in his eyes and felt an overwhelming love for him. But somehow it wasn't a joyous love; it felt sad, almost pitying.

'I do love you,' she whispered, saying it properly

for the first time. And it was the truth. She just hoped it was enough, not so much for him, but for herself.

His face cleared, a broad grin driving the despair from his eyes. 'God, it makes me so happy to hear you say it. I thought . . . well, maybe I was a disappointment to you this time around. Without the whole macho adventure-climbing thing . . .'

She laughed. 'I never loved you because you were a mountaineer, Fin.'

'Didn't you? But that was part of it, no? Part of the package?'

She leant into his body. 'Part of who you are, so yes, I suppose part of what I love. But you don't have to be a climber for me to love you.'

Fin held her close and gave a long sigh. 'That's just as well. Because from what the doctor said, it's looking less and less likely that I'll be able to do the mountains seriously again.'

CHAPTER 14

8 December

'I need to beg a favour. Can you do this Saturday night?' Mary asked, when Flora got to work on Monday morning. 'My sister's coming over from Dublin for the weekend.'

'Of course.' Flora heard the hesitation in her own voice.

'I can ask Rene to find someone else if it's a problem? Or get Pia to do it . . . although I'd rather not.'

'No, no, it's fine, really.' She didn't relish the thought of night duty, never had, but she owed Mary.

'Sure lover boy'll be able to do without you for one night?' Mary joked.

'Sure.'

Fin was in the shower when she got home.

'Don't worry,' he called. 'I've done the supper. All ready to go.' He came out in a T-shirt and sweatpants, kissing her before he went to turn the hob on under the pan of vegetable soup. He smelt of ginger body wash, deliciously damp and clean.

'I have to do a night on Saturday. Mary's got her sister over from Ireland.'

Fin groaned. 'Why can't they get someone else to do it? You work all week as it is.'

'I suppose they could, but Dorothea wouldn't know them. And Mary was so good about doing my shifts when we went to Scotland.'

She sat down, watching Fin getting the bowls out, cutting the bread, grating the cheese, dressing the salad.

He brought over a glass of red wine and handed it to her.

'It must be a health and safety issue, the amount of hours you all do. Isn't the old lady's care compromised by overworked nurses?'

She laughed. 'I won't do much except sleep. She only wakes once or twice on a normal night. And it's money.'

'Well, if she only wakes twice, why would it matter who was there? She'd hardly notice. And anyway, we were thinking of a pizza and movie with Bel on Saturday. Remember?'

'We could do it in the afternoon. I don't have to be there till eight. I'm sure Bel won't mind.'

'Will you ask, though? See if someone else can do it?'

'I've told Mary now.'

'But it's not up to her to find a replacement nurse, is it? Surely that's Rene's job?'

'Fin, can you drop it please? It's only one night.'

But he was shaking his head.

231

'It's not the night itself, it's the principle. You're her nurse, Flo, not her daughter. You shouldn't feel obliged to spend so much time worrying about whether she's happy or not.'

Flora put her glass down on the table. She was tired.

'I know you're right, but it *is* different from most jobs. I suppose I've got too attached.'

'You wouldn't be expected to do twelve-hour shifts if you were in an A&E department, would you?'

'No, true.'

He seemed to be waiting for her to concede more.

'I don't know what to say, Fin, except this is my job at the moment. Sometimes I think you're jealous of Dorothea.' She spoke lightheartedly. But his expression didn't lift in response.

'Am I being ridiculous?' he asked finally, giving her a sheepish grin. 'It's just the days seem so fucking long. I sit here all by myself and I get maudlin I suppose.'

'Is the soup OK?'

He rushed to rescue the pan.

As they sat eating their supper on the sofa, Flora asked, 'Have you thought any more about going up north?'

Fin nodded but didn't say any more.

'And?'

She saw him take a deep breath. 'I will go, for a week maybe. But I'm worried if I do you won't want me back.'

'What on earth do you mean?' She was amazed. Fin had always been independent – sometimes to a fault – and here he was, sounding almost scared of being separated from her for a few days.

'Look, I know I've been a pain recently. I take it out on you all the time, I do realise that. I wouldn't blame you if you didn't want me around.'

In the silence, her thoughts flashed back to how it had been between them in the past, before he had left her. But all she could remember was him being away for weeks at a time and the thrill of him returning, lean and bronzed, full of his adventures. How they would fall into each other's arms, make love as if for the first time. They seldom argued about anything. And whereas she'd loved her job, it was Fin who consumed her thoughts – her life. How real had it all been? she asked herself now.

'Do you think she'll die before Christmas?' he was asking.

'Oh, Fin . . . I have no idea. Christmas is only about two weeks away. Can you stop hassling me about her.'

'I suppose you'll be working?'

'No, actually. Mary always does Christmas Day and Boxing Day. She likes it, she says. Rene comes over. It's much like any other day for Dorothea I expect. She hates fuss.'

Pia opened the door to Flora on Saturday night, giving her a sweet smile. Flora remembered Mary

233

saying that the Filipina nurse made her teeth hurt, and understood what she meant.

'Everything OK?' Flora asked.

Pia nodded. 'We have nice day. Miss Dorothea is happy happy . . . we go to the park. She is very well.'

'I'll just go and say hello.'

She knocked, and went into the old lady's bedroom. Dorothea was lying facing the wall and Flora thought she might be already asleep as she didn't reply when Flora said hello. She laid her hand gently on her shoulder, but Dorothea flinched, quickly withdrawing her arm away from her touch.

'Dorothea, it's me . . . Flora.'

She felt her patient go still for a moment, then turn cautiously to face her.

'Flora . . .' Dorothea blinked up at her. 'Is it Monday?'

'No, it's Saturday night. I am doing tonight instead of Mary. She has her sister visiting from Ireland.'

The old lady reached out and clutched her hand. 'You're staying?' She looked past her towards the door.

'I'm staying tonight, yes.'

Dorothea sighed, still clinging to Flora's hand. Flora looked intently at her patient's anxious face. This is what Mary had been talking about. 'I'm just going to have a word with Pia.' She tried to extricate her hand, but the old lady clung on.

'You're staying . . . now?'

Flora stroked her hand. 'Yes. I just have to speak to Pia for a moment. I'll be straight back.'

'She's going?'

'Yes.'

Dorothea searched her face, then slowly relaxed her grip.

'She seems very anxious to me,' Flora told Pia, who was waiting in the kitchen.

'I think she tired now. Is my fault. We have lots of fun and maybe it too much for her.'

'So what did you do besides going to the park?'

The other nurse's face lit up. 'Oh, we have tea. I bring cake for her. We watch old movie on TV. We chat chat all day. I think she not used to it.'

Flora wondered if there was an implied criticism here, about how Flora looked after her.

'Sounds good.'

'I write it all down in the book,' Pia said, tugging her fringe across her forehead and patting it into place.

'OK, well, thanks. See you in the morning.'

When the nurse had left, Flora went back into Dorothea's bedroom.

'Has she gone?' The old lady looked wide awake.

'Yes. Dorothea . . . tell me what happened today.' Flora perched on the bed and took her patient's hand again.

'Happened?'

'Yes, with Pia, the nurse. What happened? You seem so keen that she leaves. Did something happen?'

Dorothea lowered her eyes. 'I don't know what you mean.'

Flora squeezed her hand. 'You can tell me. Tell me why you're so anxious.'

'Am I anxious?' The old lady gave her a quick look.

'Yes, you seem to be. So what did you do today?'

Dorothea didn't reply immediately.

'We . . . went to the park . . . nothing really.'

'She says she made you a cake.'

At the mention of cake, Dorothea's eyes suddenly blazed.

'She makes me a cake . . . every time.' The words were almost spat out. Perhaps seeing Flora's startled look, she got herself quickly under control again, but her mouth was still working away, her lips twisting nervously.

Flora remembered the outburst a few weeks back when she'd offered tea to the old lady.

'And you don't like it?'

Dorothea wouldn't look at her. 'It's very kind of her . . .'

'Dorothea!' Flora couldn't help raising her voice in frustration. 'Please, tell me what's wrong. Say if you don't like Pia. I promise I won't tell her.'

For a moment the old lady was silent. 'I never said I didn't like her.' Her tone was resolute.

'OK . . . but it's clear to me you don't.' She got up. 'If you'd only tell us why, we could do something. If she's unkind to you, we can get rid of her, you'd never have to see her again. Rene can find you another nurse.' She began to lift her forward so she could plump up her pillows.

'I don't think she would.'

Flora looked hard at Dorothea. 'What do you mean? She could, easily. Tomorrow if you'd like.'

Dorothea stared back and Flora held her breath. She could see her patient wavering, trying to make a decision. Tell me, just *tell me*, she thought.

'I . . . don't want to put Rene to any trouble.'

'It's no trouble. There's an agency. She just has to ring them and they'll fix it up. It's really not a problem.'

Dorothea sank back onto the pillow and closed her eyes, her face suddenly lax with exhaustion.

'I would rather you left things as they are,' she whispered.

Flora wanted to shake the truth out of her, but she knew she couldn't badger her any more. She tucked the old lady's arms beneath the duvet and turned out the light.

'Good night,' she said. Dorothea didn't answer.

Flora watched television till around ten o'clock, then changed into a T-shirt, tracksuit bottoms and a pair of Fin's climbing socks. The nurse's room, next to Dorothea's, had a single bed. Flora lay down gingerly where so many nurses had slept – despite Mary having changed the sheets. The bed had probably been bought pre-war; the mattress was ancient horsehair and iron-hard, the rusty springs making uncomfortable lumps which she had to negotiate in order to find a place to lie. The polyester filling in the narrow duvet wasn't nearly warm enough for the cold December night. She knew she wouldn't sleep much and wondered how Mary put up with this night after night.

She must have dozed off, because she woke with a start to the sound of Dorothea's bell. She got up, dazed, acutely aware of the cold.

'I'm here,' she told the old lady, not turning the main light on, but able to see in the light from the hall. 'Do you want to go to the toilet?'

Dorothea nodded but made no attempt to sit up. 'I . . . I don't feel very well.'

'Do you feel sick?'

Flora saw the old lady shake her head on the pillow. 'Hot . . . I feel hot . . .'

She placed her hand on Dorothea's forehead. It was burning. She quickly turned the light on. Her patient's cheeks were flushed, her eyes glittering with fever.

Flora fetched the thermometer and put it gently in her ear. It read 39.2.

'Have you got a headache?'

Dorothea looked confused for a moment. 'I . . . have.' She raised her hand to her face and held it against her cheek. 'I don't think I can get up.'

'Don't worry, you don't have to, I'll bring the bedpan.'

Flora looked at her watch. It was just before midnight. Should she ring the doctor? Dorothea's temperature was very high. It could be flu, she thought. Was that what had been bothering her earlier? That she hadn't been feeling well?

She settled the old lady and decided she had to call the surgery. She knew Dr Kent was on call some nights, and although she was loath to wake him if he was, she had never trusted the doctors who did locum work at night. They could be so brusque and uncaring, impatient unless it was a case of life or death.

But her call was immediately patched through to Simon's mobile.

'Hey, Flora,' he said, his voice thick with sleep. 'What's the problem?'

She told him and he said he'd be over in ten minutes.

He arrived in jeans and a navy jumper under his tweed coat.

'Bloody freezing out there.' He rubbed his hands together briskly, then he put his bag down and took his coat and scarf off.

'Sorry to drag you out in the middle of the night. I just thought over thirty-nine was a bit high.'

'Absolutely. Let's take a look.'

'Hello . . . Flora tells me you don't feel so well.' The old lady gave him a wan smile as he began to examine her gently. 'Do you have a sore throat?' She nodded, swallowing with difficulty then beginning to cough.

'When did you first notice she had a temperature?' he asked Flora.

'Just now. She was fine when she went to

sleep . . . at least, there weren't any signs of fever then.'

'I think it's probably flu, she's got all the symptoms. I'm going to start her on Tamiflu.'

'But she had the jab in September.'

'There's quite a virulent strain going round at the moment. It's not hit the *Daily Mail* yet, and I've only seen a couple of cases, but a colleague in the Midlands has been inundated.'

Back in the hall he hesitated. 'You wouldn't do me a cup of tea would you?'

'God, sorry. Of course. I thought you'd want to get back to bed as quickly as possible.'

'I'm not on till the afternoon tomorrow, and I know I won't sleep yet.'

They sat together in the sitting room, each with a cup of tea. The low light from the single lamp and the isolating stillness of the night made for an unusual sense of intimacy.

'I promise and swear that I won't bang on about my problems this time,' Flora whispered.

There was silence.

'You see? If we don't talk about you and the leopard, we have nothing to say to each other.'

'That's because it's a weird relationship.'

'Ours?'

Flora nodded. 'We're sort of not quite colleagues or friends. And we have to be professional around each other. I broke the code by telling you about my boyfriend.'

'So should we stick to the price of incontinence pads then?' He looked amused.

'Not sure how it works. If we were in a hospital or an office we'd be properly working together on stuff. But here we just stand in the hall and whisper.'

'I suppose.'

'This flat's a limbo place, it creates a bizarre sort of family,' she went on. 'We're thrown together for a while, then it's over and we never see each other again.'

'I don't like the thought that we . . .' He stopped.

She sipped her tea. 'Tell me about your ballroom dancing.'

He grinned. 'Nothing much to tell. I'm not very good, I just love it.'

'I'm sure you're being modest.'

'Promise I'm not.' He paused. 'Come on, get up. I'll give you a demo.'

She laughed. 'No way. I told you, I can't dance. Anyway, we'll wake Dorothea.'

'Come on, I'll be really, really quiet.' He was pulling her to her feet. Before she had time to object any further, he had put his right arm around her body and taken her left hand in his, stretching her arm outwards. She was intensely aware that she had just a thin T-shirt on, no bra. 'You know how to waltz?'

She pulled a face.

'OK, left foot back . . . right to the side . . . just

follow my feet.' He began softly humming John Denver's 'Annie's Song' – she remembered her mother loving it and playing it over and over – and took off between the furniture, spinning her round at a smooth, dignified pace in the half-lit room. 'You fill up my senses . . .' he sang. 'Don't look at your feet . . . relax.'

His arm brought her closer. She was laughing now, trying to follow his steps, stumbling sometimes, but picking it up with his confident instruction. Very soon she fell into the rhythm and began to enjoy herself, swept up in his firm embrace, singing along with the doctor: 'Like a night in a forest . . .'

'You're a natural,' he spoke in a stage whisper as they stopped, breathless and laughing, falling onto the sofa together.

'That was brilliant!'

'You should come along one day. You'd love it.'

For a moment they sat in breathless silence.

When she glanced across at him, she found he was gazing at her, a dark, penetrating stare from his brown eyes that made her feel intensely vulnerable and exposed. She crossed her arms around her body, realising that she was blushing.

Noticing it, his own expression suddenly clouded with embarrassment.

'What am I like, dancing in my pyjamas in the middle of the night.' She spoke lightly to deflect the sudden tension.

He smiled but didn't answer, bending his head to his cup.

Flora was aware of the raised beat of her heart in the still, shaded room. Simon Kent met her eyes and the look between them held for a long second.

'It was . . . fun.' His voice was no more than a murmur. He drained his tea. 'I'd better get home.' He pulled himself off the sofa.

Flora got up too, shyness making her next remark sound stilted and formal.

'Listen, thanks for coming out. It could probably have waited till morning.'

'Nope, it couldn't. She needed to start the Tamiflu as soon as poss if it's going to have any effect.'

The atmosphere was once more professional between them, merely doctor to nurse.

'You know what to do. Keep her fluids up, plenty of rest, light diet. Keep an eye on her temperature. See how she goes.'

'Of course.'

'I'll drop by tomorrow evening, after surgery, but obviously call if there's any deterioration.' He pulled on his coat, wrapping his scarf hastily round his neck as if he was suddenly desperate to be gone. 'Thanks for the tea . . . and the dance.'

She went to check on Dorothea after he'd gone. The old lady was asleep, her cheeks still flushed with the fever, and Flora crept back to bed. What went on there? she asked herself, trying to get warm under the synthetic duvet. Did I imagine that look? She remembered her own response to it and immediately rejected the memory. She fell asleep to the strains of John Denver's song still playing in her head.

Dorothea was restless all night, constantly calling out, even if not for assistance, as if the fever were giving her bad dreams. But each time she called, Flora woke and went to see if she was alright, pushing fluids, checking that she was comfortable. By the morning they were both wan and exhausted.

Flora got dressed just before Pia was due to arrive. She didn't want to leave Dorothea, ill as she was, with the day nurse, but Pia was full of concern and sympathy for the old lady.

Flora went in to say goodbye to Dorothea, Pia following close on her heels.

Dorothea looked at her as Flora took her hand.

'You're not going are you?'

'Yes. I'll be back tomorrow.'

Dorothea looked past her at the smiling Pia, then looked away again. The Filipina nurse bustled into the room and sat on the bed.

'Hello, Miss Dorothy. Flora says you not so well today.'

Dorothea forced a small smile.

'I think it best you stay in bed till you feel better,' Pia continued, stroking the old lady's hand with her own plump one.

Dorothea looked down at her hand, not returning

the nurse's touch. She glanced at Flora, who had moved towards the door.

'When are you coming back?'

'Tomorrow. If I can, I'll drop by later to see how you are.'

'You no worry, I look after Miss Dorothy very well.' Pia's concern seemed genuine.

'I'm sure,' Flora replied, wondering if the clear antipathy the old lady had towards Pia was just one of those paranoid fixations that older people sometimes get about certain people – even blameless sons and daughters – convinced they are trying to steal their money or sell their house, do them harm in some way.

'I hope you feel better soon,' Flora said.

'I . . . don't think I will,' Dorothea said, a note of reproach in her voice.

When Flora got home, Fin was still asleep, although it was nearly nine-thirty. She got undressed quickly and crawled in beside him. He was deliciously warm as she snuggled against him. He half woke up and drew her into his side, kissing her on the top of her head.

'Good night?'

'No, lousy,' she replied, making a decision not to mention dancing with Dr Kent around Dorothea's sitting room in the dead of night. It was innocent fun, she told herself, at the same time knowing there was an edge of something more than that in the doctor's eyes.

'Go to sleep then,' he ordered, stroking the hair back from her face and kissing her gently on the lips, 'before I stop you.'

It was nearly midday when she woke, the bed empty beside her.

She padded through to the sitting room to find Fin in his usual position on the sofa. He got up to make her some coffee. As she related the events of the night, he kept shaking his head.

'Poor you. You're exhausted and you have to go back to work tomorrow. I thought you said you'd be able to sleep.'

'It was unusual last night. She was ill.'

'But you look terrible. I think next time Mary wants a night off you should ask the agency to sort it.'

'Please, can we not have another conversation about the iniquities of my job? It doesn't help.'

He looked at her as if he were battling with a decision about whether to go on arguing or not.

'No, you're right. Sorry. We're together, that's all that matters.' He came towards her, holding his hand out to her as she sat on the sofa. 'Why don't you go back to bed for a bit?'

But she couldn't respond because she suddenly felt really nauseous. She held her breath, waiting, hoping that it would go away.

'Flo?'

She heard his voice as if from a long way away as she made a dash for the bathroom, where she was violently sick.

Fin was right behind her. 'Flo . . . Flo, are you alright?'

She groaned. 'God . . . I don't know where that came from.'

He hovered over her. 'You've probably got Dorothea's bug.'

'I bloody hope not.' She filled the tooth mug with water and rinsed her mouth out. 'I still feel sick.'

'You'd better get back to bed.'

He tucked her in and sat beside her, his expression contrite. 'I didn't mean to hassle you . . . I just look forward to the weekends with you so much.'

'I look forward to them too. This weekend was an exception. It won't happen again.'

'I was just being childish.'

He was searching her face, looking for forgiveness, and she was willing to give it. She took his hand and kissed it. But she knew it was increasingly a pattern between them. He would pick a fight, she would get upset, he would apologise. She lay back, holding her stomach, waiting for the nausea to go away. She didn't want to live like this, and she knew he didn't either.

Dorothea was not looking much better when she arrived for work. The fever had abated and her cheeks were no longer flushed, but now she looked chalk-white and listless.

Flora let her stay in bed again. She had little appetite, but Flora poached some haddock for her lunch, just in case. She laid the fish in the saucepan with a little milk and put it on to boil, but when she took the lid off the pan, she was suddenly over-come with nausea again and had to rush off to the bathroom. She wasn't actually sick, but she retched repeatedly over the toilet bowl. She felt cold and shaky and leant against the basin for support. The bell rang. She dragged herself to the door, cursing.

'God, you look like death!' Dr Kent immediately took her by the elbow and steered her into the sitting room, pushing her gently onto the sofa.

'I felt sick, but I wasn't sick. Just retching.'

She sank gratefully against the cushions, gave him a rueful smile.

'I'd better call Rene, get another nurse on board,' he said. 'Do you have her number?'

Flora nodded. 'Listen, I'll be OK in a minute. It happened at the weekend as well, and I was completely fine later.'

'Do you have a headache, sore throat?' He sat by her and took her pulse, laid his palm against her forehead.

'No . . . nothing.'

'You don't seem feverish. He was looking at her questioningly. 'Umm . . .'

'Umm what?'

'Just a thought . . . might you be pregnant?'

'Pregnant?' The word fell like a whisper between them, carried away by the sheer improbability of the idea.

'Only a suggestion.'

'I can't be.'

Simon Kent raised his eyebrows. '"Can't be" as in totally out of the question? Or "can't be" as in I can't believe I am?'

Flora thought back to that one night in Scotland when they hadn't had a condom. He didn't come inside her, but still . . .'

She felt a flush rise to her cheeks.

'It is possible, I suppose.'

'Have your periods been normal?' He was being very professional with her, his expression neutral.

She thought back. 'No . . . but then they never are, haven't been for a few years now. I had a slight bleed a couple of weeks ago, but now I think about it, it wasn't a proper period.'

He got up. 'Perhaps you should take a test.'

She stared at him, remembering the dancing, the odd moment between them on Saturday night. But his face was shut down, she had no idea what he was thinking.

'You should definitely call Rene and get another nurse. You can't work if you're feeling nauseous all the time.'

'I'll call her in a minute,' Flora told him, knowing that she wouldn't. She didn't want to go home yet, not until she knew for certain.

'Would it be good news?' Dr Kent was asking.

'Yes,' she said quickly. 'No . . . well . . . it's not brilliant timing.'

The doctor looked as if he were waiting for her to say more, but she couldn't speak, she was just holding onto herself, almost breathless.

She thought he said he would look in on the old lady, and she thought he called goodbye, but she was in too much of a daze to know for certain.

'Just nipping to the chemist,' Flora told Keith. She had waited till she was sure the doctor was well away before checking on Dorothea, then grabbing her purse and her coat. She felt cold with shock, her heart fluttering uncomfortably in her chest.

'How's Miss H-T getting on then? Haven't seen her about since last week.'

'Got the flu.' She was dying to just get the kit, do the test, stop the unbearable suspense. But the porter was in a conversational mood.

'She's a tough old bird . . . bit of flu's not going to bother her for long. You don't get to ninety by being a wuss.'

'I'm sure you're right. Anyway, better get on. Don't want her waking up when I'm not there. You OK?'

Keith grinned. 'Bloody marvellous is the truth. Got a gorgeous woman in my bed at last!'

'Way too much information, thanks!' His chuckle followed her to the main door.

She gazed blankly at the boxes of pregnancy test kits, going over and over in her mind the number of weeks since that night in Scotland. Five and a bit, if you didn't count from the most recent period, which had only lasted two days. She grabbed the most prominent brand and went to pay for it, suddenly flustered in front of the girl at the till, self-conscious about the implications of her purchase. The girl merely scanned the box through.

'Like a bag?' She asked in a bored monotone.

Flora nodded, not wanting Keith to see what she was carrying.

When she got back to the flat, Dorothea was awake and ringing the little bell by her bed.

'Sorry, I had to pop out for something. How are you feeling?'

'I think . . . very tired.' She tried to sit up. 'I need to get out.'

For the next hour, Flora was tied up with her patient. It wasn't until Dorothea was settled again, a cup of weak tea beside her bed, that she had time to go to the bathroom.

Scrabbling with the packet, giving a hurried glance at the instructions, she peed on the stick, watching the tip go pink. She checked her watch. Two minutes, they said. The second-hand pottered agonisingly slowly around the face. But as she sat on the edge of the bath, her eyes darting between her watch and the small results window on the white plastic wand, she was certain beyond any doubt that what she'd see would be a clear blue plus sign.

CHAPTER 15

17 December

Rene's voice nattered on as she sat beside the bed, holding her friend's hand. Dorothea had been asleep most of the afternoon and looked to Flora as if she wanted to go to sleep again.

'It's been a bit of a nightmare day. I had a terrible argument with Alan about the clematis – the gorgeous pink one along the bottom fence, remember? He claims it's on its last legs, but he's always such a Jonah about my plants, even though he's employed to look after them. He wants to rip it out, plant a new one. But it's been there since we got the house, twenty-seven years ago. I'm not letting it go without a fight . . .'

'Oh dear,' Dorothea muttered. 'So what will you do?'

'As little as possible. I said he was on no account to touch it. I know it wasn't at its best this summer, but the weather's been so strange. I said we should leave it another year, see how it goes. But he's so bad tempered about it.'

'Perhaps you should find another gardener?' Dorothea suggested mildly, looking as if she were struggling to get involved in the conversation. She had Flora's sympathy. As she finished massaging E45 cream into the dry skin on the old lady's legs, pulling the bed covers back into place, her own thoughts were in turmoil; the precious secret buzzing round her, threatening to burst into the open at any moment.

Rene was shaking her head vehemently. 'Heavens, no, I can't do that. He's Christine's cousin. I'd never hear the last of it if I sacked him.'

The old lady said nothing, probably, like Flora, having no idea who Christine was and not having the energy to ask.

'Anyway, my dear, I must love you and leave you, get back home and put the supper on. Rosie's coming round with her latest beau.' Rene rolled her eyes. 'Hope he's more articulate than the last one.' She bent to kiss Dorothea on the cheek. 'So nice to see you a bit better today. I'll try and pop in again tomorrow.'

Dorothea smiled up at her friend. 'Thank you so much,' she said.

Flora went with Rene to the front door.

'What do you think?' Rene asked.

'She's weak, and still very tired, but she doesn't have a fever any more. I think Dr Kent caught it in time.'

'What a gem he is,' Rene said. 'I can't believe how much attention he pays her. He's always round here, and he's not even private. We're so lucky to have him.'

Flora heard the main door of the flats slam behind her at the end of her shift with a huge sigh of relief. Now she could think. She walked up Gloucester Road instead of taking the bus. It was mild for December, a light sleet making the pavements oily. She welcomed the cool, damp night air on her face.

'I'm pregnant,' she kept whispering to herself like a mad woman. 'I'm pregnant.' But the words made no sense. She had wanted a baby for so long.

But hard on the heels of her euphoria came the cold hard facts of her situation: living on what amounted to her sister's charity, in a tiny flat, with an unemployed climber who was reluctant to have children. Not to mention the perils of actually keeping the pregnancy at her age. How will Fin react? she wondered, her stomach knotted with nerves as she trod down the slippery area steps to her flat.

Fin was frowning in front of the television, the volume muted. He smiled at her as she came in. 'This stuff is such crap,' he said, yawning, and stretching his long arms towards the ceiling. 'I don't know how they have the bloody nerve to make these ludicrous shows in the first place.'

She laughed. 'Why watch it, then?'

'Bugger all else to do.' He got up and gave her a kiss. 'I saw Prue today,' he went on. 'She was banging on about Christmas. Says it's going to be about twelve of us.'

'Usually is.' She took off her coat and hung it on the stand. 'Did she say who she's got lined up for us this year?'

Fin shook his head. 'Bound to be hideous. I was thinking . . . suppose we go up to Scotland instead? If Mary's going to be there, you've got at least five days off if you include the weekend. It would be better than making nice to your sister's pompous friends.'

Flora thought of his father's house, freezing in December, the damp sheets, the musty smell, the avocado-coloured bath, but she decided not to have the argument with him just now.

'Fin. Sit down. I've got something to tell you.'

The discontent and lethargy on Fin's face was immediately replaced by a wary interest. 'Go on.'

'Sit down first,' she repeated, receiving a puzzled frown from Fin. He threw himself back on the sofa and looked at her impatiently as she settled herself in the chair opposite, trying to find the right words. But her nerves wouldn't stand prevarication.

'I'm pregnant,' she said flatly.

'Pregnant?'

'Yes. I did a test this afternoon.'

He stared at her in silence.

'Say something,' she urged.

'It can't be mine.'

'Fin! Of course it's yours. Who else's could it be?'

Fin shrugged. 'That man you were seeing before

I pitched up? You had sex with him presumably?' His voice was flat with tension.

'Once. But that was months ago, and we used a condom.'

He got up and started pacing around behind the sofa. 'So do we. Every time. And the only time we didn't, I didn't come inside you. There's no way it can be mine. You said yourself it wasn't possible, that night in Scotland.'

Flora realised she was shaking. She hadn't expected him to be overjoyed, but to deny he was the father?

'I said it was unlikely, not impossible.'

Fin shook his head but didn't say anything.

She got up. 'Fin. This is your baby. The test says I'm only five weeks gone.'

'I just can't believe it.'

'Nor can I. But it *is* your baby.' She went over to him and took his hands. His gaze was bewildered.

'OK, OK . . . I believe you.'

They stood silently, staring at each other. His patent lack of enthusiasm clutched at her heart.

'I know it's not great timing, but . . . I . . .' She could feel the stress of the day finally catching up with her, tears gathering hotly behind her eyes.

'Sorry, sorry.' He pulled her into an embrace. 'It's just a massive shock for me.'

'It is for me too, but I'm still happy.' Was this true, she wondered. She was dazed, incredulous, but she realised she had waited to enjoy the moment until she'd spoken to Fin.

'Come over here,' Fin pulled her across to the sofa, sitting her down and holding her close against him. 'It's great, amazing. I was trying to think it through, that's all. I'm just not sure how we're going to manage when you can't work any more . . . three of us cooped up in this tiny flat.' He glanced down at her. 'It's going to be hard.'

She drew away from him. 'You are pleased though . . . just a bit . . . aren't you?'

He began to speak, then stopped.

'Fin?'

He hesitated again.

'Alright: I'm not going to lie to you, Flo, it's too important. I don't want a child right now. Not yet, not until we've had some time together, got our lives on track with somewhere decent to live. This is way too soon . . . you know it is.'

Tears were pouring down her face. 'You sound as if you're blaming me.'

'I'm not . . . but it was you who said we should keep going, even though we didn't have a condom that night in Dad's house . . . if that's when it happened. I've been so careful all the other times.' He sounded almost peeved, and Flora suddenly felt an irrational desire to hit him.

'Fuck you.'

She shot up from the sofa and walked out, shutting herself in the bedroom. Lying there, she felt her heart pounding through her chest wall, but anger stifled any more tears. She would have the baby whether it suited Fin or not. She would do it alone, somehow she would, even if they had to live off the state. She clutched her stomach, trying to get a sense of the minute cluster of cells that would eventually make up their baby.

It was a long time before Fin appeared by her side. She felt disorientated by his face suddenly so close to hers.

'Flo . . . Flo? Please, let's not fight.'

She pulled herself upright, but she didn't know what to say to him as he sat awkwardly beside her on the bed. She fiddled with the tissue she'd been clutching.

'Look at me,' his hand went under her chin, gently drawing her head up. 'Listen. I know I should be more enthusiastic, and I will be, I promise. I just need time.' His grey eyes looked almost bruised.

'I can do it myself if you won't support me.' Flora knew it was a childish declaration, even if fundamentally true. She had no desire whatsoever to bring up the baby without Fin, alone and in poverty.

'Of course I'll support you. I never said I wouldn't. Please, stop being stupid and let's have some supper. You're going to have a baby, you need to eat.' He was smiling now, but she could see the effort it cost him.

Later, as she lay next to him in bed, she couldn't sleep. For the first time she questioned whether she really loved this man. His response had profoundly shocked her. Not the initial denial, or stunned surprise, that was fair enough – he was nearly fifty and had managed to evade fatherhood thus far – but the complete lack of love in his face when she had told him she was carrying his baby. Because this wasn't a one-night stand with a woman he barely knew. He said he loved her, said he wanted to spend the rest of his life with her. But she could see, in that moment, that he hadn't been thinking about her at all, or about the baby, or even about them as a couple. He'd been thinking exclusively about himself. Where was the love in that?

Bel sat next to Flora on the bus taking them to Westfield.

'Remind me. Why, exactly, are we going to some grisly shopping centre on the Saturday before Christmas?'

Her niece giggled. 'To shop?'

'Hadn't thought of that.'

'It'll be fun. Like a zoo and totally hectic, and we won't find a thing before our legs are reduced to bleeding stumps, but it's what you *do* when it's Christmas.'

'I've bought all my presents.'

'Oooh, smug. I suppose you bought them at a summer fair like old people do,' Bel teased. 'Well, I've got everyone's except Mum's. You have to help me. You know how hard it is to find something she hasn't already got.'

Flora was pleased to be away from the flat and Fin. In the first few days after the revelation, they had been careful around each other: he being over-solicitous about her health, she making light of the whole thing. But neither of them had the will to really sit down and discuss what they might do in a practical sense. So the baby was like a looming, but mute, presence over all their conversations. Flora was the first to break.

'We have to talk about this, Fin,' she'd said, as they sat having coffee and croissants at the weekend.

'I'm not avoiding it.'

'I didn't say you were.' There was a tense silence. 'Let's not argue.'

Fin tore off another piece of his croissant, but instead of eating it he just looked at it then laid it back down on his plate, rubbing his hands together to get rid of the pastry flakes.

'I've thought about nothing else since you told me, but I'm getting nowhere. We're in a mess. And if you can't work because of the baby, I don't know how we'll support ourselves in London.' He gave a heavy sigh. 'The only solution I can see is one you won't even contemplate . . . moving up to Inverness.'

'I have contemplated it.'

'And?' His look was cautious, but he didn't wait for her reply. 'I could get work up there quite easily, guiding people, or in one of the millions of climbing shops around, until I'm fit enough for bigger things.'

'We could try it out,' she conceded.

His look was surprised, bordering on suspicious. 'You'd do that?'

She didn't answer, no longer able to avoid the fact that it wasn't the house itself, or its location, that was the problem. She pushed the thought away.

'It'll be a while before I can get back into hospital work . . . I couldn't even begin to until she's at least six months old.'

'She?' Fin asked. 'It's a girl, is it?'

She hadn't realised what she'd said. 'I'd like a girl.'

Fin looked away and she immediately felt awkward, aware that any baby talk met the same blank wall. He just didn't want to engage in the baby as a real person.

'We'll sort the house. It's a good space, I can fix it up in plenty of time for the baby. Make it really nice.'

He reached over for her hand. 'You'll see, Flo. It's a wonderful place to bring up a child. Plenty of fresh air, a safe environment. He . . . she would have the perfect childhood.'

She nodded, knowing it was probably true.

'When are you going to tell Prue?'

'I'd like to tell her today, but I think we should wait. At my age there's quite a risk of miscarriage.'

'Would it be dangerous for you if you miscarried?' He looked suddenly anxious.

'Not for me.'

He frowned. 'I couldn't bear it if something happened to you, Flo.'

She resolved to start thinking seriously about the move to Scotland. It did make sense. And if they stayed in this flat, with or without a screaming baby, they would eventually stab each other . . .

Bel was digging her in the ribs. 'We're here.'

They took off around the circuit of shops lining the packed shopping centre. It was a bewildering place, loud, hot and stressful, milling with anxious people darting from store to store in their search for last-minute presents.

'OK, so what are your options for Mum?'

Bel looked dispirited. 'Dunno. I can't afford the expensive stuff she likes in the perfume or cream department. And clothes are a no-no, she'd never wear anything that wasn't designer . . .'

'What about a pretty box, or a nice coffee cup?'

Her niece pulled a face. 'Boring.'

'Or a soap dish, a wine glass . . . bath stuff?'

'Boring, boring, boring.'

They paused in front of a shoe shop.

'Those are cool,' Bel said, eyeing a pair of heavy black boots with buckles up the side.

Flora pulled her away. 'How about a CD? Your mum's got quite broad taste. You could find some funky band . . .'

Bel snorted. 'Yeah, good one. I can just see Mum chilling out to Dizzy Bats or the Dum Dum Girls.'

'No, not quite your mum's cup of tea, perhaps. Can we have a sandwich and think about it?' Flora

262

was suddenly feeling incredibly tired. Thank goodness she didn't have to work now till Thursday, the day after Boxing Day. She hadn't been sick any more, but she felt queasy a lot, and just strange – sort of buzzy and out of her body at times.

'Crayfish and avocado salad and a cappuccino!' Bel shouted. This was their favourite salad in Pret a Manger.

'Crayfish and avocado it is,' Flora agreed, then remembered she shouldn't eat shellfish or drink too much coffee. 'Or mushroom soup?'

Bel pulled a face. 'Nah . . . crayfish for me.'

She eventually bought her mother a plum-coloured mascara and a case for her BlackBerry, decorated with a silver and cherry diamanté butterfly.

'Didn't I do well?' her niece asked, as they squeezed into the bus seat.

'Perfect.'

Bel looked at her sideways. 'You don't think they're stupid?'

'No, I think they're great. If anyone can get away with plum-coloured mascara, it's your mum.'

'Can sex cause a miscarriage?' Fin asked, as they lay in bed on Christmas morning. They hadn't made love since she'd told him about her pregnancy. She'd been feeling fragile and tired, but she also sensed his lack of confidence around her body.

'No, you can have sex all through pregnancy, if you want to.'

He looked over at her. 'Do you?'

'You look almost scared of me,' she smiled, and pulled herself up to kiss him. 'I won't break, promise.'

'It's just . . . it makes me nervous . . . that I'll, you know, do something while we're making love and it'll hurt the baby.'

'So you do care about the baby.'

'Of course I care.'

'It's just that you haven't said a word about how you feel.'

'No, well, not my style is it? Banging on about that sort of stuff.'

He was silent for a moment. 'I can't imagine what sort of father I'll make.' His voice was low, as if he were talking to himself. 'I mean, what does it involve, apart from the practical stuff?'

'Just love, I think. You had a good father. Be like him.'

'He never hugged me . . . never really touched me at all. It was Mum who did the hugging.'

'I'm not sure my dad did much either.' Flora tried to remember her father on the brief visits he made from Saudi. All she could see was an image of him laughing with a glass in his hand. 'We must hug our baby lots,' she said, still unable to picture herself and Fin with a child.

The normally immaculate kitchen, pungent with the aroma of roasting goose, was a sea of preparation: bread crumbs for the sauce lay in a heap on the marble work surface, alongside apple peel and cores; a colander full of half-boiled potatoes; a plate of bloody giblets from the goose; squeezed lemon halves, torn foil, the inevitable Brussels sprouts still in their net bag; a pile of silver serving spoons waiting to be polished, a half-full bottle of red wine.

Prue wore a large butcher's apron over her pink tracksuit, and sweat poured from her flushed face.

'Thank God you're here. This is a bloody nightmare. I thought goose would be way quicker than turkey to cook, but it's still practically raw. We won't sit down for at least another two hours at this rate.'

She wiped her forehead with the back of her hand.

'Nobody minds on Christmas Day,' Flora soothed. 'We can just ply them with booze and quails' eggs when they arrive. Tell us what to do.'

Fin was set to peeling sprouts, Flora to polish the silver.

'Where are Bel and Philip?'

'I sent them out to get some brandy butter for the pud. God knows where they'll find any – not the sort of thing corner shops stock. I'm absolutely sure I bought some, but I've searched high and low.' She groaned. 'I've been so busy on this Pelham Crescent house, I don't know if I'm coming or going.'

By the time the guests arrived, Prue had calmed down, changed into an elegant mulberry wool Nicole Farhi dress and downed a couple of glasses of Prosecco.

'You didn't ask Jake did you?' Flora asked as the bell rang for the second time.

'I did actually.'

'Prue! What were you thinking?'

Her sister gave her a surprised look. 'You and he parted on good terms didn't you?'

'Yeah, but that's hardly the point. It'll be bloody embarrassing in front of Fin.' Jake had texted her a couple of times over the previous months. Just friendly hope-it's-going-well messages, which she'd replied to in kind. She would be happy to see him; she just didn't know how Fin would react.

'Because he doesn't know about him?'

'No . . . because . . . well, just because.'

'Oh, don't be silly. No one cares about that sort of thing. It was just sex, and before Fin came back anyway. He can't expect you to have been celibate all this time. I'm sure he wasn't.'

Flora said nothing, just focused on her task of turning every potato in the large roasting tray before putting it back in the oven. Her sister had always held a pragmatic view about sex. 'Never apologise, never explain, even when there are photographs,' was her favourite saying when told about a friend's infidelity.

Prue was peering into her face. 'You look a bit . . . stressed.'

'Do I?'

Her sister put her head on one side. 'Yes. Well, perhaps not stressed exactly. Maybe just a bit peculiar . . . something not quite right, anyway.'

'I'm fine, honestly.' It was on the tip of her

tongue to blurt out the truth to Prue, but Philip came into the kitchen just then, towing behind him a painfully thin woman in her forties, wrapped in extensive charcoal cashmere, with dark hair to her shoulders and sharp, pale-blue eyes.

'Marina! Happy Christmas!' Prue went over to give a carefully controlled air kiss to her friend's cheek. 'You know my sister, Flora, and her boyfriend, Fin McCrea?'

Marina's eyes lingered on Fin, and Flora could see why. He looked so handsome, rugged and athletic – even though he was convinced he'd 'gone soft' – quite a contrast to the more effete professionals and media types who frequented Prue and Philip's parties.

'No, I'm not sure I've had the pleasure,' the woman said.

Flora noted Fin's response with surprise. All week he'd been moaning about having to be polite to her sister and brother-in-law's 'pompous' friends, but now, almost instantly, he gave Marina a dazzling smile such as she hadn't seen in ages. And as he did so, he seemed to straighten his spine, draw up his head, as if he were shaking himself free of a burden. So different from the brooding, almost resentful expression that she witnessed on an almost daily basis.

The other guests arrived in dribs and drabs over the next hour. Jake was the last. He looked cute, carefully dressed in his usual black and white.

'Hey, Flora. Happy Christmas.' He gave her a

hug. He smelt of a spicy sandalwood aftershave. 'Good to see you again.'

'And you, Jake.'

Prue did the introductions as they all stood around in the large kitchen. 'You know Billy . . . and my friend Ginny . . . Marina Bell, Jean-Pierre all the way from Paris, John and Victoria from next door. And this is Flora's other half, Fin McCrea.' Her sister took a quick gulp of champagne from the glass on the work surface. 'Jake's responsible for my gorgeous kitchen, so if anything goes wrong with the lunch, we can blame him.'

They all laughed and waved acknowledgements, including Fin, who reached across and gave Jake a friendly handshake. He's forgotten I told him his name was Jake, Flora thought, letting out a long breath of relief. Fin had been very jealous in the past, especially of the doctors she worked with, although she'd never given him cause.

Everyone got steadily more and more drunk as they waited for the goose to be cooked. Flora had met most of them before and had very little in common with any of them, except Jake. She did her best, for Prue's sake, but the rich smell of the goose was making her feel a bit queasy and she struggled to join in.

'How's it going?' Jake asked, pulling out her chair for her as they finally sat down. The table had been decorated by Bel with hundreds of silver candles – in amongst lurid pink reindeer, pulling sleighs piled high with silvered pine-cones and crackers.

'Yeah, good.'

Jake's eyes flicked towards Fin at the other end of the table. He lowered his voice. 'Worked out this time?'

'So far.'

He grinned at her, his blue eyes deliberately flirtatious. 'Well, offer still stands if he does another runner.'

'Thanks!'

Marina, it turned out, was an editor and partner in a small publishing company, Grayson Bell, that did mostly travel and lifestyle books. Fin had been entertaining the table with his mountain adventures through most of the goose course, and Marina, seated next to him, hung on his every word.

'God, I can hardly survive the winter inside my centrally heated flat,' she commented, as he finished telling his most recent escapade. 'Let alone braving minus forty-something. And the terror of being perched on an almost vertical ice slope . . . why on earth do you do it?' She smiled up at him.

'Because I enjoy it I suppose,' Fin replied. 'It seems more frightening when you don't know what you're doing. But I've trained for years, since I was a kid really.'

'Yes,' she purred, 'but it's so brave to even *train* for something so dangerous.'

'It's not brave. It's just what I love most in the world.'

Flora felt her heart tighten with sadness at the almost religious conviction in his voice. She didn't look at him, and no one challenged his words. If they had, he would have protested that of course he hadn't meant he loved climbing more than Flora. But she knew that in his heart he did.

'No, he's right, it's not brave,' Prue chimed in, her tone loud and argumentative from too much wine. 'It's bloody stupid. Climbers are worse than drug addicts. They need a fix even if their personal life is falling down around their ears.'

Fin laughed, then pinned Prue with a cynical stare. 'And you're not addicted to anything then?'

To Flora's astonishment, Prue looked uneasy and actually blushed. 'You mean work,' she said after a moment.

Fin nodded slowly, still staring at her sister. 'Yeah, that's exactly what I mean.'

Flora saw Prue shoot a glance in her direction, but turn quickly away when she met Flora's eye.

'Have you thought of writing some of these stories down?' Marina was asking him. 'We're always on the lookout for that sort of book. People never tire of inspiring tales of heroism, and climbing's hot now.'

'Is it?' Philip queried.

'Definitely. Nick and I were looking at the BMC figures only the other day. Membership has tripled in the last twenty years, apparently – probably helped by all those climbing walls.'

'I've written the odd thing in the past.' Fin was seemingly unaffected by his peculiar exchange with Prue. 'I had a gig doing reviews for climbing equipment for a while – it's a good way to get free stuff. And I wrote one piece about climbing as a boy in the Lake District.'

Marina's eyes sparked up. 'Great. Well, why don't you jot some ideas down and come in after the holidays? Our office is in Great Portland Street. I'll introduce you to Nick and we can make a plan. You two will definitely get on, he's nuts about mountains.'

Flora, still puzzled, took some plates through to the kitchen. Bel was standing against the marble island, texting on her phone.

'Having fun?' Flora asked.

Bel pulled a face. 'Alright for you, you've got Jake. My side of the table's bum. That French guy sounds as if he's trying to keep his teeth in – can't understand a word he says – and the grisly neighbours just sit there, getting hammered and moaning about house prices . . . like, what part of that do they think is interesting?'

'Not all larks my side either. Ginny has monopolised Jake, and I'm stuck with Billy telling me about the sprinkler system on his back lawn.' Billy was a sad, rather overweight journalist who'd lived next door to Philip and Prue in their old house in Pimlico. They only ever saw him at Christmas, where he was a permanent fixture.

Bel grinned. 'Wish we could creep off down to yours and watch *Some Like It Hot*. Dad put it in my stocking.'

'Wish we could too.'

271

Flora bent to put the rinsed plates in the machine, but when she came up she suddenly found her head spinning. She reached for the side and clung on, hoping she wouldn't be sick.

'Flora? Flora, are you alright?' Bel was at her side, guiding her to a chair. 'You've gone green . . . I'll get Mum.'

'No . . . no, don't. I'm fine. I had a bug and it's not quite gone. Please don't get Prue, she's a bit over the limit and she'll just make a fuss.'

Bel looked worried. 'Are you sure?'

'Quite sure. I feel better already. It was just coming up too suddenly from the dishwasher.' She managed a smile, wiping away the clammy sweat from her forehead. 'Will you tell Mum I've gone to lie down for a while? Don't make a big deal of it.'

'Can't I come with you?'

'I think I just need a sleep.'

Bel looked disappointed. 'OK. But text me if you need me.'

Fin came clattering down the stairs minutes after Flora had taken off her clothes and was about to get into bed.

'What's up, you look rough.' He stood in the doorway to the bedroom, his face flushed, a stupid expression on his face as if he were trying to control his features.

'I felt a bit dizzy.'

'But you're alright now?'

She nodded, although she still felt lightheaded. He stood watching her for a moment, then came towards her. 'God, you're beautiful.' He pulled her to him, his hand cupping her breast roughly. 'Look at this, so perfect . . .' he pinched her nipple hard then bent his mouth to it.

She winced. 'Ow!'

He pulled back. 'Christ, Flo, can't I even make love to you any more? We haven't touched each other since you found out you were pregnant.'

'Just be gentle. I told you yesterday, my breasts are really tender.'

'This is how it's going to be from now on, isn't it?' His tone was heavy with resignation.

She slid past him and got into bed, pulling the duvet around her shoulders.

'You'll always have some excuse. Every man I've ever talked to says the same thing. As far as a woman's concerned, once she's pregnant it's Job Done. Sperm's safely collected, man totally redundant.'

'Don't talk rubbish.'

He raised his eyebrows. 'Is it rubbish? So you'd be happy for me to make love to you now, would you? As long as I'm "gentle".'

'No, because you're drunk,' she said, turning her back on him.

He groaned. 'So what? That never stopped us fucking each other's brains out in the past.'

'You've forgotten. You never used to drink in the past.'

Fin swore under his breath and she heard him leave the room, then stomp upstairs and slam the door.

It was after nine when he came back, sheepishly clutching a foil wrap of goose and a small Tupperware pot containing apple sauce. She was watching a cheesy American romance on Sky.

'Hey.'

'How did it go?'

'You know. More drinking. More food. But I haven't had a drop of alcohol since I last saw you.' He sat down beside her. 'I'm so sorry, Flo. I was a pig earlier. You were right, I was drunk, but that's no excuse for being beastly to you.' He picked up her hand and dropped a kiss on it. 'Forgive me?'

'Of course.' She leant against him. 'I'm sorry too. I don't feel myself.'

'I don't either.'

She laughed. 'Pregnancy by association – nasty condition.'

'You're a nurse, you should have warned me.'

This time it was she who kissed him, pulling him down onto the cushions until they lay against each other. They made love without bothering to turn off the television, the trite dialogue burbling on in the background heard by neither of them.

It was only later, when she was making some goose sandwiches with brown toast and apple sauce, that she remembered her unease at the jibe Fin had launched at her sister.

'What did you mean when you accused Prue at lunch of being addicted?'

Fin was beside her, putting the kettle on for some tea. He hesitated.

'Well, she is, isn't she? . . . totally addicted to work.'

'She looked so embarrassed though, as if you'd found her out in some dodgy sexual practice.'

'Ha! Didn't notice.'

'Didn't you? She actually blushed.'

He had his back to her. 'She was probably just flushed from all that bloody Prosecco. Hate the stuff, it gives me raging heartburn.'

'I wish I'd been drunk. Those things are hell when everyone else is and you're stone-cold sober. I felt like a sodding gooseberry.'

CHAPTER 16

28 December

Flora sat beside Dorothea, holding her hand. The old lady was in her chair in the sitting room, tucked around with a wool rug. She looked tiny and frail, her skin almost transparent – she'd had barely enough strength to make the journey from her bed to the sitting room on the frame.

'She's been sleeping a lot,' Mary had told her the morning before. 'You'll see a big change in her just in the five days you've been away. That flu really took it out of her.' The night nurse had shaken her head. 'Not sure we've got much longer.'

'So you had a good Christmas?' Flora asked Dorothea now, her heart going out to her, wondering how it felt to be so close to the end of your life.

'It was . . . lovely . . . Rene came to see me and brought her daughter . . . Rosie I think it was. I can . . . muddle her up with her sister.'

Flora let out a long breath. 'Personally, I'm quite glad it's over.'

The old lady looked at her keenly. 'Don't you enjoy Christmas? People don't.'

'Sometimes . . .'

'But not this year.' Dorothea paused. 'May I ask why not?'

'Oh, just family stuff. It's a bit stressful at home at the moment.'

'I hope it's not that young man of yours . . . causing trouble.' She suddenly looked rather fierce.

'He doesn't mean to,' Flora replied, giving in to the intimacy of the moment, the quiet room, the sympathetic ear of a person who had no axe to grind. 'But he's having problems with his life and it makes him cross.'

'Men can be so . . . childish sometimes,' Dorothea was saying.

Flora smiled. 'Can't they just?'

'Never be put upon, dear. Stand up for yourself.' There was a spark in Dorothea's washed-out blue eyes now, and her voice took on a new vigour, all hesitancy vanished. 'My generation never did. Men took terrible advantage.'

'In what way?'

'In every way. We were . . . chattels . . . really no more than that.'

Flora was astonished by this feminist declaration from the ninety-three-year-old.

'At least we earn our own money now.'

Dorothea nodded. 'That helps, I'm sure. But habits . . . die hard.'

In the ensuing silence Flora realised she no longer cared about the boundaries she'd so carefully maintained in the nurse–patient relationship. She'd known Dorothea for a long time, and so intimately; they understood each other.

'I'm pregnant.'

The old lady's eyes widened. 'Pregnant?' she asked, clearly not sure if she'd heard right.

Flora nodded. 'It's very early days . . . but yes.'

'That's . . . marvellous. What a wonderful thing.' She gave Flora such a loving smile that it brought tears to her eyes, making her suddenly long for her own mother. She wanted so badly to share this time with her, when she herself was becoming a parent.

'It is wonderful.'

She didn't feel rested from her days off, just tearful and disorientated. The holiday had consisted of nothing but arguments about their future, interspersed with oases of sex, which acted as a temporary balm and only served to confuse her . . . She got to her feet. 'I'd better get the lunch on. There's a shepherd's pie, do you fancy that?'

'Not much.'

As she reached the door she heard the old lady add softly, 'I probably . . . won't be here to see your baby.'

Flora stopped and turned. They looked at each other across the quiet sitting room. The words 'Don't say that' sprang to her lips, and died.

* * *

278

'My new best friend is determined to make me a star,' Fin told her that night, his voice tinged with cynicism. 'I think she sees a TV spin-off. Me as the new Bear Grylls. You know, leaping barefoot from icy peak to icy peak, beating off grizzlies, fearless and alone in the hostile wilderness . . . except for a ten-person camera crew of course. She was all over me like a rash.'

'Why not? You're better looking than Bear.' Flora smiled. 'You could do it. Did she say how much she might pay you?'

'She said they never pay authors much up front unless they're famous. They'd rather spend it on the marketing.'

He handed Flora a bowl of Spaghetti Bolognese and a fork.

'Thanks.' She carried it over to the sofa. 'What did she mean by not much?'

'She didn't say, she said she'd have to talk to my agent about it. Which I told her could prove tricky, seeing as I haven't got one.'

Fin picked up his own bowl of pasta. 'She told me to get in touch with a guy called Jonathan. Said she'd put in a good word for me.'

'That all sounds hopeful.'

Fin sat down in the chair opposite her. He gave a theatrical sigh. 'Does it? Seems like a lot of hard work that I won't enjoy, for precious little reward, if you ask me. I mean, it's flattering, and she's promising the stars, but as Prue says, the chances of the book taking off and making me any money are pretty slim.'

'You've talked to Prue about it?'

'Yeah, I thought she'd know more about the whole publishing scene than we do.'

'And she didn't think it was even worth a try?'

'She didn't say that exactly, just pointed out how much time writing a book takes if you haven't done it before . . . the downside of not earning much money.'

They ate their supper in silence.

'Uh . . . I've got something to confess, Flo . . .' Fin looked nervous. 'Don't be angry with me . . . but I sort of mentioned the pregnancy thing.'

'You told Prue?'

'It just came out, when we were talking about the book. I'm really sorry.'

Flora shrugged. 'I'm glad she knows. How did she take it?' She was relieved in a way that Fin had taken the burden of telling her sister from her. She thought that Prue would be happy for her, but she also knew that it would trigger a ton of nagging about how they would cope with a baby.

Fin pursed his mouth. 'She was a bit upset that you hadn't told her yourself, but I said it was really early and you were worried something might happen. I suppose you could say she was cautiously pleased. She's out tonight, but she said to go up first thing on Saturday.'

'So what will you do about the book?'

He shrugged. 'To be honest Flo, it's not my thing. I'm a mountain man. I need to be outdoors.'

'But you haven't even tried, or found out how much they might pay you. And even if this one doesn't make much, it might lead to other books, and articles – things you *could* earn money from. The stuff you wrote before was good.' She sighed, exasperated. 'Fin, you've said it yourself, you might not be fit enough to be a professional climber any more. No one's suggesting you give up climbing altogether, but you've got to start thinking of other things to do as well, just in case.'

His face closed down. 'Well thanks, Flora, thanks a bunch.'

'What?'

'Like I'm not depressed enough without you rubbing it in.'

'I'm not saying anything we haven't said before.'

'I don't need reminding of it though, do I? Especially not from you, who should be on my side.'

Frustrated by his lack of purpose, she was too tired to be conciliatory.

'We've got to have an income.'

He stood got up. 'Christ! Like I don't know that. You talk about me as if I'm on the scrap heap, that I should be grateful for any crumbs thrown my way.' He slammed his bowl in the kitchen sink. 'It's this bloody pregnancy. We were fine before that. Now you're permanently ill and neurotic. I can't have a sensible conversation with you that doesn't involve where we're going to live and how I'm going to support you and the baby.'

'That's rich! You're the one who's always nagging me to make a decision about Inverness.' Flora felt her body suddenly flush uncomfortably with heat. 'You sit there all day, never lifting a finger, then as soon as you're given a real opportunity – and a rare one at that, which could open up a whole new career for you – you dismiss it out of hand because you need to be "outdoors"?'

'If it wasn't for you, I'd *have* a job. I'd be in Scotland and living in luxury in my father's house instead of crammed up here like a fucking sardine, waiting for your old lady to die. You conned me. You said it was OK that night. I never wanted a bloody baby in the first place.'

There was a deadly silence. They stared at each other in horror.

Flora was first to speak.

'I think it would be a good idea if you did what you suggest. Go to Scotland and get a job if that's what you want.' Her mouth felt sour and ashy, as if she had swallowed dust.

'I'll go in the morning.'

She got up, her limbs like water. Without looking at him, she went into the bathroom and was sick.

In the early hours of the morning she woke from her disturbed sleep to Fin climbing into bed next to her.

'Flo . . . Flo.'

She lay there, not replying.

'Please, listen to me.' He was propped up on

his elbow in the half-light, his face looming over her. 'What I said was unforgivable. I didn't mean it. Of course I want the baby. I was just angry because you were reminding me, quite rightly, what a useless fuck I am. And I didn't want to face it.'

She felt no satisfaction in another of his endless apologies, just an overwhelming fear gnawing at the pit of her stomach.

'Say something Flo, please.'

'I don't know what to say.'

'But you know I didn't mean it . . . about the baby?'

'You left me once because I said I wanted a child.'

She heard him give a long, slow sigh. 'But that was in the abstract, when we didn't have one. Now you're pregnant, things are different. You're carrying my baby.'

He brought his hand up and stroked the hair back from her face. His touch made her want to cry.

'Flo, I love you. You believe that, don't you? And I'll love the child too, totally, of course I will. Please, can we forget about what we both said tonight? Start with a clean slate? I'll go up to Scotland tomorrow and put Dad's house on the market – I know you don't really want to live there. We can use the money as a deposit on a place in the country somewhere. Prue and Philip will help us out I'm sure, now they know you're pregnant. Or we can rent out Dad's place, use it to find somewhere down here. I'll write the bloody book. I'll do anything if you'll just forget what I said.'

'Maybe we should talk about it in the morning,' she replied.

Flora couldn't think straight. She was tormented by the growing realisation that she and Fin might never be happy together. But every cell in her body rejected this prospect, crying out for his presence beside her, protecting her, supporting her in the difficult months to come. The thought of being alone again made her sick with fear. This is bound to be a tough time, she told herself. They'd only been back together a few months. Wouldn't it settle down as soon as they had their own place?

Fin moved closer to her, his arm across her body, his head beside hers on the pillow.

'I love you,' she heard him whisper into the darkness.

In the cold light of Saturday morning, they said very little to each other. Even sex, normally the panacea for their rows, would be wholly inadequate as a means to erase the words spoken, and they both tacitly knew it. Flora had barely slept. Now she felt a terrible, leaden despair. She waited till after breakfast before telling him that she was going upstairs to see her sister.

'OK, I'll just get dressed.'

'I think I'll go on my own.'

He glanced over at her. 'Why?'

She didn't reply.

'So you can tell her what a bastard I am?' His grey eyes were sharp with pain. 'She knows that already.'

'Please . . . I just want to go on my own.'

Fin got up and came over to her, taking hold of her arms. 'Flora . . . don't treat me like this. I've said I'm sorry.'

She looked into his face. It was a face she had held in her dreams for most of the past ten years. Now, as she saw his pain, and knew that her own was probably reflected back, she knew she had run out of the will to make it better. For a brief second she rested against him, the feel of his body so seductively strong, yet so fundamentally unavailable to her for support at a time when she desperately needed it. As he brought his arms round her, she gently slipped from his embrace.

'I won't be long.'

'I can't believe you didn't tell me!' Prue was beaming at her across the marble island. 'Come here, darling.' She hugged Flora so hard that she was almost winded. 'Such brilliant news.'

'I thought we should wait before telling anyone.'

Prue shook her head. 'Not even an issue. I totally understand why.' She held her at arm's length, looking her up and down. 'I knew there was something odd about you . . . on Christmas Day, remember? I thought you were stressed about Jake being there.'

Flora laughed, feeling a sudden burst of joy. 'I still can't believe it.' For a moment they stood looking at each other, their faces alight with excitement. Then there was a clattering on the stairs and Bel rushed into the room.

'Mum told me! It's so cool, I'm going to have a cousin at last.' She threw herself into Flora's arms.

'It's very early days,' Flora warned, but she was still unable to stop smiling.

'Yeah, but it'll be OK won't it?' Bel asked.

'When's the exact due date?' Prue wanted to know.

'First week of August, the doctor calculated, but that isn't certain yet, because my periods have been weird.'

'That's ages.' Bel looked disappointed, then whooped and began dancing round the kitchen. 'I'm going to have a cou . . .sin, I'm going to have a cou . . .sin.' She stopped. 'Boy or girl, do you think?'

'I'd like a girl . . . but I don't really give a toss.'

'And Fin?' Prue asked.

'He's . . . not really said.'

There was a puzzled silence. Her sister frowned.

'He didn't seem too thrilled yesterday when he told me.'

Flora exhaled slowly. 'He's taking a bit of time to get his head round it. I think he's worried about how we'll cope . . . in London . . . if he's not working.' She turned away from her sister, not wanting her to see the tears.

'You're not going to live in Scotland are you?' Bel's voice was suddenly small. 'You can't.'

'I don't know what we'll do,' Flora said. 'It's all been such a shock. And sort of difficult timing.'

'Oh, darling.' Prue came over and put her arm round her. Her BlackBerry buzzed insistently, rocking around on the black marble, but she ignored it. 'Please, don't get in a state about it. You know we'll help out if necessary.'

'Thanks . . . thanks, Prue,' Flora mumbled, blowing her nose. 'But you've done enough. I've ligged off you for three years now.'

'Nonsense. We can have a family conference if you like. Work out the best plan.'

Flora shook her head. 'Maybe later. Fin's going up to see about the house.'

When Flora got downstairs again, Fin had been as good as his word. He'd booked a ticket to Inverness on the sleeper, a reclining seat – the cheapest option – for the Wednesday after the New Year.

'How did Prue take it?'

'She was thrilled. So was Bel.'

'Good.'

'So how long will you be away?'

Fin shrugged. 'A week?'

Flora felt a huge sense of relief at the prospect of having a few days on her own. Fin must have sensed it.

'Can't wait to get rid of me, eh?' His laugh was hollow.

287

'Maybe we just need a bit of a break,' she said.
'A break? What do you mean?'
'Just a few days to think things out without winding each other up.'

He looked cautiously relieved. 'Yeah . . . maybe. God, Flo, I can't bear what's happening between us. Where did all the fun go?' He smiled at her. 'Can we have some fun over New Year? Promise each other we won't mention Scotland or babies or jobs until I get back?'

She nodded, smiling too. 'We could try.'

CHAPTER 17

4 January

Dominic was back. This time with a cheque for three hundred pounds for the Bowman landscape. Dorothea seemed hardly to notice the piece of paper he'd put in her hand. They were just finishing tea when the doorbell went.

'That'll be Dr Kent,' Flora said.

'Oops, better get out of the way.' Dominic heaved his body off the sofa, handing Flora his cup and saucer and wiping his hands on his yellow handkerchief, pulled from the top pocket of his tweed jacket.

'You don't have to go. He said he was dropping something off . . . although he might just check to see how she is.'

'And she's in rude health, aren't you Aunt Dot?'

His ludicrous statement hung in the air as they both glanced at Dorothea, almost invisible under the rug, her features washed out, her body hardly more than skin and bone.

Flora let the doctor in. He handed her a plastic

carrier bag. 'They're disposable bed pads. We had a salesman in the surgery yesterday, and he left us a few packets. I thought they might come in handy.'

'Brilliant. That's so kind of you.'

'Incontinence pads – don't tell me I don't know the way to a girl's heart.' He gave her an amused smile. There had been a certain constraint between them since the day he'd suggested she might be pregnant, and she was pleased to be able to laugh with him again.

'How is she?'

'She's . . . she just seems to be fading away.'

The doctor nodded. 'Often happens, as you know. They get ill and just give up. I'll stick my head round the door, say hello.'

She followed him into the sitting room. Dominic was hovering, checking out a pretty silver dish on the top of the drop-leaf desk.

Dr Kent went over to Dorothea and took her hand. But the old lady was still clutching the cheque her great-nephew had given her.

'Someone been paying you off?' the doctor joked, and elicited a shy giggle from his patient.

'Aunt Dot has commissioned me to do a bit of a clear-out.' Dominic paused. 'Well, not "commissioned" as such. I wouldn't dream of taking any payment.'

Simon Kent nodded. 'So what was this handsome cheque for?' he asked Dorothea.

She handed it to him. 'I . . . think it was the

painting . . .' She pointed to the wall, where a pale square marked the place the landscape had hung.

'I remember it well, a farmyard scene. It was lovely. Remember, we discussed it?' He looked at Dorothea. 'As I told you then, I'm a bit of a fan of John Bowman.'

Dominic looked surprised. 'Really? Very few people have heard of him.'

'I have a collector friend who has about six of his. I'd love one myself, but he's a bit beyond my price range.'

'I didn't manage to get very much for Aunt Dot's, I'm afraid,' said Dominic. 'But you can't give landscapes away right now. It's all Chinese, Chinese, Chinese – anything oriental just runs out of the sale room.' He shook his head at the iniquity of it all, then hurried over to Dorothea and dropped a kiss on her cheek.

'I'd better be off Aunty. Lovely to see you as always. I'll come again soon.'

'Don't leave on my account,' Dr Kent said. 'I was just delivering something to Flora. I'm not staying.'

'No, no. I'm late already. I've got stuff to pick up in the West End and the traffic will be murder in half an hour.'

He smiled breezily at Flora and hurried away.

'Was it something I said?' The doctor looked puzzled.

'Maybe it was . . .' Flora replied.

When she got the doctor in the hall, away from Dorothea, she asked, 'When you say that a Bowman painting is beyond your price range, you didn't mean three hundred pounds, did you?'

He raised his eyebrows. 'I certainly didn't. Denis never gets them for less than two thousand, and that's the bottom end. He tried to flog me one for three and a half a couple of months ago. That guy must have put it in a general sale, where no one knew who he was. Bowman would need a specialist sale to get proper money.'

'I think I need to have a talk with Rene,' Flora muttered.

'Things going well . . . with you?' the doctor asked as he put his coat on, shaking it first. Flora could see it was wet, and the smell of damp wool was curiously reassuring. It reminded her of her childhood, and coming in from the garden when they'd been playing in the rain.

'Yes. I've seen my GP. All's well, she says. I've got to make a decision about whether to have a CVS and an amnio.'

'It's a difficult choice. What does Fin say?'

'He doesn't want the baby at all.'

She'd said it without thinking, almost to herself, but when she saw the shock on Simon Kent's face she felt instantly ashamed of her disloyal remark. In the couple of days since Fin had been away, she'd had time to think, and his attitude weighed heavily on her. She wanted to be joyful, to celebrate – as she had done with Prue and Bel – to feel her heart sing with his about this miraculous thing they had done together. But there still seemed to be no joy on his part, only a forced insistence that he cared.

'Sorry, I shouldn't have said that.'

Dr Kent nodded, picking up his bag. 'Don't panic. He'll get there. When he sees the baby he won't be able to resist it. Jasmine took my breath away, she was completely astonishing.' His face softened as he thought of his daughter. Please, thought Flora, please let that be how Fin feels when the baby is born.

'Hmm . . .' Rene fell silent on the other end of the phone. 'This isn't right,' she said eventually. 'He shouldn't be allowed to get away with it. But I bet you when I talk to him, he'll say there was a tear in the corner, or it wasn't signed properly, or it had been restored badly. Some excuse for his paltry cheque.'

'Dr Kent said he probably put it in a normal sale instead of a specialist one where there'd be Bowman collectors.'

'Well, that *could* account for it I suppose. He may be doing his best and simply be incompetent – he always seems a bit of a numpty to me, but it's still not right.' Flora heard Rene give one of her weary sighs. 'One bit of news,' she went on. 'I just got a call from the agency. Pia is going home to be with her sister, who's been taken ill. She doesn't know when she'll be back. This is her last weekend with Dorothea.'

'Thank God.' Flora made no attempt to hide her relief.

'Be careful, Flora. We have no evidence whatever of Pia being anything but loving to Dorothea. I know there was a time when we were suspicious, but it was our mistake – nothing else was ever proved. You and Mary mustn't go about saying unpleasant things about her.'

Flora put Dorothea to bed before supper – she seemed too tired to sit upright any more. She brought the wheelchair through so the old lady wouldn't have to walk, and as she pushed her past the desk, Dorothea pointed up to the space on the wall where the painting had hung.

'I think . . . I rather miss it.'

'Oh dear. Perhaps you shouldn't let Dominic sell any more of your things. You don't need the money and it's nice to have stuff around that's familiar to you.'

Dorothea didn't reply at first.

'I think he likes . . . doing things for me.'

'Yes, but don't let him take your favourite bits.'

The old lady waved her hand. 'I don't think I really mind.'

On her way home, she bumped into Keith in the hall.

'Hey, Florence. You look happy.'

'Do I? I'm certainly pleased about one thing. That nurse, the one I asked you to check out on the CCTV? She's leaving next week, going back to the Philippines.'

'Oh . . . but she *was* doing what she said, wasn't she?'

'Sort of . . . yes, I suppose. But there's no question that Dorothea didn't like her for some reason. Now I expect we'll never know, which is annoying.'

Keith gave her a mischievous grin. 'I could give it one more go . . . try and catch her at it this weekend?'

'That's a bit childish. Isn't it?'

'Yeah . . . but that doesn't mean we can't do it.'

Flora smiled. 'No harm in one little visit, I suppose.'

'Right. Will do. I'll call you when I've been up . . . probably Sunday.'

'I'm sure she'll be baking muffins and cuddling Dorothea.'

'Sounds gross.'

Flora went home to her empty flat with guilty relief. She was aware that she'd begun to dread coming back to Fin's growling, unpredictable energy, never knowing what sort of mood he would be in, having always to walk on eggshells to avoid confrontation. The New Year had been difficult, but not because they fought. As promised, they had put a moratorium on any mention of the future and tried to create an indulgent cocoon of love-making, old movies, walks in the park. And Fin seemed quite happy with this. But she found all she wanted to talk about was the baby. She wanted to fantasise with Fin about the colour of its eyes, whether he or she would have hair; work out the sort of birth she wanted; discuss how they would parent together. She felt resentful that she couldn't do this with her baby's father.

'Think you better get over here . . . now, if possible.' Keith's voice was grim when he called on Sunday afternoon.

'What's happened?'

'Just get here. And tell Mrs Carmichael to come too.'

When Flora got to the flat, Keith and Dorothea were alone. She was in bed, lying with her face to the wall.

'What happened?'

Keith, his face a mask of suppressed fury, pushed her out into the hall.

'I did as we'd agreed and let myself in about half an hour ago, around four o'clock. That bitch was in the sitting room with two of her friends. They were laughing and drinking and had all sorts of food – it's still in there on the table – and Dorothea had been plonked in her wheelchair in the corner by the window, her back to the room.'

Flora felt her whole body tense with rage.

'She had a piece of cake on her lap the size of a house – she couldn't possibly have eaten it all in a million years. And she was cold as ice. I put her straight to bed, but she'd wet herself and I had to change her and while I was doing it Pia and her mates scarpered. Fucking bitch. You should have seen her face when I walked in.'

'What did she say?'

'She said she was having a leaving party for Dorothea, and these were her friends who Dorothea had met before and loved.'

'She's always got an answer.'

'And when I challenged her and asked why she was sitting with her back to them then, she said the old lady'd nodded off and so she'd turned her round so she wouldn't be disturbed. But she could see how angry I was. I think she was scared about what I'd do.' He shook his head. 'The three of them began to gabble in their own language, obviously guilty as shit.'

They stood in shocked silence for a moment, then Keith pulled his phone out of his pocket. 'I'm going to call the police.'

'They won't be interested. To anyone else, she was just having a leaving party, like she said.'

The porter hesitated, phone in mid-air. 'But abusing an old person must be a crime.'

'If you have actual proof that someone hit her or tortured her. But what proof do we have? Even if Dorothea told us, which she hasn't so far, she'd never tell the police.' Flora sat down. 'Christ . . . this is my fault. I knew there was a problem. I should have followed my instincts, looked into it more thoroughly. I'd like to kill her. She can't just get away with it . . .'

'Looks like that's exactly what she'll do.'

'Rene's been in Dorset for the weekend, but she's on her way back. She said she'd come straight round. I'd better go and see to Dorothea. God, I feel so bad about this. Mary and I knew all along that something was up.'

'Yeah, but what could you do if Miss H-T wouldn't dob her in?'

'I don't know. But something.'

Flora went into Dorothea's room. The old lady spun round at once, her face a mask of anxiety. Flora laid her hand gently on her arm.

'It's OK, Pia's gone. For good.'

But the old lady still looked past her, as if she expected the other nurse to come through the door.

'I promise she's gone, Dorothea.' She sat beside her patient. 'I'm so, so sorry. Mary and I knew you didn't like her, we just didn't know why.'

Dorothea blinked furiously, clutching at Flora's hand.

'She . . . she made me eat that disgusting cake . . . all of it.' Flora saw the tears fill her pale eyes. 'She wouldn't do anything for me . . . until I'd . . . eaten it.'

'And she did this all the time?'

Dorothea shook her head. 'Sometimes . . . she would be nice to me . . . very kind. But then she would . . . leave me . . . refuse to take me to the bathroom or give me . . . a drink.'

The tears trickled down the papery skin and Flora reached for a tissue and gently wiped them away.

'I . . . didn't know what she might do.'

'Why didn't you tell me? We all suspected her, but we had no proof.'

Dorothea didn't reply for a moment, her mouth working away, twisting nervously.

'She said . . . if I told . . . that no one would believe me. That I was . . . a silly old woman.' She paused, gathering her breath. 'And if they did believe me, Rene would sack all the nurses and . . . put me in a home.'

'Rene would never do that.'

She stared at Flora for a moment. 'I . . . wasn't sure.'

'Oh, Dorothea, I'm so sorry.'

'I sometimes find . . . it difficult to . . . get things straight. I thought . . . maybe Rene was . . . fed up with looking after me.'

'She'd never put you in a home in a million years.'

Dorothea sighed. 'It was horrible . . . the cake. It made me feel sick.'

Later, Keith and Flora were in the kitchen having a cup of tea. Flora had washed the old lady, settled her, and now she was asleep.

'So Pia'll get off scot free.'

Keith shrugged his broad shoulders. 'She'll do a runner before anyone catches up with her is my guess. Probably never come back.'

'Not much consolation.'

'The nurses' agency can blackball her, but what difference will that make if she stays in the Philippines?'

They fell silent, both simmering with rage, lost in thoughts of revenge and, in Flora's case, guilt that she hadn't followed her instincts. She imagined how helpless Dorothea must have felt, pinned in her own home at the mercy of Pia, not able to stand up to her, and not daring to tell anyone for fear of the consequences. The cruelty of it made her want to cry.

Flora broke the silence. 'Rene will be gutted too,' she said. 'And how will she choose another nurse? Pia seemed so sweet and kind . . . although Mary never, ever liked her.'

'I promise I will kill her if I ever set eyes on her again,' Keith growled helplessly.

When Mary turned up that night, Flora worried smoke was about to pour from her head, she was so angry.

'The cruel bloody bitch! What did I tell you? What did I bloody tell you? We've got her address, I've a good mind to go round and beat her to a pulp.'

'There's a queue.'

'She should be locked up and tortured, the abusing bitch. It's sick. And I *knew* it. I knew it all along. I kept saying, didn't I? I kept telling you all.'

'Shhh, keep your voice down. Dorothea will hear you.'

But it was a while before the Irish nurse calmed down.

★   ★   ★

Fin had barely rung her since he'd been away, nor she him. When they did talk it was as if he was on a high, rattling on about all the guys he'd met at the climbing wall, the training he was getting into, the relief at being in the open air again. When she asked how it was going with the house, he seemed evasive, even though he insisted he was sorting it. He rang that night when she was finishing her supper. She was still shocked and distressed about what had happened to Dorothea and wanted to talk to him about it.

'How's it all going?' she asked.

'Great. I was talking to my new friend, Neil, the guy at the wall, today. He says there's a fantastic expedition he thinks I should get on if I'm fit enough. In Nepal, the Annapurna circuit. I've always wanted to do it. It's not till the autumn, so I reckon I should be fit enough by then if I really train hard – it's not as punishing as a lot of the climbs over there. And it's coming back, Flo, my strength. Slowly, but I already feel energised from just a few days up here.'

She laughed. 'Haven't you forgotten something?'

'What?'

'Oh, just a small matter of the baby.'

There was silence at the other end of the phone.

'Yeah . . . but the trip isn't till early September. It'll have been born by then, won't it?'

Flora was lost for words.

'Flo? Won't it, if it's due the first week of August?' His voice sounded suddenly urgent.

301

'It'll have been born, yes, but are you really suggesting you abandon us as soon as it has?'

Another silence.

'Obviously I'll be there for the birth, I'm not going to miss that. But I won't be much help when it's small, will I? I haven't a clue what to do with a baby. I can't even feed it. You'll have Prue . . .' His voice tailed off, as if he'd finally realised what he was saying.

Flora quietly put the phone down. She was too stunned to cry. She sat in blank astonishment for a time, not knowing what to be most upset about. Apart from the fact that he was considering abandoning her as soon as the baby was born, he had clearly no intention of getting the house organised to sell or rent. He was assuming she would still be here, near to her sister for help, because it suited him now. So all the talk about being together in their own place in time for the baby – whether in Inverness or not – was just so much hot air in the face of a possible mountain adventure.

He phoned back immediately, twice, three times, then texted her. But she didn't respond, she didn't know what to say. In the end she called him back, just to stop the endless barrage of messages.

'Christ, Flo, the phone went dead and I thought something had happened to you. I imagined you lying on the floor in a faint. Why didn't you answer the phone? I've called a million times. I was just about to ring Prue and get her to check on you.'

'Sorry. I was upset.'

'Upset? About what?'

'About you going off just after the baby is born.'

'God . . . I didn't . . . I mean I don't *have* to go, I suppose. I might not even get onto the trip if I can't raise the money. I just thought I'd be in the way in that small flat, and fucking useless. I thought it'd be better to get out of your hair. By the time I go, if I do, it'll be at least three weeks old.' He spoke as if this was perfectly reasonable.

'So what happened to the place we were going to get in time for the baby?'

She heard a long sigh. 'Yeah . . . well, it's complicated. I've talked to a couple of agents and they say it'll be hard to rent out the place, and mad to try and sell it. And doing it up to a good standard for a baby is going to take cash, which I don't have.' He paused. 'So perhaps it's better to stay where we are until we can get things moving.'

Flora knew he was lying. She knew he hadn't been near an agent, or given the house a moment's thought. All he'd been doing was getting back into his old life, his old habits. She and the baby could whistle for it.

'Listen, I'm tired. We can talk when you get back.'

'But you're OK now? I don't want you worrying about stuff. I'll be back soon. I just need a bit more time to get this fitness thing under way. Love you.'

It's like talking to a junky back on smack, she thought, wincing at his glib show of concern.

'Bye, Fin.' As she sat there, the phone still in her hand, she realised she had caught Fin at a unique point in his life, when he'd been involuntarily ripped from his addiction by force of circumstance. It hadn't made him happy, but it had made him dependent, unable to just take off to access his habit. His obsession with the mountains had worked for her before, when she had such a demanding life herself. But now she was asking for something more, and Fin didn't like to be asked.

Dorothea was going downhill fast. She was refusing to eat much, losing weight by the day, and her skin was beginning to break down from lying on her stone-hard mattress. Rene organised a proper hospital bed, which was higher and wider and had the mechanism to raise the head or the foot, together with a state-of-the-art waterproof air mattress. The men put the bed in the sitting room on Rene's instructions.

'She'll be much better off in here than in that poky bedroom. She can see out of the windows, have a bit of space.' Flora could see that Rene was still sad and angry about the Pia fiasco. Like Keith, she had wanted to involve the police, but there was no evidence that Pia intended harm. They both had to accept she would be long gone by now.

'What's that thing doing here?' The old lady looked confused, waving her hand at the huge bed.

'We thought you'd be more comfortable.' Rene went over to the wheelchair and took her friend's hand. 'It's got an air mattress to stop you getting sore on your bottom and your heels.'

Dorothea looked unsettled. 'But . . . shall I be sleeping in the drawing-room?'

'Yes. You'll have lots of space, and the nurses will be able to look after you more easily.'

Dorothea glanced at Flora. 'Where will I go during the day?'

'You can stay in here, in your usual chair. But when you get tired the bed's right there.'

She eyed the bed as if it were an unwelcome intruder. 'I'm not sure I shall like it.'

Rene gave her an encouraging smile. 'You might feel a bit strange at first, but you're going to love the mattress. Your one in the bedroom must be pre-war.'

Dorothea nodded, clearly not seeing anything wrong with this. 'It was my mother's.'

Rene rolled her eyes at Flora. 'Well, try this one out and see how you get on.'

'How's the new bed?' Keith Godly was in the doorway. 'Saw them bringing it in. Wow! Looks more like an ocean liner than a bed, eh?' He winked at Dorothea.

'I . . . don't think I like it.'

'Well, if you don't want to sleep in it, I shall.'

She looked up at him, then gave a whispering laugh.

'I think perhaps you should,' she told him.

'Need any help?'

Flora and Rene shook their heads. It took them an hour to make the bed and settle Dorothea in it. She barely seemed to make any impression as she lay there on the vast expanse, very still, her transparent skin as pale as the white sheet, her tiny frame hardly denting the alarmingly puffy air mattress.

'So . . . is it comfy?' Rene asked.

Dorothea turned her head on the pillow. 'I . . . think so.' She smiled at her friend, then her eyes closed and she slept.

'This will make your life a lot easier,' Rene whispered, as they left the room. Flora agreed, but Fin was coming home today, and her thoughts were elsewhere.

Fin grabbed her as soon as he came through the front door and hugged her close. He looked well, his eyes bright and laughing. Kissing her hard on the mouth, he dropped his hand down her back as he fondled her bottom, dragging her hard against his body.

'God, I've missed you.' He pulled back and looked at her. 'How are you?'

She laughed, breathless from the onslaught. 'I'm OK.'

'How's the old lady?'

'Still alive, but she's really weak now.'

Fin pulled her over to the sofa. For a change he didn't seem interested in whether Dorothea's death was imminent or not.

'Can you tell how fit I am from a week in the mountains? I feel like a different person.' He began to kiss her again.

It reminded Flora of those times when he used to come back from an expedition, leaping on her as soon as he came through the door, insatiably hungry for sex. And now she responded as she had then, giving herself over to the intense pleasure of his touch.

Later, as she lay in a warm bath, Fin standing propped in the doorway, a big grin on his handsome face, she felt torn. Sex with Fin was so confusing. Their bodies were such a perfect fit, always matching in desire, fulfilling each other's passion. How could she reconcile such a synergy with their very different requirements for life?

CHAPTER 18

17 January

Dorothea's flat had taken on a strange stillness. The old lady was sleeping for much of the day now. She was only sitting out for short periods, such as the time it took to make her bed each day with clean sheets; she spoke very little, having occasional bursts of conversation which quickly faded. Flora could see that she was retreating from the world, floating on her air mattress in the big bed, required to do nothing, go nowhere, perhaps dreaming of some distant past when she had lived and loved out there in the world. She seemed at peace.

'How long do you think she can go on like this?' Flora asked Dr Kent on one of his morning visits.

'Hard to say. She seems comfortable. She's being well looked after, fed what she needs . . . she could go on a while yet, although I don't think she will.'

'What happens if she gets some sort of infection . . . pneumonia, bronchitis? Rene's told us that she's got a living will, not to resuscitate etc, and to die at home. But does that mean we don't give her antibiotics?'

The doctor thought for a moment. 'In Dorothea's case, if she gets pneumonia, I would advise antibiotics. Dying because you can't breathe is a pretty traumatic way to go. And they won't prolong her life noticeably, just make it more comfortable for her in the short term.'

Thank God Dorothea's got Simon Kent as her doctor, Flora thought, remembering a number of bullying, arrogant members of the medical profession she'd had dealings with in the past. She knew they could trust him to put Dorothea's sensibility first in any treatment he prescribed.

'I'm off dancing tonight,' he was saying. 'Sure you don't fancy another spin around the floor?' His look was teasing, and almost tender.

'I'd like to try it when I'm dressed properly one day.'

'Oh, I don't know. Those socks were very fetching.'

Flora laughed. 'Right. Well, you didn't even have any on.'

'Both a bit sartorially challenged perhaps.'

He suddenly seemed to collect himself.

'Better get going.'

'Thanks for dropping in.'

'Just more of the same for Dorothea.'

'What? Why are you looking at me like that?'

Flora had been upstairs on Saturday morning

collecting some leftover stew her sister wasn't going to eat because they were going to stay with friends for the weekend. She put the heavy blue Le Creuset pot down on the work surface before turning back to Fin, who was by the front door, holding a black plastic bag of rubbish.

'I've just seen Prue. She told me. She said she'd promised you she wouldn't, but she felt I ought to know.'

He seemed to go very still.

'Did you really think she'd keep it secret?' Her voice was leaden. She was furious with him, not only for begging money for his Nepal trip from her sister – and without asking her first – but because it showed how determined he was to go, regardless of her or the baby.

The colour had drained from Fin's face. 'Christ, I knew this would happen one day. Why the fuck did she tell you now? It's ancient history for God's sake.' He seemed to be almost shaking. 'We were just . . . it was mad . . .' The rubbish bag thudded on the floor.

'What was mad? What are you talking about?' She felt her stomach turn over, the look on his face really scared her.

'You said . . .' he faltered. 'What did Prue tell you?'

'That you'd asked her to sponsor you to go to Nepal in September.'

Fin threw himself down on the sofa.

310

'Oh . . . yeah. It just sort of came up in conversation and . . .'

'What did you think I was talking about?'

He didn't reply, just sat there, completely still, covering his face with his hands.

'Fin?'

Finally he looked at her, his eyes pleading. 'Please, forget about it, Flo. It's nothing. I got confused. The Nepal trip . . . I should have told you. It was a spur-of-the-moment thing. I didn't think you'd mind.'

She stood watching him. 'Ancient history? What did you mean?'

'Fuck . . . fuck . . .' he muttered.

'Tell me, for Christ's sake.'

She waited, hardly able to get her breath.

'OK . . .' He let out a low groan. 'OK, if you must know . . . Prue and I had a thing . . . years ago, before I went off . . .'

'A *thing*?' Flora whispered.

'Yeah . . . it was just a mad moment. It meant nothing, Flo, honestly. We were both in a weird place and . . .' He stopped, his eyes dull with despair.

'Wait . . . are you telling me you had sex with my *sister*?' She heard the words as she spoke them, as if they were coming out of someone else's mouth.

He nodded dumbly.

'You . . . you and Prue? I don't believe you.'

When he didn't answer, she found herself asking, 'Once? Twice? How many times?'

311

'Umm . . . not . . . I don't know. A few times.'
He lurched upright, came towards her, tried to take her hands, but she quickly put them behind her.

'Where? Where did you do it?'

'Oh, God. Why does it matter where? It was a stupid, pointless thing that meant nothing to either of us. Please . . . please don't look like that.'

'Tell me where, Fin.'

'Here. In the bedroom at the top of the house.'

Flora tried to clear her thoughts, but her brain seemed to have become fuzzy and slow, the information she'd requested made no sense.

'When did you have the time? You were always away.'

He sighed heavily. 'I came up on the bike . . .'

The image of Fin astride his Triumph, riding up to London to his clandestine liaisons with her sister, was too much for Flora. She felt suddenly lightheaded and dropped down to the sofa.

'Flo?' He was beside her, not daring to touch her, his face white with alarm. 'Are you OK?'

'How long did it go on for?'

'Please, these details are pointless. Don't torture yourself.'

She stared at him. 'I need to know.'

But he wouldn't answer her. He lay back on the sofa beside her, closed his eyes.

'How long?'

'About a year . . . but not very often. Hardly at all.' His voice had taken on the monotonous tone of a zombie. He was no longer trying to persuade her to stop. 'That's the main reason why I left. She got angry with me when I said we should end it and I dreaded you finding out. I just had to get away.'

'So it was nothing to do with me wanting a baby?'

'The baby stuff made me realise what an appalling thing I was doing. I couldn't be starting a family with you while I was . . . and I meant to come back in a couple of weeks. But then I thought that by that time she'd have told you herself and I didn't dare.'

Flora was having trouble understanding. Like a slide show in her head, she watched snapshots from the year before he left: times when they themselves made passionate love; times when they walked by the sea hand in hand, scuffing the pebbles with the toes of their boots; times when they sat opposite each other drinking coffee in the café on the corner; times when he looked into her eyes and said 'I love you.' And all through these innocent images wove other, unspeakable ones; his square, callused hands cupping her sister's breast as he did her own, his mouth against Prue's carmined lips, her legs wound round his lean body. She heard the cry her sister must have made as she climaxed, echoing in her head like a fiend in the night.

'Why?' she asked, her voice cracking. 'What was it . . .?'

'Flo . . .'

She searched his face, pinning his gaze so that he couldn't look away. She tried to read what he was thinking, but his grey eyes were fixed and unblinking. There was nothing there, nothing alive anyway.

'You just can't help yourself,' she said.

There was what felt like a very long time when neither of them spoke or moved or even appeared to breathe.

'What will you do about Prue?'

Flora shook her head slowly.

'For Bel's sake . . .' He stopped, knowing, perhaps, that he was on dangerous ground.

She didn't say anything. The scale of the betrayal from the two people who were supposed to love her more than anyone else in the world – except Bel perhaps – was too huge to comprehend.

'Can you go away please,' she begged him, knowing that she couldn't hold on much longer with him in the same room.

'Go away? Don't say that. If I go, I know you'll never speak to me again. We have to talk this through, Flo. Look at me. It was three years ago, a lifetime. It was just a sort of madness, a stupid mistake, not anything important. And we didn't mean to hurt you . . . we both vowed you'd never ever find out. All of us had too much to lose.' He paused. 'We still do.'

But Flora barely heard what he said.

'Please . . .'

'I don't want to leave you like this.' He stood up. 'I'll come back in a couple of hours.'

'Don't.'

'Are you chucking me out?' The disbelief in his voice made her look up.

'You really think I can be with you now that I know what you did with my own sister?'

He sank to his knees in front of her. 'Flora, please . . . please don't say that. You're upset. You can't throw away everything we've got together for some stupid mistake three years ago. We love each other. We're having a baby together.'

At the word 'baby', Flora let out a long howl. Feral and tortured, the sound was foreign to her ears. But once started, she had no control over it. It was like a solid force pressing up through her body and out of her mouth. Fin shrank from it, staring at her in horror.

The silence that followed echoed with her cry. He got up.

'Come on. I'm putting you to bed.' He lifted her bodily off the sofa, cradling her like a baby and carried her through to the bedroom. The touch of his arms around her was an agony – it felt like the last time she would ever be held so close by him. Because, while half of her wanted to kill him for what he had done, the other half longed to sink against him and be safe, forget everything that he'd just told her.

★   ★   ★

Flora woke from a drugged sleep to the stark reality of Fin's – and Prue's – betrayal. She looked at the clock: ten past four. She'd slept for over two hours. The flat was silent. Heaving herself out of bed, she tiptoed, shivering, into the sitting room. It was suddenly much colder, nearly dark outside. She poured a glass of water and drank it straight down, then just stood there, propped against the draining board, with literally no idea what she should do.

Normally she would have called Prue. But she couldn't do that, couldn't even confront her sister about her betrayal until she got back from the country. And then only if she could talk to her without Bel hearing. That was one thing she did know. She had no desire whatsoever to break up her sister's marriage and ruin Bel's life. Neither Philip nor her niece would ever hear it from her.

Where's Fin? she wondered. Had he taken off, as she'd requested, maybe to Inverness? If he came back, could she face him? She lay on the sofa in front of the TV, the duvet tight around her cold body. She didn't care what she was watching – some old cowboy movie – she just wanted to get rid of the silence and stop herself from thinking.

Later, she made herself some toast, but the food choked her. She heard Prue and the family arriving back from the country, Bel shouting to her father as he went to park the car to bring her scarf from the back seat. She hoped none of them would drop in.

Round about ten o'clock, the door opened. Fin was standing in front of her, his face pink with cold, his hair shining wet from the icy drizzle that had been coming down all day.

'Hi.'

She sat up, pleased, despite herself, to see him. Her solitude had begun to frighten her, to remind her of the days after Fin had left her before, when she had done just as she had today: lie almost immobile under the duvet, speaking to no one, for hours at a time.

Fin hovered, not even taking his pea coat off, obviously unsure of his welcome.

'Can I stay tonight?' he asked quietly.

She nodded, and saw the immediate relief on his face. Then, for the first time, she began to cry. Her sobs tore into the silence. Fin was beside her in a second, wrapping her in his arms, holding her head tight against his chest, rocking her to and fro as he too cried.

The 'sorry, sorry, sorry' that dropped into her hair meant nothing to her. Of course he was sorry – sorry for everything all the time. But he could say it till doomsday and it would never alter the fact that he loved himself and his mountains more than he loved her. Nor would it change the fact that she wanted more from a partner than he would ever be able to give. His affair with Prue might be the final nail in the coffin of their relationship, but she had to accept that it was only the last in a long line.

'Have you eaten?' he asked, looking down at her as he continued to hold her. She shook her head.

'You must.' He didn't mention the baby, but she knew that was what he meant. 'I'll make you some scrambled eggs if you like.'

CHAPTER 19

21 January

The conditions on Monday morning were treacherous. The rain from the weekend had turned to light snow and frozen overnight into patches of ice, making the roads and pavements like a skating rink. Flora crept along the street to the bus stop, terrified she would fall.

Fin was leaving today.

'Good weekend?' Mary put the kettle on as soon as Flora arrived. 'I wasn't sure you'd make it through. Cold as a witch's tit it was last night.'

'How's the new nurse?'

'Lakme? Yeah, nice girl. Indian, young. She didn't say much, seemed a bit shy. But Dorothea was perfectly happy when I came on. Not like she was before.'

'So she's safe with her? That's all we need to know.'

'I reckon so. And there's none of that sugary bollocks we got from the evil Pia.'

Dorothea was having a good day. She'd sat out

for a while in the morning and didn't seem keen to go back to bed when Flora suggested it.

'Will you . . . choose something,' she suddenly asked Flora from her armchair.

'Choose . . . what for?'

The old lady waved her hand around the room. 'I'd like you to have something . . . of mine.'

'That's very kind, but I don't think I should.'

'Why ever not? I may get muddled a lot nowadays, but these are my things . . . aren't they?' She raised her eyebrow, her tiny, birdlike frame suddenly animated.

Flora laughed. 'Of course. I just don't want people thinking I've been taking advantage of you.'

'If that were true, you wouldn't . . . perhaps be the only person to do so.'

Does she mean Dominic? Flora wondered.

'But you've been so kind to me,' Dorothea added.

'Well, I would love something to remember you by . . . not that I'll ever forget you.'

Dorothea gave a self-conscious shake of her head. 'I think . . . I should like to go back to bed now.'

When the old lady was asleep, Flora went into the nurses' bedroom and curled up on top of the polyester duvet. She felt almost calm, as if the events of the previous day had happened to someone else. Fin will be packing his things now, she thought. He was going back to Inverness that night. Going, he said, until they'd both had time to think. And she held onto this. Not the end, she kept telling herself over and over. Not . . . *not* the end.

When she thought of her sister, she felt a helpless despair. Prue was her mainstay, her family, her rescuer, her friend. The cowardly part of her wondered why she should even tell her that she knew? What good would it do? Her sister would just repeat what Fin had said: it meant nothing, we were in a weird place, we never wanted to hurt you. All probably true, and all complete self-serving rubbish.

The day seemed very long, but even so, she didn't want it to end. She knew what awaited her: a cold, empty flat and the task of confronting her sister. So when she left, instead of hurrying to the bus, she dawdled in the cold air, happy to exist in any limbo that delayed her homecoming.

'Hey, Flora?' The shout came from across the road. She turned and saw Simon Kent weaving through the traffic towards her, wrapped in his heavy tweed overcoat and red wool scarf. Her heart sank.

'Hi.'

'Thought it was you. You off home?' His breath clouded the night air between them.

'Yes. Long day.'

'I'm sure. I don't suppose you fancy a quick drink, do you?' he said, then shook his head. 'No, stupid of me. You'll want to get home to Fin.'

'Nope.' She didn't trust herself to say more.

He waited.

'OK, why not?'

Without another word he pulled her into a pub on the corner. The warmth and noise were bliss to Flora, a welcoming cocoon of anonymous humanity.

They found a couple of stools on the edge of a larger table, occupied by two men and a girl huddled in an intense conversation about their boss.

The doctor brought her a glass of lime and soda, and half a lager for himself.

'I won't be very good company,' Flora said, eyeing the lime juice with disdain. She wanted nothing more at that moment than a massive margarita.

'Shall I ask you why not, or should we stick to the safety of our incontinence-pad dialogue?'

Despite herself, she laughed. 'Devil and the deep blue sea, I'm afraid.'

He shot her a cautious glance. 'At least call me Simon. We've known each other for more than two years and you always call me Dr Kent. Most colleagues these days call each other by their first names.'

She smiled. 'Right . . . Simon it is.'

'It's quite odd to see you out of that flat, you know. You only exist for me in the twilight world of Miss Dorothea Heath-Travis.'

'A strange world indeed. I sometimes think

people would give us a wide berth if they knew what we'd been up to all day.'

'You mean the pee, poo and snot issue?'

'For me it's cleaning the false teeth every night.' She shuddered. 'Old food and denture fixative . . . yuk.'

They sipped their drinks in silence, Flora resisting the impulse to tell him the tale of her humiliation. She couldn't bear the flood of pity and concern guaranteed to follow.

'Tell me something trivial and stupid,' she said.

'Stupid? You mean a joke? I only know one.'

'Go on.'

Simon shifted on his seat, clearly not at ease with her request. 'If you insist. So, a man walks into a bar with a duck on his head. The bartender looks up and says, "Where did you get that ape?" The man says, "It's not an ape, it's a duck." Bartender says, "I wasn't talking to you."'

Flora couldn't help smiling, not so much at the terrible joke but at the deadpan way Simon Kent delivered it.

'Lame, isn't it?'

'Most jokes are.'

'I think if you have the knack of telling them right . . .'

Despite wanting to laugh with him, to have a normal conversation, she found she was only half-listening to what he was saying. And he knew there was something wrong, she could tell

323

from the cautious glances he kept throwing her way. But she was grateful to him for not pressing her.

'Listen . . . *Simon* . . . thanks for the drink, but I think I'd better get home.'

He nodded, making no objection.

'If you ever want to talk . . . I'm not just an idiot who tells bad duck jokes and makes you waltz in your pyjamas at midnight. I can listen.'

She smiled her thanks. 'I know.'

They stood huddled on the corner in the biting wind saying their goodbyes, but she suddenly felt unable to take another step.

'I think I'll get a cab.'

He peered at her. 'You look terrible. Go back into the pub. I'll find one.'

She didn't argue.

Once home, she was restless, pacing around the furniture, everywhere noticing bits of Fin that he'd left behind: a dog-eared map of the Highlands, a sock poking out from under the sofa, the cup he must have drunk coffee from that morning. And each time it brought a new pain. She looked at her watch. It was after nine-thirty. Prue might be home.

Can you come down? I need to talk to you. She texted her sister and sat down, phone clutched in hand, to wait. When she heard the upstairs door open, she quickly stood up, not wanting to be at a disadvantage.

'Hi, darling.' Prue scuffed down the steps in the

pink woollen slipper-socks that Flora had given her for Christmas. As her head emerged into the room she grinned. 'What's up?'

Flora could feel her heartbeat pounding in her ears. The words would be irrevocable, she knew that. By saying them she would seal her own fate and that of her sister.

'Fin told me.'

Prue didn't understand the significance at first. She plonked herself down on the sofa. 'Told you what?' She looked up at Flora questioningly.

'Told me about you and him.'

Prue stared at her. For a moment their eyes locked. 'Bastard. I knew he'd cave eventually.'

Flora watched her shoot to her feet, just as Fin had done, coming towards her as if to embrace her. She wanted to back off, but she found she couldn't move.

But her sister stopped short of touching her. She just peered into Flora's face, her own frowning, mouth twisting.

'Darling, listen. I know it sounds really terrible, and if I were you I'd be upset, of course I would. But you've got to realise, it was just a meaningless thing.'

'So that's it, is it?'

Prue shrugged. 'I hate myself now for having done it, but at the time we just got carried away. Flora, please . . . it was a pointless, stupid moment. Just sex. You should never have found out.' She looked around the flat. 'Where's Fin?'

'He's gone.'

'Oh, darling. You haven't split up because of this have you? That's madness. You're having his baby.'

'How often did you see him?'

She saw her sister hesitate, probably wondering what Fin had said. 'Just a couple of times. He was the one who drove it, not me.'

'Funny, that's exactly what Fin said about you.'

'Well, he would. He's never exactly been Mr Truthful, has he?'

'He said it went on for a year. You say it was just twice. Who do I believe?'

'A year! That's ridiculous.' Her voice was shrill and tinny. 'It was a couple of times over the summer, that's all.'

That's all? Flora thought. *All?* She didn't believe her anyway. Fin, in his entirely selfish way, had seemed to be the one telling the truth. She wondered why she needed to know the details. They were hardly relevant, but they seemed all she could grasp onto in this unbelievable scenario.

Prue sighed. 'I'm so sorry you had to find out. But please, I beg you, don't wreck your child's future because of a stupid infidelity over three years ago.'

Flora didn't reply at once, her thoughts with the baby growing inside her. What sort of future will I be able to give her? she wondered.

At last, she said, 'Me and Fin . . . it's not just

about what happened with you. That's just the icing on the cake, if you like.'

Her sister continued to gaze at her, an irritating look of concern on her face, as if Flora were the one at fault here, for caring so much.

'Umm . . . about Philip and Bel . . .'

'Don't worry,' Flora cut in, 'your secret's safe with me. I wouldn't put either of them through that. Not that you deserve it . . . or them.'

'Oh, come on, Flora. Don't be pious. I'm sorry, really, really sorry. It's horrible to see you so upset and know that I'm to blame. And I agree it was a bad mistake. But in the end it was just sex.'

Flora gasped at Prue's nonchalance, even knowing her cavalier attitude to sexual relationships in general. 'You don't seem to think it's important at all! My sister fucks the man I love and he leaves me, and you think I should just roll over and forget about it?'

'I didn't say that. But that's exactly my point, it *wasn't* important.' She gave a frustrated sigh. 'You can't blame me for him leaving. That was entirely his decision.'

Flora suddenly had a moment of blind fury.

'Go, please . . . just go away.'

Prue looked shocked. 'Alright . . . OK . . . but I did warn you about that man. I told you not to get involved with him again, that you'd never be able to trust him. But you wouldn't listen, and now look what's happened.'

Flora turned away. She could no longer look at her sister. Prue seemed almost baffled by her distress. And worse, she seemed to blame her, Flora, for the whole thing.

As she worked through the week, mostly on a sort of numb autopilot, Flora wondered what she should do. She hadn't spoken to Prue since their talk, and she didn't want to, refusing to reply to her sister's many attempts to call her. Her problem was how she could go on being normal in front of Bel and Philip. And how could she continue living in the flat and taking her sister's patronage? She wanted to pack her things and move out. But she had nowhere to go, and no money to rent anything more than a room in a flat-share on the outskirts of London, miles away from work.

Her predicament created a permanent state of anxiety, gnawing away at her gut day in, day out, with no appreciable let-up. Her current job would end soon and she wouldn't be able to work for many more months anyway, because of the lifting involved. She would have maternity pay from the agency – she'd checked that – but it wouldn't be enough to be independent of Prue. She had no savings, and Fin wouldn't be much help. But the worst aspect of it all was not the practical one. It was that she felt terrifyingly alone. The two people she most depended on had disappeared from her life almost overnight.

How would she cope through the long months of pregnancy, the birth, the first weeks of her baby's life, without the support of her sister and Fin? Or anyone else?

'I'm going to get you out while I do the bed.' She began lifting Dorothea's now feather-light frame until the old lady was sitting upright, then swung her legs over the edge of the bed. She was still in her nightdress and her legs were exposed, thin as matchsticks and mottled a purplish-pink in places.

'Dominic is coming today,' Flora told her.

'I'm glad . . . it's him,' she said. There had been a flurry of visitors that week. People from her past who must have been informed by Rene that the old lady was fading, and whose conscience required they see her one more time: the old man from down the hall who was almost completely deaf; a couple from her church; the woman who used to clean for her before the nurses took over; Reverend Jackson, the bumptious vicar. The visits had been awkward. Most people didn't really know how to be with a dying person, Flora had long ago discovered. They either sat mute and anxious, eyes swishing in search of potential help. Or they talked and talked about their own lives with determined jollity, but with scant reference to Dorothea lying in the bed beside them. Dominic, with his self-important but familiar bluster, would be a relief to them both.

Dorothea perked up when she saw her great-nephew. He employed his usual flattering banter with the old lady, but, although Flora was pretty sure she saw through him, she seemed to enjoy his company. He made a point of entertaining her as she lay propped up regally in her state-of-the-art bed; he pranced round the room, cup and saucer in hand, giving them both chapter and verse on the various antiques dotted about the room.

'Take this,' he said, picking up the little silver dish Flora had chosen as the piece she would like to have after Dorothea died. 'This is such a pretty bit of Arts and Crafts.' He turned it over and examined the side of the dish, running his finger across the rubbed hallmark. 'Birmingham 1919 . . . A.E. Jones. Jones was such a talent, and so little is written about his work.'

He waved the bowl at his great-aunt. 'This would get a fair old price at auction, Aunt Dot, if you've a mind to sell it.'

Dorothea waved her hand. 'I . . . think . . . I have given Flora that one.'

Dominic spun round to where she was packing up the tea tray.

'Flora?' He gave her a suspicious stare. 'I don't understand.'

'Dorothea insisted I choose something that I liked, to remember her by.' His expression made her feel almost guilty.

'I see. And you chose this one. Good choice.' He raised his eyebrows just a fraction.

'I had no idea it was valuable. I just liked it,' she told him in a whisper, while picking up the tray. As she walked towards the door she addressed the old lady. 'Please don't hang onto the silver dish because of me, Dorothea, if you'd like Dominic to sell it.'

But the old lady shook her head firmly. 'I have . . . given it to you.' She waved her hand at him. 'You can find something else I'm sure.'

Dominic followed her into the kitchen.

'Flora, I, er . . . don't take this the wrong way, but should you be taking presents from Aunt Dot? I'm not being funny, but as you said before, it'd be easy for someone in your position to take advantage . . . once you cross that line.'

She was about to reply, her face scarlet with indignation, when he rushed on.

'Of course I know you'd never do that. I just think it looks bad . . . if you let her give you things, sort of sends the wrong message to the other nurses. You get what I'm saying?'

Flora had to take a deep breath before replying, tempted as she was to say something seriously rude.

'Your great-aunt begged me to choose something of hers. I said I didn't think it was appropriate, but she absolutely insisted. It was impossible to refuse, and I think she'd have been hurt if I had. Like I didn't care about her.'

Dominic nodded his head in his wise-owl manner, pushing his glasses up his nose.

'Hmm . . . I see. Yes, perhaps you were put in a tricky position. And of course, it's not something you have to follow through on when . . . you know.'

Flora put the cup she was washing down on the draining board and turned to face him full on.

'I never wanted or asked for anything from Dorothea, but these are her possessions, Dominic. Don't you think she has the right to give them away if she chooses?' She could hear the quietly controlled tone of her voice and was proud of herself. 'She's still completely compos mentis . . . and Rene knows.'

Dominic held his hands up, palms towards her. 'Please, I wasn't accusing you of anything, Flora. You look upset, but I think you've got the wrong end of the stick. You're a very special person doing a brilliant job, no doubt about that. I was just concerned that maybe Aunt Dot was on a bit of a spree . . . you know, handing out stuff willy-nilly to anyone passing.' He blinked his eyes as if he were fighting back the tears. 'I'm like you, I'm just trying to protect that darling woman.'

She nodded. 'Yes, well, I don't think you need to worry on that score. The only things belonging to Dorothea that have left this flat have been those you yourself have taken away to sell.'

His pale eyes looked at her, considering her words for a moment as if he were uncertain as to what she was implying. Then he obviously decided to take her at face value.

332

'Good-good. That's a relief.' He forced a thin smile to his chubby cheeks. 'Sorry to have brought up something so unpleasant, but one has to face the fact that old people are hugely vulnerable.' His tone was so pious and preachy she wanted to smack him.

'True. Rene and I are very aware of that.'

Dominic moved into the hall muttering to himself. 'Right then, better be off. Bye, Flora. Glad we had the chat.'

'Has Dominic gone?' Dorothea wanted to know. 'I . . . thought I heard his voice.'

'Just now, yes.'

Her eyes looked up at Flora, suddenly beady. 'He's a dear boy . . . but his mother rather spoilt him. He was an only child you see.' She smiled at Flora, 'One child, three fools, my mother used to say.'

Arriving home later, she paused in the street a few doors down from the house. She was worried that Prue, who knew exactly when she got home in the evening, would be lying in wait for her. And perhaps it would be better to swallow her pride and make some sort of peace with her sister. As it stood, she was no longer at ease in her own home.

But it was Bel who came bursting through the upstairs door before Flora had time to take her coat off. She rushed at her aunt and held her in a tight embrace.

'I've been watching out for you,' Bel said, when she had released Flora. She could see the distress on her niece's face.

'What's happened?'

'It's Mum and Dad. They haven't spoken to each other since Monday when they had this terrible row – I could hear them shouting at each other downstairs after I'd gone to bed. Dad's moved into the spare room, but they won't tell me why or anything. It's really, really horrible.' The words came in a rush, followed almost immediately by tears. Bel just stood there in her light grey sweat-shirt and black leggings, her arms folded tight across her chest, making no attempt to wipe them away. Flora went to get a piece of kitchen towel and handed it to her.

'Are they going to get a divorce?' Bel's voice was very small.

'Come and sit down.' She drew her over to the sofa.

'You must know what it's about, Flora. Mum tells you everything. What's she said? Has Dad done something wrong? Please, please tell me.'

Flora was paralysed. It seemed obvious that the row must be about Fin, but she didn't know for certain that it was. And why would Prue suddenly confess when Flora had promised she wouldn't say anything?

'I haven't spoken to Prue since the weekend, darling. I honestly don't know what's going on between them.'

'But you'll find out won't you? Please. Talk to Mum, you've got to. I'm scared Dad will leave.'

Flora tried to still her heartbeat by taking long, slow breaths.

'I'm not sure . . . if your mum hasn't said anything . . . whether I should interfere.'

Bel looked exasperated. 'But you and Mum don't have secrets. Why hasn't she talked to you?' She threw her arms up in the air. 'You see? This is why I'm worried. If Mum can't even tell you about it . . .'

'Alright, I'll call and ask her to come down.'

'Now?'

'Yes. You go back upstairs. She won't talk if you're here.'

'And you'll get her to tell me what's going on? I really need to know. It's driving me crazy.'

'I'll ask her to. But I can't go behind her back, Bel.'

Her niece hung her head. 'Nothing's been right in this house since Fin came back.'

Flora held her breath.

'Did your mum mention Fin's name in the row?'

'No . . . I don't know, maybe. I couldn't hear what they were saying – I didn't really want to – but you know how weird Mum's been since he pitched up.'

Flora picked up her mobile from the table and brought up her sister's number. Prue replied almost immediately.

'Flora?'

335

'Can you come down?'

Prue didn't reply immediately. 'I'll be there in a minute.' Her voice was uncharacteristically subdued.

'Go on.' Flora gave her niece a quick hug. 'I'll do my best.'

'Thanks, thanks . . . I love you.'

'Love you too.' Bel scooted up the stairs.

Her sister's face was drawn and pale, although the make-up was still in place. She threw her phone onto the sofa beside her and gave out a low groan as she leaned back against the cushions. Flora waited, but Prue said nothing. They hadn't given each other the usual hug, just manoeuvred around the space until they were sitting on opposite sides of the coffee table.

'How did Philip find out?'

Prue raised her eyebrows, puffed out her cheeks. 'I . . . oh, God . . . it was a stupid row. I mentioned that I'd sponsored Fin's Nepal trip, and he got angry, said I was really letting you down encouraging him in he-man activities when he was a new father. He wanted to know why I was suddenly being so nice to the man when I'd been slagging him off from here to kingdom come ever since he showed up.' She sighed. 'He said I kept flirting with Fin at Christmas, accused me of fancying him. Said it was embarrassing.'

'So you told him?' Flora was incredulous.

'Not at first. But I can't stand sexual jealousy. I said . . . I said Fin was more of a man than Philip

336

would ever be.' She shrugged. 'Just to taunt him. And . . . oh, I don't know . . . it all just came out.' Her sister drew herself up, suddenly proud. 'Philip doesn't own me. I don't ask who he fucks.'

'I'm sure he doesn't fuck anyone except you.'

'Who knows?' Prue said tiredly.

'Bel's worried. She thinks Philip's going to leave . . . that you'll get a divorce.'

Prue's expression was instantly anxious. 'Did you tell her anything?'

'No, of course I didn't, but she has to have some sort of explanation. She's going mad.'

'But what can I say? I can't tell her the truth, she'd be devastated.'

'What's Philip's position?'

'Much the same as yours.' She gave Flora a sideways look, which she didn't respond to, and said, 'It's Fin that's the problem. If it had been anyone else I don't think he'd have taken it so hard.'

Flora didn't answer. She felt a cold, hard nut of anger whenever she thought of their treachery. And, like her brother-in-law, not just for the crime per se, but for the cruel and casual choice of partner in that crime. Why choose her sister? Why choose her lover? Now, though, that nut turned to pity. How agonising would it be to have to tell your daughter that you'd cheated on both your sister and your husband . . .

Prue suddenly got up. 'That bloody, bloody bastard.'

'It was your choice too.' Flora spoke quietly, but she could feel renewed anger spike through her gut at her sister off-loading the blame.

Prue's eyes flashed as she snatched up her phone. 'Yeah, yeah. Well, I tell you what. I'm pretty much over apologising. Because it'll never be enough, will it? You two saints will make me suffer for ever for what I did . . . I'll never be allowed to forget it.'

'That's unfair.'

'Is it really?' Prue's face was flushed. 'Well, be sure and let me know when I'm forgiven, OK?'

Ignoring the last remark, Flora asked, 'What will you tell Bel?'

'That's my business. I'll work it out.' She turned on her heel and stomped away up the wooden staircase.

Flora sat for a long time on the sofa, contemplating the mess that her family had become. I've got to get out of here, she thought again. And again there seemed no way that she could. She kept picking up her phone to call Fin. She wanted to hear his voice, to know how he was. But she didn't. Could she get past this, forgive him for what he had done? For the sake of their baby, shouldn't she at least try?

'You're *pregnant*?' Mary's mouth hung open. 'You're kidding me. When's it due?'

Flora told her.

'Well, that's grand. So yer man came through.'

Flora nodded, she couldn't begin to tell Mary about her situation.

'You can't be working when this job ends.'

'I'll have to for a while. I haven't told the agency yet.'

'You've got to be careful. The old lady's OK, she's so light. But suppose you got some great galumphing fella who can't get out of bed on his own?'

Flora sighed. 'I know.'

'He'll have to stump up, keep you in the style you should be accustomed to.'

'So how is she?'

Mary shook her head. 'Not so good last night. She's got a bit of a cough this morning and her temperature's slightly raised. Don't like the look of it.'

'Chest infection?'

'I'd say.'

Simon Kent leaned over Dorothea, poking his stethoscope inside her nightie, first on her chest, then on her back. The old lady looked flushed and feverish, barely acknowledging the doctor's presence. She'd deteriorated fast during the morning. He tapped her chest in various places then turned to Flora.

'Her lungs are rattling away.'

Dorothea began to cough, the spasms tearing at her frail body. When she finally stopped, she was breathless, her eyes wide with anxiety as she tried to get air into her lungs.

'I think it's pneumonia,' Simon said in a low voice, his large hand gently covering the old lady's wisp of a one for a moment.

He walked away from the bed.

'Will you give her antibiotics?'

'I think I'll have to . . . not to prolong her life . . . I know she's asked not to have unnecessary treatment, but it's going to be hell for her if she can't breathe.'

'I'll call Rene.'

'I'll rustle up some oxygen too. She'll need that.'

They stood and watched the small figure lying there, her eyes closed, nostrils flared in her attempt to breathe.

'It's not looking good, Flora,' he said gently, noticing perhaps that her eyes had filled with tears. She swallowed hard, clearing her throat. She realised that the old lady was the only reliable thing in her life at present. Always there, always kind, never judgemental or demanding of her what she couldn't provide. She couldn't bear the thought that she would no longer be with her every day.

Simon laid his hand on her arm.

'Listen, I'll be here as much as I can.'

She smiled at him. 'Thanks. It's not . . . I knew this was coming, of course. But . . . well . . .'

'I'll be back later.'

★   ★   ★

340

'I . . . I feel very cold.'

Flora got a quilt from the spare-room cupboard and put it over the duvet. The old lady was staring at her as she worked, her eyes bright with fever.

'I want . . . to get out.' She tried to raise herself from the pillow, but she couldn't and fell back. 'I need to see Peter . . . he's not well.'

'Best not to go now. Wait a while and see if you feel stronger.'

Dorothea shook her head, her eyes blinking anxiously. 'But . . . he needs me . . . Peter. I must go to him.'

'Who's Peter?' She wondered if he was the man who'd jumped off the bridge.

'Peter? You know . . . where is he?' She closed her eyes, tossing her head to and fro on the pillow, opened them again. 'Is he here?'

Flora held her hand. 'No.'

She sighed and her eyelids drooped. When she opened her eyes she seemed surprised. 'Flora? I thought . . . for a moment . . . you were someone else.' The old lady squeezed her hand. 'Stay with me will you?'

'I'm here.'

The room went very quiet. Winter sun poured in through the French windows, creating dusty paths of light. There was no noise except for the soft, rasping breaths, so shallow and quick, coming from the figure on the bed. Occasionally Flora gave Dorothea sips of water, but mostly she just

341

sat with her, holding her hand, which lay on top of the pale pink eiderdown.

Simon came back in a couple of hours. He held out a brown medicine bottle.

'Start her on this. I got the liquid in case she can't manage capsules. The oxygen should be delivered in the next hour or so. Have you given her any painkillers yet?'

Flora nodded. 'I gave her some paracetamol earlier. She's been quite disorientated, asking for someone called Peter . . . thinking I was him.'

Dorothea was asleep, so Flora and Simon went into the kitchen. She put the kettle on.

'I could do with one of your jokes right now.'

'You must be desperate.'

Flora gave him a rueful smile. 'I'm going to miss her. It'll be very strange.'

'What will you do?'

'Find another job . . . I'll have to, for a few months.'

'Do you really have to?'

'Yup.' She handed him his tea.

'I suppose it'd get boring, just sitting waiting.'

'It's not that . . .'

He looked at her for a second or two. 'You know you can always ask me . . . well, if you need help . . . of any sort.'

'Thanks. I won't, but thank you.'

There was a heavy silence. She didn't want him to be so kind, without any reason; it made her feel helpless.

'Everything's great,' she added, her tone deliberately bright.

By the evening the oxygen cylinder was in place, the plastic moulded mask over Dorothea's face secured by a thin piece of elastic behind her head. She kept reaching and pulling it away, her cheeks flushed, as she began to cough. Rene had been there for hours, sitting beside her friend, and had only gone because her husband was ill at home.

Flora didn't want to leave the old lady. She rang the night nurse and told her what was happening.

'I think I'll stay. You don't need to come in.'

'You'll be buggered if you're up all night after a day's work, especially in your condition. We can both be there,' Mary said, and Flora didn't argue.

Mary took the first shift. 'I'll wake you at two.'

Flora thought she wouldn't sleep, but she did, and it was after four when Mary finally roused her.

'You looked so peaceful, I didn't like to disturb you.'

'You should have. How is she?'

'Quiet. She's slept off and on. The mask irritates her, and the coughing's bad. I don't think she's got much longer.'

Flora dressed, made herself some tea and went to sit beside her patient. Mary had gone to bed. She had a book, but couldn't read. Holding Dorothea's hand, she sat watching the tired old face as she struggled to get sufficient air. It seemed cold in the room, although the heating was turned up high, and Flora shivered in the chill. The feeble light from one small lamp and the stillness of the hour made her feel as if she was in a cocoon, like the time she and Simon had danced. But tonight it was just her and Dorothea.

'Is that you?' Dorothea's eyes were open. She looked confused. 'I . . . thought . . . it was . . .'

'It's me, Flora. How are you feeling?'

Dorothea managed a weak smile. 'Not so good. I . . . think I was dreaming . . . of him.'

'Peter?'

'Yes. Did you know him? I can't remember.'

'I didn't, no. Was he the man you loved?'

The old lady's eyes clouded. 'The man . . . I loved.' She didn't say any more, just nodded slowly. 'He was so beautiful . . . so . . . very dear.'

Flora felt her own eyes fill with tears.

'I think . . . I shall see him . . . soon now.' She sighed, but her face suddenly seemed to relax, the breathing easier for a minute, the furrows in the thin skin of her brow smoothing out.

Silence descended again, broken only by the soft hiss of the oxygen and the old lady's breathing: in, out, in, out . . . Flora found herself transfixed by the rhythm.

The next time she woke, Flora tried to give her some water. But after one sip she pushed the glass away, as if she were impatient to speak.

'Love . . . love is all that matters . . . in life.'

Flora nodded.

Dorothea stared at her, and Flora watched as her gaze lost its focus.

She felt a small squeeze of Dorothea's hand, then her breathing began to slow. The periods between each breath became longer and longer as Flora looked on. She almost held her own breath, anticipating the old lady's next one. Holding Dorothea's hand in a gentle grasp, stroking her arm, eyes fixed on her patient's face, Flora could do nothing but wait. And finally, after what seemed like a long while, there was only silence. The next breath never came.

Flora, hardly realising what was happening, did nothing for a few moments. The point of death was so hard to take in. She could see, however, that whatever had been the essence of Dorothea was very clearly gone, a peculiar absence of self in the frail physical body on the bed.

Rousing herself, she let go of Dorothea's hand and got up to turn the oxygen off, removing the mask carefully from the old lady's head. She bent to kiss her forehead, still warm from life.

'Goodbye,' she whispered, stroking the white wisps of hair back from her face. 'I hope you find your Peter.'

Flora felt empty and cold. She placed both the old lady's arms inside the sheet, and pulled it up to her chin before going to wake Mary.

Mary crossed herself and mumbled a quiet prayer as she stood beside the bed.

'Dear old thing. I'm glad she didn't linger.'

The bureaucracy of death swiftly took over: Simon Kent to certify it, Rene to set in motion the undertakers, Flora and Mary to lay Dorothea out. Keith popped in, all of them there without their usual purpose, milling around under the sombre reminder of mortality.

'It feels so strange, not to have to think about her needs,' Flora told Simon as they stood together in the kitchen for the last time. 'And knowing this is my last day here.'

'It'll take a bit of getting used to,' Simon responded, putting his mug down on the draining board and looking at his watch. 'I'd better go and shower and get to the surgery.'

But he didn't go, he hovered. Flora had a sudden dread that she would never see him again. Never see any of them again after today. There would be no reason to.

'Well, goodbye then, Flora,' Simon said at last. 'Good luck with the baby.' He moved towards her as if he was going to embrace her. And she wanted him to, wanted to rest for a moment in his arms. She felt so bereft. But he stopped short and held out his hand, giving her a firm handshake instead.

'Bye, Simon.'

*   *   *

When Flora got home later that day, she didn't know what to do. The job with Dorothea, in her quiet, womb-like flat, had been part of her rehabilitation after her depression. She'd been able to work in a safe, unchallenging environment, doing a job that felt important – at least to her. Now, the anchors of her life had all come loose. Prue, Fin, Dorothea, the people she'd worked with . . . even her relationship with Bel and Philip was threatened by the rift playing out upstairs. The only thing she had to cling to was the new life growing inside her. Every tiny thought of the baby, even in this sea of chaos, brought a sort of cautious anticipation, almost a taste in her mouth of something tempting and just out of reach.

CHAPTER 20

4 February

'Come in and see me,' Cheryl from the agency said.

'Umm . . . OK.'

'We can review what you want to do next. Not sure if you're interested in hospital work?'

'Not really.' She knew she should tell Cheryl that she was pregnant. And she knew she should face the potential safety issues herself: heavy lifting, infectious diseases, long hours, potentially violent dementia patients. But she was like a rabbit in the headlights. It was nearly a week now since Dorothea had died. She needed to work, but she had no idea what else she could do to earn money during her pregnancy. Or how she would support her child once it was born. Asking for help from her sister was completely out of the question.

'I could see you tomorrow morning, around eleven?' Cheryl said, and Flora told her she would be there. But she wasn't optimistic about the outcome. She'd be unlikely to get such a relatively easy gig again, not on nurse's pay at least. Most people like Dorothea – who were old rather than ill – were looked after by carers, who were paid much less, but Rene had insisted on employing nothing but qualified nurses for Dorothea, even if it wasn't really necessary. Flora doubted she'd be so lucky again.

And hovering at the back of her mind as she went over and over her dismal options, was Fin. She missed him. However much she tried to cut herself loose with thoughts of his treachery, she still found herself dwelling on their lovemaking, the laughter in his grey eyes, the way he said 'I love you.' She ached to be in love with him as she had once been – feel that heady, unquestioning, naïve madness that spiralled her out of herself and denied all reality. Should she try and make it right between them, take off to Inverness and live with him in his father's house, give their child a proper home? But when she allowed herself to see past their sexual chemistry, reality brought her back down to earth. Trying to commit to someone who was so obviously allergic to commitment was senseless and exhausting.

Tired of listening to the tedious treadmill in her brain, she got dressed and went out. It was still bitterly cold, but at least there was some fitful sunshine between the February clouds.

'Flora?' Prue was standing on the doorstep – immaculate in one of her black Donna Karan trouser suits – hugging her arms to her body in the chilly wind as Flora emerged from the basement.

'Hi.'

'Come in for a moment will you?'

The invitation was decidedly unfriendly, but she went up the steps. Her sister didn't ask her through to the kitchen, just stood with her in the gloomy black and white marble-tiled hall. It had been nearly two weeks since they'd spoken. Flora thought she'd lost weight; her face was drawn, set in angry lines.

'Why aren't you at work?' she asked.

'Dorothea died last week.'

Prue raised her eyebrows briefly. 'Oh . . . Anyway, I thought you ought to know, Philip and I are having some time apart.'

'Really?' Flora was surprised. She thought Philip was more sanguine, more realistic about his wife.

'It's not him. I'm the one who's asked for it.' Her sister shook her head. 'We both said some very bad things to each other over this Fin business. Neither of us can get past it at the moment.'

Flora didn't know what to say.

'He wants me to be something I can't be.'

'Is this about fidelity?' Flora wondered for the first time if Fin was the only one. And if Prue had foolishly mentioned this to her husband in the heat of the moment.

'Isn't it always?' Prue bit off the words, her breathing fast. 'Isn't every marital row in the history of the human race about sex? Men are so

350

fucking territorial. Philip thinks he owns me. And he fucking doesn't.'

'Where's he going to go?'

'Flat in the Temple. Belongs to a judge – some friend of a friend who's only there one night every three weeks or something. Usual cosy boys' club bollocks.' Prue could hardly keep the sneer from her face. It's as if *she's* the victim of *Philip's* infidelity, Flora thought, not the other way round. But her sister had always been good at manipulating a situation to put herself in the right.

'And Bel? What does she know?'

'Nothing. And I'd like to keep it that way. We've just said we're having a few problems . . . that we'll sort it out.'

'And will you?'

'Who the fuck knows?' The anger had been replaced by an artificial nonchalance. 'Have you got another job yet?'

Flora shook her head.

But her sister was not interested in anything but her own problems at that moment. She just shrugged and looked at her watch. 'Christ . . . I'm late.'

Prue was shutting her out, blaming her, ridiculously, for all that had happened. But although Flora found it hard being on the receiving end of such unfair resentment, she was also relieved not to be dealing with the still raw subject of Prue's relationship with Fin. Every time she was on the verge of phoning Fin, it was the thought of them

351

together that stood in her way, her reluctance compounded by the fact that neither he nor Prue really seemed to understand why everyone was so upset.

'I am the resurrection and the life, saith the Lord. He that believeth in me, though he were dead, yet shall he live . . .'

Reverend Jackson's voice boomed out, ringing around the large church in dramatic echo. The ten or so mourners were seated in the front two rows; Rene, sporting a large black hat, Keith in his three-piece suit, Mary wrapped in a heavy black overcoat, Dominic in dandyish black corduroy and a fedora. Flora shivered as she looked at the coffin.

Footsteps rang on the stone floor and she glanced round, pleased to see Simon Kent making his way down the aisle. She'd thought he wasn't coming. He chose her pew and sat down next to her.

'Bloody nithering out there,' he whispered, squeezing her hand briefly. 'You OK?'

She nodded, but she wasn't OK. The last few days she had spent completely alone, hiding under the duvet, unable even to keep her appointment with Cheryl to talk about another job. She felt paralysed with loneliness. She didn't have one friend she could pour her heart out to; Prue had been her best and only one. She knew she should get up, get out, that lying there could be dangerous for her, pre-empting a slide into real despair that she would find it hard to come back from. But she couldn't bring herself to move further than the kitchen to make yet another slice of toast, or boil the kettle for yet more tea. It had been touch and go this morning as to whether she could make the effort to get dressed and go to Dorothea's funeral. But she'd known she had to.

She filed out after the coffin with the others and was greeted by Reverend Jackson's enthusiastic handshake, his big paws closing round Flora's cold hand as he beamed his Christian smile. She smiled back mechanically, desperate to get home, back to the safety of the sofa – back to oblivion.

Rene was travelling with the coffin to Mortlake Crematorium, but she didn't want the others to come. 'It'll be quick, Dorothea stipulated no fuss,' she'd told Flora. The others were going back to the flat, where Keith had organised refreshments.

'Coming, Florence?' Keith, who was standing with the doctor, offered her his arm.

'Listen,' she said, 'I think I'll get off home.'

'Oh, come on. We can't have a wake without you,' the porter insisted, grabbing her arm and marching her along the pavement.

'So d'you think the old girl's watching us?' Mary the night nurse glanced heavenwards as she put on the kettle in Dorothea's kitchen.

Flora actually managed to laugh. 'I hope so,' she said, but the flat already felt diminished and lifeless, dank without the heating. There were boxes already in the hall, the big hospital bed had gone, and the furniture in the sitting room was tagged with coloured stickers indicating their destination.

'Bless her,' Mary said quietly, as she arranged mugs on a tray.

'Isn't Dominic coming?' Flora asked, as they all stood awkwardly in the hall with their tea. She had waved hello to him in the church, but he'd appeared to ignore her and turn away. She thought perhaps he'd had a row with Rene over the silver bowl and was blaming her. Not that she cared. It was a relief not to have to see the man again.

'He said he had to get back to work,' Simon said. 'He looked upset. But then I suppose he was very close to Dorothea.'

'Was he?' Flora queried. 'I mean, he visited quite often and gushed all over her, but I got the feeling he was just waiting for her to keel over.'

'Ooh, that's not very nice, Florence. Not about our very own Prince Charming,' Keith said. He had had a couple of run-ins with Dominic over his high-handed demands for the porter's help in carrying his swag to the car.

'Still, can't believe what a rubbish deal he got for the Bowman,' Simon commented. Flora thought he was avoiding her today. He talked mainly to Keith or Mary, and after one cup of tea and a sausage roll, he began his goodbyes. She hoped he would ask for her number, but he didn't, and she couldn't find the words to ask him to stay in touch.

* * *

354

The next week was the same as the last for Flora. More duvet, more toast, more mind-numbing television, few showers, little sleep. The February weather was particularly dreary, and the small flat permanently in gloom, matching her increasingly despairing reflections. Bel had gone skiing with the school for half-term, Prue didn't call. Neither did Fin. Flora knew she needed to earn money, and be fit and healthy for the baby, but even these imperatives failed to stir her from her lethargy. Next week, she promised herself. Next week. But the thought of next week – and the week after and the one after that – only brought churning fear, tears and a sense of utter hopelessness.

One morning, as Flora lay and contemplated the dreary prospect of another day by herself, she was aware of a tiny fluttering in her stomach, fleeting and barely perceptible. She stayed very still, her fingers resting lightly on the small swelling. Nothing happened for an age, but then she felt it again. She held her breath, almost in awe. Her own baby, moving inside her, growing and flourishing through all this misery. It brought her up short. How could she be so indulgent, so utterly selfish? She should be out exercising, breathing in fresh air, eating healthy food, not slumped on the sofa, existing on a diet of toast and tea.

She got herself out of bed quickly, showered, dressed, bundled herself up against the weather, and set off for the park before she could change her mind. She felt dazed at being out, but the late

February sunshine was wonderful on her skin. There was even a hint of spring in the purple and white crocuses that poked up around the bottom of some of the trees in the park. She walked for half an hour, then settled in the park café and ordered some scrambled eggs and camomile tea. She opened the paper for the first time in weeks. No one was in the café this early – the mums and babies would arrive later.

Flora glanced up from the paper at the heavy sound of the café's glass door opening. Her heart leapt. It was Simon Kent. He hadn't noticed her yet, and she watched his smile light up his handsome face as he ordered a coffee, always so polite, so respectful. She realised how much she'd missed seeing him every day.

He was turning to go, his takeaway coffee in his hand, when he spotted Flora. For a moment his face was inscrutable, she sensed almost a reluctance in his expression, as if he were unwilling to engage with her. But then he smiled.

'Flora, hello. Didn't see you there.' He came over to her table. 'How are you?'

'I'm fine,' she said.

There was an awkward silence.

'Everything alright with the baby?'

She nodded. She wanted to ask him to sit down, but found herself hesitating.

'It's odd, none of you being there to drop in on.'

'And for me too . . . join me if you like,' she said finally.

He hesitated for slightly too long. 'Umm . . . OK, I've probably got a minute.' He took his overcoat off and threw it on the spare chair.

'Are you working again?'

'Not yet, but I must soon.'

There was that look again, the one that seemed to see more than she wanted him to. 'You look very pale.'

'Do I?' she said with unnatural brightness. Then the effort of the morning overtook her and she felt herself sliding, collapsing into herself, the false energy that had propelled her out of bed and into the park suddenly running dry. 'I've been . . . not really myself,' she mumbled, embarrassed under his scrutiny.

'You must miss Dorothea.'

She shrugged. 'I suppose . . . yes. I don't know . . . it's everything.'

He didn't speak, and the silence seemed to stretch between them until it was almost unbearable.

'Fin and I aren't together at the moment.'

'At the moment?'

'He's in Scotland.'

Simon was clearly confused, but perhaps wasn't sure if he should question her further.

'I think we may have split up.'

'Really? I'm sorry. But you say "may have", so it sounds as if there's hope.'

'Perhaps.'

'And with the baby . . .'

'I can't stay with him because of the baby,' she said, hearing her defensive tone and regretting it.

'No, no, I didn't mean to imply that.' He looked baffled by the conversation, but she didn't know what to say to explain the unexplainable.

For a moment they looked at each other. She'd forgotten how beautiful his eyes were.

'Well, I suppose I'd better get going. Surgery's about to start.'

She nodded, wondering where the easy banter that used to exist between them had gone.

They said their goodbyes and he turned to go, looping his coat over his arm as if he didn't want to take the time to put it on.

'Simon . . .' Flora called after him and he came back. She wanted to ask him to be her friend, to meet her occasionally for coffee or a walk. She wanted to tell him that she really liked him, that she'd missed him. But the words died on her lips. 'Great to see you,' she muttered.

'And you,' he said, his brown eyes suddenly intense and almost sad.

Flora wandered home, angry with herself for being so tongue-tied with the doctor. All her resolve about getting her life back on track for the sake of the baby had ebbed away, leaving her with no more ambition than to get back under the duvet.

The week stretched on, Flora sliding even further into a paralysed stasis. Part of her felt that it was pointless to move, to eat, to live; pointless to kick against the inevitable despair. But something had to be done. She had to earn money.

Cheryl, the owner of the nurses' agency, sat swinging from side to side in her black high-backed chair, the fuchsia-painted nails of her right hand tapping lightly on the desk top.

'Obviously you shouldn't be doing private nursing. Not being pregnant at your age.' She was fiftyish, overweight, her shoulder-length hair dyed an improbable shade of aubergine. There was no small-talk with Cheryl, everything was businesslike and to the point in the well-run agency.

'I know. But I have to work. And I'm not qualified for anything else. Please . . .' She felt intensely vulnerable under Cheryl's professional stare.

'It's not just *your* position though, is it? If I send you to a client and you're suddenly taken ill, or aren't able to lift or something because of your pregnancy, that person's care is compromised as much as you are.'

Flora just sat there, unable to work up enough spirit to argue.

Cheryl sighed, her tough manner suddenly dropping away.

'Listen, there is one possibility, if you're up for it.' She paused, her mouth working as she considered her proposition. 'We've been let down by the maternity cover we got in for Kelly. The bloody girl just didn't come in this week, and no one can contact her. She was useless anyway.'

Flora waited.

'You know what Kelly does. Books jobs, interviews nurses and carers . . . it's not rocket science. But we'll need someone till July, when Kelly's supposed to come back.' She raised her eyebrows when Flora didn't immediately respond. 'It's a desk job. Compatible with pregnancy.'

Flora nodded, realising the gift she'd just been handed. 'God, yes, thank you, that would be great.' She paused and repeated, 'Thank you so much, Cheryl.'

As she headed home, Flora knew she should feel happier. She was immensely grateful for the job, which would start the following Monday and at least solve her financial situation till the baby was born. But the thought of sitting in that dreary, airless Holborn office, under harsh strip lighting for eight hours a day, breathing in Cheryl's sickly perfume and ringing nurses to find out if they were free to work, was dismal.

This is for the baby, she told herself. But when she got home she just crept back to bed and spent the next few hours in a miserable doze – she often napped during the day now, because at night she was wide awake, her sense of loneliness further enhanced by the conviction that everyone else in the city was snuggled up comfortably with someone else.

Flora struggled through her first weeks at the agency and almost died of boredom. Working a twelve-hour shift with Dorothea had gone twice as quickly as eight long hours in that stuffy office. Tina, the only other employee, was in her early twenties and kept up a relentless monologue about boys, clothes, haircuts and how wasted she'd got, as if Flora was a kindred spirit. Flora kept reminding herself that she was very lucky to be working at all, but it didn't make the time go any faster. By the weekend she was always exhausted. Mary asked her for tea one Saturday. Keith offered a drink. Even Jake texted: *wanna margarita yet?* But she turned them all down, despite her desperate loneliness; being sociable was an impossibility. She knew she was sliding, that the baby was the only thing between her and despair. But as the weeks went on, and February became March, March became April, bringing the Spring, even the baby didn't seem to be enough.

'Flora?' It was Rene.

Flora, still half asleep in front of Saturday morning television, had reached automatically for her phone, although most of the time now she avoided all calls. Rene had called three times already this week, but she hadn't picked up, hadn't replied, and regretted doing so now.

'Hello, Rene.'

'Have I woken you?'

'No . . . no. I was just . . . checking emails.' She hauled herself upright.

'I need to have a chat with you. I'll be at

361

Dorothea's tomorrow, sorting things out. Could you pop round?'

'Umm . . .that might be difficult. I have to meet up with someone for lunch.' She hoped her lie was convincing. It was hard enough getting herself together for work, without having to go out at weekends too.

'Right . . . well, maybe afterwards? I shall probably be there most of the day. Or before?'

Flora knew she wasn't going to get out of it. 'OK . . . can we make it after, then?'

'Does fourish give you enough time?'

'Yes, that's fine. I'll see you tomorrow.'

After Rene had hung up, Flora groaned quietly. She'd sounded as if it were urgent, but then Rene always did. What did she want to talk to her about anyway? She probably needed help clearing out the flat so that the grisly Dominic could get his hands on it, she decided. But if Rene were offering a few days' work over a weekend, she wasn't in a position to turn it down. She went through to the bathroom and peered at her face in the small mirror. A pale, drear image looked anxiously back at her, heavy dark rings beneath her gold-brown eyes, hair straggling, unwashed and uncut, past her shoulders. I look like a bag-lady, she thought, turning quickly away and putting the shower on before she lost the impetus.

'Come in, come in.' Rene ushered her inside. 'I've made some tea.'

They picked their way through the boxes in the hall to the sitting room, which was partially packed up, pale dust-sheets making odd shapes of the furniture, more boxes piled by the windows, pictures stacked against one wall. Only the sofa stood uncovered, the dust-sheet folded neatly over one arm.

Rene poured the tea in silence.

'All looks very organised,' Flora commented, her eyes sweeping round the room, remembering the daily image of Dorothea sitting peacefully in her chair by the window. She felt a pang of loss.

'Well, it's getting there. Still a lot to do.' Rene handed Flora a mug and took the other one herself, cradling it between her hands in the cold room.

'Right . . . no point in beating about the bush. I've got something very important to tell you.' Rene paused, her look significant. 'I'd have told you before, but there were a number of things to sort out.'

Flora waited. 'Dorothea has left this flat to you. And a small legacy to go with it.'

Flora's mouth dropped open. 'What?' She felt a shiver down her spine, felt the blood drain from her face.

Rene nodded enthusiastically. 'Yes. Marvellous isn't it? The flat is now yours. And fifty thousand pounds.' She gave her a broad smile.

'But . . . wait . . . to *me*? I don't believe it. What about Dominic? I thought she'd left everything to him.'

'She had. But she changed her will. She's left him a substantial legacy, of course. He should be pleased, but of course he's not.'

Flora was speechless, suddenly understanding why he'd snubbed her at the funeral. 'Why? Did she think he was cheating her?'

'She never said as much. You know Dorothea, she wouldn't have said a word against him. She was just determined that you have the flat. She was extremely fond of you.'

'I was very fond of her too.' Flora's eyes filled with tears. She swallowed hard. 'But can I really have it? Won't Dominic challenge the will?'

'He certainly planned to. He was livid. He demanded a meeting at the solicitor's. Called both of us some pretty horrible names. But I said we had proof that he'd been cheating his great-aunt for months, selling off her stuff for a fraction of what it was worth. I told him in no uncertain terms that if he made a fuss, all that would come out.'

'But we don't have proof . . . do we?'

'Not as such, but it wouldn't be hard to get. The clincher was when I asked to see the bills of sale from the auction houses for all the items. He went quiet after that.'

'So you don't think he'll take it further?'

'Look, she left him a hundred thousand pounds and all the most valuable furniture. More than he deserves. He'd be mad to risk his reputation – for what that's worth – by taking us to court. Whatever his justification, he was nothing more than a common thief.'

Flora sat in stunned silence. She looked at Rene. 'Let me get this straight. Dorothea has left the entire flat . . . to me. And fifty thousand pounds?'

Rene laughed, reaching over to pat her arm. 'Hard to take in, eh?'

'When did she do it? Change her will, I mean?'

'About two months before she died. She suddenly got a bee in her bonnet about it. I had to arrange all the signing on a Saturday, when you weren't here. Ironically it was Pia who witnessed her signature. And she's left something to Mary and Keith. The flat's leasehold, I'm afraid, it's only got twenty-eight years to run. You'd have to renew the lease fairly soon if you wanted to sell it for what it's really worth.'

Rene rattled on. 'Obviously probate will take a while with regard to the money, but as Dorothea's executor I can give you the keys to the flat now. I don't know what you intend to do, but I would suggest you don't leave it empty for too long. Houses quickly develop problems if they're not lived in.'

Flora looked around the room. This is mine? This is really mine? It was impossible to take in. And it felt even stranger that she wasn't able to thank Dorothea in person.

Rene got up. 'You sit there for a bit, absorb the good news. I need to get on with things, tackle her bedroom. Then we should talk about what, if anything, you'd like to keep of the stuff not going to Dominic.' She bustled out of the room.

Flora leant back against the cushions and closed her eyes. Dorothea, she called silently into the ether, her hands pressed together in her lap. Dorothea . . . please be there, please hear me. Thank you a million times for what you've done. It's unbelievable. You've literally saved my life. There was no sound in the still room, but she fancied, in her euphoric state, that Dorothea did hear her, her kind smile lighting up those pale old eyes. The tears were hot behind Flora's lids, but she welcomed them, her sense of relief too much to contain.

For the next two hours, she and Rene worked side by side, a roll of bin bags between them gradually being filled with all that remained of Dorothea's life. But Flora felt disassociated from her actions, her speech. They went on automatically while she floated separate, buoyed up by the first breath of hope she had experienced in months.

'You'll have to get insurance sorted out. I'll send you a copy of the lease and one of the will. You should come in and talk to Andrew Houlting, my solicitor, the one who's dealing with probate. He can tell you roughly when the money will be available, and arrange the necessary paperwork if you need a loan against it.'

Flora listened and nodded and agreed, all in a daze.

When she left Rene, she didn't know what to do with herself. She walked up towards the bus and home, then changed her mind. She didn't want to go and sit alone in the flat, bursting with the incredible news she'd just received, and no one to share it with. So she walked back down to the arcade and Waitrose. She would treat herself, buy some decent food for a change. Her heart wouldn't slow down; every time she thought about the flat, the money, it leaped and jumped in her chest as if it were doing a jig.

She rang Fin as soon as she got home. She was dying to tell someone.

'Flo?'

'How are you?'

'I'm great! Been on one, exercising like a bloody nutjob. When you're in the zone the rest of the world doesn't exist.' He drew breath, obviously hearing what he'd just said. 'Not you and the baby of course . . . I didn't mean you don't exist . . .'

'It's OK, Fin. Listen, something amazing has happened to me.'

'Amazingly good or amazingly bad?'

'Amazingly amazing.' She found herself laughing to herself.

'So are you going to tell me?'

'Dorothea left me her flat.' Flora spoke the words with complete disbelief. 'And some money.'

'Christ, that is amazing! So the old lady came through.' There was a long pause. 'Will you sell it?'

She didn't answer at once. There had been no

moment when they had made a finite decision about their future together. And she had no idea what he was thinking.

'No,' she said, suddenly very clear about what she herself wanted. 'I think I'll live there.'

'OK.' He went silent. 'So you and me . . . does this mean . . .?'

'I don't know.' She could hear his breathing on the line and didn't know what she wanted him to say.

'I can't . . . it's hard to think we won't be together. I'd sort of thought you'd be here, with me. You and the baby. You still could be, Flo. You know I love you. If it's the Prue thing . . .'

For a very long time neither of them spoke.

'I think we want different things from life, Fin.'

'I suppose we do,' he muttered eventually.

Flora ended the call awash with conflicting emotions: the bubbling excitement about Dorothea's flat, relief at the thought of the legacy, and a leaden sadness that she and Fin couldn't make it work together.

CHAPTER 21

4 June

In the weeks since Flora had got the keys to the St George's Court flat, she had gradually, with the help of Bel and Keith, and recently Simon Kent, begun to transform the cluttered and tatty interior into a clean, light space. She'd been sleeping in the flat for a couple of weeks, and Dorothea's old bedroom was now bright and clean, the ancient carpet long since consigned to a skip, the floorboards sanded, polished and covered in a colourful rag rug, the heavy curtains replaced by a calico blind. The rest of the flat still had a long way to go.

It was Flora who had made the decision to get in touch with Simon again. She knew they would be neighbours and would bump into each other in the street, but she thought they could also be friends and had wanted to dispel the awkwardness that was so apparent when they'd seen each other in the park café.

One morning, a month or so after she had got the keys to the flat, she'd left a text on his mobile: *Give me a ring when you have a moment. Flora.*

He hadn't responded for two days, and she was saddened at the thought that he didn't want any contact with her. But on her way to work at the agency, walking from Holborn Tube station in the din of the rush-hour traffic, her phone rang.

'Flora, hi. It's Simon Kent.' He didn't sound unfriendly exactly, but as if he was in a hurry, his breath quick as he walked.

'Hello . . . How are you?'

'I'm fine.'

Though discouraged by his tone, she'd ploughed on. 'Um . . . I just called because I thought you should know, we're going to be neighbours.' She told him about Dorothea leaving her the flat.

'How wonderful. She obviously adored you.'

'We're just giving it a basic makeover.'

'Well, good luck with it all. I hope you'll be very happy there.' He'd paused. 'Probably see you around and about then.'

'Drop in if you have a moment. I'm sort of living there now, although it's a mess because there's still masses to do. Keith's helping.'

For what seemed like a long time, he hadn't replied. Then eventually he said, 'And Fin too, I expect.'

'Fin and I aren't together any more.'

Another silence. 'Oh . . . I'm sorry.'

'Yeah, me too.'

'So you'll be living there by yourself, then.'

'Yup.'

There was a pause.

'OK . . . well, I'm good at wielding a paintbrush

if you need more help.' His reserve had finally softened. 'And the baby?'

'The baby's fine.'

Since then, Simon had often come round, sometimes to help paint or clear things out at weekends. He'd occasionally accompanied her and Bel to choose baby clothes and equipment – being the only one with previous baby experience, he said. He'd even driven them both to IKEA for nursery furniture – the real test of friendship in Flora's book. But although she felt totally at ease with him and the three of them were never short of things to say to each other, sharing a lot of laughter, she and Simon were still nothing more than friends. Flora sometimes caught him looking at her in his quiet, intense way, and wondered how he really felt about her. For her part, she knew only that she had come to look forward to seeing him, that his presence was becoming an essential part of her life.

'It's a bit of a creepy colour.' Bel pulled a face as she eyed the paint tin sitting on the dust sheet.

'"Creepy"? What on earth do you mean? It's just a very soft green. I thought it would be restful in the sitting room.'

'Hmm. S'ppose it might look better when it's on the walls.'

'Well, let's finish the baby's room first. You can't object to Linen White!'

They were sitting on sofa cushions on the recently sanded floor of the sitting room – the rest of the furniture was still stacked in the hall – each sipping from a takeaway carton of mixed-berry smoothie from the café opposite.

'So how's it going with Mum?'

Bel rolled her eyes. 'Pretty rubbish. She's stopped shouting all the time. Now she just wanders about, looking as if she's going to cry. Hate it.'

'And your dad?'

'Yeah, I see him a lot, but never with Mum. He says she still won't speak to him. And when I asked Mum if they were getting a divorce she just said 'Of course not', as if it was, like, totally obvious they wouldn't. I wish she'd just tell me what went wrong.'

Flora shifted uncomfortably on her cushion. 'They'll sort it out, Bel, I'm sure they will. It's horrible for you, but give them time.'

'So you keep saying. But she's not even talking to *you* – you haven't seen her for months – so it's got to be really, really bad.' Her niece eyed her suspiciously. 'You must know what happened, Flora. Please . . . please tell me.'

Flora met Bel's pleading glance. It wasn't the first time Bel had asked her, and each time she was forced to fob her off with some platitude about things being alright in the end. Eventually Bel had given up asking, but she wasn't stupid.

'Look, Bel, I've said before, it's complicated. Your mum's going through a difficult time. I don't think it's any one thing, just a weird phase in her life when she's not coping with stuff.' Her

372

words, as usual on this subject, sounded thin and evasive.

Bel raised her eyebrows. 'Yeah, well, that's pretty much what Mum and Dad always say . . . basically nothing, nada, zip.' She sighed, sucking the last of her smoothie noisily through the straw.

'I'm sorry.'

'No, I get it. You all think I'm a dumb kid who's too young to hear the truth. But hey, I'm fifteen. And it's *my* family.'

Flora saw the tears and reached over to take her hand. 'Come on. Let's paint. It'll take your mind off your stupid parents.' She hoped Bel never had to hear about her mother and Fin.

For a while they painted. The walls were done, it was just the gloss along the skirting boards and around the sash-window frames that needed finishing. The room would be lovely: light, airy, calm. Flora thought of her baby lying cosily in the cot – which was still in a flat-pack awaiting Keith's construction skills – and felt a frisson of anxiety.

'Is Dr Simon coming round?' Bel asked, as they paused to check their progress.

'He said he'd try and drop by later, but he's on call.'

Bel was suddenly fixing her with a strange look. 'He's so totally cute.'

Flora laughed. 'Simon?'

'Doh . . . yes, Simon. Who else?' Her niece was still eyeing her. 'Don't you think he's cute?' Bel obviously liked the doctor, they had developed a teasing friendship over the previous weeks while helping with the flat.

Flora didn't answer for a moment. 'OK . . . yes, he is very cute.'

Bel looked triumphant. 'So?'

'What do you mean?'

'So what are you going to do about it?'

Flora shook her head, pointing down to her swelling stomach. 'Bel, I'm pregnant, in case you hadn't noticed. You can't think about that sort of thing when you're pregnant.' She saw Bel raise her eyebrows. 'Trust me, you can't. Simon and I are just friends. And anyway, who says he's interested in that way?'

'I says,' her niece grinned broadly and turned back to the paint tray.

That night, as she lay in bed, Flora thought about that conversation. Was Bel right about Simon? Flora had seen those looks he gave her sometimes, but no one would consider romantic involvement with a heavily pregnant woman, or relish the prospect of dealing with another man's child . . . would they . . .? She loved his dark eyes, his kindness; he made her laugh. But surely if he'd felt anything more for her, he'd have said something by now. She wondered how she would feel if he did.

Oxford Street on a Saturday morning was a dumb idea, Flora realised, as they wove their way through the crowds. But she was working all week, she didn't have much choice.

'Do I really need all these things?' she asked Simon, gazing at the bewildering array of safety equipment, from socket covers to fridge locks to door-slam stoppers. Simon picked up a starter pack of safety equipment.

'Not sure you need to worry about it raiding the fridge any time soon.'

'Or banging its head on the corner of the table. Did you have all this stuff for Jasmine?'

Simon gave her a wry smile. 'We had a nanny instead.'

He seldom talked about his four-year-old daughter, but Flora knew that Carina, his ex-wife, made it really hard for him to see her.

'I'm not going to get any of this stuff.' She made the decision, putting the packet firmly back on the shelf. 'The flat isn't big, I'll hear her cry without a stupid monitor. And all this stuff won't be needed till she's way older, if at all.'

'Good plan. Parenting's just another marketing scam these days,' Simon said. 'Come on, I'll shout you tea at Sketch. It's got comfy armchairs and deliciously decadent macaroons.'

Once in the plush, exotic surroundings of Sketch, Flora sank into her chair with relief. 'Shall we share a cream tea . . . *and* some macaroons? Eating for two!'

'And a blueberry éclair?' Simon grinned up at the waitress taking their order. 'Even though I'm not.'

'Oh, I think pregnant dads can indulge as well

as pregnant mums,' the waitress joked. As she disappeared towards the till, there was a brief awkwardness between them.

'I suppose we do look like a couple,' Simon said.

Flora gave an embarrassed laugh. 'I suppose.'

They sat in silence, during which Flora suddenly realised that she would love it if they were. But the realisation made her even more self-conscious; she couldn't even meet the doctor's eye.

'Have you thought about what sort of birth you want?' Simon asked eventually, obviously searching for a safe topic of conversation.

'Pain free?' They both laughed. 'I'm a coward, I'm afraid. I know I should be doing the NCT thing, but I want drugs – loads of them – and epidurals. The lot.'

'Yeah, what you really want is for the baby to appear by your side like the Angel Gabriel.'

Flora smiled, then suddenly shivered. 'God, it's scary. Not just the giving birth – that's bad enough – but then there's the whole responsibility thing.' She held her hand against her belly, gently stroking the growing bulge.

Simon watched her, chewing the corner of his index finger absentmindedly. 'I suppose Fin will come down for the birth? But if . . . if he isn't there for any reason, and you want someone to hold your hand . . .' He shot her a quick glance.

'He says he will . . . but thank you. Thank you, Simon. That's very kind.' She was more than touched by his offer, guiltily pushing away the hope that he might be there with her instead of Fin.

After another awkward silence, they began to talk about a film Simon had seen the previous week.

Flora stood next to the paint tins in the sitting room and sighed a big sigh. The room looked suddenly much bigger than she thought, and she was tired. The flat seemed to be taking ages to finish. All she wanted was to sit on the sofa in the pale green sitting room and relax. It was such a beautiful spring evening.

The bell rang. She wasn't expecting anyone, and decided not to answer it. She couldn't face a visitor right now. But it rang again, and she gave in, cursing under her breath.

'Bad time?' Simon Kent gave her a keen glance. 'You look exhausted.'

She smiled. 'I do feel a bit tired. I think it was seeing the vast expanse of wall I have to paint.'

'Want some help?'

'I wouldn't mind your opinion about the paint I've bought. Bel thinks it's "creepy".'

Simon chuckled as he knelt on the floor to check the side of the tin. 'Hmm, Sea Urchin 6 . . . interesting.' He prised off the lid with a paint-stained chisel belonging to the porter, and peered at the contents. 'She could have a point, your niece. Looks a bit subterranean.'

Flora frowned.

'You don't like it? I thought I couldn't have plain white in the sitting room, it'd be too cold. And this is very pale . . . more a greeny blue.'

Simon put his head on one side. 'Sort of reminds me a bit of an operating theatre.' He grinned up at her.

Flora frowned. 'Stop it!'

'Listen, it's your flat.' He stood up. 'If *you* like it, that's all that matters. My opinion doesn't count.'

She nodded, but it wasn't quite true. She knew she wanted him to be happy in it too. 'Yes,' she said now, 'but I don't want a clinical atmosphere. I want it to be warm and cosy.'

'Well, it might be. Come on, let's do a wall. See how it looks.'

The French windows were wide open, letting the warm spring breeze into the empty room; the radio played quietly in the background as they stood side by side, each with a roller, smoothing the operating-theatre green over the stripped and sanded surface. Glancing sideways at the doctor in his jeans and grey T-shirt, a smear of paint on his forearm, Flora couldn't help smiling. She was actually happy – really happy – for the first time in months, maybe years. Simon must have sensed her look, because he turned to her and smiled back.

'Not looking too bad so far. You're right, it's not as green as I thought.'

'So it doesn't summon swabs and scalpels to mind?'

'Not at first.'

They worked on until the wall was finished, then stood back to examine their handiwork.

'Not sure I'm convinced,' Flora said.

'It's not dry yet. Might end up lighter?'

'Maybe. I'll make some tea while we wait.' It was beginning to get dark outside, and she turned on the small lamp plugged into the socket nearest the door.

When she came back with the mugs, Simon had brought two wooden kitchen chairs – Dorothea's – in from the hall and placed them alongside each other, facing the just-painted wall but at a distance from it.

'Looks like we're about to watch a movie,' she said, handing him his tea.

'We're going to sit and watch the wall, absorb the atmosphere, imagine it's a normal evening and we're here, talking about the day, with a glass of wine . . .' He stopped, looking suddenly embarrassed by the intimate scenario he had outlined. 'Just to try and see if it's a colour you can live with,' he added quickly.

They lapsed into silence and began staring at the wall. Then, from the radio came John Denver's lilting voice: 'You fill up my senses . . .' and Flora was vividly reminded of Simon humming the song as he waltzed with her that night, all those months ago, in this very room.

'They're playing our song,' Simon said, with a small smile, holding his hand out to her. 'Flora Bancroft, would you honour me with this dance?'

He pulled her to her feet, and they took off around the empty room, their socked feet swishing on the polished boards as he gently guided her, his steps flowing and confident, their bodies close. The words rang in her brain . . . 'come, let me love you . . .' It was a song that spoke of a man completely inhabited by his love for a woman.

The music finished, but they went on waltzing for a few more turns of the floor. When they finally stopped, they still stood together, Flora's hand resting on Simon's shoulder, his arm around her waist, their other hands clasped. She glanced up at him in the soft glow from the single lamp, and saw his eyes so full of emotion as he looked at her that it took her breath away. Her heart began to race.

'Flora . . .' he whispered, hesitating for only a moment before bending to kiss her softly, tentatively on the lips. And she felt in that moment, as his mouth met her own, that she never wanted the kiss to end, never wanted to leave his embrace again. For a long time they just stood there, holding each other, not speaking.

'I've wanted to do that for what seems like a lifetime to me . . . but I hope you don't think . . .' He glanced down at her swelling figure. 'I mean, it's probably not the right time.'

In answer, she reached up and kissed him again.

Flora woke the next morning to find herself smiling with happiness. She and Simon had stayed up late – camped on the sofa in the hall – talking and laughing together, sometimes holding hands, a bowl of hummus and pitta bread between them, until he had finally taken himself off home across the road. She didn't quite believe – after all this time as colleagues, then friends – what magical thing had happened to them both last night, but she felt as if a dam had burst, all the pent-up embarrassment and constraint between them swept away by his kiss.

She got out of bed, examining her belly in the bathroom mirror as she did every morning. At around seven months it was still quite neat and compact, but it seemed vast to her as she stroked the smooth curve. She was aware of the strange flutter of movement often now, and the image of the tiny body growing safely inside her made her quietly happy.

As she was getting dressed, the doorbell rang. Simon, she thought, running to answer it. But it was Fin's voice that greeted her over the intercom.

'Fin! What are you doing here?' Shocked, she stood back to let him into her flat. He was deeply tanned, his hair bleached gold, and was pounds lighter than when she'd seen him last. His light eyes smiled down at her.

'Wow! Get you. You look gorgeous.' Before she had time to stop him, he had swept her into his arms, planting kisses on her neck and her face. 'Pregnancy certainly suits you,' he added, releasing her.

'What are you doing here?' she repeated. 'You should have rung.'

Fin shrugged. 'I thought I'd surprise you.' He looked around the flat. 'This is great.'

'It's not finished yet.' She didn't know what to say to this man. Obsessed with him for over a decade, she found he was almost a stranger to her now.

'So . . . I had to come down to sort out the visa and stuff for Nepal, and I thought I'd spend a few days with you.' He gazed at her. 'I've really missed you, Flo.'

'You can't stay here.' Her voice sounded sharp with panic.

Fin looked taken aback. 'Oh . . . can't I? Why not?'

'Because . . . because we aren't together any more.'

'Yeah . . . but that doesn't mean we can't spend time with each other. That's my baby you've got in there.' He grinned, reached to touch her belly, but she moved back.

'Flo? What's the matter?' Then his brow darkened. 'Have you got someone else here?'

'No.'

'Well, what's the problem then?' He went over to the sofa and flung himself down on it, patting the cushion. 'Still the same old couch. What memories this has, eh?' His suggestive glance was one Flora was entirely familiar with. But whereas in the past it might have triggered her own desire, now it made her feel uneasy.

'Shall I make some coffee?'

'That'd be good.' He got up and followed Flora into the kitchen. As she stood at the sink filling the kettle, he came up behind her and leant against her, putting his arms round her body.

She shook him off. 'Please . . .'

'Whoa, what's the matter? OK, I should have called and warned you, but you used to like me surprising you.'

She poured coffee grounds into the cafetière. 'That was in the past, Fin.'

'Fair enough. But you don't seem very pleased to see me. I was hoping we could make plans for the birth and stuff. It's not so long now. I'll come down the week it's due and stay till it's born if you like. Then we could see how it goes. Obviously I'll have to take off early September for this Nepal trip. But we could have a few weeks together, let me get to know my daughter. If it *is* a girl, of course.'

Flora looked away, not wanting him to see the alarm in her eyes. She knew, of course, that Fin would have to have some involvement as a father, but she hadn't really thought through how it would work in practice. She'd just assumed his lack of commitment would make him no more than a vague presence in their child's life. Yet here he was, suggesting he stay with her; be with her for the birth – and for weeks after?

'You said you'd be useless with a small baby. That was your excuse for going to Nepal.'

'Yeah, well, I've had a chance to think since

then. It wasn't a good time for me before, Flo. I wasn't myself.' He paused. 'I was thinking . . . you and me. Perhaps we should give it another go? With the baby coming . . .'

She pushed the plunger down on the grains, wondering what she should say.

'You're not still angry with me about the Prue thing are you?' he was asking.

The 'Prue thing', as he put it, was still a thorn in Flora's side. As Bel said, she and Prue hadn't spoken in months. Flora had decided she didn't have the extra strength to try to rebuild her relationship with her sister right now – and Prue obviously felt the same – but it was an ongoing sadness that Prue wasn't involved at all in her preparations for her baby's birth. And she hated what the family furore was doing to poor Bel. But as far as Fin was concerned, she tried not to dwell on what had happened any more.

'So have you got the baby's room ready?' Fin was asking. He seemed relaxed and at home, as if his visit were an everyday occurrence. The renewed confidence he'd got in his physical strength had brought such a change from the depressive, growling malcontent she'd lived with. And Fin was a wanderer by nature; he put roots down more quickly than most. Flora shook her head.

'Will you show me?'

'It's still in boxes. We only finished painting yesterday.'

'We?'

'Yes. Keith and Bel . . . Simon Kent, Dorothea's GP . . . have been helping me.'

Fin was staring at her. 'Keith? That porter guy who works in the block?'

'Yes.'

'OK . . . well that's very convenient.'

'It is. He comes up and helps after work sometimes, or weekends. He's been great,' she said, ignoring the innuendo.

'I'm sure he has.'

'Meaning?'

'Oh, come on, Flo. You can't hide it from me. I know you too well.'

Flora gave a short laugh. 'You don't know anything about me any more.'

But he was suddenly up close, his light eyes full of suspicion. 'So you and this Keith guy have been getting it on over the Crown Emulsion, eh? Very cosy.' He reached for her, pulling her close, stroking the hair back from her face. And suddenly he was bending down, his mouth on hers, his tongue forcing its way between her teeth. She tried to pull away, but he was powerful in his jealousy, his grasp on her arms painful.

'Hey, Flo.' His voice softened. 'Come on, don't fight it. You know what we've got together.' He drew back, but kept a tight hold on her. 'Our bodies are meant for each other. I bet this Keith guy doesn't come close.'

She finally wrenched herself free. 'I wouldn't know, we aren't in a relationship.' She was shaking.

Fin raised his eyebrows. 'Hmm . . . but you'd like to be, right?'

They were interrupted by the doorbell. Flora didn't move.

'Do you want me to get it?' Fin turned towards the door, but Flora got there before him. It was Simon.

She opened the door. 'Hi. Fin's here.'

Simon looked at her and then at Fin. She was flustered, knowing the doctor couldn't help but notice the sexual energy between them, even though it was negative.

'Simon Kent.' He slowly held his hand out, suddenly the professional doctor she remembered from when Dorothea was alive. Fin reluctantly shook it, casting an inquisitive glance at him. 'Umm . . . perhaps I'll come back later,' Simon muttered.

Flora looked at him pleadingly, the pleasure of the night before playing over in her mind. Please, please don't think what I know you're thinking, she implored silently. But she could see the devastation on his face.

'I'll ring you,' she said, but he left without another word.

As soon as the door was shut, she turned to Fin. The fury building in her chest was like no other Flora had ever experienced. Nothing that had happened between them in the past came anywhere close.

'Leave. Just go, get out.'

His face registered astonishment. 'Hey, what have I done?'

'You don't even know, do you? Christ, Fin, your life is just one endless, self-centred roller-coaster of indulgence. You come, you go, you help yourself to whatever you want whenever you want it, and you don't give a flying fuck who you hurt along the way.' She was trembling with rage. 'How dare you force yourself on me like that. How dare you even touch me any more. Just get out. GET OUT.'

He continued to look at her as if she had lost her senses. And indeed she felt as if she had.

'GO!'

He held his hands up. 'OK, OK . . . keep your wig on. God, I've heard pregnant women can be over-emotional, but this is a bit extreme, Flo.' He picked up his daypack. 'I'll talk to you later, when you've calmed down.'

She couldn't speak, tears were choking her, but she wasn't going to let him see it. She opened the door and, with another baffled shrug, Fin McCrea walked out of her life.

When she'd had time to calm down, she phoned Simon. He didn't pick up but she left a message. 'Please call. He's gone.'

Then she waited, but he didn't ring back.

She sat miserably through that Sunday afternoon, trying the doctor's mobile every hour or so, unable to concentrate on anything. But there was no response. *Please ring*, she repeated over and over, checking her phone obsessively in case she'd missed his call.

She was shaken by her outburst with Fin. But she knew it had not been just about the kiss, or about jeopardising her relationship with Simon. It was cumulative, a pent-up force of anger for all his betrayals, his selfishness, which until now she had never properly vented.

It was nearly six when Simon rang the bell.

He looked tense and subdued.

'I won't stay.'

She saw him take a deep breath as they stood together in the cluttered hall. Looking her directly in the eye, he said, 'Listen, I think we should cool it for now. Not see each other. I quite understand if you still have feelings for Fin . . . he's the baby's father, for God's sake. But my own feelings for you . . . as I'm sure you've worked out by now, are so strong that I can't deal with it. I'd like to be your friend, Flora, but I just don't think I can do that.' His words sounded almost rehearsed.

Flora held her breath. 'Fin and I are totally finished, Simon. There's nothing unresolved. What you saw was real and I know how it must have looked. He got jealous about Keith of all people, when I said you'd all helped me paint the baby's bedroom, and he came on to me, forced a kiss on me without my consent, just before you arrived. . . .'

Simon didn't reply. His handsome face was twisting with anxiety.

'The thing is, I spent months trying to put you out of my mind after Dorothea died, knowing you were with Fin. That's why I was so weird with you in the park café. I knew that it would churn up all those old feelings again.'

'Simon, please. You've got to believe me. It's over.'

He sighed heavily.

'I've been so insanely jealous myself . . . all day. I haven't known what to do. It's been pure hell. If you still have even an iota of feeling for that man, please . . . please tell me now.'

Before she had time to repeat her assurances, he'd rushed on.

'It would be perfectly reasonable if you weren't sure if you still loved him. I'd understand. I just need to know.'

'Simon, stop! Please, look at me. I – do – not – love Fin McCrea.' And hearing her own words, she knew it was completely true, that she was finally free of her decade of obsession. She reached for his hand and held it lightly. 'I literally couldn't bear it if you walked away from me now,' she added, in no more than a whisper.

He stared at her. 'Maybe you need some time, though. It's not so long since you split up. And perhaps your feelings will change when you have the baby together.'

Flora shook her head emphatically. 'They won't. I don't suppose he'll even be there when the baby's born. He was only here this time to get his visa for Nepal, and needed somewhere to crash. He didn't even ring to say he was coming, just burst in on me.'

Simon didn't seem quite to believe her, although he still held onto her hand. 'This isn't meant to sound disrespectful to pregnant women, but maybe you shouldn't be making important decisions right now.'

Flora gave a short laugh. 'Fin assumes I've lost it too. But he had reason, I yelled at him like a banshee.'

He finally smiled.

'It wasn't pretty.' She paused. 'I know what you're saying, but where you're concerned, I think I know my own mind. You can't invent what happened between us last night; it was extraordinary, Simon.'

'I certainly couldn't invent it, no.'

'And it's not as if we're even having sex, or moving in together . . .'

The doctor grinned. 'Yet,' he said.

EPILOGUE

September 2013

'This is bonkers,' Flora whispered. She looked around her in awe. The long ballroom with its polished wood floor, padded plush velour walls – shabby now – and unique barrel-shaped dome of a ceiling was lit by a bizarre mix of dozens of French chandeliers and glowing red clusters of Chinese lanterns. At one end were tables and chairs, some on a raised dais, at the other a small curtained stage. The faded, almost tawdry grandeur of the place was at once exotic and intimate.

A number of couples were already doing the quickstep to the loud strains of 'Puttin' on the Ritz' and Flora, despite herself, found her foot tapping.

'Sit here,' Simon instructed, finding a table on the raised dais where Flora could get a good view. 'I'll get you a drink.'

She watched the dancers as she waited for him to come back; some of them were impressive, gliding slickly around in perfect harmony, backs beautifully arched, elbows high. At the other end of the spectrum were those who hardly knew the steps and constantly tripped, stopped and laughed, and began again. But everyone was enjoying themselves.

This was the first time Flora had been out without the baby. Thea Sarah Bancroft was six weeks old now and currently in the safe hands of Prue and Bel – who was so in love with her little cousin that she spent most of her spare time round at Flora's.

Flora had wanted to call her Dorothea, but Bel pointed out that she'd always be nicknamed Dot or Dotty. And Simon agreed. It was her niece who'd suggested Thea. Sarah was for Fin's mother – Flora thought it important that the other half of Thea's genes be acknowledged in some way. But Fin hadn't seen his daughter yet. He was long gone on his Annapurna trek, and had said he was too busy training to be there for the birth.

They'd hardly spoken since Flora's outburst back in May, even though she'd apologised. She felt guilty at how thoroughly relieved she was, and guilty, too, because she knew that Thea would never really know her father properly. But she had to remind herself that Fin had never wanted a baby in the first place, despite his numerous dissemblings over the years. And Thea, she hoped, had Simon.

The baby had also healed the rift between her and Prue. The day after Thea was born, her sister had arrived at the hospital with a huge basket of flowers. They had held each other for a long time in silence. Neither of them, it was clear, had any desire to rake over the painful past.

It was Simon who had paced with Flora through the early labour pains, driven her to the hospital, held her hand as she screamed abuse at him and the nurses when the pain got too hard to bear. And it was Simon who had held Thea in the crook of his arm and gazed at her as if she were his own.

She had asked him time and again during her pregnancy if he could ever accept Fin's child as his, and he had always replied that he didn't know. But in the event the bonding between him and Thea had seemed to happen naturally. Flora had yet to meet Jasmine, his own daughter. Her mother had taken her to America for the summer to visit relatives. Flora was nervous of how the little girl would react to her, but she was determined to try and forge the same bond with her as Simon had with Thea.

'I've been dying to show this place to you,' the doctor said as he set down her lime and soda, his Coke. 'It started as a cinema, but the kitsch decor is pure Fifties. Isn't it heaven?'

'I love it. Some of the dancers are brilliant.'

'Yeah, and some of them are dire.' He pointed to a young guy stumbling over his partner's feet just beneath their table.

Flora laughed. 'That'd be me.' She had vowed she wouldn't, *couldn't* dance tonight. She had only come along for the ride. But now she was here she knew she wouldn't be able to resist.

It almost made her dizzy, being away from Thea, out in the loud adult world again, her breasts tingling at every thought of her baby, the song-beat drowning out conversation and thought.

'We won't stay long. I know you'll worry. But let's have a couple of dances . . . when you're ready.'

'Make it a waltz,' she said, 'it's the only one I have any idea how to do.'

When 'You Light Up My Life' came on, Simon grabbed her. 'Now or never!'

They stepped onto the dance floor, Simon expertly manoeuvring her between the other couples. Flora did little else but press herself against him, cling to him, let him lift her round . . . her feet, for the most part, obeyed his own. After a while she stopped worrying, just gave herself up to the moment.

'You . . . light up my life,' Simon sang in her ear, 'you give me hope . . . to carry on . . .'

She looked up at him, and for a second they were suspended in that sea of movement, looking into each other's eyes for what seemed like an eternity. He smiled, and dropped a quick kiss on her mouth, then swept her off again, round and round across the polished maplewood floor.